SOMEONE HAS TO DO IT

I'd had a few brushes with how absolutely power could corrupt. The Wardens were built on solid, idealistic principles, but somewhere along the way some of us—maybe even a lot of us—had lost the mission. There were a few faithful, altruistic ones left (I didn't dare count myself among them).

It's never been my job, or my nature, to worry about whether or not what I was doing was right in the grand scheme of things. I'm a foot soldier. A doer, not a planner. I like being useful and doing my job well, and so far as the lasting satisfaction goes, owning a killer wardrobe and bitchin' shoes doesn't hurt.

I never wanted to be in an ethical struggle. It shouldn't be my job to decide who's right, who's wrong, who lives, who dies. It shouldn't be *anybody's* job, but most especially not mine. I'm not deep. I'm not philosophical. I'm a girl who likes fast cars and fast men and expensive clothes, not necessarily in that order.

But you do the job you're handed.

CHILL FACTOR

BOOK THREE OF THE WEATHER WARDEN SERIES

Rachel Caine

A ROC BOOK

ROC
Published by New American Library, a division of
Penguin Group (USA) Inc., 375 Hudson Street,
New York, New York 10014, USA
Penguin Group (Canada), 10 Alcorn Avenue, Toronto,
Ontario M4V 3B2, Canada (a division of Pearson Penguin Canada Inc.)
Penguin Books Ltd., 80 Strand, London WC2R 0RL, England
Penguin Ireland, 25 St. Stephen's Green, Dublin 2,
Ireland (a division of Penguin Books Ltd.)
Penguin Group (Australia), 250 Camberwell Road, Camberwell, Victoria 3124,
Australia (a division of Pearson Australia Group Pty. Ltd.)
Penguin Books India Pvt. Ltd., 11 Community Centre, Panchsheel Park,
New Delhi - 110 017, India
Penguin Group (NZ), cnr Airborne and Rosedale Roads, Albany,
Auckland 1310, New Zealand (a division of Pearson New Zealand Ltd.)
Penguin Books (South Africa) (Pty.) Ltd., 24 Sturdee Avenue,
Rosebank, Johannesburg 2196, South Africa

Penguin Books Ltd., Registered Offices:
80 Strand, London WC2R 0RL, England

First published by Roc, an imprint of New American Library,
a division of Penguin Group (USA) Inc.

First Printing, January 2005
10 9 8 7 6 5 4 3 2 1

PUBLISHER'S NOTE
This is a work of fiction. Names, characters, places, and incidents either are the
product of the author's imagination or are used fictitiously, and any resemblance
to actual persons, living or dead, business establishments, events, or locales is
entirely coincidental.

The author wishes to thank:

Good fortune, Godiva chocolates, and Slim-Fast

My long-suffering, long-haired Cat.

Jo, Kel, Glenn, Jackie, Pat, Annie, Circe, and a host
of other wonderful friends too numerous
to name here.

Lucienne Diver, for her magnificent support.

My friends and colleagues at LSG Sky Chefs.

Musical support: the great Joe Bonamassa,
Eric Czar, and Kenny Kramme!
www.jbonamassa.com
(And thanks to all the JB fans out there who've
made me welcome in their family!)

PREVIOUSLY . . .

My name is Joanne Baldwin. I control the weather.

No, really. I was a member of the Weather Wardens. . . . You probably aren't personally acquainted with them, but they keep you from getting fried by lightning (mostly), swept away by floods (sometimes), killed by tornadoes (occasionally). We try to do all that stuff. Sometimes we even succeed. It's amazingly difficult, not to mention dangerous, work.

I had a really bad week, died, got reborn as a Djinn, had an even *worse* week, and saved the world, sort of. Except that in the process I let a kid go who may be a whole hell of a lot worse than just a few world-scouring disasters.

Oh, and I died *again*, sort of. And this time I woke up human.

At least I *still* have a really fast car. . . .

ONE

The sky overhead was blue. Clear, depthless, cloudless blue, the kind that stares back at you like Nietzsche's abyss. Not a cloud in sight.

I hate clear skies. Clear skies make me nervous.

I ducked and leaned forward again, trying to look straight up from the driver's seat through the most tinted part of the windshield. Nope, no clouds. Not even a wispy little modesty veil of humidity. I leaned back in the seat and adjusted my hips with a pained sigh. The last rest area I'd spotted had been a broken-down, scary-looking affair that would have made the most hardened long hauler keep on truckin', but pretty soon cleanliness wasn't going to matter nearly as much as availability.

I was so tired that everything looked filtered, textured, subtly wrong. Thirty hours since I'd caught three hours of sleep. Before that, at least another twenty-four of adrenaline and caffeine.

Before *that* I'd been on the road, driving like a madwoman, for three weeks, poised on the knife edge between boredom and panic. In a very real way, I'd been in a war zone all that time, waiting for the next bullet.

I was desperate for a bathroom, a bath, and a bed. In that order.

Instead, I edged a little bit more speed out of the accelerator.

"You all right?" asked my passenger. His name was David, and he was turned away, soaking up the sun that poured through the side window. When I didn't answer, he looked at me. Every time I saw his face, I had a little microshock of pleasure flash down my spine. Because he was gorgeous. High cheekbones, smooth gold-kissed skin, a round flash of glasses he didn't need but liked to wear anyway as protective camouflage. He wasn't bothering with disguising his eyes just now, and they flared a color not found anywhere in the human genome . . . warm bronze, flecked with orange.

David was a Djinn. He even had a bottle, which currently rested in the pocket of my jacket, cap off. And that whole three-wishes thing? Not accurate. As long as I held his bottle, I had nearly unlimited power at my fingertips. Except it also came with nearly unlimited responsibility, which isn't the supersized bowl of cherries it sounds.

He didn't look tired. It made me feel even worse, if that were remotely possible.

"You need to rest," he said. I turned my attention back to the road. I-70 stretched on to the horizon in a flat black ribbon, stripes faded to ghosts by the merciless desert sun. On either side of the car, the landscape bristled with more spikes than leaves—Joshua trees, squatty alien cacti. To a girl from Humidity Central, also known as Florida, the thin, dry air seemed too light to breathe, so hot it scorched the lining of my lungs. And it was all blurring into sameness, after days of playing cat and mouse out here in the middle of nowhere.

"Oh, I'm just peachy," I said. "How are we doing?"

"Better than we have," he said. "I don't think they've noticed us yet."

"Yet." A sour taste grew in the back of my throat, not entirely due to the lack of toothbrush and minty freshness. "Well, how much farther do we have to go?"

"Exactly?"

"Approximately."

"Miles or time?"

"Just spill it, already."

"We just passed a town called Solitude. Six more hours, give or take." David leaned back in the passenger seat, still looking at me. "Seriously. You okay?"

"I have to pee." I fidgeted again in the seat and glared at the road. "This *sucks*. Being human *sucks*, dammit." I should know. I spent a semiglorious, spectacular, brief period as a Djinn. And I'd *never* had this embarrassing need to pee in the middle of nowhere.

He kicked back in the seat and tilted his head up at the blank car roof. "Yes, so you've said."

"Well, it *does*."

"You didn't mind being human before."

"Hadn't seen how the other half lives, before."

He smiled at the roof. Which was a shame, because the roof couldn't appreciate it the way I do. "Want me to conjure you up a bathroom?"

Bastard. "Bite me."

He gave me that raised-eyebrows expression again, over mockingly innocent eyes. "Why? Would it help?"

He was taunting me with the whole bathroom thing. Oh, he could conjure one up, that wasn't the problem; hell, he could probably conjure up one with Italian marble tile and hot and cold running Perrier. But I couldn't let him, because we had to keep a low profile for as long as we could, magic-wise. David was doing all he could to keep us unnoticed, but any big, flashy conjurations would certainly light up the aetheric like a supernova.

And that would be bad. To put it mildly.

I pulled the car over to the side of the road; Mona protested, powered down to a throaty growl, and shivered to silence when I turned the key. In seconds, heat pushed through the windshield like a bully. Had to be in the nineties already, even though it was barely mid-April. I felt sticky, unwashed, cramped, and frazzled. Nothing like a little two-thousand mile trip and spending three weeks in a holding pattern—driving nearly the whole time—to make you get that less-than-fresh feeling.

"Are you okay?" David asked me.

"Fine, already!" I snapped back. "Why wouldn't I be?"

"Oh, I don't know. Let's see . . . in the past two weeks, you've been infected by a demon, chased across the country, killed, become a Djinn, been reborn . . ."

"Got shot," I put in helpfully.

"Got shot," he agreed. "Also a point. So there's plenty of reason for you not to be okay, isn't there?"

Yeah. I was a few clouds short of a brainstorm, as

we like to say in the Wardens. I'd thought I was dealing well with all of the craziness that had become my life, but being out here, alone, with all of this desert and huge empty sky . . .

. . . I was beginning to realize I hadn't dealt with it at all. So, of course, I insisted. . . .

"I'm fine." What else could I say, realistically? *I suck, this is awful, I'm a complete failure as a human being and a Warden, we'll never pull this off?* Hell, David already knew that. It was a waste of breath.

David gave me a look that said he plainly thought I was full of crap, but he wasn't going to argue. He pulled a book out of his coat pocket. This one was a dog-eared paperback copy of *Lonesome Dove*, which somehow seemed appropriate to the current circumstances. One benefit of being a Djinn . . . David had a virtually limitless library of reading material available to him. I wondered how he was on DVDs.

"I'm waiting here," he said, opening the book. "Yell if a rattlesnake bites you."

He settled comfortably in the seat, looking every inch the normal guy, and refused to respond to my various irritated noises. I opened the door of the Viper and stepped out onto the shiny black asphalt of the shoulder.

And yelped, as my sexy-but-sensible heels promptly sank into the hot surface. God, it was *hot!* Forget about frying an egg on the sidewalk; this kind of heat would fry an egg inside the chicken. Waves of it shimmered up from the ground, beating down from the hot-brass sky. I tiptoed over to the safety of gravel, skidded down the embankment, and tromped off into the dunes.

Open-toed shoes and desert: not a good combination. I cursed and shuffled my way through burning sand until I found a likely looking Joshua tree that had just enough foliage to function as a privacy screen to the highway. It smelled astringent and sharp, like the thorns that spiked it. There was nothing gentle about this place. Everything was heat and angles and the hot stare of a clear, unwilling sky.

No way around it. I sighed and skinned down my panties and did the awkward human stuff, worrying all the time about rattlesnakes and scorpions and black widow spiders. And sunburn in places that didn't normally get full western exposure.

Surprisingly, nothing attacked. I hurried back to the car, jumped in, started Mona up. David kept reading. I pulled the car back out into nonexistent traffic, shifting gears smoothly until I was cruising at a comfortable clip. Mona liked speed. I liked giving it to her. We weren't even approaching the Viper's top speed, which was somewhere around 260, but in about thirty seconds we were rapidly gaining on 175. It was a tribute to American engineering that it only felt like we were going about, oh, 100.

"Much better," I said. "I'm okay now."

"You don't feel okay," David said, without looking up from the book. He flipped a page.

"That's creepy."

"What?"

"You ought to say, 'You don't *look* okay.' Not, you know, *feel*. Because you aren't—"

"Feeling you?" He shot me a sideways look; those oh-so-lovely lips eased toward a smile. "I do, you know. Feel you. All the time."

I understood what he meant; there remained this *vibration* between the two of us, something radiating at a frequency only the two of us could feel. A low-level, constant hum of energy. I tried not to listen to it too much, because it sang, and it sang of things like power, which was way too seductive and frightening. Oh, and sex. Which was just distracting, and frustrating, at times like these.

When I'd been a Djinn I'd existed in a whole other plane of existence, accessing the world through life outside of myself. The Djinn don't carry power of their own; generally, they act as amplifiers for the world around them. When they're paired up with someone like me—a Warden, someone with natural power of her own—the results can be amazing. David swore, and I believed him, that what we had going on between us now was something other than that, though. Something new.

Something scarier in its intensity.

"You feel me all the time," I repeated. "Careful. Talk like that will get this car pulled over."

"Promise?" He leaned over and adjusted my hair, pushing it back from my face and hooking it over my ear. His touch was fire, and it sent little orgasmic jolts through my nervous system. *Jesus.* He was studying me very intently now, as if he'd never seen me before. "Joanne."

He rarely used my full name. I was surprised enough to edge off the accelerator and cast another quick glance at him. "What?"

"Promise me something."

"Anything." It sounded flippant, but I meant it.

"Promise me that you'll—"

He never got to finish the sentence, because the road curved.

Literally.

It heaved and bucked, black asphalt rippling like the scales of a snake, and I yelped and felt Mona rise up into the air, engine screaming. A sonic boom like a cannon going off slammed through the air, so loud I felt it shudder my heart in my chest.

Oh, shit.

"Levitate!" I screamed, which was about all I had time for, and instantly I felt that vibration between me and David turn into a full symphonic thunder of power. It cascaded out of me, into him, transformed into a nuclear explosion on the aetheric, and forged itself into a matrix of invisible controls.

The world just . . . stopped.

Well, actually, *we* stopped. Mona paused, hanging tilted in midair about three feet above the road. Her engine was still screaming, her tires burning the air, but we weren't going anywhere. Weren't falling, either. Below us, I-70 continued to ripple and flow like it was trying to creep off to the horizon. I wasn't sensitive to this particular frequency of power, but I knew what it was.

"Shit," I said. "I guess they found us."

David, solemn and unrattled, eased back in the seat and said archly, "You think?"

The guy doing this to me was named Kevin, and I couldn't really hate him. That was the worst part of it. You really *ought* to be able to hate your archnemesis. I mean, it's only fair, right? Feeling sorry for him, and just a little responsible . . . that just sucks.

Kevin was a kid—sixteen, maybe seventeen—and

the fact that his generally punk-ass personality was hard to like had something to do with his having lived a real fairy-tale existence. The bad fairy tales. His stepmother had been something right out of a Grimm story, if the Brothers Grimm had written about sexpot-stripper-wannabe–serial killers. What she'd done to Kevin didn't really bear close scrutiny unless you had the cast-iron stomach of a coroner.

So it was no surprise that once power came his way, Kevin grabbed it with both hands and used it exactly the way an abused, near-psychotic victim would: offensively. To keep people at a distance, the way a scared kid with a gun pointing it at anything that moved.

Trouble was, the gun—or power—that he'd grabbed was named Jonathan, and if you could measure Djinn with a voltage meter, Jonathan would melt the dial, he was so intense. I liked Jonathan, but I wasn't really sure Jonathan returned the favor; he and David had a close friendship that stretched back into—for all intents and purposes—eternity, and I'd jumped right in the middle.

Jonathan was *not* somebody you wanted to be on the wrong side of. And now that he'd been claimed by Kevin, just like any other Djinn, the whole master-servant relationship was in force. Which was trouble enough, clearly, but I was beginning to get the very clear idea that while most Djinn had the skill of working creatively around their masters' commands—it was like negotiating with the devil—Jonathan either hadn't mastered the craft or just plain didn't care.

He was certainly not averse to causing *me* trouble, at least.

So. We hung there in midair, and watched the landscape below rise and fall like the ocean. Mona slowly evened out from her tilt to a nice, even hover.

"Do I need to ask?" I asked. My voice was more or less steady, but my skin was burning from the sudden rush of adrenaline.

"Earthquake," David said.

"It was rhetorical."

"So I gathered." He looked icy calm, but his eyes were glittering behind the glasses. "Jo. You can slow down now."

Right, I was still pressing the accelerator through the floor. I let up and, for no apparent reason, shifted to the brake. My legs were shaking. Hell, my whole body was shaking. I couldn't get my hands off of the wheel.

"You know, there are three kinds of waves associated with earthquakes," I said, in an attempt at nonchalance. "P waves, S waves, L waves. See, the sonic boom is caused by the primary waves—"

"And the ancient Chinese believed it was the dragon shifting in its sleep," David interrupted me. "None of that is very useful right now."

Again, he had a point. "Okay. What if I order you to stop it?" I asked.

David shook his head, looking down at the continued waves moving through the ground. "Power against power. It would only make things worse. I can't oppose him directly."

"So it is Jonathan." As if I had any doubt. We'd been playing keep-away with the state of Nevada for nearly three days, circling around. And every time, there'd been something to stop us. Hail the size of basketballs that I'd barely been able to keep from smashing the Viper into scrap. Lightning storms. Wind walls. You name it, we'd run into it.

And from it.

I'd spent a considerable amount of my time and energy fixing the careful balance of the ecosystem. Kevin/Jonathan didn't seem to give a crap that tossing fireballs at us might seriously screw up the entire matter-and-energy equation, or that whipping up a tornado might rip apart the stability of the weather half a continent away. Kevin I could understand; he was a kid, and kids don't think of consequences. But Jonathan . . . I knew he had the capacity to balance the scales. He just hadn't.

Hanging in midair wasn't getting us anywhere. I sucked in a deep breath and said, "Plan B, I guess."

"I think we're midway through the alphabet," David replied. "Jo, I really thought we could get through to Las Vegas, but we're not even coming close. Maybe we should—"

"I'm not giving up, so don't even think about saying it."

I *couldn't* give up. Kevin and Jonathan were a partnership made in hell, and it was my fault. I'd given Kevin the opportunity to do that. Also, I should have been able to stop Kevin from stealing the powers of the most gifted Warden in the world, my friend, Lewis Levander Orwell.

So I was *not* giving up now. The cost could be incalculable in lives and property, and one of them I knew personally. Lewis would die. He was dying right now, the same way he'd die if somebody came along and ripped important biological parts out of him that his

body needed to keep functioning. Lewis was so powerful magically that magic was part of him. He couldn't
do without it.

However, the trouble was that Kevin now possessed
so much power that David and I—and any other poor,
stupid, magically talented idiot trying to make it to
Las Vegas—were as obvious and vulnerable as black
bugs on a pristine white floor. No place to hide. Nowhere to go, except onward, hoping we'd be able to
avoid the giant's crushing power.

We had, so far. But clearly they were just playing
with us.

I had a dreadful thought. "Is there anybody else on
this road?" Kevin, I knew, wouldn't go out of his way
to rack up civilian casualties, but I was far from convinced he'd go out of his way to avoid it, either.

"Not in range. I can dampen the vibrations a little,
at the outskirts, and he's focusing it right beneath us.
No one's been hurt." The unspoken *yet* made me
wince.

"How long can he keep it up?"

David shot me a look. "You're kidding."

"As long as he wants?"

"Exactly." From the desert-dry tone, David was
feeling a little inadequate. "We'll have to wait him
out." Again.

"So," I said, and forced a little lightness into my
voice, "how *will* we pass the time?"

David wasn't in the mood for banter. He watched
the road writhe like a living thing below us and said,
"Catch some rest while you can. I'll keep watch."

Not exactly what I was hoping for, but I got his

point. I was tired, and unlike David, I was only human these days.

Not that I was bitter about that, or anything.

Much.

Weather is nothing but the practical application of quantum mechanics. There's no way to make quantum mechanics simple, but ultimately it boils down to the interactions of particles so small they make atoms look big. Everything is divisible by something else, down to particles so small the human mind can't grasp them or even measure them in any way except by the effects they leave behind. Particles behave like waves. Nothing is what it seems.

Controlling quantum interactions is a macro/micro science, or magic, or art—or the true marriage of all of those. When you're controlling the weather, manipulation occurs at subatomic levels, gaining or losing energy, annihilating quarks against antiquarks or protons against antiprotons, and it's both destructive and clean. It can mean the difference between a sunny day and a gentle spring rain, or a thunderstorm and a killer F5 tornado. It can mean flood or drought. Life or death.

It's a lot of responsibility, and I'm afraid the Wardens don't really take it all that seriously sometimes. We're human, after all. Like everybody else, we've got lives, and families, and all the normal human complement of sins and vices. Hey, nobody likes getting the four A.M. call from the office, especially if it's to fix somebody else's mess.

And sins, yes, we've got plenty of those. Greed, for

one. Greed and power have always been really good bedfellows, but greed and magic are the deadliest of evil twins.

I'd had a few brushes with how absolutely power could corrupt. The Wardens were built on solid, idealistic principles, but somewhere along the way some of us—maybe even a lot of us—had lost the mission. There were a few faithful, altruistic ones left (I didn't dare count myself among them).

It's never been my job, or my nature, to worry about whether or not what I was doing was right in the grand scheme of things. I'm a foot soldier. A doer, not a planner. I like being useful and doing my job well, and so far as lasting satisfaction goes, owning a killer wardrobe and bitchin' shoes doesn't hurt.

I never wanted to be in an ethical struggle. It shouldn't be my job to decide who's right, who's wrong, who lives, who dies. It shouldn't be *anybody's* job, but most especially not mine. I'm not deep. I'm not philosophical. I'm a girl who likes fast cars and fast men and expensive clothes, not necessarily in that order.

But you do the job you're handed.

I couldn't sleep. I mean, could you? Hanging in midair over an earthquake, waiting for the other shoe to drop? Even as exhausted as I was, fear kept me from closing my eyes for more than five seconds at a time.

So we were hanging there, watching the road ripple in the bright merciless sun, when something occurred to me and made me sit up straight, blinking.

"Can I fly this thing?" I asked. As if we weren't already hanging a ton of steel in midair without benefit of an airplane engine. *D'oh!* "I mean, move the car to another highway. Without them knowing."

That got David's complete attention, with a slight puzzled frown. "It's not exactly built for gliding, but yes, I suppose. Why?"

"Because if you can keep an illusion on the aetheric of us staying here, I can move the car with wind power to another route, and maybe we can gain some time before he figures it out." I hesitated, then asked the question I'd been afraid to put into words. "He could kill us, right? Anytime he wants."

David's eyes were mercilessly clear. "He could try. Eventually, he'd succeed. I can't fight Jonathan power-for-power. But he doesn't want to kill you. If he did, you'd be dead already."

I noticed the change in pronoun. *I* was the one in danger of dying. The worst that could happen to David was that while the car was being crushed like a beer can and my bones shattered, the bottle in my pocket would break and he would be set free. Jonathan would no doubt consider that a bonus. Which, leaving aside how I felt about David and hoped he felt about me, wasn't an unreasonable point of view. I wasn't exactly comfortable with the whole master-slave dynamic of things, either.

"Can you hold him off?" I asked.

"For a while. If he attacks directly."

"Long enough for me to—"

"Save yourself," David finished. "In a game like this, you're playing Kevin, not Jonathan. I can block

Jonathan, but the strategy has to be misdirection, not direct defense. We have to keep moving. If we let them pin us down, we're finished."

I nodded, noting little details: white lines around David's mouth, tension around his eyes. This was hard for him. *Very* hard. The scope of his friendship with the Djinn named Jonathan stretched back to an age when they were both human and breathing, dying together on a battlefield in the dim mists of prehistory. Saved by a force so primal it could suck the life out of thousands, maybe millions of living things to create a creature like Jonathan—a living, thinking being composed of pure power. Even among the Djinn, he was something special, and that was no small statement.

And now he was on the wrong side. At least, the wrong side of me.

"We can't hurt him," I said. David shot me a surprised glance. "Right?"

"I don't know of much that could. And nothing that you'd want to mess with."

"But he could hurt you."

"He won't."

"He could." The reason he could hurt David was, essentially, *me.* David had spent his power freely to pull me back from the dead and put me in a Djinn form; he still hadn't entirely recovered from that.

In the tradition of lovers everywhere, we didn't talk about it.

David shrugged, glanced down at the undulating I-70, and said, "We'd better get moving, if we're going to move. It's just a matter of time before it occurs to Kevin to order Jonathan to swat us down."

That was the saving grace of all this—we had the

power of a nuclear weapon in the hands of a petulant child, but at least he wasn't what you might call a great thinker. Jonathan, though bound to serve him, wasn't bound to give him advice, and so far hadn't taken it upon himself to act as general in this fight. Thank God.

I nodded, took in a breath, and shut my eyes. Drifted out of my body and up to the higher plane of existence we among the Wardens knew as the aetheric level . . . the plane where the physical dropped away, and only the energies of the world were displayed. Human senses could see only certain spectrums; when I'd been a Djinn, the aetheric had shown me a hell of a lot more, and deeper, but I was trying to be satisfied with what I had.

Just now, the aetheric was showing the road below me lit up like a giant glowing runway, glittering with power that three-D'ed down below the surface deep into bedrock. The little idiot was destabilizing the whole region. I couldn't stop him; my powers related to wind and water, not earth. Somebody else would have to balance those scales. In fact, somebody's cell phone in the Warden's organization was probably ringing right now.

Time to make the kind of trouble that was my specialty. I reached out into the still, arid air, went high, carbonated air molecules in one place and stilled them in another. The by-product of that is heat. That's all wind is, the interaction of hot and cold, of hot air rising and colder air rushing to fill the void that nature really does abhor. I rolled down the car window and felt the first freshening breeze blow warm against my cheek; a little more energy and the breeze became a stiff wind. I felt the car rock lightly.

"Get ready," I said aloud. "I'm going to have to push pretty hard."

"He won't know we're moving," David promised.

I increased the range of heat, focusing the power of the sun in a massive surge, and saw the wind shear building up on the aetheric. It came boiling at us in an invisible, syrup-thick wave.

It hit Mona broadside, spun us around, and then we were *moving*.

I yelped, tightened my grip on the steering wheel, and felt the sickening sense of falling for a full two seconds before we steadied out again, moving fast. I stretched myself farther on the aetheric, spinning atoms, holding chains of force together. This thing was as slick and slippery as glass.

To magical eyes, the halogen-bright glow of the car stayed where we'd been. It was a complicated illusion, requiring massive amounts of directed power that had to be hidden and buried in the natural processes occurring around us; I could feel that power pouring out of me like blood from an open wound. David was amplifying and redirecting it, but it was at a huge cost to both of us.

"How long?" I managed to stammer, and held out my hand. He grabbed hold. His skin was fever-hot.

"Half an hour, maybe," he replied. No sign of strain in his voice, but I felt a fine vibration through his skin, felt it in the bond between us. "Don't worry about that. Worry about the wind."

He was right. The kind of power I was using was treacherous, all too easy to go wrong. Wind has a kind of intelligence—slow, instinctual, but predatory. The stronger the wind, the more cunningly it can manifest, which is why working with major weather systems is reserved for the most powerful of Wardens. It's not just physics. It's lion taming.

And I could feel this particular lion starting to lick its chops in anticipation.

Below us, the Utah desert moved in lazy, deceptively gentle increments. We were traveling through the sky at better than a hundred miles an hour—slow for a plane, but dangerously fast for the air currents I was handling. David was holding Mona steady. I hoped he also had a little attention to spare to keep us unnoticed from the ground; seeing a Dodge Viper do a Chitty Chitty Bang Bang in the desert sky might be a little hard to explain, even for UFO nuts.

I spotted a small, likely looking back road at the edge of the horizon, and concentrated hard on slowing us down. That involved a risky and complicated series of adjustments—cooling the air behind us, warming the air in front, creating a collision of forces that would stall out the wind shear. Luckily, there wasn't enough moisture in the air to have to worry about creating a storm. I had to bleed off the buildup of energy as well, because that had to go somewhere, and leaving it roaming around looking for a place to discharge was a rookie's mistake. I crawled it over telephone lines in bursts of blue plasma to discharge it into the earth.

Unfortunately, the wind didn't *like* the idea of slowing down.

"Shit," I whispered, and reached deeper, trying to grab hold of the fast-moving molecules. Hot processes were always more difficult to stop, things moving too fast, on too big a scale. I steadied myself, listened for the tone of the wind, and spread myself out on the aetheric. It was like becoming the wind, like melting into it. Once I was inside of it, I could slow it down. . . .

And then David said sharply, "Hold on."

It hit us from behind, a shockingly powerful slam like a giant's palm on the bumper. I bit back a scream and felt the car shoot forward, faster, starting to tumble out of control. *Fuck!* That was the wind, hitting back. I'd given it too much energy to work with. Behind us, the energy was starting to spiral in on itself. I saw the sand begin to rise up, painting the outlines of the biggest damn dust devil I'd ever seen. Not a tornado, not in the traditional sense, but up high where we were, it was far more powerful than down on the ground.

I felt strength flooding back into me as David stopped his draw. I snapped into the aetheric to gather up the shattering chains of control. It was like playing marbles with a dump truck, chaos dancing in gleeful abandon. *I can't.* Panic threatened to overwhelm me, make me lose what control I had.

And then I felt him, on the aetheric, wrapping himself around me, supporting me, steadying me. *You can,* he whispered through that silent, strong connection between us. *Trust yourself.*

And something inside me went still, and the chaos no longer looked like chaos. There were patterns, beautiful sparkling patterns, *life*, life everywhere, in the wind, in the ground, in me, in David.

There was no chaos. For an instant I saw it, *knew* it on a level that only the true Djinn could perceive, and I reached out and took control.

And the wind obeyed. Tamed its fury with a sigh, dropped its coating of dust, coiled around us like a pet.

Mona touched down gently on hot asphalt that shimmered off into the distance like a black mirage.

I opened my eyes, blinked away the lingering euphoria, and felt Mona's engine still purring and trembling through the grip of my hand on her steering wheel. I was holding on to David, or he was holding on to me, or we were holding on to each other.

I had to let go to ease Mona back into gear. My hand shook violently on the gearshift, but I just held on until the shakes went away.

He'd just shown me how the Djinn see the world. A sight I'd had, and lost.

I hadn't realized until this moment how deeply I mourned it.

We played cat and mouse with earthquakes all the way to the Nevada state line. I could only imagine how nuts it was making the normal world, not to mention the poor Earth Wardens who were supposed to be keeping the world safe for regular folks; my cell phone kept ringing, but I didn't have the time or energy to answer it. The caller was Paul Giancarlo, who was temporarily acting National Warden for the U.S.—our previous fearless leader having been corpsified in the line of duty just about a week ago. Another thing I hadn't been able to stop, even as a Djinn. I could only imagine how worried Paul was, but it wouldn't reassure him to hear my status reports. His Djinn would tell him we were alive. That was about all the good news there was.

"Highway Six," I said. I was shuffling maps, which was something I could do while David drove. He wasn't as good a driver as I was, but I tried not to hold that against him. He was holding Mona to the road, and we were burning rubber, trying to get as far as we could before Kevin and Jonathan locked onto us again. I knew that anytime now, Kevin would just lose patience with the game and say something unequivocal, like, *Smash that car into junk, right now.* At which point it would be Jonathan versus David, in the battle for my life, with the winner a foregone conclusion.

"Highway Six turns into Highway Fifty," I said, following the route with my finger. "Loneliest road in America." Which was all to the good, for us; I didn't want to be on a congested highway with the wrath of Jonathan coming down on me. "Unfortunately, it doesn't take us where we need to go. On the upside, maybe that means they won't come after us for a while. I don't know about you, but this crap is getting ridiculous."

He made a noise that could have been either agreement or indigestion, except that I didn't think Djinn could get indigestion.

"It also means we could pull over for the night," I said slowly. I'd lost count of how many hours we'd been in the car. The little sleep I'd been able to catch had left me grainy-eyed, subject to nervous caffeine-sponsored tremors, and having post-traumatic stress flashbacks to the last soft mattress I'd slept on. Of course, that had been a hospital bed, and I'd been recovering from a gunshot wound to the back. Hence, the PTSD.

"We could stop," David agreed. Nothing in his voice. Not looking at me for a long beat, and then cutting his eyes over at the last second. "You should rest."

"Start fresh in the morning."

"There's nothing more we can do now."

"Probably true. Wouldn't hurt to catch some sleep while I can."

We were both quiet for a few seconds, and then I let out a slow, tired breath. "I can't. I can't just sleep while they're out there doing God only knows what, to God only knows who. . . ." We hadn't been able to see anything beyond the wall of Jonathan's power. For all I knew, they'd turned Las Vegas into one giant beach party, like eternal spring break. That would be about Kevin's speed.

"We would've heard if there had been anything spectacular," he pointed out. "There's been nothing on the radio so far; it's business as usual for the regular mortals out there. And even if Kevin is doing something, you can't stop it by burning yourself out like this."

"David, they've *killed Wardens*." At last count, while I'd been lazing around in my hospital bed, two Wardens and their Djinn had gone into the no-man's-land around Las Vegas, and hadn't returned. Plus, there'd been no contact from either the Wind or Fire Warden in Nevada. The Earth Warden, probably feeling like the only target left on the shooting range, was justifiably nervous. "Jesus, I can't just . . . relax!"

David's voice was low, warm, and gentle. "I know." And he reached out with one hand and brushed his fingertips against my skin. "Sleep now."

And before I could protest, I was gone.

* * *

My dreams were haunted.

I was standing in the desert, staring off to a limitless flat horizon. Sand drifted lazily around, but I couldn't feel any wind . . . couldn't feel *anything*.

No, that wasn't right. I could sense the external pressure of the breeze against my skin, feel it ruffling my hair . . . but I couldn't *feel* it. Not inside.

I had no sense of the weather at all.

Blind. I was blind. Panic ripped through me, and it felt both overwhelming and weirdly unreal, the way things do in dreams . . . intense and disconnected.

This is what is.

But it wasn't. I was a Warden; I had powers; I was alive and kicking despite the odds.

This is what is coming.

"It's beautiful," a voice said. I turned my head, and there was a woman standing next to me—tall, glorious, with waves of white-gold hair and amethyst eyes. Her pale, diaphanous robes whipped in the wind I couldn't feel, and she raised her face to the sun and drank it in like a happy child.

I knew her. She'd saved my life not so very long ago, just before she'd given up her own existence, damaged and flawed as it was. She'd once been a Djinn like David, but her love for a human had undone her. Made her into an Ifrit, a creature built of shadows, manifesting in its Djinn form only when it had drawn enough power out of another. Ifrits were vampires at best. Cannibals at worst.

She'd clung to that half-life for hundreds of years, to stay with the one she loved. And she'd given it up for me.

I still didn't really know why.

"Hey, Sara," I said, like seeing her was the most normal thing in the world. She didn't open her eyes, but her smile deepened and a dimple appeared on her cheek. "Where are we?"

"At the end of the world," she said, and took my hand. Her skin was Djinn-hot, pale and perfect as ivory. "Where all the rivers run."

There weren't any rivers. I pointed it out. Her Mona Lisa smile didn't diminish.

"Figure of speech, love," she said. "For now . . . how is David?"

"I burn for him all the time," I said, in the obscure honesty of dreams. "If I lose him I'll die."

"You won't."

"I will." Just the idea of it brought on a massive, black wave of grief that threatened to cripple me. Sara squeezed my hand, as if she knew, as if she could feel what I felt. I gulped down a hot, acid breath. "Where's Patrick?"

"Here."

"Where?"

"Close your eyes."

I did, and instantly I was in the aetheric, or the dream-aetheric, anyway. And it wasn't Sara holding my hand. The Djinn who did was drawn in shades of power, lines of tragedy, but there were ice-cool blues and greens shimmering around his aura. An aurora borealis of peace.

Somehow, I wasn't surprised. "Oh," I said. "There you are. Hey, Patrick." Not that it was possible to talk on the aetheric plane, as such, but my dream, my rules. Patrick's form turned toward me, and somehow it overlaid itself with the semblance of humanity he'd worn for more than three hundred years . . . a big man with an energetic explosion of white-blond hair, eyes as bitter and intoxicating as absinthe. Santa Claus, but the kind who'd drop presents on the ground to look up women's skirts as he bent over.

"I've missed you," he said, and an incorporeal hand grabbed my ass.

"Wrong! Wrong touching!" I yelped, and jumped away. He grinned like a naughty schoolboy.

"Can't blame me for trying."

"You're dead," I accused him. "Shouldn't you be giving up bad habits?"

"Seems a bit late to reform. So. You're here to ask what you should do."

"No, I'm having a dream."

"Are you?" He folded his arms across his chest. It made for a weird overlay; it was like seeing a two-dimensional paper cutout held in front of a glowing angel. "You should turn around and go back, love. Can't fight this battle. It's like a wildfire. Even the densest Fire Warden knows that sometimes you have to let the flame burn itself out."

"This kid's going to kill people, Patrick. I can't let that happen."

He reached out and thumped me on the forehead. It hurt. "Ow!" I opened my eyes, and suddenly I was looking at Sara again, beautiful sunlit Sara, who was just putting her hand back at her side. No longer smiling.

"It's raining," she said, and turned away from me. A gust blew her dress back into a set of wings that shimmered in the light.

It wasn't raining. There wasn't a cloud in the sky, not a drop of water anywhere.

She was facing west. Far to the horizon, I saw a tiny smudge of black, a miniature lick of flame that might have been lightning.

It started as a whisper, grew to a mutter, then a rumbling thunder like a million horses running in panic.

And then the flood came in a midnight wave, thundering down canyons below us. It was a thick, muddy wave with a crown of black mist, churning with the smashed remains of homes and businesses and corpses. It was vast, and it was sweeping the human world clean. Nothing could escape it. It slammed into the mountain where we stood, and I felt the world shudder. A cold, wet sigh spread over me, and then the wave split and went around us, thundering past and down, down into the black chasm of infinity.

"Where all the rivers run," Sara said. Her eyes were terribly sad, terribly lethal. "Go home, child. Don't come here to die."

The spot on my forehead where she—or Patrick— had thumped me flashed white-hot, burning, and then I felt myself losing my balance.

Screaming.

Falling toward the churning, foaming, stinking flood of death below.

I jerked back away to the smell of ozone, and the prickly-sharp presence of a close lightning strike. David was still driving, but the sky had turned dark gray. There was a thick purple-black center to the clouds that told me trouble was coming, even without the benefit of using Oversight to look up on the ae-theric. Rain lashed the road in thick silver waves. I glanced down reflexively at the speedometer, and found that we were still blazing along at nearly a hundred miles an hour.

The hair standing up on the back of my neck wasn't just from the lightning strike.

I turned my head and worked out a painful kink, ran my fingers through my hair (or tried to; it needed some major shampoo and a monster-class conditioner), and tried to swallow the cotton-mouth I'd acquired during the nap. More lightning flashed on the horizon, blue-white with a delicate fringe of pink. It shattered into ribbons, striking four or five targets at once. The words of an elder Warden came to me: *If you're close enough to see it, you're close enough to worry.*

David said, "I think we should stop for a while." He gave me a quick, impersonal once-over. "A meal, a shower, a good night's sleep. Doctor's orders."

"There's a difference between *being* a doctor and *playing* doctor, you know." Reflex banter. I wasn't trying to argue against it; the dream had knocked all the fight out of me. It had, in its extremely obscure way, been trying to tell me something. Not surprising that I'd dream about Patrick and Sara, the two who'd given up their existence to bring me back to the mortal world . . . but I could do with a lot less vague prophecy. How come the sage advice never came in plain language, anyway?

David nodded at a blaze of green neon up ahead. "I'm pulling in."

The chiaroscuro blur resolved into a Holiday Inn,

and as another bolt of lightning tore its way out of the heavens and into the earth, resetting the delicate polarity of the battery of life, I realized that I hadn't even asked the logical question.

As David turned the ignition off, I turned toward him and said, "Is all this coming for us?"

Another bolt of lightning lit his face ivory, turned his eyes into hot orange-gold flares.

He said, "Isn't it always?"

TWO

When I scampered through the pneumatic doors of the Holiday Inn, a rain-lashed, bedraggled mess, I had one of those shivery, disorienting déjà vu moments. Everybody gets them, and of course the important thing to do is just forget about it and keep moving on.

Except that I took about six steps into the lobby, spotted the faux-rock fountain with its floating rings of silk flowers, and realized it wasn't déjà vu at all. It was memory.

I really *had* been here before. Six years ago.

"Crap," I whispered, and fought a deep, clawing instinct to get back in the car and just keep driving. But outside thunder rattled plate glass, and there really wasn't any point in trying to get away from this particular past.

Besides, I don't run from bad memories.

I straightened my back and walked to the front desk. It wasn't quite a sashay, because of the squishing shoes, but I held it together. I didn't recognize the girl behind the desk—staff must have changed over several times since the tight-assed blonde I remembered handing me my last room key. This one—brunette— stopped popping her gum and straightened up, smiling sympathetically.

"Wow," she said. "Real mess out there, huh?"

"No kidding," I said, and wiped strands of hair back from my face. "Hope you have a room available."

"Yep," she said. "Nonsmoking, is that okay?"

"Does it come with a hair dryer?"

"Definitely."

"Perfect."

We did the credit card thing, and she made me a cute little electronic key, and I squished out toward the stairs, past the gently tinkling fountain. No such things as ghosts—at least, I hope there aren't—but I couldn't help but feel a very cold, very real chill as I passed the spot.

Charles Spenser Ashworth III.

Man, I *so* didn't want to be here. Not now.

David was waiting for me when I unlocked the door to the room. He was dressed in a casual blue-checked flannel shirt, blue jeans, sneakers . . . his WWI-vintage olive-drab coat was draped over the arm of the chair, and he was kicked back on the bed, lying flat with his hands under his head. I kicked the door shut and stood there staring at him.

Dripping.

Without a word, I went into the bathroom and stripped off my wet clothes, cranked the shower on hot, and had a luxurious, spine-melting wash, with complimentary shampoo and cute little soaps. Two ap- plications of hotel-provided conditioner made it barely possible for me to work the complimentary comb through my uncomplementary hair. Which was curling again, drat it. In my original human incarnation, I'd had glossy, straight, jet-black hair. Since my rebirth, I'd acquired a disturbing tendency to Shirley Temple curls. I used the hair dryer and worked, teeth gritted, until I had everything straightened to my satisfaction.

When I came out, my clothes were dry, folded, and put away in drawers, and David was still lying on the bed in exactly the same position, only bare-chested and covered by the sheets. I set his unsealed bottle on the nightstand, next to the clock radio.

He smiled, eyes closed, and his chest rose and fell as he breathed me in. "You smell like jasmine."

I dropped the towel and slid under the sheets next to him. "Hotel soap. I hope it's an improvement."

He rolled up on his elbow to look down on me. What I saw in his eyes took my breath away. Sweet, hot intensity. Djinn are made of fire, and passion, and power. Having one feel that way about you . . . it's like nothing else on earth. His skin wasn't touching me, and it didn't matter; he was touching me in ways that were more intimate than that. A sweet burn of pleasure ignited somewhere near the base of my spine and worked its way up.

"How far are you willing to go with this?" he asked me. Which was not what I was hoping for him to say, and I blinked to indicate I had no idea what he was talking about. David read my confusion and continued. "Kevin's afraid. He's young, he's stupid, and he's scared. I think there's every reason to believe that if he wasn't insane before, he probably is by now. So how far are you willing to go to get him?"

Something flashed past me, something from the dream in the car. Wildfires, burning themselves out. I shook it off. "As far as I need to. Somebody's got to take him down."

He moved a lock of hair back from my face. "Others can."

"In time to save Lewis's life?" I asked, and saw a slow cooling of those molten-bronze eyes. "Don't. This isn't about personal feelings, David. He's important. Lewis is important to . . . hell, to *everyone*. And what Kevin's done is killing him."

"You need to ask yourself something," he said softly.

"How far I'm willing to go? Because I just said—"

"No." His gaze held me still. "Why it always has to be *you*. Are you that powerful, or just that arrogant?"

I froze. Then I rolled over and pulled the hurt close. I felt his warm fingers lightly caress my shoulder. His voice was a bare whisper against my ear, soft and textured as velvet.

"I'm scared for you. I lost you twice already, Jo. Please. Stop trying to save the world. Can you do that for me?"

I had to be honest with him. "I don't think I can. Not this time. It's our fuckup, David. I have to try."

I felt the warm puff of his sigh. "That's what I thought." His lips pressed gently on the bare skin of my shoulder. I took a deep breath and turned toward him . . .

. . . but he was gone. Disappeared. Vanished like the Djinn he was.

Don't go, I need you, please stay. . . . I really did need him, especially tonight, especially here. But I was a tough girl. Tough girls don't beg.

I closed my eyes and tried to sleep, but the memories kept coming back.

Now that I'd remembered being here before, I couldn't forget the circumstances, and the circumstances started with Chaz.

You probably know somebody just like Charles Spenser Ashworth III. Maybe not with as fancy a name or pedigree, maybe not as rich, but you know him. He's the guy without much talent but with a whole lot of mouth, a fast-talker with flashy ideas. He never follows through, because that's hard work. He's all about the *ideas*. *Ideas*, he will tell you, are much more important than *execution*. Because anyone can do the grunt work. Men like Chaz are usually successful, because there's an entire business culture out there who buys into the notion that actual work is cheap and somehow déclassé. He's usually a consultant, or an executive, and he usually has a flashy car (but one without any real performance), a mistress, and at least one ex-wife and the associated ex-children.

My Chaz was a Warden. I had the misfortune of being assigned to audit his work.

First of all, understand that being a Weather Warden in Nevada isn't exactly the world's most stressful job. The surrounding states are the ones with the big problems; by the time the shit hits the fan in Nevada, the Wardens have generally had plenty of chances to slow it down or stop it. The place is strong in Earth Wardens, not Fire or Weather. So for a Weather Warden to get audited in that state is pretty . . . well, unusual. But for about two years prior to my assignment, there had been some funky things going on.

It was luck of the draw as to who would get the free trip to Vegas, and it turned out to be me. Florida, California, Texas, Oklahoma, Kansas, Missouri . . . those are the hot-weather experts, and we do get tasked for this sort of thing on occasion. If he'd been in Montana, somebody from the Vermont or Alaska regions would have been given the treat.

But *no*, it had to be me. Lucky me.

I knew I was in trouble when I arrived at McCarran International Airport in Las Vegas and found that Charles "Call Me Chaz" Ashworth hadn't bothered to pick me up. I mean, if you were being audited, and you were asked to arrange transportation, wouldn't you try to make a good impression? Not Chaz. He left a message for me to rent a car, and told me that he'd reserved me a room at Caesar's. Since I fully intended to charge Chaz for the car, I rented a Jaguar, drove down the Neon Mile to the trashy-cool Roman extravagance of the Palace, and pulled into the valet spot. There was a wait. I hesitated for a few seconds, then flipped open the folder that I'd been reviewing on the plane.

Even though Chaz was nominally based in Las Vegas, that wasn't where the questionable weather behavior was being registered. It was up in the lonely northern part of the state, the empty expanses. Too many storm fronts, coming too close together, and usually at odd times. Interesting. And—not so coincidentally—it looked like he had some property up there in that area.

The valet knocked on my window. I looked up, smiled at him, and hit the power switch to roll down the glass.

"Sorry," I said. "Changed my mind."

I drove through and checked the courtesy map that came with the Jag, eased back in the blood-warm leather seats, and decided to take a road trip.

The epicenter of the trouble was a place named White Ridge, which was a dot on the map so small that it looked more like a printing error than a population center.

I headed for it without delay.

It was a four-hour drive through hard, bright, merciless country, and at the end of it I found a town that had a Wal-Mart, a deserted downtown, one decrepit diner, and—just at the edge of it—a small Holiday Inn. I parked in the lot, pulled my cell phone from my purse, and consulted the file for a phone number. I dialed and got voice mail, and Charles Spenser Ashworth III's smooth, radio-announcer voice. *Please leave a message and I'll get back to you. If you're a single lady, I'll get back to you sooner.* Oh, he just oozed charm. Or maybe just oozed. I left him a businesslike message that said I'd arrived, where I was, and that I expected him to meet me as soon as possible.

It was white-hot outside when I walked in through those automatic doors at the Holiday Inn. I was wearing a white pantsuit, and a neon-yellow halter top under the jacket. Kicky yellow shoes. The outfit was disappointingly pedigree-free, but then I was on a budget, saving up for couture in the future. It was still big-city enough to draw looks.

I trundled my sturdy wheeled travel case up to the counter and booked a room. Cooled my heels in my new temporary home, flipping TV channels and trying to figure out why all hotel pillows are either too hard or too soft. Two hours later, the hotel phone rang.

Chaz was in the lobby.

I descended the somewhat rickety steps, past the fountain, and there he was. Unmistakably a Chaz, not a Charles. Tall, solidly muscular, deeply tanned, with wavy dark hair and sparkling blue eyes. An artificially white smile, perfect teeth. He looked like he belonged out in Hollywood, hanging poolside, especially considering the casual Polo shirt and Dockers, loafers without socks. Altogether too preppy, but I wasn't going to hold that against him.

Much.

He looked me up and down in blatant appraisal—not the usual fast I-shouldn't-be-doing-this-but-I-can't-help-it appraisal that polite men tend to give, but the kind that ought to be reserved for Friday nights around closing time at the strip club. His stare centered on my breasts. Okay, I know, don't wear the halter top if you don't want the attention, but jeez, it was 120 in the shade. Bulky turtlenecks were right out.

"Joanne? I was expecting you to wait for me in Las Vegas. I was coming into town later." He didn't wait for my response. He captured my hand and gave me an extravagant kiss on the back of it, staring deep into my eyes the whole time. "Charmed."

"Mr. Ashworth—"

"Chaz, please. Really, you wasted a trip; this is just where I have my country house." He made it sound like he was a landowner back in the old country, titled and bursting with noblesse oblige. "Honey—"

"Joanne." Two could play the interrupting game, and I'd already had it up to here with Mr. Charm. "Please refer to me by name, if you don't mind."

He flashed me a smile that was too toothy to be apologetic. "Joanne, yes, of course. Sorry. Look, there's just no reason for the Wardens to send somebody all the way out here. No deep, dark secrets in the attic. Not that I'm not thrilled to have your company."

I reclaimed my hand. "I'll be needing your records."

"Certainly." Another toothpaste-ad smile. "But they're back in the city."

"You don't keep anything at your country house? Seems like you spend quite a bit of time here." I spread out the folder on the counter and found the maps I was looking for. "When I mapped the weather patterns, it sure looked as if a lot of the manipulation occurs from this location, *not* from Las Vegas. So it stands to reason that you'd have an office here, wouldn't you? If you're keeping proper records."

He lost the smile. "I haven't got anything to hide."

My Aunt Fanny! From every note in the file, everybody knew there was something weird out here, but the prior three auditors sent to investigate hadn't found a thing. My mission was to investigate and find something to bust his ass, so that there could be a formal inquiry, and he could be removed from duty.

Protocol. Even in the supernatural business, you have to follow strict human resources procedures.

"Then you won't mind if I audit the records at your home office," I said.

"I don't have a—"

"Chaz," I interrupted, and held on to a thin, don't-screw-with-me smile. "I *know* you have a home office. Let's not spend more time on that, okay?"

He didn't look happy.

"Let's go," I said, before he could throw out any more lame pickup lines, and led the way out to the Jaguar.

I kept silent all the way out to his house, a good half hour's drive even at excessively indulgent speeds. I virtuously resisted the urge to smack him, which surely must qualify me for some kind of sainthood . . . believe me, he was annoying. I could easily see why they'd sequestered him out here in the middle of nowhere. Mouthy, hyperactively on the make, shallow, and none too smart. I couldn't tell how talented he was, but even the biggest store of power in the world wouldn't make him a good Warden.

And then I realized that *I* could also be accused of being shallow, hyperactively on the make, and mouthy. I hoped I was smart, though. Smarter, anyway.

We turned off on a paved road and passed under a big wrought-iron gate decorated with—I'm not kidding—the chromed silhouette of a nude woman, the exact copy of what you see on taste-free truckers' mud flaps. The name over the entrance was FANTASY RANCH. Oh, yeah, this was going to be fun.

The house was an overdone Tudor style, ridiculous out here on the prairie. There was a struggling, desperately green lawn in front that looked suspiciously like it might have been freshly spray painted. A garage with three cars, all crap-year Corvettes. All red, of course. In the corner, a gold pimp-trim Cadillac Seville, maroon.

He kept chatting me up all the way up the front walk, but I wasn't listening; I was looking into the aetheric. Oversight gives you a nice lay of the land, particularly since there's a fourth-dimensional time layer to it that represents the past. The history of Chaz's pad was nothing to be proud of. On the aetheric, the place showed its true character. A shell of a place, barely there . . . overlaid with shadows. That was kind of sad. Even the place where he lived didn't make much of an impression on the world.

Neither did Chaz himself. People tended to manifest on the aetheric in visual representations of their self-image; his looked pretty much like a sad, faded image of his physical form. I wondered what he saw when he looked at me. People tended to get the oddest expressions.

Well, the only good news was that Chaz wasn't likely to be a serial killer, not with a basically boring aetheric presence like this. Not that I couldn't defend myself, but it was nice not to have to worry about it. I had plenty of other things on my mind.

His house was self-consciously tacky—retro-seventies without any semblance of a cool factor. He made reference to the water bed. I shut him down and made it clear that I expected to be shown to the home office.

It was at the back of the house, and it looked like he'd set it up from some office catalog rather than to suit any kind of actual work process; everything was expensive, but nothing was very good. The filing cabinet was some exotic handcrafted wood, but the drawers stuck. Inside, there was a chaos of unmarked folders, piles of haphazard papers, crap mixed in with vital documents. I'd heard he hadn't filed quarterly reports in a year; they were probably here, stuffed in with downloaded porn photos. The records I found . . . well, *threadbare* would have been a generous description.

After two hours I was ready to scream and blow the whole place away with a tornado. Instead—reminding myself that I was a professional, dammit—I grabbed and boxed up everything that looked remotely interesting, while Chaz's smile got thinner and thinner, and wrote him out a receipt for what I'd taken.

The Jag's trunk was roomy. I got six boxes in there, added the remaining four to the backseat, and headed back to the hotel.

Time to settle in with room service tuna salad and pay-per-view movies while I struggled through the paperwork.

It was going to be a long, long audit.

I drifted back to the present, and realized that instead of lulling myself to sleep I was lying in the dark, staring up at the ceiling and watching rain patterns ripple across the spackle. The light out in the parking lot was a bright blue-white, like sustained lightning.

I considered doing something about the rain, but so long as it didn't develop into something devastating, I decided to let it ride. There were Weather Wardens aplenty roaming around the country; the Wardens Association was on the verge of chaos, what with the senior leadership being dead and all hell breaking loose out here in the desert. I was here with a specific job, and I ought to concentrate on it.

Like last time. And look how that had turned out.

I closed my eyes on a vision of blood and tried, uselessly, to sleep.

I woke up, not remembering drifting off, to find myself on my right side, staring into David's face. He was watching me. I yawned, stretched, and inventoried the need for a good toothbrushing, not to mention mouthwashing—more things I hadn't needed to deal with when Djinn. Those halcyon days were making resuming normal life one giant pain in the ass.

"Sleep well?" David asked.

I hadn't, and he knew it. "Where'd you go? . . . No, I take it back, I don't really want to know. *Why* did you go?"

"We were going to fight." He lifted a hand and traced a fingertip up the outside of my arm to my shoulder. "I didn't see any reason it had to happen. You were just tired and discouraged."

"Fighting can lead to other things." It had before. Our first real lovemaking had happened as the result of a fight in a hotel. I saw the memory move in him, too.

"No need to fight to have that." His voice had dropped an octave, gone even quieter, but there was a tension behind it that made him seem even more alive, even more intense. The light glide of his touch on me took a left turn, followed the line of my collarbone.

"Close the curtains," I whispered. Behind him, the

curtains snapped shut, all on their own, blocking out the frowning clouds and the steady, mournful pulse of rain. It occurred to me, late and with an electric jolt to the spine, that David was under the covers with me, and he'd already done away with the bother of clothes. His glasses lay carefully folded on the nightstand, next to the fragile blue glitter of his bottle.

Nothing between us but skin, mine real—whatever that meant—and his manifested by will and magic. And all the more real for that, because he'd chosen this. Chosen *me*.

I felt cold. As if he knew it, he put his arms around me and pulled me close to his heat. His lips pressed a burning kiss on my forehead, a benediction I didn't deserve, and slowly traveled down to my mouth. Sweet, slow, leisurely kisses, gentle as the rain outside. Healing the chill inside me, filling the empty places.

He murmured something into my open mouth—words I didn't know, in a language like liquid fire. I pulled away a little, looking into his eyes. So much passion in him, constrained by so much will.

"What did that mean?" I asked him. He traced the line of my lips with his fingertips like a blind man memorizing the shape of my face, and didn't answer. "David, what did that mean?"

I felt him go tense against me. The lazy focus of his eyes sharpened. "Don't," he warned me.

"What did that mean?" I was being very specifically repetitive, and I felt the surge of power as the Rule of Three kicked in. He was compelled to answer me truthfully, but of course, the truth with Djinn could be fluid. It wouldn't be outside the boundaries for him to reply to me in another language. We could play this game all day, if he felt inclined. Owning his bottle didn't mean I owned his soul.

But he didn't try to avoid it. His eyes went the color of dark, tarnished brass, almost human, and his hand went still against my cheek.

"It's part of a ritual," he said. "The literal translation is that I will mourn you when you're gone. Because you're mortal, and you take stupid risks, and I'm going to lose you. I hate it, but I know it's going to happen. Because you won't be sensible."

There wasn't a breath between us. Skin on skin, sealed together with sweat as body heat rose. My whole body was aching and throbbing for him, but my mind kept struggling.

"What kind of ritual?"

"Joanne—"

"What kind of ritual?" No answer. "*What kind of ritual?*"

This time, the words were in that liquid-fire language again. The language of the Djinn, but with a rough edge to them that sounded human. He pulled me to him again, put those burning lips to the column of my throat, and made me arch uncontrollably against him. It wasn't exactly clear in this relationship who owned who, I thought when I was capable of thinking. And he wasn't going to answer me. Not in words.

His hands were everywhere on me, shivering my skin into goose bumps, making me moan with need and delight. *Too long, it's been too long. . . .* He rolled me over on my back, settled his weight on top of me, took hold of my wrists, and pinned them on either side of the black spill of my hair, tormenting me with kisses and friction that didn't put him where I needed him to be.

"God, David, please . . ." I whispered. I wasn't sure what I was asking, whether it was for the white-hot surge of flesh between us or the answers to my questions. Or something else entirely. I felt like crying, and I didn't know why. My heart hammered like a cheap toy, fragile and unreliable, one beat at a time between me and the end of things. I hadn't faced the crashing, intimate knowledge of my own mortality, because I couldn't. I was always hiding from it in action, chasing after what came next.

Not David. He'd faced it. He'd been afraid of losing me, of having every moment between us threaten to be the last. I'd made a being of fire and power *afraid*.

He looked merciless staring down at me, except for the vulnerability in his eyes. The odd, unexpected humanity. "Please don't ask me what it means."

There was something in it that made my heart break. I whispered, "I won't," and felt the tension ease out of him. "Because you're going to tell me."

"You have to trust me."

I choked on a laugh. "Who's on top here?"

He let go of my wrists, sat up on his knees. The sheet slid away. The lamps gilded his skin, and I felt my breath catch and tear something inside of me. Some last shred of resistance.

His hands, hot on my thighs. Moving them.

"You have to trust me," he repeated. It was only a whisper now, and his eyes had kindled a bright new flame. "Can you do that?"

"Yes."

"You're sure?"

"Yes!" I pushed myself up on straight arms, looking into his eyes. Slowly bent my knees and drew them up, drawing him in with the motion.

His teeth lightly grazed the skin of my shoulder. I put my arms around him, holding him, feeling the waves surge and break. Waves of power, transforming and pure.

He whispered words against me that broke me apart, destroyed me, rebuilt me as we moved, and I didn't recognize a word of it, and it no longer mattered, because now I *understood*. The way flesh accepts touch, or lungs accept air.

He was telling me he loved me, the way Djinn say the words, and it was more beautiful and more terrifying than the banners of war.

I fell asleep in his arms, safe and warm and untroubled, and there were no dreams.

I woke up to thunder. Reflex action: I checked Oversight, and found nothing out of the ordinary out there, then realized that the thunder was knocking, and there were people outside of my hotel room.

"Jo!" A man's voice, rough and authoritative. "Open the damn door. Right now!"

I knew the voice. I let my head fall back against the pillow of David's warm skin, and said what he already knew. "Great. The boss is checking up on us."

David pulled away from me and I could feel the fury burning through him, see it boiling in his eyes. This could get *very* unpleasant.

"Go," I told him. "Let me handle it."

His hot eyes scorched me, just for a second, but

behind the anger I saw worry for me. I kissed him, fast and hard, and felt him mist away.

The door slammed open. I yelped and crawled backward, clutching the covers over myself, until my naked back met the cold headboard.

My boss, Paul Giancarlo, flanked by three other Wardens. One of them was Marion Bearheart, the woman who scared me most in the world; nice lady, frightening powers, and the right and responsibility to use them.

I flipped up into the aetheric plane to get a quick reading, and saw Paul in his avatar form—his outline had the unmistakable suggestion of a knight in armor, sword in hand. In the real world he looked more like a refugee from *The Sopranos*, complete to gold chain peeking through dark chest hair, and a stretch golf shirt that didn't make him look like anybody who chased a ball around the back nine for fun. Sexy, and dangerous as hell.

Marion's bronzed features were expressionless here in the real word, turned sharper by her gray-and-black hair being pulled back in a thick single braid. She was wearing a black leather jacket with fringe blurring the edges, blue jeans, black cowboy boots. Up on the aetheric, I caught the flare of eagle wings in her aura.

I didn't know the other two except on a nodding acquaintance. Both were seniors, both from outside the country. One was from Canada, one from Brazil. Their presence in my hotel room was not reassuring.

Paul gave me his most impersonal look, and that meant something really, really bad. Paul always took time to notice and appreciate the little things, like a naked woman in bed.

"Get dressed," he said. "Hurry."

He turned and left. Marion stayed behind, shutting the door after the others. She crossed her arms and watched me. I watched her right back.

"A little privacy?" I asked. She cocked her head to one side, eyes bright as a raven's, and smiled a refusal. I threw the covers back and walked naked across the floor to pull open drawers on the dresser. David had left my clothes neatly stacked.

As I dressed, Marion kept her eyes on the bed I'd just abandoned, and finally she said, "It's wrong, you know."

I didn't play dumb. I just asked, "Why?" as I fastened my bra.

"He's at your mercy. Even if he loves you, Joanne— and I have no doubt he does; I've seen enough to know that—inevitably, it'll turn to something else. A slave doesn't love a master. A slave *endures* a master. This will twist and sicken. It can't do anything else." Her voice dropped lower. "You'll lose him. And even if you don't, it makes you terribly, terribly vulnerable."

"It's not like that." Even as I said it, I felt the lie turn in my mouth, sticky and sour. It's what I'd been afraid of in the beginning. Why I hadn't ever wanted to claim him as a Djinn. What was between the two of us was fragile, and I was human and stupid. It was easy to screw it up.

She transferred her gaze to me. The look was too wise, too compassionate, and it made me feel cheap.

"Not yet, maybe," she said. "Give it time. I do speak from experience, you know."

Interesting. I'd never seen Marion's Djinn; I didn't know of anyone who ever had. She had one, of course; at her level, it would be impossible for her not to. And yet . . . she was extremely private about that relationship. Those short sentences were, from her, a bombshell confession. I knew, without looking over my shoulder, that David was manifesting behind me. Not afraid to show himself now that he knew the game was up. I felt a little better for the support, though I knew there was only so much he could do in this situation.

Only so much either of us could do, actually.

"Thanks for the advice," I said. My chilly tone was a little undermined—and muffled—by the fact that I was pulling my black knit shirt over my head at the time. I tested my shoes and found them dry—another silent gift from David. I stepped into them and headed for the bathroom.

Marion, who'd taken a step farther into the room, got in the way. I stopped and frowned. "Look, no matter how urgent this is, it's not so urgent that I can't pee and swig some mouthwash, right?"

She looked doubtful. That scared me.

"I'll be thirty seconds," I said, and ducked around her.

Just to be rebellious, I took a full minute.

The saving-the-world confab took place downstairs in the Holiday Inn lobby, next to the tinkling artificial fountain where I'd first met Chaz. Paul had taken the liberty of rearranging the furniture, pulling sofas and chairs into a tight little group. Circling the wagons. The desk clerks looked oblivious; I guessed that Paul had used his Djinn to put a glamour around us, make us unnoticeable. (It was, as David constantly reminded me, a hell of a lot easier than making us invisible.) I clopped down the lobby stairs, following Marion; David was no longer visible. I never could tell when David was gone, or just pretending to be gone. That was a sense I'd lost along with my Djinn union card.

Paul was pacing. Not good. When Paul paced, it meant things were getting serious. I could see that responsibilities were already wearing on him; a month ago, Paul had been content to be a Sector Warden, overseeing a big chunk of the East Coast, reporting directly to the National Big Cheese. But the events that had taken a hand in making me a Djinn, and then unmaking me, had changed the landscape of the association. So far as seniority, Paul was one of the few left standing who could take on the additional work. And there was, God knew, a hell of a lot to do. The stress had already given him shadows and bags under his eyes, and I didn't remember the fine tension lines at the corners of his mouth.

I was shocked to see him out here, chasing after me. The situation with Kevin was bad, no doubt about it, but he had a national organization to run, and it wouldn't run itself. I hoped he wasn't putting personal feelings ahead of business.

I took a seat on the couch, next to Marion, and Paul stopped prowling long enough to say, "Joanne Baldwin, you know Marion. Meet Jesús Farias and Robert West. Brazil and Canada."

Two heads nodded at me. I nodded back. Neither looked happy to be here.

"The kid you're after—" Paul continued.

"Kevin," I said. Paul's eyes fastened on me for a second, then moved on.

"Kevin," he corrected. "He's got wards up around Las Vegas. Great big ones. He's been fucking with weather systems across half the country to play keep-away with you, and that can't go on. We're killing ourselves trying to keep the peace out there."

"Sorry," I said. I was. "There's not a lot of choices to this, Paul. Either we leave him alone, or we go after him. But either way, it's not going to be good news, and I thought we agreed—"

"We did," Paul interrupted. "We agreed that you should come out here and stop him, but Jo, you *haven't* stopped him. You haven't even gotten close. Your Djinn doesn't have the power to go up against this punk nose-to-nose, and all that can come out of this is disaster if you cowboy around out here any more."

The Canadian, West, put in, "Your boy Kevin is destabilizing more than the weather. We're reading a huge pressure buildup along the Cascadia Subduction Zone. If we can't stop it, your problems out here will seem very small indeed."

Oh. Right. He wasn't Weather; he was Earth. "How bad?"

"At current levels, we think we can expect a mega-thrust earthquake along the Cascadia line. That's off-shore, around Vancouver and Oregon. It could potentially be as small as a nine-point quake, but we think it's probably going to be worse. A lot worse."

As *small* as a nine-point quake? The one that had just killed 25,000 in Iran had been a 6.5. "How much worse?"

"The amount of energy increases by a multiplier of forty times for every point on the Richter scale. This is probably going to register higher than the scale counts. Hypothetically, perhaps an eleven. Using the Mercalli intensity scale, it's a twelve, total damage, buildings thrown into the air—"

Big enough to scare the holy shit out of the Wardens, in other words. "I don't mean to tell you your business, but what about using smaller quakes to—"

"Bleed off energy? Useless. That amount of energy can't be bled away, not without spreading the devastation farther." His eyes were chilly. "And you're right. You shouldn't tell me my business."

The Brazilian weighed in. His English was excellent, spiced with a slight musical intonation. "Also, we estimate that the temperature all over this region has been raised by a mean of five degrees since this boy began his attacks; he has no conception of how to bleed off energy and balance the system. If it continues to rise, we won't be able to hold the network. Things will shift. And with the equations alread so far off scale . . ."

Paul stopped pacing and looked directly at me. "We're talking about melting icecaps, Jo. Floods. Climatic devastation. Earthquakes worse than we can possibly control, even with Djinn. Which we have too few of, by the way. I don't know if you're aware of it, but things are getting critical on that front. We lost Djinn we couldn't afford to lose, back there in the vaults. We barely have enough to keep things together as it is, and we keep on losing them. Wish to God I knew where they were going. . . ."

Marion shot him a look, a clear *we-don't-talk-about-that* message. I covered a flash of surprise. The Wardens were losing Djinn? I knew they were in short supply—they always had been—but I'd been under the clear impression that they knew exactly where their Djinn were, all the time. Of course, it made sense that there would be attrition. Once a Djinn's bottle was shattered, it disappeared. For all the Wardens had ever known, they left our plane of existence for someplace more exotic and safe . . . they'd never known what I knew, that many of them stuck around as free-range, unclaimed Djinn. Hiding in plain sight.

I wasn't about to tell them.

"All this could be followed by another ice age," Farias continued somberly. "One which we may no longer have enough trained personnel to stop. We've lost too many, both human and Djinn."

It sounded wacky. A teenage kid raised the temperature in Las Vegas by a few degrees, and boom, ice age. But weather's funny like that. The point wasn't the amount the temperature was raised; it was that it caused chain reactions. Altered rainfall. Shifted wind patterns.

El Niño on a global scale.

The last time a serious, out-of-pattern weather shift had happened, the Mayan Empire died of thirst, and crop failures in Europe sparked chaos that killed millions. Some say it caused the Dark Ages. It had taken the Wardens generations to control things again, put the systems back in balance. Or some semblance of it, at least. When the entire world system wobbled, it was the work of several human lifetimes to correct it.

I sucked in a deep breath. "So if you don't want me to keep going after him, what do you want me to do?"

Paul sank into a chair, leaned forward, and clasped his hands together. The gold chain around his neck swung free. It was a Saint Eurosia medal, patron saint against bad weather. I was reminded that when his relatives had sit-downs like this, it was sometimes to talk about whom to whack.

"The kid's scared," Paul said. "He knows things are out of control, but he won't talk to us. I'm pretty sure he thinks we're going to kill him."

As if we weren't. Yeah, right. "So what's the plan?"

"I'm ready to bring the full power of the Wardens down on him if I have to, but I don't want to go to war here. It's too dangerous. People are going to die if we do it the hard way."

"So you want to make a deal with him."

"Yes."

"And you what—want me to be your middleman? That's bullshit. He's been spending the last three weeks trying to keep me the hell *away* from Vegas."

They were all looking at me . . . Paul with a dark, sorrowful intensity, Marion with compassion, the other two with a mix of contempt and curiosity.

I suddenly knew, on a very visceral level, that I really wasn't going to like this conversation at all.

Paul said, "Jo, give me your Djinn's bottle."

Silence ticked on, dragging the seconds with it; I felt blood start to pound loud in my ears. "What?"

"Your Djinn. David." Paul leaned forward, elbows on knees, looking earnest. "C'mon, Jo, it isn't like you have him officially anyway. You got him by accident; he was Bad Bob's originally. If we had a calm minute around here, we'd have asked you to turn him over to the pool anyway. You're not authorized to handle a Djinn yet, and we need every single one right now to keep the systems stabilized."

I sucked in a breath of air that felt thin and hot. "You're kidding me."

"No." Paul held out his hand. Just held it out. Nobody else moved. "Jo, babe, let's not make this official."

"If you didn't want to make it official you should've come without the posse."

Point scored. His eyes flickered. "Please, Jo. Swear to God, I'm too tired to fuck with you right now. Don't make it hard."

"Don't make it *hard*?" I repeated, and slowly got to my feet. They all stood up, too, and flesh crept along the back of my neck. "I'm not handing him over, Paul. He shouldn't even be chained to a damn bottle, anyway. He's not—"

Instantly David was corporeal, standing behind Paul's chair, face white and eyes blazing. He mouthed one word.

Careful.

I realized, with a cold shock, what I'd almost blurted out. I'd almost told Paul about the Free Djinn, the ones roaming around loose and unclaimed out in the world. There were a lot of them, a lot more than the Wardens could ever have expected, and if I mentioned that then the Wardens would see it as their responsibility to find them and enslave them . . . for their own protection. Or some equally bullshit backward explanation that boiled down to benefiting the Wardens and no one else. Especially now, when they were running so scared. They'd use anything and everything to bail themselves—all of humanity—out.

I swallowed what I'd been about to say and finished up. "He's not going to be put in any goddamn pool. He's not a *resource*. I claimed him, and I'm keeping him."

David flickered and was gone. I felt suddenly, coldly alone, standing here with four Wardens staring at me. Four Wardens, I realized, who each had the power of a Djinn at their commands. No accident, that. Not when they were complaining about the shortages.

"You said you don't want a war," I said to Paul. "Don't start one with me, babe."

He let me make half of a dramatic exit. When I put my right foot on the staircase, beside the maniacally cheerful fountain, he said, "I get that you think you're in love with this Djinn—which is fucked-up beyond all measure of fucked-up, by the way. But beside that, which we *will* be talking about later, this doesn't end with you walking away, right?"

I didn't turn. Didn't let myself hesitate for more than a split second before I took the second stair.

Paul's voice went official. "By the authority of the Wardens Council, I'm ordering you to turn over your Djinn to us. And if you don't, I'm taking you down, and Marion's authorized to put you under the knife. You'll lose everything, Jo. Everything. Even your powers. And maybe that'll kill you, but right now I can't fucking worry about that."

At the top of the stairs, David flickered into existence, walking slowly down toward me. He had on his traveling clothes, his long olive-drab coat, and he looked young and innocent and angelic. My vision of him, imposed on him? Or his own reality? How much of him was really *him?* I didn't know. I couldn't.

He locked eyes with me for a second, then went past me down to the lobby. Hands in his pockets. The Wardens had all come to their feet, staring, and I could tell they were a whisper away from throwing their Djinn into all-out battle.

He looked back over his shoulder. The overhead lights trapped a shimmer of red and gold in his hair, and reflected sparks of hot bronze in his eyes as he smiled at me. A gentle, heartbreaking smile.

"Give them what they want, Jo," he said. "It'll be all right."

All around him, Djinn were moving like disembodied shadows. He was surrounded. Hemmed in. Trapped.

I took the bottle slowly from my pocket, felt the pulsing heat of the magic inside of it, thought about what it would be like to lose him.

I can't. Can't.

If I started a fight, it would go nuclear in minutes. Too much power here. Too many people with the ability to destroy half the continent.

Too much goddamn emotion.

I prepared to smash the bottle against the railing.

"Jo." He whispered my name like a caress, and followed it by laying fingertips gently against my cheek. "Don't. This needs to happen. Just do what they tell you."

He led me down the two steps, over to Paul. Paul held out his hand again.

I can't.

I let the bottle drop from a height of about a foot, from my hand to Paul's. David could have intervened. Could have jostled Paul, made him fumble the catch; could have, in that split second, blown the bottle across the room to shatter against faux stone.

I gave him that chance.

He did nothing.

Paul caught the glass container, and I felt the connection explode, melt away into silence. Even though David was holding my hand, he was *gone,* gone from me. Even his skin felt insubstantial.

His eyes turned dark. Human. Brown.

Sad and quiet and—hiding just under the surface—wary.

"Good choice, kids," Paul said. He looked tired and unhappy as he looked at David. "Back in the bottle, please."

I could feel David trying to fight, but the pull was irresistible, and in a sudden convulsive flicker he was gone. Paul reached out for the stopper, which I handed over as well. My fingers felt numb.

I watched as he worked the stopper into the bottle. The four Wardens seemed to breathe a sigh of relief. Paul handed the bottle to Marion, who took a black magic marker out of her pocket and wrote a rune on the bottle itself. A sign, I recognized, that was a kind of mystical DO NOT OPEN, CONTENTS UNDER PRESSURE. She opened a leather satchel sitting next to the chair and eased the bottle into special padding, then closed and locked it.

"Okay." I pulled in a deep breath and tried to put the anger aside. "Now you've got David out of the way. When do I go?" Paul looked up, startled, frowning, as if I knew something I shouldn't. "Hello? Vegas? Meet and greet with Teen Psycho?"

Paul didn't answer me. Marion said softly, "Kevin doesn't want you, Joanne. He has no reason to trust you. You can't negotiate with him on our behalf."

My mind went blank. "Then why all this—"

To get David. To get David away from me, to play us against each other.

I had a sudden premonition of disaster even before Paul said, "You're going home, Jo. Now."

"Like hell!" I rounded on Marion, on the case where she'd put David.

And I heard Paul say flatly, "Marion, take her."

THREE

I had a couple of choices—one, I could fight like hell and trash the hotel and probably kill a whole lot of people, or two, I could give up and see where it took me.

I didn't like option two, but I liked option one even less, and when Marion moved toward me, power at the ready, I just stood still for it.

"Easy," she whispered to me, and wrapped something around my wrists behind my back that felt thick and organic. At her touch it stirred, writhed, and tightened into something tough and flexible. It couldn't cut me, but I wasn't likely to be breaking loose from it, either. Wind and water don't do much against the power of living things. It was probably some sort of vine she'd cultivated for times like these. "Nobody's going to hurt you, Joanne. Please trust me."

I'd never been able to trust her. Ever. I liked her, but her agendas and mine just didn't match and never had. Her hand rested lightly on my shoulder for a second, then pressed harder, guiding me to a chair. She sat me down, took out another vine from her pocket, and bound my ankles.

"Done?" Paul asked. She nodded and stepped back. Paul—my *friend*—got down on one knee next to the chair and looked me right in the eyes. "Go ahead. Ask."

"Okay," I said. I kept my voice low and calm, even though I wanted to scream at him—it wouldn't do a damn bit of good, and I might need a good screaming voice later. Right now, they were in control. *Wait for an opportunity.* "Use your heads. I can help you; you know I can. You can't afford to ignore the opportunity here. C'mon, guys. Wise up."

He was sweating, I noticed. Paul, the iceman, was sweating bullets, and there were dark patches under the arms of his nice, neat golf shirt.

"This goes way beyond personal feelings. Sorry, babe, but we don't have a choice here. We thought we could contain the kid, but things are too serious now. We need to deal, and with Jonathan on his side, he'll know if we're not playing straight. So you go home. This gets done without you."

"Who had *that* brilliant idea?" I shot back.

"I did." A new voice, coming from the corner. Paul looked over his shoulder, and I saw someone step out of the shadows from beneath the stairs.

It was old-home week at the Holiday Inn. I looked up into the tired, drawn face of Lewis Levander Orwell, my friend, once upon a time my lover, and saw the bleak, black acknowledgment of just how fucked-up all this was. And then I *really* saw, because he wasn't walking on his own. He had a cane, a fancy carved affair that had dragons running up the sides. Extra long, because he was pretty damned tall.

He'd lost more weight, gone from lanky to thin and fragile. His skin had a translucent ivory cast to it, as if he were fading away like a Djinn.

It was an effort for him to walk the four short steps to the chair across from me. No one tried to help him, but I could feel the weight of their attention, their concern. He sank into the plush brown velour with a sigh, propped the cane against the arm, and folded his hands together as he looked at me.

"You look like shit," I said bluntly. I surprised a thin smile out of him.

"Right back at ya. How much have you slept?"

"Averaged out, a couple of hours a day."

"Can't survive that way, Jo."

"You're one to talk."

Silence ticked. Lewis's eyes flicked aside to Paul. "Sorry about the drama. I'd have done this on my own, but frankly, I think you could kick my ass right now."

"I could kick your ass anytime," I shot back reflexively, but I was a little appalled by the fragility I saw in him. He looked . . . breakable. I'd never seen him like this, not even when he'd been hurt.

Lewis was dying. Really dying.

"Don't blame Paul for this. It was my decision."

That got my attention. "Since when do the Wardens take orders from you?" Because even though, technically, he *was* a Warden—the most powerful one in the world—he'd been on the outside a lot longer than he'd been in. Lewis wasn't a conformist, and he hadn't exactly risen through the chain of command.

In true form, he blew past the question. "We can't defeat Kevin by frontal assault. You already understand that."

"I'm having a hard time seeing how keeping me *tied the hell up* is winning the battle!"

"We need to talk to him. Persuade him to give up. It's our only real choice."

"How the hell are you going to get him to talk at all? He's holding all the cards!"

"You let me worry about that part." Lewis shifted, as if something inside hurt him. "First things first. We have to get Jonathan out of his hands. You agree?"

I had to. I knew what Jonathan was, and how important he was to the Free Djinn—plus, Kevin wouldn't have the leverage and force multipliers necessary to destroy the world if we took his Djinn away. "Sure."

Did I imagine it, or did Lewis's knuckles turn a little whiter? "That's our bargaining chip. To Kevin, one Djinn's pretty much like another. He doesn't know Jonathan. He doesn't know how much more powerful Jonathan is than any of the others. That's why we're going to offer a trade."

"A trade?"

He held my eyes. "Jonathan for David."

"What?" I jerked upright, tried to pull my hands apart. Marion's vine compensated by wrapping tighter. The slick, living feeling of it moving on my skin made me want to run screaming, but I forced myself to relax. *Deep breaths.* "You're kidding. Tell me you're kidding." Nothing from him but that slow, steady stare. *Come on, Lewis, lie to me at least. Make a damn joke. Something.* "You can't give him *David!*"

"We'd be a hell of a lot better off," Paul rumbled. "That Djinn you've got ain't no small fry, but he's a quantum level of trouble down from the current situation. And he's been in bad situations before. He even knows the kid."

"David can take care of himself." Lewis's eyes were inhumanly gentle. "We can recover him later. It's a temporary situation."

"*You* can say that? What, like *Yvette* was a temporary situation? Like *Bad Bob* was a temporary situation? He's been through hell, Lewis. I'm not letting you put him through more just because it's convenient!"

"Jo, you need to remember that he's not a *person*; he's a tool." The compassion in Lewis's face was a cold, distant kind—the kind God might have when he looks down on all the unwashed billions. "Discussion's over. This wasn't easy, and none of us want it. But we're up against the facts now, and the facts are that people are about to die. Millions of them. And if we can trade one Djinn, don't you think it's a good equation?"

"In theory. Try standing on my side of the equal sign."

Paul spoke up. "Look, I was hoping I wouldn't have to say it, but if you screw this up for us and we all survive it, that bottle over there gets sunk in a concrete block and dumped in the deepest pit in the ocean. David goes into history, trapped in that bottle. My hand to God."

Lewis held up his hand without looking away from me. "Paul, she knows the score. No need for that."

"Screw you!" I spat back.

"I need you to do this. *I* need you to do this. Just . . . go home. Leave this to us."

Jesus in polka dots, he was *playing* me. Moving me around the board like a chess piece. I could see the calculation behind the earnestness . . . and he was right. It didn't fucking matter that I was being manipulated, or even that David was being put at risk. Again.

I swallowed a rush of bitter betrayal, and said, "Fine. I'll go, but you ought to know that Kevin's not going to keep his end of the bargain. He won't give up Jonathan. He's too scared to do that, and hell, maybe Jonathan doesn't even *want* to go. Ever thought of that?"

Lewis didn't look like he was listening. He was fixed on a spot somewhere beyond me, face blank.

"Lewis?"

He twitched. His eyes stayed fixed on the distance. I looked over at Marion, who took a step toward him.

Too late. His face went from pale to pallid, his eyes rolled up in their sockets, and his whole body went as rigid as that of a condemned man riding electric current. His face distorted, convulsed, and he slid out of the chair to thump down sideways on the area rug.

And then he began to convulse in the worst seizure I'd ever seen.

Everybody was eerily calm about it. Marion got down next to him and held his shoulders; Paul crouched at his feet. I watched Lewis's body spasm, fighting itself, tearing itself apart, and felt tears sting hot at my eyes. He was making choking sounds, and I could hear his muscles creaking.

Lewis was dying. Hell, the whole *planet* was tearing itself apart. This was just the small-scale representation of it.

The convulsions stopped after about two minutes. Marion sat where she was, stroking hair from his pallid, sweating forehead with gentle motions. Lewis stayed down, relaxed now, gasping in heavy breaths and blinking slowly up at the ceiling.

"Well," he finally whispered, "that was embarrassing."

I struggled for words. I wanted to hate him, but I couldn't. I just couldn't.

"I'll go quietly," I said. "That's what you want, right?"

He slowly focused on me, but I sensed he was too tired to lift his head. "Jo, this is so far from what I want. . . ."

"I don't need your apology."

He nodded, sucked in a breath, and blew it gently out. His eyes drifted closed. "Then I'll take a nap, if that's okay."

West murmured something sotto voce, and his Djinn appeared—a cowboy kind of guy, windburned and tough-looking—and scooped up Lewis in his arms like a broken toy. He walked away, out into the sun. I was left staring down at the empty space on the rug, on the fallen cane that gleamed black and abandoned in the hotel lights, and in the silence the mad tinkle of that damn fountain sounded as loud as thunder.

Marion said, "Lewis is the Earth. He's tied to it. We never understood that before, but there's something inside of him that can't be removed, and can't be stopped. He's dying, and it's manifesting itself around us. That's why we can't end this, even with all the power of the Djinn we have left. We need to get Lewis's powers back from Kevin, and we need to do it *now*. Jonathan took those powers away. If we get Jonathan, we can set things right. It's the only way."

I nodded and shoved away the screaming panic at the back of my mind. My voice was surprisingly steady.

"Right," I said. "I'll go home. I suppose you're going to see me to the border."

Marion let me loose from the vine, once they were sure I was in a cooperative mood. I was allowed a last meal—this one in the Denny's restaurant in the motel parking lot, accompanied by my grim-eyed Warden guards and their invisible but ever-so-menacing Djinn. Not that I was planning on a great escape; I thought Lewis had a crap plan, but it was still better than the nonplan I had. I'd tried it my way for three weeks, and I was no closer to getting the situation resolved than when I'd started. Time for somebody else to take a swing, even if it was a swing and a miss.

"So," I said around a mouthful of ham-and-cheese omelet, "which one of you lovely people is escorting me home? Because I don't think for a second you'll trust my word of honor."

Paul looked up, furious. His skin was splotched with red, his eyes bloodshot and raw. "Just stop it, will you?"

"Why?" I chewed another mouthful that tasted like ashes, and sucked coffee noisily just for the sake of annoying them. "Am I supposed to go like a lamb and say nice things about you? Screw you, Paul. You burned me."

I was almost sorry I said it when I saw the devastation on his face. This really wasn't easy for him.

I looked at the rest of them. They avoided my gaze. "Gee, guys, none of you are coming with? That's too bad, 'cause you're just so darn much *fun*."

Paul put his hands over his face and leaned his elbows on the table. Behind him, the desert glittered in sunlight, fresh and dry and clean on the other side of plate glass. Inside, the bright yellow and retro-seventies rust decor looked desperate and grubby around the corners. The omelet I was eating needed salt. I added Tabasco sauce instead.

"We've got a lot to do," Paul said. I didn't stop dispensing Tabasco. "We're meeting a couple of guys; they'll see you all the way home."

"Fabulous." I capped the pepper sauce and began mushing up the omelet to my satisfaction. "I hope you have a plan B handy, because your plan A sucks, and it's going to fall apart faster than a Yugoslavian car. I don't care what Kevin says; he's playing you. He's not giving up his Djinn."

Paul didn't have the moral courage to meet my gaze. "We've got a plan B."

"And yet this stands as the best option?" Silence around the table. I tried a mouthful of coffee. It tasted like sludge. "Wow. We really are screwed."

"Jo, quit making this hard. I goddamn well just got over the shock of you not being dead. Can you quit mouthing off and let me be glad you're breathing for a while?"

"I'll quit being a bitch if you quit selling me and mine down the river." I didn't really want to keep on hurting him, but I couldn't stop. Facing things with fortitude wasn't really my strong suit. Since screaming and crying were out, insults were what I had left.

We tacitly agreed to a mutual cease-fire, to chew in peace.

I finished up and excused myself to the bathroom. Marion started to go with me. "Please," I said, and fixed her with a smile that didn't match what I was feeling. "You *know* I'm coming back. Where can I run? Jesus, let me pee one time in private. I give you my oath as a Warden that I'll come back." I held up my right hand, palm out, and the rune there glittered blue up on the aetheric. Truth, for anybody with the eyes to see it.

Marion nodded and sank back down in the leather-ette chair. She folded her hands together and watched me gravely as I walked away, headed for the door marked with the skirt hieroglyphic. The plastic fake-wood finish had a tacky film on it, a consequence of being located too close to the fry baskets. I didn't actually have to pee, but I needed a minute alone. A minute to stare at myself in the harsh fluorescent light, at the curling, still-damp hair and pallid face, at the dark blue eyes that seemed too haunted to belong to me. When I'd been Djinn, they'd been silver, bright as dimes.

I looked tired. I tugged irritably at my hair, which was *not* supposed to curl like that, and seemed destined to be the bane of my existence for the rest of my . . . probably very short life.

"Snow White."

A cold, gravel-rough whisper. I froze and looked around. Saw nothing. Heard an almost silent laugh that sounded like sandpaper over stone.

I felt goose bumps breaking out all over my skin, and fought back a shiver. "Who's there?" I demanded. No feet under the two bathroom stalls. Nobody else in the room except my reflection.

You know. I didn't know if that voice was in my head, or put there from outside. Creepy, either way. I stared hard into the mirror, let myself float up into the aetheric, and finally spotted something that didn't quite belong. A flicker. *Use your eyes.* Except that my eyes were just plain human these days, not Djinn; I couldn't see in every spectrum, every level of the world. And what was talking to me didn't exist in this one.

Shall I lend you mine?

Something happened in my head, a sharp, tearing pain, and then I was seeing edges to things that weren't there, colors that had texture and depth and no name in the world I lived in.

In the corner, shadows flowed black into a shape that glittered like faceted coal. Spiderlike. Dangerous.

An Ifrit. A failed, twisted Djinn.

A vampire.

Sara? No, it couldn't be Sara; she'd died along with Patrick, both giving up their essences to create a human body to house me. It was someone else. Who . . . ?

Who else called me Snow White? "Rahel?"

Lumps of coal have no expression. She didn't move. I took a step toward her, saw the edges of her start to fray as if she might disappear. "Rahel, wait. Please."

Can't stay.

"Why not?"

Hungry.

Ifrits ate Djinn. I had a sudden, startling moment of gratitude that David was safely locked in the case at Marion's feet, out there in the restaurant. Much as I liked Rahel—if this was Rahel—I didn't want her munching on my lover.

My relationship with her was complicated at best. As a Free Djinn, she'd been my friend, sometimes my enemy; she'd acted to save my life at least once. And I hadn't been able to stop her from being destroyed not so long ago. This wasn't really Rahel. It was the zombie shell of her, undead and undying.

I wanted *strongly* for her to go away.

"What do you want?" I asked

She answered me silently. *Give me food. Tell you things.*

"What kind of things?"

Things to save you.

Her voice was getting fainter in my head, the edges of her looking misty. This was one hell of an effort for her, communicating on this plane of existence. Clearly she needed a recharge to continue. Too bad I didn't carry any handy snack-sized Djinn.

The bathroom door opened, and Marion came in. She ignored me and walked right to a stall, went in, and clicked the lock. The satchel with David's bottle went with her, which gave me the total willies; the Ifrit's head turned to follow her, but she didn't attack. I went to the sink and ran water, scrubbed my hands, and watched the black shadow in the corner. Rahel hadn't moved, but she was fainter now.

"Stay with me," I whispered. I saw nothing, heard nothing in my head, but somehow I knew she'd received the message and agreed. I watched her shadow dissolve completely.

"What?" Marion's voice. I shut the water off and reached for a towel.

"Nothing."

That probably wasn't a lie.

When I came back out, there were two new faces at the table. Paul nodded at them. "Jo, this is Carl Cooper and Lel Miller. They'll be taking you home."

Carl was bland. His hair was dishwater blond and thinning fast; he had thin lips out of practice for smiling. His eyes were hidden by aviator sunglasses, but I had the strong impression that he wouldn't have been any more expressive if I'd been able to see his baby blues.

Lel Miller was a different story altogether. Tall, leggy, gorgeously tanned. She had quite the salon finish, right down to the well-kept gleam of her French manicure. I held up my palm in the traditional Warden hi-there; they each followed suit, and in the aetheric, our runes glittered.

"Charmed," Lel said. She had a sexy contralto purr. She extended a hand to me, palm down, as if she expected me to kiss it.

I took it and examined the bracelet chiming around her wrist. "Nice," I said. "Velada?"

She looked impressed. She reclaimed her hand to pet the silver chain and ornaments, which were small clouds and lightning bolts. "Yes. You know your jewelry."

Paul rolled his eyes. "If it gets worn, she knows about it," he said. "Go ahead. Show her your shoes."

Lel obligingly extended an elegant leg in denim. I glanced at the footwear for a second, looked back into her lovely hazel eyes, and said, "Kenneth Cole." She gave me a self-satisfied smirk. "Knockoffs," I finished. "Probably Taiwan."

The smile went wherever bad smiles go, and she yanked her leg back out of sight. "I wasn't dressing for the prom," she shot back. I thought about pointing out that Velada jewelry was hardly appropriate for breakfast at Denny's, but gave it up. Hell, my shoes were out of pedigree, too. It happens.

Paul was going to lengths to hide a smile. Marion wasn't even bothering. "Okay," Paul said. "Sounds like you guys are going to get along great. You know the route?"

Lel nodded. Carl contented himself with gobbling leftover buttered toast. Not her, I noticed; she wasn't wasting her perfect lipstick on anything so useless as breakfast.

I didn't like her, and it wasn't because of the shoes. Something about her raised my hackles. Carl was just a cipher, but Lel I *really* didn't want to be in a car with all the way to Florida.

Speaking of which, I had a bad, bad thought. "Um, Paul? Can I take my car?"

He nodded. "Yeah, fine. You drive. They'll just ride along."

"Both of them?"

"You got a backseat, right?"

Not much of one, but I wasn't going to be concerned about their comfort. "Sure." And the minute

I could ditch my escort, I'd be heading back to pick up the pieces of this disaster. Because it *was* going to be a disaster. No doubt about it.

Carl finished the toast, swilled down half a cup of coffee with a noisy slurp, and stood. Lel followed suit more slowly.

"Jo." Paul reached out and took my hand, just for a second. "I'm sorry."

"Oh, you're not *nearly* sorry yet," I said. "Get back to me later, though."

It was the hardest thing I'd ever done, to walk away and leave David behind.

I'll find you. I promised it to him with a grim, burning fury. *I will. No matter what.*

My Viper started up with a roar.

Lel had called shotgun, leaving a disgrunted Carl in the cramped backseat. She seemed completely uninterested about why they were babysitting me on a drive back to Florida; in fact, she slipped on headphones and flipped a switch on an iPod, and ignored me completely. Which was fine with me. I backed my midnight-blue Mona out of her parking space and eased her into gear. The freeway beckoned ahead.

"So that was your Djinn, right?" Carl asked, just as we hit merging speed. Nobody on the road in either direction. I opened Mona up to eighty and kept an eye on the horizon for cops or storms. "Your Djinn they're trading over to the kid? Must suck, right?"

"Sucks," I agreed tightly. "We're not going to chat, right?"

"Long damn trip if we don't."

"Longer if we do."

He sighed and settled back. Lel bobbed her head in time with a beat I couldn't hear, and I watched the miles start to spin away.

There was a huge, gaping empty space inside me. I couldn't feel David anymore, and that was the worst part. Not knowing where he was, what they were doing with him. How *could* they believe Kevin? Were they really that stupid, or just that desperate? Kevin wasn't exactly a brilliant strategist, but he had a certain criminal cunning . . . and you could count on the fact that if he had the chance to double cross you, he would. He was greedy, he was selfish, and he'd never been treated fairly in his life. He'd believe you were going to screw him anyway, so why wait?

As a survival strategy, not half-bad. As a way to live, it was a tragedy.

I kept half my attention up on the aetheric as I drove, looking for trouble and hoping for a sign. There was a huge roiling disturbance centered behind me, in the direction of Las Vegas, but it was like an impenetrable wall of confusion.

David had told me that this had to happen. I didn't understand why, but all I could do was trust him, trust Lewis, trust in the goodwill of the universe.

Not really in my nature.

We'd gone about fifteen miles out into the big nowhere when Lel took the headphones off, looked over the backseat at Carl, and said, "This about right?"

"Yeah," he said. "Looks right."

"For what?" I asked, and that was when Carl took a gun out from under his tan windbreaker and pointed it to my head.

"Pull over," he said.

I felt a cold-hot bolt of shock. "You're kidding."

I heard a metallic snap, cold and harsh, right next to my ear. "The next sound you hear kills you. Pull the car over."

Lel was watching me with a little half smile, satisfied as a cat in a cream factory.

I drifted the car to a stop at the side of the road and stood on the brakes unnecessarily hard. My legs were shaking. I've been on the wrong end of a lot of situations, but the wrong end of a gun was a different story. *God*, I hadn't seen this coming. . . .

"Out," Carl said, and handed the gun to Lel. "Cover her."

The woman was good at it; I never felt there was a split second to take advantage of, and besides, there were two Wardens on me, and it wasn't like I could overpower them, not without David. Not without a huge, costly fight. The memory of being shot in the back overwhelmed me. I'd survived it, but not without cost, and not without pain; I didn't have any wish to try a rematch of me versus Smith & Wesson. I opened the car door and stepped out, keeping my hands up and in a helpless position.

"You understand that if I feel so much as a light breeze, you're dead," Lel said conversationally. I nodded. Strange feeling, to be so cold when the sun was so hot; my hands were clammy. I wanted to wipe them on my skirt and didn't dare.

"Look," I said, "if you want the car—"

"Shut up. Walk," Lel said, and jerked her chin out in the direction of the desert. It looked pretty much like every other part of the desert. Nothing out here but sand, cactus, and the occasional vulture. Somebody had used the road sign for target practice. The aged buckshot dings were rusted rich orange.

As we struggled through hot sand, heading over the nearest hill, I wished for some more sensible shoes to die in—crazy, the things that go through your head. I wished desperately for David's warm, comforting presence, not to mention his ability to kill these two roaches really, really dead. I wished for a lot of things that I couldn't have. *Stupid! Should've seen this coming.* Except the idea that someone might have ordered me killed had never so much as entered my mind. Who the hell were these guys working for?

The sun beat down like a yellow hammer on the top of my head. I remembered what sunlight had felt like as a Djinn—that incredible sense of pure power soaking into me. As a human, it just made me feel overheated and exhausted.

"Okay, hold it," Lel said.

"I can keep walking; I'm not really tired," I offered; my voice sounded squeaky, full of bravado. Hiking was not my fave, but it was better than . . . well, a hole in the head.

Lel ignored me. She glanced over at Carl, who was on his cell phone, turned away from us, talking softly. The wind was staying still, thankfully; I didn't doubt that she was paying attention to *that*. Or that she'd shoot me if she suspected I was trying something tricky.

We waited. I shifted nervously from one foot to the other, watching the clear skies, feeling exposed and all too defenseless. "Look," I said. "I don't know what's going on, but if it's a matter of money . . ." Not that I had it, but I'd figure something out.

She gave me a beatific smile, waking dimples in her cheeks, and smoothed her perfectly behaved hair as a very slight breeze drifted by us, trailing the sharp, hot smell of mesquite. Carl finished his phone call and turned back to us. Lel handed him the gun. No words between them; they were obviously a tightly rehearsed act.

"Um . . . what now?" I asked.

"Now we wait."

"For . . . ?"

No answer. The sun got hotter. Despite the chill that continued to pebble my skin into gooseflesh, I was sweating buckets, and I didn't dare wipe my face. My arms were getting tired from their half-mast position of surrender.

We heard the faint growl of an engine. Lel's eyes turned toward the direction of the highway as it revved and died away.

It appeared the criminal mastermind had arrived. I waited, sweating and worrying, until a tall, lanky form limped slowly toward us from the maze of dunes and spiked thornbushes.

"Lewis!" I blurted, and felt a spurt of relief like ice water . . . just as I realized that neither Lel nor Carl looked surprised to see him.

Oh, fuck.

"You look bad," Lel said to him—clinical analysis, not concern. "You sure you're up for this?"

"Yes," Lewis said. He had his cane again, and he was gripping it in a white-knuckled hand as he leaned his weight on it. His color was an unhealthy yellow-gray, and there were hard lines of pain around his eyes and mouth. Pale lips that nearly vanished, they were so colorless. "Just don't take long."

My hands had come down. A jerk from the gun made them go back up again, grabbing sky. "Lewis?" I asked it very softly, watching his face. He looked at me for a few long seconds, then down at the sand.

"It's the way it has to be, Jo."

"Wait—"

He nodded to the Terror Twins. Lel removed a test tube–shaped bottle from her coat pocket. Now *there* was a bottle I wouldn't have put a Djinn into, under any circumstances. One roll off of a table, and *poof* . . . unfortunately, I was all out of tables, and Carl was holding the gun like he seriously meant to use it.

"Lewis! Just tell me what the hell's going on! Look, I can *help*—"

"You are helping," he said without looking up. "Lel. Do it."

She popped the cork, and a Djinn misted into being next to her. Tall, dark-haired, kind of a business-class version of Raquel Welch. The Djinn's eyes had a distinct reddish tinge to them, which was unsettlingly demonic, and the red-painted nails on her flawless hands had definite talon potential. She was wearing a suit that damn sure looked like Prada to me, sleek and dark and elegant.

No shoes, disappointingly. Her legs misted down around calf level, in the traditional Djinn way. She didn't waste her energy on anything as human as feet.

I waited for Lewis to say something. *Anything.* To goddamn well *look at me.*

He moved the cane in front of him and braced himself with both hands, staring down. Absolving himself of responsibility.

"I swear to God, Lewis, I won't forget this," I said. "Whatever you're doing—"

Lel cut me off with a simple, direct command to her Djinn. "Stop her heart."

I sucked in a fast, hard breath, not really expecting to finish it, but then my lungs were full and I was holding my breath and *still* nothing was happening. The Djinn in Prada and Lel were exchanging looks like nuclear weapons.

"Did you hear me?" Lel asked through gritted teeth.

"Clarification is required," Prada said. Ah, it was like that. Apparently, Lel had done something to get on the wrong side of this Djinn. Bad timing: Djinn liked to toy with people, especially ones they didn't like. And they *really* didn't like to be used as cheap executioners.

Lel's fingers tightened around the test tube, then relaxed; she couldn't risk even a hairline crack in it. Her dimples started looking hollow instead of cute, and her eyes took on a hard, sharp shine. "Stop her heart from beating. How much more clarification can you need?" Lel's eyes cut to Lewis, but he didn't comment or move. His head was still down, his shoulders tensed.

Prada had a cruel tilt of a smile. "Specify," she purred. Carl muttered a soft, exasperated "Fuck me!" and the Djinn's smile gathered force, as if she were really very amused. I glanced frantically from Prada to Lel to Lewis, and felt a scream building somewhere like fizzy soda at the back of my throat.

"Lewis, help me," I whispered. I got an involuntary look from him, a flash of dark eyes that betrayed how much this was costing him, this stillness and silence.

And he looked away again, leaving me to my fate. My heart was hammering so fast and hard I thought it was shaking me apart; I was trembling all over, and my knees had gone the consistency of rubber bands. There was some panicked screaming going on in the back of my head, along the lines of *I don't want to die!* and if this went on any longer, I wasn't going to be able to keep my cool.

"If you're going to do it," I said in a surprisingly steady voice, "don't screw around. I'm not going to beg." Unless it went on another thirty seconds.

For the first time, Prada's reddish eyes flicked toward me. Read me like a book. I saw her face go still and blank, and then those flawlessly made-up eyelids went to half-mast and she held out a hand toward me. An open hand.

I felt her power reach out and fold around me, sink deep into my skin, my muscles, my bones. It kept moving, tightening, focusing around the panicked thick drumming of my heart.

"No," I whispered, and tried to back up.

No use. There was a second's pain, and then my heart just . . . stopped.

So much silence. I never knew how quiet it could be. The wind whispered over me, brushed black hair over my shoulders, and I knew I should breathe but breathing didn't seem that important now. *Listening* was important. There was so much to hear. . . .

I fell to my knees. I know that because I heard it happen, heard the heavy, fleshy thump and each individual grain of sand rolling and scraping.

Lel bent over me. The sun gave her a completely inappropriate and undeserved halo. "By the way, they're *not* knockoffs, bitch."

Prada kept squeezing the life out of me. I wanted to say something, but I had no idea what, and anyway, there was nothing left now, nothing but the vast silence and a burning desire to see David, one more time. . . .

It all happened so fast.

The cold black glitter of an Ifrit launched itself over me and battened on Prada like a glittering black second skin. It began to feed. Prada reflexively did the only thing that would save her . . . she translocated. Because she was still sunk elbow deep in me, stopping my heart, I felt the drag as she towed me with her.

"No!" That was Lewis, yelling. "No, not yet, not yet—"

I felt Lel reaching out, but it was too late; we were already moving, already in that *not there* space between worlds.

My last thought was, *Oh shit, my heart isn't beating. . . .*

And then I hit something, hard, and that all stopped mattering.

FOUR

I was lying on a tiled floor. It was hard, warm, and damp. The air smelled hot and moist, earthy, heady with the perfumes of a hundred flowers. I saw blackness and star fields streaming away from me, and people were running toward me.

Being dead was oddly painless. Oh, wait, I wasn't dead yet, was I? Just dying. Takes minutes for the brain to shut down, and meanwhile, I had a fixed-stare view of thick-leafed succulents rustling overhead, of a tracery of milky glass and black iron beyond that. Faces kept appearing and disappearing. They all looked alarmed.

One of them leaned over me and did something that made my ribs creak. As he leaned over, I thought, *I did not give you permission to French me,* and then I realized what was happening.

I was being revived. Chest compressions. Mouth-to-mouth.

I choked, and felt something flutter in my chest

under the painful stiff-armed pumping someone was giving me. The first hint of a heartbeat.

"She's coming back!" My rescuer had turned away, yelling; he was young, African-American, wearing what looked like an official-type security blazer with a logo on it. Nice cologne. When he turned back, I offered him a loopy smile. "Hey, just stay still, okay? We've got an ambulance coming."

"I'm fine," I said, and tried to get up. He was as strong as he looked, and I felt a good deal weaker than I should have. "What happened?"

"You collapsed, ma'am. Look, don't move. Everything's—"

Definitely not okay, I saw as I pushed myself up on my elbows. Prada was down flat on the tile a few feet away, and a black, sharp-edged shadow was crouched on top of her like some hideous gargoyle.

"Hey! Stop it!" I tried to sit up. I'd been locked in a struggle with an Ifrit when I'd been a Djinn myself; I knew how terrible it felt to have the life torn out of you. . . . "Rahel, *stop!*"

The Djinn was eerily silent, but the Ifrit was making noises—eager, whimpering noises, like a starvation victim at an all-you-can-eat buffet. Prada's face was turned away from me, so I couldn't see the agony in her expression, but I could see her whole body trembling. Shaking apart. Misting at the edges, sublimating into the aetheric.

The Ifrit began to change. Take on shape and form and texture.

Take on color.

Lel must have finally mastered her confusion and ordered the Djinn back in the bottle, because suddenly

there was a sensation of vacuum, and she was gone.
The Ifrit, deprived of her feast, fell to humanlike
hands and knees on tile, still making those raw,
wretched noises. Her form wavered, solidified,
became . . . Rahel.

"She's not making any sense," my savior in the security blazer said to an army of paramedics, who arrived wielding tackle boxes and professionally bored
expressions. One had a gurney. Not that a bed didn't
look good, but I *really* didn't have time for this.

I swatted aside his hand. "Am too." And then it
came to me, why he thought I was crazy. I was watching Rahel, and Rahel didn't exist for them. They
couldn't see her. I blinked and fell back flat, being
obliging for all the nice medical folks who took BP
and pulse and talked about various things that I didn't
understand but which sounded very official. The world
slowly came into focus around me, now that the crisis
was passing. We were in a huge greenhouse, a Victo-
rian monstronsity that stretched up at least two or
three stories in graceful arches of wrought iron and
frosted glass. The place was delirious with flowers and
lousy with plants, but every single one was perfectly
groomed. Not a speck of dirt out of place. I couldn't
tell if the birdsong and insect hum were real or prere-
corded; this was so perfect it was more like a simula-
tion of nature than nature itself. We were in the center
of the garden, near the picturesque, dignified gazebo
where tourists by the millions had no doubt taken
blurry photos to commemorate losing their shirts. I
smelled food, and spotted a restaurant about twenty
feet away. At the far end of the indoor garden, there
was a hallway leading into the hotel lobby.

This all looked familiar. *Really* familiar.

The paramedics and security were keeping gawkers at bay, but there were lots of them. People of all ages, races, classes. Tourists in tacky shirts and walking shorts, complete with fanny packs. Guys in hand-tailored $5,000 suits talking on cell phones. One woman in a dress far too cool to be anything but couture, carrying a Fendi bag and wearing a selection from the Miu Miu fall collection on her feet. Kids in Rugrats T-shirts.

Holy shit. I was in Las Vegas.

It took me the better part of an hour to get rid of the various forms they wanted me to sign. I also had to appease grimly unhappy officials, and discovered I was now a guest of the Bellagio Hotel, courtesy of scaring the crap out of them by dropping dead in their conservatory. They had no way of knowing that I'd been dumped there out of the aetheric, and I didn't see any reason to explain it. I whipped up a quick story about coming to town and looking for a good hotel, and they bought it; I accepted a complimentary key card and escaped back to the conservatory as quickly as I could, hoping she'd still be there.

And there she was. Rahel. Sitting on a park bench, waiting. She rose gracefully to a standing position, brushed nonexistent dust from the neon-yellow pant-suit she favored, and straightened to look down at me as I walked up. Her head tilted to one side, cornrows rustling like dry leaves, and in that beautiful, dark-skinned face her eyes blazed yellow as summer suns.

"Snow White," Rahel greeted me. Her voice still

sounded strained, as if she'd spent hours screaming. "Feeling better?"

"Not very." I extended my hand. She looked at it as if she had to decide whether or not to snap it off, then took it in hers, shook, and dropped it. Her skin felt hot and dry, perfectly solid. "Thanks for waiting."

"I was about to abandon you. I don't have long." She looked peeved at the reminder. "She was weak." Meaning the power she'd drained from Prada wouldn't last long, and then she'd start to revert back to the shadows. "I did what I could for you. Be mindful, sistah. You owe me."

"Definitely . . . Ah, quick question, but do you know where David is—"

"Still in the hands of your *friends*," she said. "I can help you no more. I must feed to regain my power."

I grabbed her hand, and quickly let go. It didn't feel right. It sure didn't feel as smooth and soft as it looked. "Wait. You can't, Rahel, you know that it'll wear off. You have to know of a way to cure yourself. Don't you?"

Hot, predatory eyes met mine, and I had a very hard time holding the stare. She growled out, "No. I will exist in this form, feeding from others, or I will die. *Your* doing. Yours and David's."

I remembered the last time I'd seen her; like most of the Free Djinn, she'd been trapped by the contamination in the aetheric, poisoned by pretty little blue sparklies that had eaten her from the inside. I'd watched her die, or at least I'd believed so at the time. Her disintegration had looked more like being digested than just temporarily banished.

Okay, great, she was holding a grudge. Not good,
but then, she'd just saved my life . . . at least
temporarily.

She took my silence for agreement. "There will be
an accounting. For all of those who are brought
down."

"But not now," I said. Without realizing it, I'd
started rubbing my chest, over my heart. "Right?"

Long, long stare. I broke out in goose bumps, but
didn't let her see it, hopefully.

"We will speak of it," she said softly. "If you
survive."

"Doing okay so far." It came out sarcastic. I swallowed my reflexive need to strike out. "Rahel, thank
you. Thank you for my life."

She regarded me without blinking, then turned and
plucked a bright yellow flower from a nearby plant.
The broken stem oozed clear blood; she licked it away
contemplatively, fastened the flower in her glossy
black hair, and gave me a smile that betrayed razor-
sharp teeth.

"You're welcome, Snow White," she said. "But
don't get too comfortable in your new skin. You may
not have it for long."

I held myself very still. She circled slowly around
me, walking as gracefully as a tiger, watching me all
the while. Sunlight caught in the amber beads at the
ends of her cornrows, and glinted on an Egyptian ankh
worn around her neck. Soft gold, with a look of antiq-
uity to it. The Djinn were such an odd mix of old
and new, like Socrates on a skateboard. "Your enemy
is coming."

"Which one?" That sounded flippant; I hadn't

meant it to. I mean, it wasn't like I just had the one anymore. *Lewis, oh, God, what the hell deal did you make, and what devil did you make it with . . . ?*

Rahel grabbed hold of my shoulder, leaned closer, then shivered as if she'd been caught in a mortally cold wind. The shape of her changed, hardened, grew cold, then snapped back into focus, into defiant neon yellow and elegant, tall lines. Into flawless skin and the eyes of a predator, glittering with urgency. "Your enemy is coming. Listen to me, Snow White. The Djinn need you. You must not trust . . ."

Her lips were still moving, but what was coming out was just noise: a kind of grinding, growling screech, fading into silence. Despair sparked once in her expression, and then she blurred like an out-of-focus projection and turned dark, glistening, cold.

Nightmarish and spidery.

I yanked my hand away and jumped back, driven by memories of what it had been like to fight an Ifrit, but she didn't come after me. Humans didn't classify as food for something like her. She just . . . faded away.

"Rahel?" I looked around. Filtered sunlight, glossy green leaves, the whisper of flowers and fountains. I turned in a slow circle, stunned by the beauty, by the loss, by the enormity of what I was supposed to accomplish. Just surviving seemed like a heavy load, right about now.

A family of five passed me, consulting maps and pointing in more directions than a compass. They crowded the gazebo for a picture. I had to wait for them to clear the path. I fumbled the key card to my complimentary suite out of my skirt pocket and wished to hell I'd actually thought to slip a credit card in there . . . or cash. . . .

I felt a surge of power zip along my spine, smelled ozone, and got up, fast. Something was coming my way, and it wasn't good.

Your enemy is coming, Rahel had said. Looked like he was almost here. I cast about for someplace to go, realized it would be pointless, considering who I was up against, and decided to stand my ground.

A blue static spark jumped from the wrought-iron bench across six inches of empty space, and zapped me just as the hum of insect and bird activity in the conservatory went still.

The earth stopped breathing, or at least it stopped where I was, as Kevin Prentiss wandered into the building. He saw me, paused for a few seconds, then stuck his hands in his jeans pockets and sauntered my way. Funny, becoming king of the world hadn't changed the kid much. He was still plain, acned, surly, shaggy, and badly dressed. From the aroma that wafted my direction—sweat and sour clothes and desperation—he hadn't taken personal hygiene to heart, either. He was wearing a hooded gray sweatshirt over a T-shirt that read, partially obscured, UCK YOU, with a one-fingered illustration. His sneakers—red Keds—looked battered almost beyond recognition. Greasy too-long blue jeans with the hems torn out sagged around his shoetops.

He stopped about ten feet away. Gunfighting distance.

"Been wondering when you'd show up," he said. "Where's your boy toy?" Meaning David.

That stung. I had a hard time keeping my voice even. "I'm alone."

"How'd you get in?" Kevin jammed his hands in the pockets of his sweatshirt and made belligerent fists in the fabric. "Shouldn't have been able to. Nobody can get in who's like you."

"You mean Wardens? The Wardens can't get in?"

"Just the ones in Vegas here before me." He shrugged. "Thought this place'd be fun. It's kinda boring. I mean, it's cool and all, but . . . I wanted to be away from all of you, and you just keep on coming after me. I mean, what did I do to you?"

Besides wrecking the Wardens' vault and screwing around with powers he didn't understand? "I guess they're worried you're out of control, Kevin."

"I'm not."

"And then there's Yvette," I said slowly. "Who's dead."

Kevin's eyes flew up to meet mine, wide and defenseless, and I saw the memory unfold in them. He'd done that. He'd ordered her killed, and he hadn't flinched.

He was flinching now.

"Bitch deserved it," he said. It sounded tough, but it was all 'tude. He had a huge amount of power, and nobody could tell him what to do . . . but he was alone. More alone than anyone I'd ever seen. "You'd better not cross me, yo?"

"Yo." I spread my empty hands in a gesture of surrender. "Not crossing you. But maybe there's something I can do for you."

"Yeah?" He kept it neutral, but I saw the flare of hope in his face. "Like what?"

"Like make a deal for you. You give up Jonathan, give back the powers you stole—I think the Wardens won't make more trouble for you. You just go on about your business." Not that I was empowered to make deals for them, but I was here and he was talking. And with the deep game Lewis seemed to be playing, the faster and simpler I could make this, the better.

Kevin shook his head. "No way. He's all I got."

"Sooner or later they'll get to you. Look, Kevin, I don't care how much power you've got; sooner or later they'll take you down. You *know* that. Let me—"

"I don't need your help." He took a shuffling step my direction, probably trying to look menacing; he succeeded in looking like he was going to trip over his ragged hems. "You shouldn't even be here. No Warden alive can get past the city limits; that's what Jonathan said."

No Warden alive.

Oh, Lewis. You bastard . . . you could've let me in on the plan. . . . He hadn't wanted Paul and the others to know. He'd been doing this himself, in secret. Hence the abduction by Lel and Carl, and where the *hell* did my innocent, peace-loving Lewis find a couple of hard-core killers like that? Lovely.

"Well? What're you waiting for? Go. I'm ordering you to . . . you know . . . go!" Kevin made a shooing motion. If it hadn't been so pathetic, I'd have laughed.

"I can't. Not a Djinn anymore, and I don't happen to have one on me, either." My mind was racing like an engine on idle, making lots of noise and going nowhere. "Hey, you want to send me packing, use your own."

"Who? Him?" Without looking up, Kevin made a

little circle in the air with his finger in the general direction of the roof.

I figured he wasn't talking about God. "Jonathan," I clarified. His hand dropped back to his side, but there was a flash in his eyes that might well have been fear.

"You don't want that. Maybe you should just take a bus or something. But you'd better get moving, or I *will* tell him you're here, and tell him what to do with you."

"Is he in the bottle?" I asked. Kevin scuffed a shoe on tile and looked surly. "C'mon, Kev, be a sport. Is he running around loose or did you seal him up?"

"He told me if I stuck him in the bottle one more time he'd cream me." The prominent ball of Kevin's Adam's apple worked up and down. "Not like I can't handle him, but shit. Let the old geezer have some fun, you know?"

"If he's out of the bottle, he already knows I'm here," I said. "Look, Kevin, I never hurt you. I tried to help you. You know that, don't you?"

"You've been trying to bust down the door ever since I came here. You and all of *them*." He jerked his chin in the general direction of nowhere, referring to the Wardens, I was sure. "Well, you're here now. Hope you liked the ride."

I took a step toward him. Just one. His head jerked up, and so did his hand, pointing at me in some awkward parody of a stage magician. *Theatrics*, part of my mind reported dryly. *He probably has incantations to go along with it.* Kevin had power, and he'd rubbed elbows with trained professionals, but I was pretty sure his entire understanding of how magic worked had more to do with Saturday-morning cartoons than quantum physics. He had power of his own—fire, as I recalled, and a pretty sizable talent—but by himself, he wouldn't be hard to defeat.

But he wasn't alone, and if I started a fight I wasn't going to win. Lewis wanted me here, and he'd gone to amazing lengths to get me in position; it'd be a shame to waste a perfectly good murder on something so stupid as picking a fight with Superpsycho.

I stopped, folded my hands like a good girl, and waited for him to make some kind of rational decision.

His eyes swept over me, and I was sorry again that I hadn't dressed for the occasion—if you're going to risk your life, you ought to at least look good doing it. The shoes weren't holding up well under the abuse, and they'd been no-name knockoffs to begin with— I'd blown out of New York with no time for quality shopping. Ah, for the good old days of Djinnhood, when I'd been able to conjure Manolo Blahniks out of the aetheric . . . What did heroic last stands call for, anyway? Versace? Jimmy Choo? I was still steaming over Lel's last jibe at my shoe savvy. Those had *definitely* been knockoffs.

"Come with me," Kevin said. He shot me a brief, hot sideways look. "You try any shit with me, I'll do you like I did . . . Yvette." He had trouble calling her *Mom* these days. I was amazed that he'd ever been able to choke the name out, the kind of hell she'd put him through. My sympathy for him didn't make him any less threatening.

I had a vivid red memory of what had happened to

Yvette. I didn't think I'd ever really be able to forget the sound of her skull crushing. "I'll be good."

He started to turn away, hesitated, and said, "What's your name? For real, yo. None of that Lilith bullshit you pulled last time."

"Joanne."

"Oh." A frown layered his forehead. "For real? Huh. I thought you had a better one than that."

"Better?"

A vague gesture. "You know. Hotter."

I took offense. "You mean like Vanna LaTramp or something? Some pole-dancer name?"

Shrug, and two hot little circles in his cheeks. "You don't look like no Joanne to me."

"Yeah, well, you don't look like a Kevin. Okay, you would if you had a haircut and some decent clothes. . . ." I knew my mouth was running off with me, but I couldn't stop it, and then he was turning on me, hand raised.

I froze. He didn't hit me, but it was a close thing.

"Bitch, don't act like my fucking *mother* unless you want to die like her." *Ouch.* His tone had gone opaque and steel-cold, edged with fury. So much for the light conversation. He was trying to be those dangerous, badass villains he'd watched in movies. The problem was that he *was* dangerous, and I knew it better than anybody. The image of Yvette Prentiss came back to me as she screamed out her last moments of life. Kevin had watched her die without so much as a blink. However much he might *look* like just another Generation X punk, he was more than that. Worse.

She'd made him that way.

I didn't dare push him. I gestured politely and said, "After you."

He grabbed my arm and towed me toward the lobby of the Bellagio.

With enough money, *everything* can be made tasteful. The lobby of the Bellagio was a good case in point. I couldn't imagine the mind-boggling amounts spent on this place . . . the fantastically ornate blown-glass floral ceiling for a start, which would have been beautiful if it had been two feet across, but at forty feet was so overwhelming it nearly whited out the mind. Soft, soothing carpet underfoot, edged with bright, shiny marble. Well-scrubbed tailored staffers. Endless rows of counters waiting to do nothing but serve paying customers. The place was thick with tourists, most outfitted in whatever the latest Abercrombie & Fitch ad told them would make them cool.

Too bad for me that nobody seemed to notice me, Kevin, or the way he was twisting my arm to get me to keep up with him. I wasn't sure if it was a standard don't-see-me glamour or just people minding their own damn business.

"Like it?" Kevin had noticed my look around. He sounded proud, as if he'd designed it. "I coulda stayed anywhere, but this was the best."

Like he was paying for it. "How do you know?" I asked him.

"Cabdriver said."

If there was anything that spoiled the elegance of the Bellagio's image, it was the constant musical chatter of slot machines. Beyond the lobby stretched the casino . . . and it *stretched,* filling a mall-like expanse with a sea of multicolored flashing slots and quiet harbors of blackjack tables, roulette. Dark paneling gave the place a quiet nineteenth-century elegance. Lack of windows made it eternal early evening. Bars—and there were three I could immediately spot—were doing a brisk business. The thought of a steadying drink made the back of my throat ache. *C'mon, Lewis, help me out here. Throw me a bone.* I had one faint hope: Lewis had some kind of clever, deeply ingenious plan for getting me out of this alive.

Yeah, right. You are *the bone that got thrown.* My snarky superego was probably right; the Wardens—including Lewis—weren't interested in my troubles at the moment. I was a distraction, and I was on my own.

People everywhere, moving with a purpose. This was a *very* bad place to try a confrontation, which was probably Kevin's point in choosing it. Or Jonathan's. Sounded like Jonathan logic to me; Kevin would have probably crawled into some hole in the ground and pulled it in after him, like a kid hiding his head from the bogeyman. Jonathan was the one who'd think of all of the defensive possibilities of a very public, high-profile establishment.

Kevin steered me off into the casino area, and we strolled past one bar, heading past slots, more slots, keno, blackjack. We passed a room marked PRIVATE, where, when the door opened and closed, I caught a glimpse of a poker table and some intensely silent men hunched around it. *And you think* you're *playing for high stakes, pals. Try my game.*

"Where are we going?" I asked. Kevin didn't answer. We turned left at the T intersection, away from the casino area and into what looked like (to my instant, back-brained delight) a shopping mall. A *high-class* shopping mall. Only he didn't lead me that direction; he steered me toward a massive bank of elevators, complete with polite and flinty-eyed security men who waved us through when I fumbled out my card key.

We stepped into the lift and enjoyed a silent, efficient ride up into the stratosphere.

"How'd you get in?" Kevin finally asked, as the lights flickered past the twenty-fifth floor. "Just curious."

"I was dead."

"Oh." He stared, waiting for the punch line. "Kind of extreme."

"You're telling me."

He couldn't decide whether or not I was lying, but it didn't much matter; the elevator topped out, and we exited one floor from the top.

It was a long walk down an elegant hallway big enough for the chariot race from *Ben-Hur*. The last door on the left was his.

It swung open for him at a touch, and I felt the dim, out-of-focus surge of power. Fire, this time; he'd just fooled the locking mechanism with an electric charge. Nice bit of control, that; he'd been largely untrained last time I'd seen him, mostly in the smash-and-grab phase of things.

I took a step in and realized that Kevin had appropriated the presidential suite, or at least the vice-presidential one. It was huge, sumptuous to the point of pastiche, but never over the edge. I was pretty sure the furniture was antique, for the most part; if it was reproduction, it was in the best of taste.

Kevin let go of me, shut the door, and shuffled over the wine-colored Aubusson to a fully appointed bar. He poured himself a straight glass of Jim Beam. I refrained from lecturing him about the evils of distilled spirits or reminding him of the legal drinking age.

I looked around. "Where's Jonathan?"

He rattled crystal. "Around." Which meant he had no idea, probably.

"You keep his bottle on you?"

"You smoking crack? I'm not telling you where I keep it."

"Not asking you to," I said. "Hey, would you mind . . ." I mimed pouring. Kevin splashed some JB in another glass and handed it over, and I took a sip. *Wow.* Liquid heat, turning into burning lava somewhere midthroat. Well, it was happy hour somewhere in the world.

I nearly spluttered my drink when a new voice said, "Enjoying your stay?" It came from the corner of the room, where a big leather armchair sat facing a broad plate-glass window overlooking the white spray of fountains. I set the glass down and took a couple of steps to my left to get a better look.

Not that it was any surprise, really, to see Jonathan sitting there. He looked relaxed. Fully at home. Head back, eyes half-shut, feet up on a virtually priceless Federal table that really shouldn't have been mistaken for a footstool under any circumstances. I let myself stare at him for a few long seconds. It wasn't a chore or anything; he appeared middle-aged, light brown hair liberally scattered with gray. The wiry, strong build of a habitual runner, dressed in faded blue jeans and a forest-green fleece pullover. Some kind of deck shoes on long feet. The kind of casual cool that the trend-driven shoppers downstairs could never hope to imitate.

He was the only Djinn I'd ever met who had humanlike eyes, at least at first glance. His were dark. I happened to know, because I'd looked pretty deeply into them at one point, that they weren't just dark; they were black, they were infinite, and they were *dangerous*.

Jonathan didn't have to work to impress anyone. All he had to do was show up.

"Well," he said without looking in my direction. "I leave you for a little while, and you go all human on me. You really know how to survive, I'll give you that. So. Life treating you okay?"

"Yeah, not too bad." I was shaking inside, vibrating on levels I didn't know I could still feel. Maybe there was some Djinn left in me, after all. "You?"

He quirked a funny little smile. "Fine. Hey, about all this, it's nothing personal. You know. And incidentally, way to work the angles. He said I couldn't let in any living Warden. Dying for the cause—strategically sweet." He tipped back a bottle and swallowed a mouthful of beer. "They give you some kind of performance bonus for that?"

"Gift certificates and a special parking space," I said. "Mind if I sit?"

He shrugged and indicated an elegant brocade chair a few feet away. I eased down on it, smoothing my skirt with sweaty palms. Over at the bar, Kevin was drinking his Jim Beam and looking defiant about it.

"So," Jonathan said, and smiled. I didn't like the

smile; it was cold and hard as a glacier. "I guess they sent you here to make a deal. What've you got that I might want?"

As if his master—his *nominal* master—weren't even present. That gave me the shivers. I'd known the kid wasn't up to the task of owning and operating a border collie, much less a Djinn, but . . .

"Nothing," I said. "Except I can call off the Wardens and give Kevin a chance. A better one, anyway, because you and I both know that his days of surviving this are shorter than the shelf life of a loaf of bread."

Preaching to the choir. Nothing moved in Jonathan's pleasant expression, in the impenetrable depths of his eyes.

"You're assuming I care about that," he said. "Maybe there's something else we can talk about."

I could guess. "You still want David's bottle. I don't have it anymore."

It occurred to me, rather too late, that if I didn't have David, Jonathan had no reason to keep me breathing. In fact, he had a pretty nice incentive to make sure I stopped. David would grieve, he would get over it, things would—on the Djinn scale—go back to relative normalcy; eventually Jonathan would be able to rescue him, and without the distraction of me, David would willingly go.

"I know you didn't give him up on purpose," he said. "Who's got him? Where is he?" Jonathan asked. He looked relaxed, but I wasn't deceived; I also felt something weird in the air. Kevin was standing motionless, staring at the Djinn. Like he was waiting for some kind of direction. Yeah, the whole master-servant thing was topsy-turvy on this one.

"The Wardens have him," I said. "It's out of my hands. You'll have to provoke a full-out war to get him back now."

. "You say that like it's a bad thing." Jonathan took his feet off of the antique table and stood up. He had a kind of energy to him that made me shiver—restless, intense, fueled by something I didn't fully understand. "You think we can't win a war like that."

"I *know* you can't win a war like that. But more important, a whole lot of people would die in the middle of it, and neither one of us wants that to happen." I hoped.

He walked up to me, hands in his jeans pockets, and stood there looking down at me. Lightless eyes. Something cold moving in their depths, like dying stars.

"Don't assume you understand what I want," he said. "Human life is cheap. There's only one race I have a vested interest in protecting—the one you use and degrade and throw away. *My* people. If a war with the Wardens is what needs to happen to get my point across, well, that's just very sad for you. I'm not letting you trade us like trinkets any longer."

"Hey," Kevin said. He'd moved in behind me while my attention was focused on Jonathan; it creeped me to realize that I hadn't noticed. "Wait a minute."

"Quiet," Jonathan hissed. "The lady and I are having a *conversation*."

I yelped as my chair suddenly began to slide, as if shoved hard from behind. Heading for Jonathan, who stepped out of the way . . .

. . . and then heading straight for the plate-glass window.

I felt panic grab my throat, because the chair kept accelerating and I *knew* I was going to hit the glass, crash through, tilt out over that sickening drop, and fall. And scrabbling my feet on the carpet wasn't slowing me down.

Jonathan brought the chair cleanly to a stop right at the window. I grabbed the arms so tightly I felt something crack, either wood or my fingers, and panted out the shock and fear.

"See that guy down there?" Jonathan asked, and tilted my chair up on its front legs to give me a better view. I *meeped* and clutched the chair arms harder. "No? Well, okay, granted, they all look alike from up here. Here, I'll help."

My forehead touched the glass.

It rippled like water, and I melted right through the slick, cold surface, head and shoulders. I felt fresh, hot air blast over me, fast as the jet stream, and my hair whipped back in a tattered black flag over the back of the chair. I was afraid to breathe. The glass felt molten at the edges, thickly liquid around my body. It wasn't holding me in place. There was nothing now between my tilted chair and thin air but Jonathan's goodwill, which I wasn't sure I actually had. I kept trying to push backward, but I wasn't going anywhere.

"That man down there is some kind of Warden," Jonathan said. "A leftover from before I put up the wards. Granted, he's not very good, but hey, he's what you guys are known for, right? Secondhand crappy work? That's why people die night and day from your negligence. Can't blame me for that."

"I don't," I managed to choke out between clenched teeth. "We do the best we can. And if you'd work *with* us instead of *against* us, we'd be able to help more people. But you're not about helping anyone, are you? You're about freedom at any cost. Jesus, if we free the Djinn, we can't touch the big storms, the major disasters. The ones that kill a hundred thousand at a whack. Who will? You?"

The chair thumped back down to the carpet, and the glass re-formed in front of me with a thick sucking sound. Waves rippled through it, then stilled. I looked up into Jonathan's dark, endless eyes, and remembered falling into them as a Djinn, remembered the age and seduction and limitless *power* of him.

"Nobody ever asked us," he said, and sank down to a crouch next to me. That smile was beautiful, cynical, and utterly chilling. "Not that we'd say yes, but it'd be nice to be *asked*. But never mind all that. Who sent you here?"

"Nobody."

"Let me put it another way . . . somebody made sure that you were dead enough to get by the wards and dropped you right in our laps. Who?"

"Bite me." The chair tilted again. Glass against my forehead, fluid and warm, flowing around me. I whined somewhere deep in my throat and closed my eyes. "No, really, I mean that. Bite me. Just don't throw me out the window, 'kay?"

"Scared?"

"Oh, yeah." I managed a pallid, sweaty smile. "You?"

He leaned over to study me, upside down. "You're so expendable they practically fired you out of a circus cannon. You do know that, right? I think you're a diversion. Something for me to play with while they bring in the big guns."

Kevin, in the background, cleared his throat. "Don't you think—"

"No," Jonathan cut him off. "Let me take care of this."

"But—"

"Son, this is out of your league," Jonathan said. Not unkindly. "She played you before; she'll play you again. Just let me handle it."

"Okay." Kevin sounded lost and uncomfortable and very much a kid. He'd been a lot more difficult when I'd been his Djinn, but then, the dynamics of that relationship had been a whole lot different. He'd looked on me mostly as a supernatural blow-up doll. Jonathan was, in a very real sense, the father he'd never had, and a *very* kick-ass dad he'd make.

Except I didn't think he had Kevin's best interests at heart.

I turned my head and looked straight up into Jonathan's eyes. "Don't use him. He deserves better than that. If you want to kill me, just do it; don't drag the kid into it. It's cheap and it's cruel."

I got a quirk of ash-gray eyebrows, a flash of surprise across the ageless face. "I thought he was a murderer. A rabid dog that needed killing. That's what the last Warden had to say before he took the express elevator down. You can still see the splash on the sidewalk if you look closer." He tilted my chair again. I yelped and tried to push myself through the back of the cushions. Hung on for dear life and tried to swallow the urge to beg for my life.

Twice in one day. "You really think the kid deserves a chance?"

"I think he needs to be stopped," I said breathlessly. "I don't think that necessarily means he has to be killed. And since I may be the only one who thinks that, you really ought to think twice about giving me the vertical tour."

This time the glass just disappeared. *Poof.* The legs of the chair were one inch from the window. Tilted forward as I was, my knees were already exposed to the bright Las Vegas sun. Below, the Bellagio's fountains roared like Niagara, and I could taste the metallic humidity of them evaporating under the desert's constant fixed stare.

I started to slide out, and the sunlight slid hot over my thighs, illuminated my stomach . . . I was going over, screaming.

That was when Jonathan pulled in a breath so sharp and hard it was audible over the tearing wind, and reached out to yank me back, into the seat. He let the chair thump safely back to the carpet.

Stared down at me with wide, dark, surprised eyes.

"*No,*" he said. "He couldn't possibly be that stupid."

He, who? Lewis? *Au contraire, mon ami.* I was feeling like everybody was acting fairly stupidly, including me with the bravado. I struggled to breathe without sobbing. *God*, I didn't like heights, particularly heights from which I would drop to my death and do a fast, ugly survey of thirty-five floors on the way down. I looked up through my wind-tangled hair and saw Jonathan still staring. He looked honestly spooked. It lasted for two or three heartbeats, and then he got control of his face and went back to his habitual I-don't-give-a-crap expression.

"It won't work," he said, and leaned over to get right in my face. "I don't care what he told you, it won't work. If he told you it would guarantee I wouldn't hurt you, he lied. Understand?"

I didn't. Before I could say so, Kevin said, "Don't throw her out the window. Bring her over here to me."

A straight-out order. Kevin's voice shook when he gave it, but Jonathan didn't object or try to screw with him; he towed my chair across the room and delivered it in front of the kid, then stood back, hands in his pockets. Watching me through half-closed, expressionless eyes. I could feel fury pulsing behind it, though. He was mad, all right. I had no idea why. Wasn't like I'd done anything but try not to get myself launched, and I hadn't even done that effectively.

Kevin looked fragile next to him.

"Close it," he said to Jonathan. The roaring hot wind coming in the open window suddenly cut off. Shiny, flawless glass back in place. Some tense, panic-stricken part of me kept on screaming, but I forced it to shut up.

"What happened to the other Wardens who were sent?" I asked. Kevin slumped those narrow, sharp-edged shoulders and studied the carpet.

"They came before I told him to keep them out."

"You had him kill them?"

"I didn't tell him to."

"Did you tell him *not* to?"

Shrug. I closed my eyes briefly to block out the sight of Yvette dying, screaming. "How can you possibly think you're going to get out of this alive, the way you keep screwing up? You can't *kill* these people; they'll never let go of you!"

"I know." Kevin looked forlorn. A little boy again. "It was just the one; I just scared the rest and they said they'd stay away. I just wanted them to leave me the fuck alone. Why can't they do that?"

"Because you have something that doesn't belong to you." *And you're using it incredibly badly . . . or it's using you.* "The Wardens don't know what's going on in here. They've sent people; they haven't heard back. They're afraid you're killing people in here. Kevin, if you'll just tell me what you've done—"

"Nothing!" He still had the crystal tumbler in his hand, half-full of Jim Beam; he launched it across the room to take out an elegant table lamp with a crunch of porcelain. "Jesus! I'm just trying to have some fun, that's all . . . don't I deserve that? Not like my life hasn't sucked hard enough . . ."

"Baby?"

We all came to a complete halt at the new voice . . . female, soft, high-pitched. Blurry with sleep. I twisted my head and saw that the door to the bedroom had opened, and there was a girl standing there. There was a lot of her on display, since the sheet she was covering herself with didn't exactly drape properly— lots of pale skin, some of it tattooed in dark blue Celtic patterns along the left arm and thigh. She had light hazel eyes, and her red hair was cut short in a straight-out-of-bed tangle that salons would work for hours to achieve. Not pretty, really. A wide jaw, narrow eyes, prominent cheekbones—and then she turned her attention away from me toward Kevin, and the light caught her face just right. Beautiful. Beautiful in a narrow, starved kind of way, a heroin-hungry elegance.

"Oh," Kevin blurted, and blushed. "Uh . . . nothing you need to worry about. Business." He pulled himself up straighter. "Just go back to bed, okay? I'll be there soon."

The hot hazel eyes wandered back toward me. "Who's she?"

"Nobody."

"Looks like somebody." She pouted, and shuffled toward the door dragging the Egyptian cotton sheet along with her. "Come back to bed, okay?"

"In a minute."

"Now?"

"In a minute!" His temper flared, and I saw the hurt explode in her eyes in response as she looked back. "Jesus, Siobhan, just go back to bed, okay? I'll be there in a minute!"

She turned and went back into the other room, the door closing quietly behind her. I looked up at Kevin, who was staring after her, and said, "Siobhan?"

His cheeks flushed dark red. "Never mind."

"You pick her up out on the strip? Or did you get Jonathan to conjure her up for you?"

"Shut up, okay?"

"She's real. Not Djinn." I kept staring at him, forcing him to meet my gaze. "Kevin, tell me you didn't kidnap this girl. And how old is she? Sixteen? God!"

"I didn't kidnap her! She was on the street." The red flare in his cheeks was turning purple. "You know. There were these cards. Dropped on the sidewalk."

Hooker cards. Of course. "You're paying her?"

Jonathan, who'd resumed his comfy chair with his feet up, snorted and said, "No, she's with him for his witty personality."

"Shut up!" Kevin yelled. Jonathan picked up his half-empty beer and took a long pull. It must have warmed up while he was tormenting me; mist floated off of the bottle as he chilled it down again. "Look, she's . . . she's just company. Never mind her. She doesn't matter."

I wondered if she knew that. I thought about the hurt I'd seen flash in her eyes. "All right. Let's talk about you. You want to get out of this alive?"

"Depends." He settled into a mulish, utterly teenage expression. "Don't mind dying. I'm not afraid."

Unbelievable. I looked from him to Jonathan, who raised his eyebrows and gave me a lime-bitter slice of a smile. "Don't look at me," he said. "I'm just the help."

Right, I was the Church Lady. "If you want me to make a deal with the Wardens, you've got to give to get. What are you offering?"

Kevin cut his eyes toward Jonathan. "I'll turn him over if they let me go." He threw it out like a challenge.

Jonathan had no apparent reaction as he took a swig of beer. "Don't do it," he said mildly. "They'll screw you. It's what they do."

"Yeah, well, *you* don't listen to me!" Kevin looked even more stubborn, and turned his attention back on me. "You want him? Fine. Just let me go."

I felt the words wash over me like an ice-water

shower, and tried to keep the expression out of my face. "So you'd just . . . turn him over. Give me his bottle."

"I don't need him." Like hell, but maybe he really believed it.

"Fine. You hand me the bottle; I'll find a way to get it to them." I kept it casual. Hopefully, he wouldn't realize that once I held Jonathan's bottle, I'd be in control of him . . . and that would be the end of Kevin's little joyride. I'd put Lewis's powers back where they belonged, set things right, smash the bottle, and be out of this whole damn affair. Then they'd *have* to give me David's bottle back.

Or maybe I'd keep Jonathan's bottle until he *made* them give David back. Yeah. That could work.

Kevin was thinking it over. "You swear? You'll let me go?"

"Absolutely," I lied without a qualm. "Trust me."

He was going for it; I could see it in his eyes.

"Okay," he said. "I'll get the bottle. You stay right here."

He took a couple of steps away, faltered, turned back.

"Oops," Jonathan said. He took another drink of beer.

"What?" I asked, and then I felt the air go odd and dead in the room.

I sucked in a startled breath, saw Kevin's eyes widen, and he asked, "You *bitch*, I said I'd let you—" He broke off into a sickening gagging sound and reached for his throat, whooping in a deep breath. I felt a burning, clawing sting in the back of my mouth, tried to scream, and realized that if I did I was dead. I turned toward Jonathan, who was watching us with mild interest.

"Can't let him do that," Jonathan said. "I've got things to do. People to see. If you know what's smart, Joanne, you'll stay the hell out of my way."

"Help—" I croaked. He shrugged.

"You're a Warden. Help yourself."

Kevin was already passing out. He pitched to his knees, clawing at his throat. His face was scarlet.

In seconds, he was down. Unconscious or dying.

I needed to breathe, and breathing wasn't an option at the moment. A stupid little rhyme ran through my mind, the punch line of which was *what he thought was H_2O was H_2SO_4.* Chemical humor. My brain cascading uncontrollably, trying to find the answer in the rummage cupboard of my memory.

I let go of my body and felt it thump down on the expensive burgundy carpet, thick enough to qualify for mattress status, and launched myself hard into the aetheric. Reached for clarity. The air turned solid around me in a three-dimensional glittering cube, and I plunged deeper, deeper, hunting for what I knew would be there.

Two molecules added to the complex chain that made air breathable. Just two.

No problem, I could do that. I was good under pressure.

I stretched out power like a thousand hands and began crushing those molecules—or, more accurately, shaking them up like soda pop, changing their electromagnetic signature and rendering them unstable. Crushing them would have meant too much energy being released, and with the kind of poison that had been formed around us, that would have killed us just as fast. Us and most of the top three floors of the hotel.

This shit was extremely flammable. Jonathan really didn't care, did he? This was just another exercise for him; he wanted to see me jump through hoops. Maybe he was mad because I'd actually made Kevin agree. . . .

Quit dicking around and work fast. That voice in my head was entirely unnecessary; I knew how little time I had before either Kevin or I sucked down too much of this crap to survive it. I wasn't enough of a biology geek to know what it would do to me, but I figured it would be fatal and it probably wouldn't be an easy way to go. *Come on, move it. . . .*

God, I needed David. . . .

No, you don't. You did this fine on your own before. It's not big enough to need a Djinn. Need was such a subjective thing. *You did this in training, remember?*

Yeah, well, in training sessions I wasn't trying to *breathe* it while I was altering it.

I realized that my fingers—at least the aetheric representation of them—were getting clumsy, and I dropped down partly into Real World land to form a pocket of pure oxygen around my body, then around Kevin's. I felt myself gasp, felt the rush of relief that followed, and went back up to patiently continue the work.

Something prickled along the back of my neck, which up there wasn't really my neck, or really a prickle; if Jonathan had done this to us, why wasn't he trying to stop me from fixing the problem? And why go to such lengths? He could have just put Kevin to sleep if he'd wanted.

I abandoned the repairs, which were mostly complete anyway, and dropped down into my body like a speeding bullet, breathlessly fast, got to my feet and stumbled for the door . . .

. . . and ran into a man coming into the room.

A man with a gun.

I'd describe him, but really, the only thing in focus for me was the gun. I knew some fancy Fire Wardens who claimed to be able to block the ignition sequence in the firing chamber of a gun, but that took guts, mad skill, and a liberal dose of luck, none of which I had at the moment, and besides, I wasn't even a Fire Warden. My lungs and exposed skin were still aching from exposure to the poison-soup air.

I put my hands up and considered knocking him over with a gust of wind, but the steady stare of the gun made me abandon the idea. He looked like a guy who could shoot straight through a hurricane, if necessary.

He gestured silently. Sign language for *get your ass out here*. I shuffled cautiously out, hugged the wall, and stared at the gun some more. It was an automatic, I knew that much. It looked black, angular, and deadly efficient.

"You Joanne Baldwin?" he asked me. He had a nothing kind of a voice, not deep, not high, not impressive. A trace of a West Coast drawl, maybe. I nodded. I couldn't seem to take my hand away from my aching throat. "Good," he said. "You got the bottle?"

I shook my head and coughed. My lungs throbbed.

The gunman reached over and shut the door. "Poison gas, right?" he asked. "Damn. Guess it's not a good idea to go in there and toss the room just now."

I shook my head. He holstered the gun and held out his hand, and just like that, he came into focus for me. A wallpaper kind of guy with black hair, a clever face, and light brown eyes. Two-day growth of beard.

"Nice to meet you. My name's Quinn," he said. "I'm here to rescue you."

FIVE

Some rescue.

When it became clear I wasn't the damsel in distress—or at least not the kind Quinn could save me from with his heroic .45—he grabbed me by the elbow and hustled me down the hall, into the elevator, and out through the casino in record time.

I was getting tired of being hustled.

As we stepped outside onto the wide portico, with its huge sweep of overhang and constant stream of limos and taxis dropping off money, I yanked myself loose and stepped back, hands in fists at my sides. *At last.* Out in the open—more or less—and breathing natural air.

"Hey!" I snarled. Quinn's eyebrows did a funny little up-and-down jerk, and then his face went reflectively impassive. "Pal! Back off, will you? I don't need your damn help! I had things under control!"

"Yeah, it really looked like it," Quinn said. He calmly reached into his pocket and took out the gun again, in full view of the uniformed doormen. One of

them looked alarmed and reached for a phone; Quinn
also moved his coat and revealed an official-looking
gold badge in a black holder snapped over his belt.

Quinn was a cop.

"Let's take a drive, sunshine," he told me, and
steered me out into a holding pen reserved for taxis
and cars for hire. A dark brown Ford Taurus sat
among them, shiny as a roach, and Quinn popped
open doors and put me in like a criminal with a hand
on my head, into the backseat. I immediately tried the
door, but of course it didn't open. Childproof locks
had a lot to answer for.

Quinn's driver's-side door opened, and he bent over
to fix me with a look out of those light toffee-brown
eyes. "Play nice," he said. "Don't make me cuff you."

I put my hands pointedly in my lap. The car's upholstery groaned slightly as he got in, and then the engine
fired and we were moving down the long driveway
into blinding Las Vegas sun, heading for a huge sign
that spelled out the current Bellagio attractions in
glowing starlike lights.

"I'm under arrest?" I asked. "What's the charge?"

"Criminal stupidity," Quinn said.

"And you're full of shit. I told you, I didn't need
rescuing, and if I'm not under arrest, Detective
Quinn—"

"Consider yourself a material witness in an ongoing
investigation."

"An investigation of what, exactly?"

He took a right turn onto Flamingo Road, negoti-
ated with a Lexus for a lane change, and headed the
car down Las Vegas Boulevard. "Murder," he said. "I
had a guy pitched out of that window about a week

ago, you know. Messed up my sidewalk something terrible. I guess you know that nobody else can see those
knuckleheads up there. You must be a Warden, right?
Wardens can see them."

Now that the panic was starting to subside, I felt
tired and achy. Groggy with leftover adrenaline. "And
you? You're a Warden?"

He held up his right hand. I made a pass in the air,
concentrated, and saw the telltale sparkle of wards
reflected on his skin. Quinn's aetheric tattoo was an
ankh, the Egyptian symbol for life. Which didn't
match the stylized sunburst I'd expected to see.

"*Not* a Warden. What the hell are you?"

"Need to know, sunshine."

"As in, I don't need to?"

"I know you thought you were being all clever and
shit, but the kid wasn't giving you Jonathan's bottle.
Oh, he was going to give you *a* bottle, but it was one
with a nasty toy surprise inside. He already pulled that
on one other poor bastard." Quinn's glance in the
rearview mirror was grim and assessing. "I take it you
have some experience with Demon Marks."

Where the *hell* had he heard that? Not even the
Wardens knew much about it. The Djinn knew, but
this guy wasn't Djinn; I'd have been able to tell that
much. Not a Warden, not Djinn, but *something*.

And yet, when I took a look at him in Oversight,
he was just a guy. Nothing special. Not even any powers to speak of.

Quinn could tell I wasn't going to offer any color
commentary. "If he'd given you the bottle, you'd have
uncorked it to order Jonathan in," he said. "Only

problem is, that would have let something else *out*, and we've got quite enough of that kind of problem going around right now. So sorry, but I had to stop you."

I felt a flush of cold through my veins. It was *possible* Quinn was right; Kevin's brain worked that way. If he could have found a way to screw things up, he'd have done it. And giving up . . . It wasn't really his style, was it? Taking out the enemy in the most horrifically violent way possible, *that* was his style. And if there really had been a booby-trapped bottle . . .

During Kevin's escape in New York three weeks ago, he and Jonathan had released from their bottles at least three Djinn who were infected with Demon Marks, which meant that they were clinically insane, at the mildest interpretation; I knew that two of them had been located and recaptured, safely labeled as hazardous materials, and stored in some underground vault in Colorado. The third remained on the loose. It figured that Kevin might have grabbed up one of the other unbroken bottles as insurance. He could have passed one of those to me, and that would have meant passing me the Demon Mark when I opened up the bottle. Yippee. Been there, done that. Really didn't care for a return engagement.

"Where are you taking me?" I asked. Useless question. He didn't even bother to glance in the rearview. There was no plastic divider between me and Quinn, and I was starting to wonder what the effects of a decent wind gust would be inside the passenger area of a Taurus, but then Quinn took an abrupt right turn, up a long, wide drive.

Toward the gleaming glass pyramid of the Luxor Hotel, guarded by the massive golden bulk of the Sphinx.

"Oh," I said. "Cool. I always wanted to stay there."

The Luxor was like the Bellagio, only different. I kind of liked the Egyptian theme better, but then I've always been pretty ostentatious in my fashion sense, and besides, in the cluster of high-end shops by the entrance I spotted evidence of Jimmy Choo, Prada, *and* Kate Spade. That plus all the ornamental gold and enamel . . . well, I almost forgot about Quinn's gun and badge and hand on my arm.

For a minute.

The gaming area was virtually identical to the Bellagio's; only the wallpaper and carpeting and uniforms were different. The money was universal, and so was the mingled, vibrating sense of euphoria and desperation. I couldn't resist; I let myself slip the leash of the material world a little and rose up into the aetheric, just enough to catch a peek.

When I was a Djinn, the aetheric had registered in patterns and wavelengths of light. These days, human senses limited me to the surfaces of things, and a kind of broad psychological interpretation of auras. On the aetheric plane, the casino was almost a photonegative of how it appeared on earth. Instead of brilliant and glittering, it was dark, shadowy, peopled by ghosts whose auras fired in flares of manic excitement or despair. I don't mean that everybody there was addicted . . . far from it. But there was a *shine* to it that reminded me unsettlingly of the way the blue sparklies had looked, up on the aetheric, when the route had been open from the Demon Realms into our own.

I wasn't sure what that meant, but I decided I didn't have time to solve the world's problems, anyway. One problem at a time, and mine was towing me through the casino at a relentless pace.

"Hey, you're not going to take me back to your presidential suite and hang me out a window, are you? Because that's so last half hour ago . . ."

"Quiet," Quinn said absently. He strong-armed me up to one of those areas labeled PRIVATE, guarded by not one but two strong-looking guys in discreet blazers with not-so-discreet bulges under their arms. They nodded to him. He nodded back. One of them jerked a chin at me. They all gave me the once-over.

All in silence.

I gave myself the once-over, too. Clingy shirt, short skirt, high heels that were just short of being quality . . .

"In your dreams, guys," I said. "It's not what it looks like."

"She's with me," Quinn said.

"Watch it, Quinn," one of them warned. They were virtually identical—Buzz Cut Number One, Buzz Cut Number Two. Number Two had a slightly thicker neck. Number One had cool, chilly gray eyes. "Don't make us come in there."

Quinn fixed them each with a look, and I mean a *look*. Whatever he'd been using with me had been his friendly-puppy act, because that look was outright scary, promising evil and death in man-sized portions.

"Gentlemen," he said, and Buzz Cut Number One slid a key card through a slot and opened the door for us.

Beyond was a small, smoky room. In another setting it might have been labeled *intimate*, but in this one it was just small. Low lighting in the faux-Egyptian sconces along the wall, plush dark carpeting underfoot. A full bar at one end, with a uniformed bartender on duty.

In the center of the room, a round table, and five men sitting around it.

Playing cards.

The cards were floating in midair in front of each player; as I watched, an older gentleman who looked like he'd been made a CPA in the days of the pharaohs decided to fold, and lowered his hand facedown to the green baize surface. The room smelled of cigar smoke and sweat-soaked money. I didn't know how much the pile of chips on the table represented, but it was a lot. A *lot*. I didn't dare peek into the aetheric this time. Some things—I knew this instinctively—really shouldn't be seen.

"Quinn," the accountant grunted, and the rest of the players looked up. I was staring at the hand of the man directly in front of me; the floating cards showed he had eights over queens.

"Sir." Quinn's demeanor had changed again, this time to the respectful public servant. He let go of my arm. "Joanne Baldwin. Joanne, this is Myron Lazlo."

"Charmed," the accountant said, and nodded in my direction without getting up. "You're a Warden, correct?"

"Weather," I said. "You?"

He had a lived-in face, lined around the eyes. High cheekbones that made him look like he'd stored a couple of tight, small apples in them for the winter. The suit—what I could see of it—was easily a four-grand tailored job, probably from Saville Row or Rome. Beautiful gray wool. The tie was a Villa Bolgheri silk, knotted to perfection.

I revised my estimate of his total net worth up by seven figures.

"I'm not a Warden," Myron Lazlo said. "Neither are these other gentlemen, I assure you."

"So you're what, ankh guys? What's up with that?"

He gave me an unamused, unwelcoming smile. "Quinn, you're being unmannerly. Bring a chair for the lady, please."

Quinn moved without comment, came up with a straight-backed chair, and moved it into position away from the table.

"If you'd be so kind as to wait a moment," Lazlo said. "We're almost finished with this hand."

I sat down, crossed my legs, folded my hands, and waited. Quinn and his gun and his dead-eyed stare kept me honest, as did the idea of the Buzz Cut twins outside the door. Plus, whether they wanted to call themselves Wardens or not, these guys had something . . . defying gravity wasn't something that most people, not even *my* people, casually went around doing. I had the unsettling feeling this was just a parlor trick, so far as they were concerned. I spent my time trying to figure out how they did it. No Djinn in evidence. I concentrated on the air, but it was following the normal flow patterns dictated by the forces of the room—the silent current of the air-conditioning coming from the top left-hand corner, swirling into corkscrew eddies as it was drawn down by gravity toward the floor. The hotter flow was a shimmer of yellow, filtering the opposite direction. Some kind of filter system in operation, technology I didn't recognize that attracted the chemical chains of the smoke in the air and funneled it away. As smoky as this room was, I realized it could have been much worse. Five men, each puffing away on cigarettes or twenty-dollar cigars for hours on end . . . made me gag nicotine to think of it.

I didn't see any signal, but a sigh went through the four remaining players, and three folded and one raked in chips. Lazlo gathered the cards and neatly shuffled them back together before handing them off to a Luxor-uniformed factotum. The dealer put the cards into an envelope, pulled a self-seal, and labeled the outside of the envelope with the date, time, and some kind of code number. So there could be analysis done later, I assumed, in case of an allegation of cheating. Nice.

He put a fresh, unbroken deck on the table and stepped away to stand like a statue in the corner, near the bartender.

"Now," Myron said, and gave me that parsimonious smile again, "let's talk about you, Ms. Baldwin. What brings you to Las Vegas?"

If he could ante up that fake a smile, I could see it and raise him on wattage. "Sun, fun, shopping . . ."

"Could it be that you're here to make a deal with Mr. Prentiss on behalf of the Wardens?"

I looked at Quinn. He was leaning up against the

wall, arms folded, watching me with bright, uninformative eyes.

"Could be," I said. "Could be I'm here to kill him. Could be I'm just in the wrong place at the wrong time. That happens more than you'd think."

Myron laughed. "My dear lady, I can also see into the aetheric, you know. And while you are intemperate and occasionally unwise, you lack the necessary ruthless detachment to be able to execute young boys. Even in pursuit of the greater good. And besides that, the Djinn would stop you, you know. However, I think you actually believe you might do it, so I'll give you the benefit of the doubt and not consider it a lie." The laughter faded out of his eyes and left them chilled and scary. "You do not want to lie to me, my dear. Really, you do not."

Okay, now I had a creepy bad feeling. They knew about the Wardens. They knew about Kevin. They knew about *Jonathan*. Was there anything these guys didn't know?

"Your attempt to stop him is foolish," one of the others continued. He was a short, gnarly-looking little man, approaching middle age but not yet arrived: slicked-back black hair, rimless glasses, eyes of no immediate impact behind them. "The Wardens need to stay out of this. They caused this mess, just as they've caused hundreds more in the past thousand years."

"Oh, okay. We'll just pick up our toys and go home." I smiled at Gnarly Guy, saw a faint flush spark high in his cheeks. "You *do* know about the temperature rise, don't you? Global warming? Impending ice age? Earthquakes? You *do* think we should do something to stop that, right?"

Silence. They all looked at me, and then Myron Lazlo said gently, "Actually, my dear, no. We don't. And that is our difficulty. The Wardens long ago exceeded their authority when they began to enslave the Djinn and force the world to their own uses. The system has long been out of balance, which is why you have to work so hard to keep it going. What you're speaking of is simply the logical result of so many mistakes. It can't be corrected by working even harder to control it."

"Then how can it be corrected?" I asked.

"By letting go," he said. "By giving up the illusion of control and allowing the world to right itself. That is the only way we can find our balance again."

"And how many millions is *that* brilliant strategy going to kill?"

"As many as it takes, my dear. If the Wardens had followed the right course a thousand years ago, we'd not be facing this kind of apocalypse now, but they refused to believe. More power, they said. More power will fix what's broken. But it won't, and you know that on some level, don't you?"

Things started to fall into place. "You've been fighting us."

"No," Myron said. "We've been correcting you. We stand on the side of the Mother. On the side of balance. We are Ma'at."

I stared at them, blank. They stared back. After a long moment, Myron smiled beautifully and nodded at the bartender.

"I believe our guest might require a drink," he said. "You favor whiskey, I believe? Although I find a gin and tonic to be quite refreshing at moments like these."

I ordered something, no idea what it was even as I was saying it, because my whole attention was fixed on what was opening up before me. Another world. The answer to the difficulties the Wardens had been facing, the reason the damn world didn't *cooperate.*

I was looking at an enemy the Wardens didn't even know they had. And dammit, they didn't even *register* as Wardens. As anything at all. How the hell could they do anything against us?

Silence reigned until the uniformed bartender pressed something into hand. I sipped. Not whiskey. Something bitter and bracing, cool as limes on my tongue.

Myron said, "We are the keepers of the balance, Miss Baldwin. I trust you have some understanding of what I'm saying?"

"I don't care if you call yourself the Justice League of America, you're screwed up," I said. "Don't you realize that you're playing with *lives*? People are dying out there. *Millions* will die."

"And that is a very natural thing," put in another player. "Sentimentality should have no place in an analysis of the environment. Things die. It's the nature of the world. You acknowledge that sometimes fires must burn so that the forests may be renewed. Surely you apply the same standard to the entire world."

"So now humanity is a forest and you're going to let a fire burn us out? Kill to cure?" I gripped the sweating glass hard in my hands and strove to keep my voice steady. "I stand corrected. You're not screwed up; you're insane."

"We have a long view," Myron admitted. "To you, it might seem cruel, but I promise you, my dear, it's the best thing in the end. The more power you expend preventing the Mother from correcting the balance, the more violent the correction will be when it comes. And even the Wardens understand that you can't stop everything you identify as a disaster. Far from it."

"Yeah, thanks to you guys, I'll bet." I took another fast drink. The stuff was strong, judging by the numbed feeling in the back of my throat; I set the rest of it back down on the floor, but before it touched down another uniformed flunky was there to grab it and carry it safely back to the bar.

"It was the Wardens who forced things out of alignment thousands of years ago," Myron said. "The system began to fail the moment that they discovered they could force the Djinn to their service, instead of asking for their cooperation. Which brings us to the sorry state of affairs we find ourselves in. Djinn no longer act for us; they act against us, in constant subtle ways. The earth itself struggles to throw off the chains. And the Wardens are so oblivious, they simply tighten their grip around their own throats."

"Wow. That's poetic," I said. "So you brought me here to lecture on the evils of the Wardens?"

Myron looked amused. So did the rest of them, even Gnarly Guy, who looked like he wasn't amused by much this side of the grave. Myron passed the unbroken deck of cards to his left and nodded to the table. As if he'd given some signal, the rest of them scooted around, leaving space for another chair.

"No. We brought you here to play cards," he said. "Join us, Miss Baldwin. We could use a bit of feminine strategy in this room. Don't worry. We'll play it the normal way, out of courtesy to you."

I shot a look at Quinn, who was a statue against the wall; he had a long-distance stare that didn't seem to see me anymore. I stood up and instantly one of those suit-coated big men picked up my chair and carried it to the card table.

Myron indicated the place with an open hand. I tried another pleading look at Quinn. It was like pleading with a statue of Stalin.

I took the seat, and the new dealer—an elegantly put together little man with big Coke-bottle glasses—expertly snapped the seal on the deck, fanned the cards for inspection, shuffled, and began the deal. I was about to say that I had nothing but my shoes to bet with, but before I could draw the breath someone—I looked up and saw it was Quinn—had put a rack of chips down in front of me.

"I trust you know how to play," Myron said.

I gave him my very best innocent smile. "I went to a couple of casino nights in college." I fanned the hand I'd been dealt. It sucked, naturally. That didn't matter. I was about to teach these masters of balance something about tipping the scales in your own favor. "I'm in."

We played Texas Hold 'Em, and they cleaned my clock.

Two hours later I was sweating, broke, back down to betting my shoes, and out of the game. Quinn politely carried my chair back to its proper interrogation distance; when I looked mutinous about sitting down, he put a hand on my shoulder. Not that he pushed, exactly. Just put a hand on my shoulder, with authority.

I sat. Besides, my feet were starting to hurt, and my pride was bruised.

The old men played another three hands, silent except for raising and calling, folding and grunting in satisfaction when they won. It looked to me like Coke-bottle Glasses was winning. Nobody seemed bothered.

At some invisible signal, they just stopped playing. Myron gestured to the Luxor-uniformed factotum, who came around, counted chips, and handed over handwritten notes. Once the green baize table was clear, they passed their slips of paper around to Myron, who read each one and put them in some kind of order. Then he folded his hands on top of them.

"The vote is concluded," he said. "Mr. Ashworth holds the right of decision in this matter."

Vote? *Vote?* They voted by playing poker?

It hit me two seconds later what name he'd used. *Ashworth.*

That could be a coincidence. There were lots of people named Ashworth.

Coke-bottle Glasses stood up to his lofty height of about five feet, straightened his nondescript but highly expensive gray suit, and took off his glasses. Without them, he had a dignified if sharp-featured face. He fixed a fierce gaze on me.

And I knew. There was a family resemblance, no question about it.

"I believe you knew my son," he said. "Charles Spenser Ashworth the third. I am Charles Spenser

Ashworth the second. You may call me Mr. Ashworth."

I opened my mouth to say something, no idea what, but he stopped me with one upthrust finger and an intensely unpleasant look.

"Joanne Baldwin," he said, "I have won the right to decide what is done with you. Do you understand that?"

I managed to nod. I was too busy looking over his shoulder at Quinn, who'd come to full alert. Quinn had some features about him that reminded me of Carl, back in the desert. Adaptable to the situation, even if the situation called for death and mayhem.

I was unexpectedly nostalgic for the Bellagio hotel room, and the hair-trigger tension of Jonathan and Kevin. At least I'd been among friends.

Ashworth was talking. ". . . avoided telling the truth six years ago. You will not avoid it this time."

I wet my lips. "May I say something?" I got a terse, jerky nod from Ashworth. "I was cleared of charges by the Wardens."

"By the Wardens, yes." His contempt was clear. "We do not acknowledge the—how shall I put it?— *impartiality* of the Wardens. The venally corrupt should not be judging the guilty."

"Hey! Did we miss the part where I was *not guilty*?"

"I'm sorry, my dear, but you see that we may not necessarily agree with the decision," Myron said. "You were responsible for the death of one of our own. And now you must answer for it."

"To his *father*? Call me crazy, but what's impartial about that?"

Myron spread his hands in an elegantly helpless gesture. "You saw the game, my dear. He won the vote. In fact, you even participated. You had the opportunity to win your freedom. You failed."

These guys were insane. "I didn't know I was playing for it!"

"Would you have played more skillfully if you'd known?" He studied me for a long moment, then reached in his pocket and withdrew a white-gold cigarette case, tapped out a cancer stick, and lit up. "Continue, Charles."

"You will tell me," Ashworth said. "You will tell me how my son died. Now."

Oh, I *so* didn't want to do this, especially not now. "Look, this is *six years old,* and we have a real problem, don't you get it? That kid over at the Bellagio has the power to—"

Somebody electrocuted me.

A charge zipped up from the carpet, the metal leg of the chair, into my flesh and bones. I lost control. My body convulsed in a galvanic response, frozen by the current. Electrocution doesn't hurt, in the strictest sense of the word; there's no way to feel pain when every nerve in your body is frying into carbon.

It isn't until it *stops* that your brain gets the signal and you feel the pain.

The second the current cut out I pitched forward, gasping in great whoops of air, shuddering, feeling as if I'd dived into a lake of fire. Someone's hands kept me from sliding out of the chair. Not Quinn's. He was still across the room, doing an imitation of a statue. I felt a bright sting of panic inside at the thought that they might do that to me again, but I kept myself from babbling. Somehow. I just panted and shuddered and tried to keep my muscles from twitching.

Myron blew out smoke, took another leisurely drag on his cigarette, and said, "I really don't think you should concern yourself with Kevin Prentiss just now, my dear. Please attend to the matter at hand. Charles really has very little patience."

"Tell me how you killed my son." Ashworth's voice had dropped lower, gone gravelly.

I looked at him from underneath tear-matted lashes. "Trust me when I say you don't want to know."

They were going to do it again. No problem. All I had to do was control the situation . . . disrupt the particle chains as they formed, kill the electric charge and dissipate it, preferably through the carpeting so that it would shock the crap out of all these self-righteous little—

I thought I was prepared for it, but I wasn't. The hands on my shoulders released, and before I could get hold of the whip-fast chain of linking charges the banquet chair became Ol' Sparky again, and I was riding the lightning. I wish I could say that my mind whited out but it wasn't like that. When it was over, I felt every frying nerve and misfiring cell. I couldn't hold back the tears and the sharp-edged whimpers, any more than I could stop the involuntary convulsions that continued in my back, legs, and arms. I smelled something burning. It was probably me. They held me upright in the chair.

And in my ringing ears, Charles Ashworth's calm order came like the voice of doom. "Tell me how you killed my son."

"I'm not a fucking Djinn; the Rule of Three won't work. And I'm not telling you a thing, you son of a bitch," I managed to gasp.

Quinn spoke from across the room. "Joanne, just tell the man. He really will kill you."

"It would be a shame," Lazlo said. He'd stubbed out his cigarette sometime during the last eternity, and was staring down at his clasped hands.

The others around the table looked to be in various stages of discomfort, but nobody was banging a fist and demanding for my torture to be stopped. Even the bartender was still as a ghost in the corner. The duties of the silent employees might even cover body disposal.

I tried to bring myself under control, and reached for wind . . .

. . . and slammed hard into a barrier that was as complete as anything I'd ever encountered. Somebody had this place locked down. *Tight.* It had the smell of Djinn to it.

"Please," Lazlo said. "There is no need for this unpleasantness. All you have to do is tell us what happened. Surely there's nothing you object to in that. I'm certain you already told the story to the Wardens. Why not to us?"

Because I didn't want to remember it.

There was a warning zap through the chair, just enough to sting and make the tears in my eyes break free. I gasped in shallow breaths. Hell, they probably already knew the story, I told myself. They knew everything else. Clearly, fighting wasn't getting me anywhere except a fast trip to a largely hypothetical afterlife. I wasn't ready to die again. Not yet.

I sucked in a deep breath, managed to straighten myself up, and tried my voice. It sounded weak, but steady.

"I'll tell you," I said. "But don't blame me if you don't like it."

I hated Chaz from the first moment I laid eyes on him, and I couldn't really say why. Ever have that happen? Makes you feel ridiculous and prejudicial, but it's nothing you can help. It's some cellular process of repulsion that you have no control over.

That was me and Chaz. Repulsion at first sight. The act of being pleasant to him for more than a minute at a time made me ache like I'd been mining granite with a teaspoon. After an entire day of poking through the chaotic mess of Chaz's confiscated records, enduring enough paper cuts that it constituted human rights violations, I called back to the office and complained about the assignment. I wasn't trying to get out of it, exactly, but I had myself a good whine and begged for help. My boss, John Foster, gave me reassurances and platitudes in his warm Southern voice and told me not to kill the bastard.

One thing I *did* figure out, from the mess of recycling piled on my bed. Chaz had too much money. *Way* too much money. I'm not talking about personal funds, like being born rich, although he probably had been; I'm talking about income. I knew how much a Warden of his pay grade should make—I had the pay tables with me. He had five times that coming in and going right back out again, to not-very-well-concealed Cayman Island accounts.

Chaz was definitely dirty. It was just a matter of

determining the kind of dirt it was. After mapping the weather patterns, over and over, I decided it had to do with smuggling. Somebody was paying him to make adjustments at specific times, on specific dates. Recurring patterns, too. Classic.

I needed to catch him in the act, though. The Wardens were notoriously forgiving, unless you were caught red-handed; I intended for Chaz to be dead to rights.

Mainly because, as previously stated, I just couldn't stand the little prick. He kept showing up at my motel room, trying to sleaze me into bed, as if that would somehow magically convince me not to hang him out to dry.

On the fourth day, I threw back the curtains and discovered that morning had dawned early and cold, the way it does in the desert; there was something inviting about the emptiness stretching toward the blue blur of mountains.

According to the patterns I'd been mapping, today would be a day Chaz would be trying some manipulation. No use looking in the direction the storm would be blowing; you had to track it upstream, to the point at which it provided cover and protection. It was a good three miles out in the desert, as the vulture flew. No way the Jaguar was made for off-roading, so it was going to be a hike.

I could do with burning off some frustration, I decided, not to mention the carb load I'd built up while chowing down on tuna-fish sandwiches and fries. I had bikini season to worry about. Plus, going on foot would give me an advantage of stealth.

I changed into a jog bra and sweatpants, threw on

a thin white T-shirt, and laced up running shoes. There was coffee down in the chilly lobby; the fountain was still tinkling madly away. Somebody—probably a late-night partier—had added a floating Budweiser cup to the extravaganza of dusty silk plants and spray-on stone. I chugged down some heavy-duty caffeine, liberally diluted with fake creamer, and waved to the desk clerk on the way out.

I paused inside the glass doors to adjust my shoes, and as I did, I felt weather shifting. I looked up and found the sky clear, laced with a few high-riding cirrus clouds and reflected orange sunrise. Chaz was already starting up, amazingly enough; I'd honestly thought that he might postpone things, considering he had an auditor sitting right in a ringside seat.

He thought he was good enough that I wouldn't notice. Idiot.

The wind was shifting to the east. I could clearly feel the tug of power from that direction. I braced myself with one hand on the wall and drifted up to the aetheric. Chaz was working quietly to slow a high, fast-moving airflow, creating a cool air mass to the north. That was what caused the wind shift . . . warm air flowing into the downdrafts. Subtle, and effective. He was creating a hell of a lot of chop that extended in about a five-square-mile radius over my little patch of desert.

I went back to the desk and called Chaz's home office. No answer. I tried his cell phone, too, and got voice mail. He was out there, all right, working on site. Good. I'd be able to get a look at what was going on.

I walked outside, braced myself against the building, and stretched my tendons. Overhead, a small plane buzzed the blue, making erratic circles; it gave up and headed off to the south. Away from the interdicted area affected by the weather shift. I couldn't tell what kind of plane it was, but traffic patrols were common over this expanse; it saved the cost of keeping too many state cruisers on the highways. Aerial surveillance . . .

. . . and maybe somebody had something that they didn't want that plane to see. Which explained the chop that Chaz had created a few thousand feet up.

I finished stretching and jogged out onto the shoulder of the road, heading toward the center of the problem area. It was a diagonal line from the hotel and the road, straight out into the middle of God knew where; I oriented myself by the aetheric, not line-of-sight. Getting lost wasn't going to be a problem.

The first half mile was hard as my body adjusted to the new climate; the air was sharp and brisk going down, thinner than I was used to. It tasted sweet, full of subtle dry perfume. No sign of the surveillance plane, which had evidently decided to go surveil somewhere more comfortable. Up on the aetheric, Chaz was still making changes to keep things balanced, but balanced in his favor. I could undo that with a little judicious application of force, but until I knew better what I was up against, there was no reason. Besides, there was no advantage to letting him know that I'd even noticed.

Running in sand was twice as tiring as on a flat surface, but I relished the burn. Sunrise came in a slow, glorious explosion of color as I jogged—layers of gold, tangerine, mauve, dark blue. Nothing moved out in the emptiness; no breeze stirred the sand, and it was too early for snakes and too late for owls. Overhead, an early-rising hawk rode thermals, and out to the far eastern horizon a cloudbank brushed its heavy skirts across mountains.

God, it was beautiful. Even knowing it was being manipulated to look this way, it was heartbreakingly gorgeous.

I stopped when my tendons began screaming for relief, and walked off the cramp, stopping to marvel at the delicate little cacti, the scuttling desert beetles, a wavy line of ants marching up a dune.

I ran on and felt my body settle into a deep, satisfying rhythm. Pulse, lungs, muscles, all working in perfect harmony. I didn't think about running; I just ran. My whole attention was fixed on the center of the disturbance, which lay just ahead.

I was still jogging when I heard voices. Two, off in the distance. We were quite a ways from civilization, at least such as was represented by the Holiday Inn.

I'd finally located Chaz. I had the feeling he wouldn't be happy to see me, which gave me a little burn of contentment; the faster I could get this assignment over with, the better. I'd packed a camera with me. Nothing like Kodak memories to roast him over an open fire back at Warden HQ. I slowed to a walk, keeping mostly to the cover of bushes, ducking when I had to.

I heard two voices. Man and woman. Arguing, by the tone, but the words were smeared on the still desert air. *Chaz, you dog. No honor among thieves, is that it?*

I hadn't yet reached the top of a little hill when I

heard the woman scream. A full-throated shriek of terror, cut off so suddenly it left me cold inside. I dug in and sprinted up the loose sand, topped the dune in a spray of dust, and skidded to a halt.

There was a sun-faded dust-colored Jeep parked in the arroyo below, and the man next to it wasn't Chaz after all. Different body type—middle height, angular, wearing blue jeans and a black windbreaker with a black baseball cap. Aviator sunglasses. Pale skin, I thought, but that was just an impression, too fast to be reliable. As I came to a stop at the top of the hill, I saw that there was a woman with long black hair lying in the sand at his feet.

She'd fallen or been pushed down on the sand on her belly.

Funny how much you notice in moments like that, with the air so clear and still. The woman had on a faded pair of cutoff jeans and a white tank tee. Long tanned legs and white running shoes.

She was struggling as he knelt down beside her.

He was holding something that glinted hard steel in the morning sun for part of its length, dull red for the rest. As I watched, he plunged the knife overhand into the woman's back, and her reaching hands scratched at the sand, digging, digging, trying to dig her way to freedom.

I heard the high-pitched breathless screams.

I heard them stop.

Shock rolled over me, freezing me in place, and then it was pushed aside by an incoming storm of rage. I lifted up my arms and called the wind, felt it sigh and answer, as if it had been waiting for the chance. *You bastard, you're not getting away with this. . . .*

The man down in the arroyo looked up, and the aviator glasses flashed red in the rising sun. There was a bag on the ground next to the woman. Bottles spilling out of it, a confusion of glass winking in the dawn light.

It was a goddamn drug deal gone bad. *This* was what Chaz had been protecting. Murder.

"You bastard," I whispered, and gathered the wind in my hands to take him down.

Didn't work out that way.

Something hard hit me in the back of the head, and I remember falling, sliding weightlessly on cool dry sand down the hill, into darkness.

Six

When I woke up, I was in darkness. My head throbbed like a high-performance engine in need of a tune-up, and I was folded into someplace cramped and hot. Blood tasted burnt copper in my mouth. It took me a few stupid seconds to remember where I'd been, what I'd seen, and I saw the man plunging the knife into the woman's unprotected back with a shock that made me flinch.

Focus, I told myself. My senses reported that I was probably in the trunk of a car. A nice big one, at least. Roomy. It smelled of spilled oil and hot metal. There was a wet softness underneath me, and *that* smelled like blood. Mine. My head was bleeding like a son of a bitch, and that edgy light-headedness—that came from shock.

Judging by the road vibration, we were on the highway. I reviewed my options. One, I could stay still and quiet and hope that a ruthless killer forgot he'd stored me back here. That option didn't look so good. Two,

I could knock the car off the road with a wind strike, get out of the trunk, and rip the bastard limb from limb . . . that one was actually pretty attractive. I felt around and found nothing to use to pop the trunk— no tire iron, which was unfortunate; I'd feel a hell of a lot better with a big heavy weapon in my hand. I hadn't brought my cell phone on the run, and even if I had I doubted the coverage out here in the middle of nowhere.

The car was slowing down. I swallowed a burst of nausea and tried to put myself in the best position possible to launch myself out as soon as the trunk opened. Time to focus, get everything still and quiet inside so that I had the fine pinpoint control of the wind that I required. My pulse refused to cooperate. I'd worked under pressure before, but that had been when I was fighting nature, not a cold-blooded killer. I kept seeing the woman, the knife, the blood. I kept picturing myself facedown in the sand, digging for freedom.

A sudden application of brakes rolled me forward. We were stopping.

I gathered the threads of control together despite the sickening pain in my head. Thermals flowing high and deep, a layer of cool air sinking toward the ground. Warm air slowly circling up. The dance of a stable, quiet system. Chaz had manipulated it to drag the surveillance plane off course, but he'd put everything back, nice and neat.

A Warden had been an accomplice to murder. That made me sick to my soul.

I felt the car shudder as the driver's-side door

slammed shut. Felt, rather than heard, footsteps crunching alongside. A key scraped metal somewhere near my nose, and I braced myself . . .

. . . and, as the dark got sliced in half by a square of lemon-yellow light, I let out a warrior's yell and lunged up, powered by feet braced against the quarter panel. I grabbed at the dark shape standing there, caught fabric, and as he flinched backward I held on and let him pull me the rest of the way out.

As my feet touched asphalt, I superheated the air above us and created the mother of all updrafts. Its power lifted us off the ground. I wrenched free of my captor and stumbled back against the trunk of the car as the man was yanked upward by the airflow, out of control.

"Wait a minute! Joanne! Help!" he yelled, and I froze and clawed hair back from my eyes.

Chaz Ashworth III, pale as milk, was hovering up there, on the verge of taking a trip to Oz the hard way. I had planned to express-train him right up to the freezing cold and low oxygen content of the higher regions, which would knock him out in seconds, but now I had a problem.

Chaz wasn't the killer. *That* guy had been shorter, thinner, scarier. Chaz just looked clumsy and ridiculous.

I slowly reversed the process, calming down the wind a little at a time, balancing forces until Chaz touched down on the gravel of the shoulder of I-70. A petulant burst of wind blew past us, stinging me with sand.

"What the hell—" I began, but he held out both hands, palm out, to stop me.

"I can explain. Everything. Just . . . don't do that again, okay?" He looked genuinely spooked. "We can't stay here. Get in the car. Please. Hurry!"

"Why was I in the trunk?"

"It was the only way I could get you out of there without . . ." He darted anxious looks at the empty horizon, the blank shimmering road. "Just get in the car, okay? Please?"

"I saw him kill that woman." I don't know why I said it; it was almost as if the words were under pressure; I couldn't keep them in. I had to get rid of that moment, that image, that horrible silent pantomime of death. "He stabbed her in the back."

Chaz's face went even whiter, if that was possible, and his eyes had a blank, haunted look. He grabbed my arm, moved me aside, and slammed the trunk. Hustled me around to the passenger side of the car, which I now saw was his roadmonster of a Seville, maroon, with pimp-gold trim and wheels. I wasn't shocked to find he'd gone with the expensive Italian leather interior. It felt cold and stiff against me as I edged inside. Chaz ran around the long hood and piled into the driver's seat, put the car in gear, and scratched gravel out onto the road again.

When the speedometer was pegged at eighty, he pulled a deep breath and said, "Look, you have a nasty bump on the head; maybe you imagined—"

"Bullshit."

"Hey, give me a chance here, honey—"

I held out a shaking finger at him. "*Not* your honey, and the next time you give me some name like *baby* or *sweetheart* I'm going to kick your ass so hard you can read your underwear label. Got me?"

He was silent. Typed a message on the steering wheel in urgent Morse code. Finally nodded.

"Who was he?" I asked.

"I don't know."

"I hate to repeat myself, but ass? Underwear label? I know you were manipulating the weather out there to drive off aerial surveillance. Drugs, right? He was making some kind of drug deal."

"I don't know!"

"You get paid. You have to know his name."

He looked really ill now. "Look, I just know him as Orry, okay? Orry."

"Know him how?"

"Business."

"And again, see previous threat."

"No, I'm serious, we have a business arrangement," he said. "I didn't know he was . . . you know."

"Killing unarmed women?" I felt sick to my stomach, but damned if I'd throw up in front of Chaz. "What kind of business arrangement?"

"He pays me to keep the weather clear for his couriers, and knock police planes off course. You know, the surveillance planes, like you said. That's—"

I interpreted. "He pays you to facilitate trafficking." Which explained Chaz's unusual weather patterns out here in the barrens. He'd been manipulating systems to create clear paths for the planes coming in, and storm fronts to frustrate the cops. "Jesus, Chaz." I rubbed my aching head. "You had to know you'd get caught."

He got a crafty look. Great. Chaz, who was monumentally stupid, actually thought he was *clever*. "Well,

I'm not the only one, you know. Everybody gets a little something on the side. It's how the Wardens work."

I stared at him, lips parted. Amazed. "What?"

"Oh, come on, drop the innocent act. Look, I agree, Orry's out of control—Jesus, I freaked when I saw what he'd done to that poor girl. The only thing I could do was get you out of there. He was going to kill you!"

"So you saved me by knocking me out and sticking me in the trunk of the car." Which made me wonder how the hell he'd gotten a maroon pimp-trimmed Seville all the way out into the desert like that, without having it become a permanent desert monument. It wasn't exactly an SUV. In fact, there was no way he'd driven this car all the way out there.

But there *had* been a dun-brown Jeep parked near the arroyo, which would have nicely done the job of carting my unconscious body back to the roadside.

It belonged to the killer. Orry.

I turned my face away from Chaz, afraid what it might say.

"How'd you get me back to the car?" I asked.

"What?"

"Did you drag me? We were a long way out in the desert. That's a hell of a distance to carry me."

"Well, I couldn't leave you out there." He tried to sound altruistic. It came off as ridiculous. "Let it go, Joanne. Look, I have money. Lots of it. Just give me a bank account number and you're an instant millionaire, I swear. All you have to do is turn in a good report to the Wardens and take the money, right? It's what all the others did." The three previous audits. He'd greased the wheels. Of course. No wonder the audits had smelled funny.

"Did the others see a woman get killed?" Her hands, scrabbling at the dirt, fumbling for rescue. "What'd she do, Chaz? Shortchange the shipment? Blackmail him?"

He sighed. "You're not going to take the money."

It would be smart to tell him I would, but I wasn't in the mood to lie. "No."

"I knew. I knew the minute I saw you. You know what you look like in Oversight? Goddamn Saint Joan the martyr. You burn real bright, Joanne, but you're burning yourself right up." Chaz shook his head. "It's the *way things work.* You take the money and you shut the hell up. Look, you do good things, right? We all do. We save people. Why shouldn't we make a little—"

"*She's dead!*" I shouted, and was a little shocked at the raw edge of fury in my voice. "And you're finished. Understand? This is over. *Over.* Nobody else dies."

Chaz sent me a pitying look. He reached down, picked up a cell phone that lay on the seat between us, and dialed a number. "Yeah, I'm on I-Seventy, coming up on the caves. Be there in a couple of minutes."

Guess I was wrong about the cell coverage, I thought stupidly. He hung up. I stared at him, at his neat pre-ppy outfit, his perfect tan, his expensive manicure.

"*You* knocked me out," I said. "*He* drove me back to your car. Why didn't you just leave me there? The two of you already killed one woman; why not two?"

"Look, you don't have the slightest idea of what's going on," he said. "I can't just kill you. If you disappear, I'm going to have to answer questions. Just . . . just take the money, okay? Take it and go. You weren't supposed to come out here in the first place; you were supposed to stay in Las Vegas."

"This was where the trouble was."

"And you go looking for trouble. Great. Out of all the Wardens, I have to get the Lone Ranger."

Unfortunately, I was terminally short a Tonto. We passed a flashing blur of a road sign that read CARLSON CAVES, 1 MILE. So I had about forty seconds to figure out what to do. The problem was that I was wounded, weak from blood loss, and I was facing another Weather Warden, which was the worst possible matchup. We could hurt each other, all right, but we'd hurt everybody else a hell of a lot worse. At least neither of us had a Djinn—that made it a little less destructive.

I eyed the cell phone. If I could call for help . . . No, they couldn't get here in time. Well, if I called John Foster, he could task his Djinn to get me out of here; that was something. . . .

I made my decision, and grabbed for it. Chaz jerked the wheel sharply to the left, tossing me against the passenger door; the phone clattered noisily against window glass and slid into the dim recesses of the backseat. *Fuck.* I was committed. Too late for caution now . . .

I called wind.

So did Chaz.

The car spun out, slammed from two different directions by fifty-mile-per-hour gusts. It skidded weightlessly, grabbed gravel, and tilted, and I nearly lost control of the freight-train blast of the jet stream I'd redirected. Airborne rocks pelted glass with snare-drum impacts, and something heavier hit and shuddered the frame. The glass on my side spiderwebbed. I pushed harder, because Chaz was reaching over to grab me, and the Seville tilted up on its side, groaned like a living thing, and rolled.

The window shattered and fell away as gravity writhed, and I yelped and hit the car again with a roar of wind, rolling it again back over on its tires. I squirmed out the broken window and ignored the hot drag of glass splinters against my skin, slithered out, and fell onto hot sand. The Seville was still moving, blasted by the jet stream, and I cowered as it was pushed over me. I hit it again with a gust, this one more than a hundred miles an hour, and it flipped up in the air and spun like I'd shot it out of a cannon. It traveled about twenty-five feet before slamming back down on its tires on top of a saguaro cactus.

I killed the wind and realized that something had happened to me. A numb feeling in my leg. I twisted around and looked, and saw a piece of shiny metal embedded in the back of my thigh, big as a flatiron, sharp as a knife. I went light-headed and gray, looked away and breathed deep.

That was when I realized that it wasn't over.

Out in the distance, something terrible was happening. A growing roar of power, thundering out of control; he'd done this, or I had, or both of us had sparked it like a match in a powder keg. I reached for the wind but couldn't grab it; it was slick as glass, moving too fast, too full of its own fury.

A smear on the horizon.

An ominous layer of haze.

A wave of brown, turning black. Breaking like surf. Birds were flying frantically south ahead of it, but I could see the wave overtaking them. I'd heard stories of black rollers from the dust bowl, but I'd never actually seen one; it was terrifying, awesome, uncontrollable. A sea of darkness blotting out the sun as it came, a horizontal tornado of lethal force. It was picking up everything in its path—cactus, tumbleweeds, fences, barbed wire, the shredded remains of animals unfortunate enough to be caught in its path.

Coming right at me.

I screamed and tried to grab for it again, but it was too much, too big; it would take a vast power sourced in Djinn to handle this thing.

Think. No time to run; it was almost on me. If I stayed where I was, it would strip the flesh off my bones, scour me dead. The wind wall inside the thing had to be upward of 150 miles per hour, maybe higher.

I did the only thing I could think of. I created a cushion of hardened air over me, locked the molecules tightly together, sealed myself in a bubble, and prayed.

The black roller roared across asphalt. I watched it strip a Joshua tree out of the earth, shred it into toothpicks, and fling it up into the impenetrable darkness. Lightning flared blue inside the darkness, static electricity flaring off of every surface capable of carrying a charge, crawling eerily on the breaking edge of the wave, flaring in hot blue lines along the telephone wires. A frantically flapping hawk disappeared in an explosion of shredded feathers.

I watched the sun disappear behind that black storm front, and closed my eyes.

Sound came distantly. Inside my hardened bubble it was one long, inhuman scream, like metal being tortured. I was afraid to open my eyes, but I knew the sand around me was gone, scoured down to hard-packed earth, eroded in patches down to bedrock. *Dear God, please* . . .

I felt a sting of hot sand spurt against my face. Static electricity zapped at me, burning; I smelled the hot snap of it everywhere around me. I struggled to hold on to the matrix protecting me, but the howling monster outside was so strong, so incredibly *strong* . . . I couldn't hold it. Couldn't . . . the pressure of the black roller was breaking down the bubble of air that was all that stood between me and being flayed alive.

I curled up tight, gasping in stale breaths, resisting the urge to add my scream to that of the insane wind out there. When I risked a look, I saw a black snake of razor wire flailing over me, held back from my skin by millimeters.

Another white-hot burst of sand broke through the shield, this one near my knees. I struggled to seal it, but the air was coming loose from its matrix, molecules spinning out of control; there were fiery strikes everywhere now, burning. . . .

And then the shield weakened, and I was on fire.

It lasted for only a few seconds, but the pain was intense, disorienting. I couldn't breathe. Instinct wouldn't let me open my mouth or eyes. Sand quickly buried me, which in a sense was a blessing against the already abraded mess of my skin.

The pressure of wind against me slowed to a bully's shove, then gusts, then a breeze.

Then silence.

The black roller had moved on.

My lungs were aching. I clawed sand away, convulsed my way up to a sitting position, and sucked in a hazy, dry breath. Coughed and tasted ozone.

It was unnaturally still. Nothing but a low-hanging blur of dust so fine it barely qualified as talcum powder, and a landscape scoured clean of everything taller than the asphalt road, which had been worn down in spots to thin gray gravel.

I rolled over, took hold of the metal spike in my leg, and yanked it free. The world wobbled and went dark, and I saw stars, felt the hot spurt of blood, and fumbled my shirt off to tie it hard against my thigh. I managed to get to my feet and limped slowly into the devastation, looking for the Seville.

I didn't recognize it at first. It had the ancient look of something that had been left out here for years, scrubbed down to base metal; the tires were shredded into thin black fibers. The hood was gone, along with the doors and the trunk lid. The leather interior was a tattered, sand-heaped mess.

No sign of Chaz. I limped around the far side and spotted a heap of rags on the other side.

He'd crawled out and tried to take shelter against the back right tire; it had been the only real cover available, but it hadn't helped. He hadn't made a shell the way I had, or if he had, it hadn't worked long enough.

He was missing his skin.

His body was a glistening red-black mess with white bone showing in places.

I sank down on my knees and wished I could cry, but there was nothing left. Nothing but fear.

"You stupid bastard," I whispered. "God, I'm so sorry."

I checked, cringing at the contact of my fingers on his raw flesh. He wasn't breathing, and there was no pulse. After a long, weary pause, I got up and limped back to the wind-scoured road, light-headed, wounded, sand-burned.

Still alive, despite everything.

Stranded under the hot glare of the sun.

I didn't tell them the rest. I ended it with Chaz's death; there was more, but it was none of their damn business. When I was finished, there was silence in the poker room. Lots of it, flowing deep and cold. Most of the card players were staring down, up, away from me.

All except for Quinn, whose eyes were fixed on me in concentration so intense it was almost sexual, and Charles Ashworth, who looked drained. Tired. Old.

"Thank you," he finally said, and turned back to the table. His voice sounded rusty and ancient. "I have no further need for her. You may do as you like."

That had a bad ring to it. I shifted slightly in the chair. Nobody was holding me down, and I was mostly recovered from the last shock; despite the presence of Quinn and the big, burly guys outside, I was giving myself pretty good odds on getting out alive if I had to fight.

"Don't be alarmed," Myron Lazlo said, in that

warm, gentle voice. "We don't mean you harm, Miss Baldwin."

I muttered something under my breath about "could have fooled me." Quinn heard. I saw the answering dark sparkle in his eyes.

"Yeah, about that, what exactly *do* you mean, Myron?" I asked. I didn't sound particularly obsequious about it. "What the hell do you *want* with me?"

Myron smiled. It was unsettling, because it looked kindly and grandfatherly and yet there was a kind of entitlement about it that made my spine try to crawl away.

"We want you to join us," he said. "We want you to report back to the Wardens and tell them all is well, the problem has been solved."

"Solved?"

"That Jonathan escaped, Kevin died. We do *not* want you to report anything about our meeting, or the existence of the Ma'at. From time to time, we will have assignments for you that will require you to act on our behalf. That is the price of your freedom."

I swallowed, wished I had a nice cold glass of water, and said, "Two problems. First, I don't take orders from *you*. Second, no matter what I say when I get back, they won't just believe me that our Kevin and Jonathan problem's miraculously solved itself."

The Ma'at, or at least as much of them as were gathered around a high-stakes table, looked at each other and smiled. Damn, they *all* looked smug. It must have been a requirement.

"My dear, we wouldn't expect they would," Myron assured me. "I promise you, Kevin *will* be dead. Quite thoroughly dead, before the end of the day. As for

Jonathan . . . well, I expect you'll just have to be convincing."

One of the others said, "She won't betray the Wardens. She's as solid as a rock. About as thick as one, too."

"Rocks are easy," Ashworth put in. He brushed imaginary lint from his suit. "All you need is a large enough jackhammer."

Boy, I wasn't going to like him any more than I had his son.

"You don't have to decide now." Myron reclaimed the conversation, leaned forward and looked presidential. "Joanne—may I call you Joanne?—you're not stupid. Surely you know that the Wardens are riddled with corruption, that the situation you faced with Chaz"—his eyes flicked to Ashworth, exchanging a silent message that contained a swift apology—"was hardly unusual. I understand that you also encountered one of the worst offenders in Florida."

"Bad Bob," I said, and immediately wished I hadn't blurted it out. I got a slow nod from all the heads at the table.

"Dangerous," Myron said. "You did the world a great favor by removing his influence."

"I didn't do it for the world." *I did it to save my ass.*

"Regardless of why you did it, the results were good. Surely Bad Bob confessed to you that he didn't act alone, that there were other Wardens engaged in illegal activities. You must be aware that it runs rampant throughout the organization. You'd have to be foolish not to have concluded that to be the case. That's part of why we were formed, and why we continue to exist. Because the Wardens have become a force for evil, not good. And they need countering."

I didn't like thinking about Bad Bob, what he'd said, what he'd done to me. I had a sudden cell-deep vision of his weathered face, his sharp blue eyes, his hands pouring a demon down my throat. I felt a sudden dry constriction in my chest, a desperate need to get out of here, away from these men who were starting to strongly remind me of that whole experience.

I stood up. Nobody panicked, not even me. Quinn stayed where he was, shoulders against the wall, arms folded. I walked over to the bar, looked the uniformed attendant in the eye, and ordered a springwater. He handed it over silently. I broke the seal and chugged it, tasting desert and fear and confusion. Handed the empty bottle back.

And then I turned back to Myron and said, "The Wardens aren't perfect. What makes you think you're any better?"

He just smiled. Wrong tactic. These guys weren't going to feel anything less than omnipotent, no matter what I said.

I tried again. "You can't kill Kevin."

"Why not?"

"He's just a kid."

Myron studied me curiously. "Yet you've contemplated killing him yourself."

"I want to take away his powers, but I don't think that means he has to die. Jeez, you guys are so damn smart, you can't come up with a way to neutralize him?"

"The Wardens failed to," said one of the poker players.

"The Wardens were shut out. *You* were on the inside." I paced the room, letting them get used to the idea of me moving. It wouldn't work with Quinn, of course; the cop was watching me with tolerant, amused eyes, but underneath that was a cold core of absolute competence. I needed Quinn on my side, or gone. What was his story, anyway? A cop, working for the anti-Wardens? There was a story there . . . and no time for me to learn it.

"Okay, assuming that I'm considering your proposition to work for you . . . what are you offering?" I clasped my hands behind my back so they wouldn't see how badly they were shaking. The carpet felt soft and springy under my feet. I put a little more swing into my hips, a little more freedom in my walk. Being the only woman in the room had an advantage, especially among older men. "Money? Power? What?"

"We're offering you the chance to do what you've always wanted to do," Myron said. "We're offering you the chance to do good."

I smiled thinly. "Oh, my. And if I don't want to take your generous offer?"

Quinn didn't move, but he suddenly got a whole lot bigger. Nothing supernatural about it; it was a body-language trick, a cooling of the expression, the warmth draining out of his stare.

"We'd have to resort to regrettable alternatives," Myron said. His eyes didn't move to indicate Quinn, but I got the point. "I'm sure you're aware that at least one Warden has already met his death here—we did not cause it, but neither did we act to prevent it. Jonathan and Kevin would do a very nice job of eliminating you, if we provided them with reason to do so. But really, my dear, there's no need for any animosity. The Ma'at are dedicated to exactly the same principles that you honor. The Wardens are no longer the saviors of humanity; they're parasites, perpetuating a cycle of violence and destruction, enslaving beings who ought by rights to be free. You can't want to be part of that."

I inched up into Oversight as I paced the room. It glittered in strings and strands of power, a treacherous spiderweb. Just now, they weren't trying to control me, but the minute I started reaching for power, they'd shut me down. Physical attack was out; I was outnumbered and outgunned at every turn.

"Miss Baldwin? I'm afraid that I require an answer."

I was about to give him an unladylike one, but then there was a discreet knock at the door and it swung open. A woman looked in—businesslike, professionally coiffed, beautifully dressed—and gave them some kind of high sign. Shut the door gently as she left.

"Ah," Myron said. He sounded ever-so-slightly disgruntled. "It appears we'll have to delay this, Miss Baldwin. Our four-o'clock is here. Mr. Quinn? Please show our guest to her room."

Quinn pushed away from the wall, walked to me, and took my arm. It looked gentlemanly, and it felt authoritarian. He steered me across the soft carpet to the door, opened it, and squired me out without another word.

I glanced back.

They were opening another deck of cards. I wasn't even a topic of conversation.

Quinn took me out past the guards. If the old men of Ma'at had a four-o'clock, he or she wasn't cooling their heels outside; all I could see was the normal business of the casino. I considered screaming *rape* or *fire* or *cardsharp,* but considering that the security all seemed to know Quinn—he exchanged friendly nods with each uniform we passed—I decided to wait for a better opportunity. Maybe Kevin would come to my rescue. That would be ironic.

The Luxor was full of things I wanted to see— beautifully reproduced Egyptian statues, the faux treasures of Tut, souvenir shops that held the glitter of gold and silver and gems—but Quinn didn't even slow down.

"Hey," I said as he hustled me past a storefront full of reproduction Egyptian furniture, "you know what all villains have in common? They don't shop. They're too busy being evil to shop. You guys need to learn the fine art of browsing."

Quinn laughed softly and put his arm around my shoulders. No sexual intent—it only meant he could steer me more effectively. He smelled woodsy, a mixture of some sharp green aftershave and a dark hint of male sweat. Maybe some gun oil, too. No tobacco. He wasn't a smoker.

"Sweetheart," he said, "you are one lovely piece of work. I gotta tell you, I've seen rich men with power over major corporations break down and cry over less than you just survived. You gave as good as you got."

"If I gave as good as I got, did good old Chuck get electrocuted? I was too busy convulsing to see."

He patted my shoulder. From some men, all of this physical contact would have been prurient, but Quinn seemed to not have any ulterior motives, not even the obvious. He was just friendly.

We arrived at a huge bank of closed steel doors. One opened, and Quinn steered me in.

Oh. Glass. I blinked and looked out at the bright glare of a Las Vegas afternoon, which was nowhere near as gaudy as a Las Vegas evening. There was something vaguely weird about this elevator, which became clear when Quinn pushed buttons and it began to rise.

It didn't go up. Well, not directly. It went at an *angle.*

"It's an inclinator, not an elevator," Quinn said. "Like the view?"

I had to admit, it was pretty. Our elevator— *inclinator*—crawled up the slope of the huge glass pyramid, each floor announcing itself with a muted whispered *ding,* and the world fell away. I amused myself by identifying hotels along the strip. Paris. New York, New York, with its roller coaster and the half-scale Statue of Liberty. The white lace of the Bellagio's fountains shooting skyward in a silent, choreographed dance.

We stopped somewhere near the top.

Quinn tugged me out, walked me down the hall, and opened up a room with the standard electronic card key.

"Well," I said, startled. "This'll do."

My room had an entire wall of windows, sharply angled, and sunlight sparked from the muted gold of faux-Egyptian furniture. The bed looked sumptuous.

Through the bathroom door, I saw a huge Jacuzzi tub facing the windows. "I'll give your side this: You know how to imprison a girl in style."

"You're not a prisoner," Quinn said, and handed me the key. "And we're not necessarily on the opposite side, either. Listen, feel free to go downstairs, hit the casinos, the spa, the pool . . . just don't try to leave the building."

I took the cool, smooth plastic. "If I do?" Quinn raised a silent eyebrow. "Right. You know I can't just hang around here, waiting for the Geezer Patrol to decide what to do with me. There's a time limit. Jonathan and Kevin are going to come after me, and believe me, I don't think anybody wants that. It'll be one hell of a show."

"You don't need to worry about the boy."

"The fact that you can say that just proves to me that you don't know dick about that boy."

Quinn reached under his coat. No change in expression. I remembered the gun, felt myself tense, wondered if it was even possible to stop a bullet with the powers I possessed . . .

. . . and he came out with another card, this one a different color of plastic.

"Have fun," he said, and handed it over. "That's worth five thousand in chips. Go crazy. I've got to get back to work."

"Quinn!" I caught his arm when he turned to go. "I can't just stay here!"

He patted my hand, removed it, and walked to the door. "If you don't," he said pleasantly as he opened it, "I'll just have to break your ankles. That'd keep you from wandering."

He shut the door with a quiet click. I chewed my lip, counted to thirty, then went to look out.

He was gone. When I raced to the window, I saw the inclinator crawling back down the face of the pyramid, and Quinn was facing out toward the view. He didn't look in my direction.

I went to the telephone, got a dial tone, and called a number from memory. Long distance, but I wasn't particularly worried about the charges at the moment. Let the Ma'at pay for it, the crusty old Republicans.

Three rings. Four.

"Bearheart," a low female voice said. I let out a gasp; I hadn't realized I'd been holding my breath.

"Marion! Don't talk, just listen. I'm inside, but there's something wrong here. A whole different set of—"

Click. The line was dead. I rattled the posts, banged the receiver helpfully against the nightstand, then hung it up.

"You know," I said to the empty air, "this would be a whole lot easier if I had some help from a friendly neighborhood Djinn. Come on, I know you're here. You've been hanging around for hours. And thanks for not saving me, by the way. I wouldn't want to get rusty."

There was a heat blur in the corner. I focused on it, and watched Rahel sculpt herself out of shadows into glittering hard angles and cutting edges. Not that the Ifrit was recognizable as Rahel, of course, but I didn't really think that any other half-Djinn would be following me around like a lost puppy.

"Can you help me?" I asked her. No answer from the black, insectile statue in the corner. "Look, you went to big trouble to come here with me. I can only assume you had a reason. Can you tell me what it is?"

She stirred. That was unsettling, because she no longer moved like either a Djinn or a human. More like a bag of razors shifting. I took a step back, found the bed behind my knees, and sat.

"Do I have any allies here?" I asked her. "Anybody I can trust?"

I wasn't sure, but that kind of looked like a nod. Maybe.

"Who?" Useless question. She couldn't speak; she didn't have enough power left from her gorging feast earlier.

An arm of hard right angles and coal-black glitter extended. Claws extruded pale as crystal from something that vaguely resembled a hand. I resisted the urge to crawl back across the bed; if she wanted me, she could get me.

I felt something tug deep inside. Panic spiked deep, and I tried to move but it was too late.

Her glittering diamond claws plunged into me. Not *me,* exactly. There was no damage to my human flesh, but as I flashed up to Oversight to view what was happening on the aetheric, I saw what she was doing.

She had hold of a glowing white-hot core centered in my abdomen, just above my pelvis. Cradling it in her claws, carefully.

I caught my breath, staring down through the crystal lattices of my aetheric body at this revelation, this glowing strange visitor inside me.

"Oh, my God," I heard myself whisper.

I'd never seen anything like this before, and yet I knew exactly what it meant.

I was pregnant.

I freaked.

First, I threw myself back across the bed, putting distance between me and Rahel's claws, instincts screaming. She didn't try to follow. I couldn't seem to get my breath, couldn't think, and as the world did a Tilt-A-Whirl spin I put my back against the hotel room door and slid down to a sitting position, head in my hands.

Impossible. This is totally impossible. I haven't . . . I couldn't . . .

I remembered Jonathan's sharp reaction to me, in the room at the Bellagio. His cryptic words: *If he told you it would guarantee I wouldn't hurt you, he lied.* Jonathan had assumed I knew about this spark of life inside me.

I gasped and looked up. Rahel was frozen across the room, still in a crouch, claws extended. Still as a black statue in the soft, filtered afternoon light. Alien as something out of H. R. Giger's nightmares.

"That bastard," I said. My voice sounded strange. "He knew, didn't he? David knew he was doing this to me. You guys don't do anything by accident."

I knew that because I'd been Djinn, recently, and I knew how much control they had over the forms they chose. David had *chosen* to put life into me—Djinn life. One thing I'd been taught in school—Djinn *didn't* reproduce. They *couldn't*. So how the hell was this possible? . . . According to the Wardens, Djinn were sterile and eternal, and they controlled them all. Except, of course, the Wardens had been dead wrong or outright lying about controlling them all, anyway. There were free-range Djinn, a lot of them. So it stood to reason they'd be wrong—or lying—about the Djinn being sterile, as well.

I knew with an absolute and unexplainable certainty that the Djinn could reproduce when they felt like it, and for some unfathomable reason, David had felt like it with me.

Of course, he'd forgotten to *ask* me first. Or even *tell* me after the fact.

Memory flashed hot. David saying, *You have to trust me,* his eyes flashing copper. And me saying, like an idiot, *Yes.*

Rahel made a move. I flinched back against the door, and she froze back into stillness, claws working as if they weren't really connected to the rest of her. Creepy. They slowly melted back into the glittering angles of her hand. Gone.

"You know what's going on," I said. Nothing. "Guess we need to find you something to eat if I want any more help out of you."

Something to eat, other than the glowing nucleus of energy inside of me. Which, to her credit, she hadn't tried to consume. Maybe it wasn't even the equivalent of an after-dinner mint yet.

"Any Djinn in this building?" I asked. Her head tilted slowly up, then down. "Let me guess. The Ma'at have some." Another slow, creaky, alien nod. "Perfect. So all I have to do is face down the opposition, steal a Djinn, let you snack on it, and I'm home free.

Assuming that you don't just walk away and let me twist in the wind."

She didn't confirm or deny, like Quinn.

I let my aching head fall back into my trembling hands.

Oh, *Jesus*, I was pregnant.

I was going to kill him *so* very dead.

To pass the time while I worked out a plan—because nothing was immediately jumping up and down, waving its little arms—I took a long, hot shower, washed my hair, dried it, applied skin moisturizers from the complimentary selection in the bathroom, then slipped into the Jacuzzi tub to bubble away my troubles for a while. I stared out at the horizon, remembering how it had looked to see a black roller crest on that flat sandy plain.

I needed a Djinn, but the Ma'at weren't about to go trotting one out in public unless they had to. That meant trouble, big-ass trouble. *Public* trouble.

Something shivery crawled up my skin, and it wasn't bubbles. Maybe the heat was getting to me, but I had an idea.

Not a good one, but any idea at all was an improvement. It had two chances of success, at least. If plan A failed, plan B was still perfectly viable. I liked that. Plan A rarely worked, anyway.

I soaked awhile longer, waiting for a better idea to saunter into my head, but nothing arrived. Night was still hours away, but the sun was burning its way down the western half of the sky. I slipped into a luxurious cotton robe embroidered with the Luxor crest, wrapped my arms around my waist for comfort, and wished I could talk to David. Scream at him, preferably. What the *hell* was he thinking? Exactly when had the whole discussion about offspring happened? I'd been unconscious a few times. Maybe he'd mentioned it then. That would be guylike.

I couldn't deal with it now. I had other things to do, and everything was risky. Too risky to be attempting with that fragile, brilliant spark of life inside me, but I didn't have that much of a choice. David hadn't damn well given me one. I didn't know the first thing about baby Djinn, and I had no one to ask but Rahel, who couldn't answer me and probably wouldn't tell me the truth even if she could.

I put my clothes back on and went shopping.

There are two things you need to be successful as a hard-core Vegas über-slut: couture and attitude. I had the second. A trip downstairs to the Luxor bazaar would ensure that I had the first.

I toured the options and decided on a discreet place that reeked of high price tags—not that it was an indicator of class, but discount stores definitely were out. I needed the best, and I needed it now.

I came in, all wrinkled and lived-in, and showed the clerk the color of my Luxor card. She was a beautiful little thing, Cleopatra-cut honey-blond hair, gray-green eyes, skin like pale spring roses. Wearing Donna Karan, which went perfectly with her body type. Good shoes, too, something from the Valentino family. I was still partial to Manolos, but I wasn't monogamous.

"Day or evening, miss?" she asked, raising perfectly

shaped eyebrows. She had a perfect, cultured, West-End-London accent.

"Evening."

"Casual or—"

"Tell you what, gorgeous, just show me what you think will make me absolutely irresistible."

She grinned, and mischief danced in those gray-green eyes. "That won't be difficult," she said, which made her my best friend ever. "Have a seat. We'll sort something for you."

Forty-five minutes later, I was standing in front of a trio of mirrors, wearing a knee-length midnight-blue raw-silk sheath dress. That wasn't anything so special, until you considered the parts that were missing. I turned slowly, gauging the effect. Transparent blue mesh from a high neck to a band of raw silk over my breasts—the parts that get you arrested, anyway—that faded into transparency again over my waist, dipping into beaded splendor low around my hips. Gorgeous. Striking. Utterly impossible to wear without supreme self-confidence.

Twenty-four *hundred* dollars, plus change. I did a slow turn again. The salesclerk draped a sapphire pendant around my neck, something large and real enough to make my heart skip a beat.

"Well," I said. "They say accessories are everything."

She gave me a knowing, conspiratorial smile and held up a pair of matching Manolo Blahnik pumps, midnight-blue raw silk, with pinpoint heels that raised me a good three and a half inches.

We high-fived. She gave me eight hundred in change from the chip card, bagged my old outfit, and promised to send it up to my room after cleaning. I tipped her generously, squared my shoulders, and called up my A-game.

Time to get to work.

I cut a swath through the bazaar, drawing stares from men and whispers from women; there were few who *didn't* look, even if they frowned. The Manolos felt perfect on my feet, completely natural; the dress clung like an expertly tailored second skin. Security watched me just like the rest of the gawkers, with a touch of assessment. They knew who I was, of course, but still, the dress had its effect.

I headed for the highest-stakes tables and came up with a likely candidate. I didn't recognize him, but he had designer clothes and two big, burly guys who were obviously bodyguards, and he had a stack of chips that could build a model of the *Titanic* without losing too much in scale.

I eased up to the table, gave him my best smile, and put down a single chip. Ah, we were playing blackjack. Cool. I was good at blackjack.

The croupier took my chip and dealt cards, and I crossed my legs as I sat down on the high stool. The man I was smiling at started smiling back. He nearly forgot his hand.

"Your play," I said, and nodded down. He focused quickly on the cards, asked for a hit, asked for another, busted, and watched about a thousand bucks travel into the croupier's territory. Then he swung around and watched me in open, frank appraisal. I pretended not to notice, checked my cards, and flipped over the ace on top of the jack. "Pay me." I salved the pain for the dealer with a smile and a wink. He smiled back.

Two professionals at work.

I got paid, a tidy little profit, and left a chip to ride as I scooped the rest back into the small, elegant bag that the saleswoman had insisted on throwing in. Midnight blue, with beadwork. Matched the shoes, of course. It wasn't Fendi or Kate Spade, but you don't get Fendi for free, now, do you?

The guy next to me leaned in closer with every turn of the cards. We did a little gambling, a lot of flirting. Drinks were free, but I had a passenger on board to worry about now, and even though Djinn were well-nigh indestructible I wasn't so sure about baby ones. I stuck to cola.

Mr. Big Spender introduced himself as a blur of syllables I didn't bother to catch. He mentioned a couple of TV shows and a film he'd starred in, none of which I'd seen. Big, broad-shouldered, dark hair and dark eyes. A face that was beautiful or brutal, depending on the lighting and angles. He liked dark colors—black, cabernet, midnight blues. We matched well.

Which was, for him, what it was all about, the look. I could tell that within seconds of making eye contact. He wasn't looking for intellectual stimulation. I wasn't sure if he'd ever actually *had* intellectual stimulation.

I was on his arm, with the bodyguards trailing behind, in about ten minutes, and suggested that the casino at the Bellagio might put out (and I might, too, with the proper application of cash or credit). We cut quite a swath through the crowd on the way to the lobby. A substantial number of tourists recognized my pickup, and stopped him for autographs; some snapped photos. He took it with good humor and used me as a poseable doll, which I suppose was the function most of his dates fulfilled both in public and in private.

We were halfway across the lobby, heading for the doors, when Quinn appeared. He took one look and knew what I'd done; fast, that boy. He didn't try to go for my date; he stepped straight up to the larger of the two bodyguards and did some whispering. *Dammit.* I was watching plan A turn to crap.

The bodyguard moved up to whisper in the pale ear of my escort, who looked nervous and gave me a twisted smile. "Ah . . ." He didn't seem to quite know what to say. We were in the lobby, nearly to the doors. "Sorry. You're really . . . that's quite a look you've got going. The dress and all. It would fool anybody. But I really don't . . . I can't be seen with . . . no offense. Really."

He nearly tripped over himself in his haste to beat a retreat back to the blackjack tables. His bodyguards closed in to let me know my presence was no longer welcome when I tried to follow.

I turned to Quinn and glared. "You told him *what*, exactly?"

He gave me a top-to-bottom look, and smiled. "That you had a little surprise for him under the pretty wrapping. Of the frank-and-beans variety."

"You told him I was a *guy*?"

Quinn shrugged.

"And he believed it?" In this dress? I think I was more upset about that than the failure of plan A.

"Some men are not very bright," he assured me solemnly. "Walk with me."

"Where?" I didn't move. Plan B was in the warm-up stage.

"Someplace quiet."

"You mean with fewer witnesses." I was too close to the exit not to take advantage. "Look . . . *veni, vendi, vici.* I came, I spent your money, and now I'm leaving. Try to stop me if you want. But in this dress, you'd better believe people are going to notice, especially when I start screaming at the top of my lungs right here in the lobby." I gave him a sweet smile. In the shoes, I was at least two inches taller than he was. "And then I'll start an electrical storm that'll disrupt every circuit in this place and fry half the computers, at least. Then I'll dump six inches of water onto this extremely expensive carpeting and short out the slot machines. Do you think they have flood insurance out here?"

Quinn wasn't amused. He gave me a hard look. "Don't be stupid, Joanne. You know I can hurt you. I can't sling around magic spells, but I can *definitely* hurt you." Great. He had a dress immunity. It figured.

I leaned closer and put my lips next to his ear. "Let me lay it on the line for you, Quinn. We're not in some private room now where your Old Republican Guard can zap me with lightning bolts out of pure spite. We're right out in the open, and I'm walking out the door. If you want to stop me, you'd better get your big guns out here, because you're going to need 'em."

He took my arm. I broke free, stepped back, and raised my voice. "Hey! Please don't touch me, you pervert! I will *not* wear your daughter's panties!" It stopped traffic and drew even more stares. He jerked his head at some security guards. I gathered power into my hands, felt the easy response of the aetheric, and sent a stiff breeze through the lobby. It rattled papers and stirred some exclamations from the clerks at the counter. Lifted a few full skirts, to feminine exclamations and male appreciation. I played to him this time, not to the audience. "Word of advice, Quinn, don't fight me. I'm not afraid of a little drama. I'm the one who ripped a hole in the UN Building in full view of the Security Council."

He stopped, staring into my eyes, and I got that sense of cold menace from him again. Quinn was nobody to underestimate. "They'll kill you, you keep this up." He flicked his gaze around. There were uniformed security closing in on us fast. "What are you doing?" Oh, he was quick. He knew I wasn't trying to get away, or I'd have broken for the doors already.

"Leaving," I lied. Leaving would just have multiplied my problems; I didn't have any expectation of walking out the door. The wind stirred my hair and teased it into a floating dark cloud. "I won't go down easy, and *you're* going to have a hell of a lot of explaining to do. Why do I get the feeling that's not a happy thing, with those guys? I'm betting they don't like failure any more than they like bad manners and displays of power in the hotel lobby."

He was silent for a few seconds, then made some imperceptible sign that stopped security in its tracks. We were no longer the center of attention; tourists were exclaiming about the wind, holding on to their suitcases as I let the air swirl and circle. Not even an F0 on the Fujita scale yet, but enough to cause a real reaction. Quinn's suit coat fluttered, outlining the gun underneath. He wasn't reaching for it, but then I wasn't under the delusion he needed to.

"I like you," he said, and flashed me a nearly genuine smile. "You know that, right? You've got style; that's rare."

"Love you too," I said. "And now I'm going. See ya!"

I turned and headed for the glass wall of doors and the gleaming ass of the sphinx outside.

Someone stepped into my path, small and neatly suited in hand-tailored excellence. Holding a silverhanded black cane, in the best tradition of his generation. Charles Ashworth II had a kind of grave dignity that wasn't affected by the wind swirling around him.

"Desist," he said to me.

"Bite me, Grandpa," I said, and kept walking. I let the wind become a gale, knocking people down, drawing shrieks of alarm from clerks and tourists. I targeted Quinn and knocked him flat, then pinned security against the walls. Sent a gust straight for Ashworth.

It didn't so much as ruffle his silver hair.

"Don't be stupid," he said. "You can't hurt me."

"News flash, Chuck, I'm not going to sit still and get fried like your chicken dinner this time." I readied my own lightning, well aware that it was destabilizing the currents inside the hotel, that it was spreading out in a dark wave of imbalance over the aetheric. "Get out of the way or I'll return the favor."

He gestured with his cane, pointing behind me, and I felt a presence taking form up on the aetheric. "I warn you, we *will* stop you. And we won't be gentle."

A Djinn. *Bingo*. Plan B had actually yielded a decent outcome, for once.

"Rahel!" I yelled, and spun around to face the Djinn that was just manifesting. "Dinnertime!"

The Djinn was familiar. I'd met him before, on the first leg of my journey to this strange place; he'd been watching over Lewis's house in Connecticut, weeks ago. He wasn't the type to bother with modern trappings; he had a Mr. Clean sensibility, with a shaved head and bare chest and *Arabian Nights* pants. His legs disappeared into mist. He was already reaching out for me.

I targeted him with a blast of wind strong enough to rip carpet from the floor and sent him flying, straight into a razor-edged black embrace. Rahel folded around him and pulled him into the shadows, both of them screaming.

Rahel was *very* hungry. I felt a sickening qualm about that, but dammit, the stakes were high and getting higher. Maybe she wouldn't be able to destroy him. Maybe.

Plan B, it seemed, was working *too* well. I hadn't actually planned on getting out of the Luxor, except under the color of an escort; on my own, I'd be a clear target for Jonathan and Kevin. Well, I'd just have to take the risk. . . .

I'd lost track of Ashworth, but he announced himself again by cracking that cane across the back of my head. I staggered, went down to one knee, and shook off the sparks. I sensed him readying for another swing and dove forward, found myself grappling with Quinn this time, who was shouting something in my ear. Ashworth hammered me with another hard blow in the back that sent sunbursts of agony up and down my spine. People were screaming, but our little tussle was lost in the general confusion I'd started. The wind was still tearing around aimlessly, fueled by my anger, and it was in danger of ripping loose from my control. The currents I'd been preparing crackled and twisted out of control, waking sparks from a row of slot machines nearest the lobby. Bells rang, lights flashed, coins poured out. Blue lightning jumped and sparked uncontrollably as the circuits discharged.

"Stop it!" Quinn was shouting at me. His face was stark and set hard as granite as he dragged me back to my feet. "Don't make me kill you!"

I put the Manolos to good use, kicking his shins with the sharp toes, digging spiked heels into his instep.

Ashworth landed another hard crack with the cane across my shoulders, and I felt a line of fire race through my collarbone. *Dammit . . .*

I twisted around. No sign of Rahel or the Djinn in the chaos. They were gone.

"Stop!" Quinn yelled in my ear. I ignored him and focused on the wind, sent it spinning through the casino area, flipping cards into the air, sending dice tumbling off of the tables. My lovely dark-haired TV star yelped as his pile of chips took flight from a blackjack table like swallows heading for Capistrano.

Chaos. There was something really, really petty about the satisfaction I felt, but I couldn't really regret it.

Ashworth's cane caught me once more in the back of the head, and everything went vague and smeared. Someone was speaking to me, whispering on the ae-

theric. But sound didn't travel on the aetheric, did it?
No, it wasn't speech, it was . . . something else. Vibration. Light. Power. Connections.

Don't fight, Jo. Let go.

I knew him. Knew the voice, or the frequency, or
the tenor of his power. Knew the whispering colors of
his aura as he wrapped me in his arms.

Please, Jo. Please let go.

It wasn't Quinn. There was somebody else there,
somebody else lifting me and carrying me away. I felt
safe and dreamily peaceful.

I felt whole.

I opened my eyes and saw David's beautiful, intense
face, those dark brown eyes flaring bright copper as
they stared down at me.

"Can't leave you alone for a minute," he said, and
his lips curved into a smile. "Love the dress."

The wind stopped. The electricity stopped arcing.

Everything stopped.

Including me, as darkness sucked me down.

SEVEN

I knew it was a dream, because obviously David couldn't be here. Dream or not, I was more than happy enough to hold on to it; I woke up cradled in warm arms, against a firmly muscled male chest, and smiled and cuddled closer and refused to open my eyes and find out that I'd imagined the whole thing.

I felt a hand smooth my hair, then touch my cheek and glide gently along my jawline.

"You're awake," he said.

No, clearly I wasn't, because that was David's voice, wasn't it? Warm and intimate as his touch, which was waking fire all over my body. I was limp and relaxed and utterly, completely dreaming.

And then his hand touched a bruise, which set off a red flash of complaint, and I realized that I wasn't dreaming at all. Not even I dreamed of having bruises. Now that I let myself drift back into the real world, I had a monster headache, pinpoints of sharp, glasslike pain all over my body, and a general feeling of having been run through the wood chipper headfirst.

I opened my eyes and looked up.

Warm copper eyes looked back, half-concealed behind round glasses.

David was seated on the bed, back braced against the wall, with me lying in his arms. I reached out to touch him. The crisp rasp of his cotton shirt felt real. So did the heat of his skin underneath.

His smile vanished as he looked down at me, replaced by a look of concern. "Jo?"

I blinked. There were two of him, both staring at me. I tried to touch one of them and jammed my fingers into the wall. "Ow."

"Dammit." He had large, sensitive hands, and one of them explored the back of my head and found that extremely sore spot, which was about the size of an egg. The words that followed weren't in English, but the venom in them left no doubt as to their meaning. David was angry. They weren't going to like him when he was angry.

"What happened?" I asked blurrily, and let myself curl up back against him. Because if it was a dream, I'd take it over my present reality any day. "Shouldn't be here."

"No, you shouldn't," he agreed grimly.

I tried again. "*You* shouldn't be here."

"Oh." He stroked hair gently back from my face. "Long story."

"Can't sleep." That was a bit of a lie; my eyelids were heavy, my body drugged by his warmth. The only escape from the crushing throb of the ache in my head was sleep, and I was starting to like the idea. "Tell me. I left you with Marion. . . ."

He kissed my forehead, and I felt the trace of a smile in it. "Once upon a time there was a Djinn . . ."

"Not kidding."

"I didn't think you were."

And I remembered something, something that made me sit up too fast and grab my aching head in both hands to steady it. I glared at him through a curtain of disarranged—and curling, dammit—hair. "You! You . . . you . . ."

He watched me with a little line grooved between his eyebrows. It was a concerned look, not a guilty one. I managed to roll off of him to my hands and knees and crawled to the edge of the bed. He sat up, following, hands outstretched. I admit, I was none too steady.

"You!" I repeated, and swallowed a mouthful of nausea at the way the world insisted on bobbing up and down. "You *bastard*! I know what you did!"

That little line cut deeper. "What exactly did I do?"

"You and Lewis . . . cooked this up. The night you left me at the hotel." It came to me like a blinding burst. "You knew Jonathan wouldn't let us in. You let them separate us."

He had the grace to look a little guilty. The worry line didn't disappear. "Jo, settle down. You've got a head injury."

"Head injury?! *You knocked me up!*" The self-righteous fury of it drove me off the bed to my feet. I swayed there, hands on my hips, trying to focus on the two of him. "Well? Nothing to say?"

"Sit down."

"Screw you! *I'm pregnant!*"

"Sit down before you—" He lunged. I didn't realize I was falling until I was in his arms, hovering a few inches above the floor—"fall down."

"Sorry," I mumbled. Tears stung hot in my eyes.

"No, not. You 'pologize first."

The world bobbled again, and I closed my eyes to stop it. Felt myself lifted and settled back on the soft bed, covers pulled over me in a warm, rustling embrace. David's hand cupped my cheek with warmth, and I opened my eyes again to see him bent over me, close enough to kiss. His lips were parted, as if he were on the verge of saying something, but then he just closed the distance and those lips touched mine. It melted me into gold, and even though my head felt like it had used as the soccer ball in the World Cup I couldn't help but respond by kissing him back. Hungrily.

"I had to protect you. I love you," he whispered into my open mouth. "I'm watching over you. Now sleep."

As if the kiss were opium, I did.

I woke up to stillness and a cold bed. The headache was at half-mast, and the bruises had faded to dull aches. No sign of David, but someone had left the hotel television playing silently on the hotel informational channel. Apparently, the PR spin was that there was a freak windstorm that had blown into the lobby through a jammed set of doors, and some shorts had erupted in the electrical system before circuit breakers kicked in. The message told me that everything had returned to normal and there was nothing to worry about.

The human race had a vast, apparently endless capacity for rationalization. It had always served the Wardens exceptionally well.

I tried to get up and winced at a sharp stab of pain in my shoulder.

"Easy," said a slightly rough male tenor voice somewhere to my right, against the gaudy glare of sunset. "Hairline fracture of the collarbone, not to mention one heck of a whack to the head."

Quinn was back. I started to ask about David, but something made me hesitate. It was still possible I'd dreamed the whole thing, that Quinn had been the one to catch me down in the lobby and carry me back up here. And I wasn't going to give him the satisfaction of mooning around over my lost Djinn lover.

I felt the weight of Quinn's body settle next to me on the bed. When I looked, he was leaning over me, staring down. He reached over and lifted my head, then probed the lump at the back with sure and impersonal fingers. I winced. "Oh, don't whine; you're going to live. And it isn't like you didn't ask for it."

"I just wanted out."

"And we put you out. Follow my finger." He moved it around, tracking my eye movements. "Any blurred vision?"

"Well, I think I'm hallucinating, because I see a big talking pile of crap."

"Funny. You're a riot, sweetheart." He sat back and lowered his eyelids to an assessing sleepy look. "Who's David?"

"Bite me. I'm not playing twenty questions; my head hurts." I was being bitchy. I couldn't help it. "You can't keep me prisoner here. I insist that you—"

His hand came down over my lips, stilling them. I continued to make cranky muffled noises for a few more syllables, then fell silent.

"You got no rights here, and you don't insist. You want to play rough, we'll play."

Quinn took his hand away from my mouth. I sucked in a breath and asked, "Why do you want me so bad?"

"Think a lot of yourself, don'tcha?" His smile was gallows-dark. "I don't. Somebody does."

"Who? Lazlo? Ashworth?" I made rude noises. "They already got their pound of electrocuted flesh out of me. Why can't I hit the road?"

"To do what? Get tossed out a window by that kid and his pet Djinn?" Quinn shook his head. "We've got a plan. You're part of it. We'll tell you the rest when you need to know it."

"Yeah. Great plan. Chock-full of foresight. Loved the whole bashing-my-brains-out part."

"I think there was something a little personal in the cane thing."

I couldn't exactly deny that one. Before I could find a suitably snarky reply, there was a knock at the door. Quinn got up and opened it, and a security guy handed over a blue canvas bag. Quinn locked the door again and rummaged around in the bag, looking for something.

"How's the head?" he asked. I shot him a filthy look. "Look on the bright side, sweetheart, you looked terrific. If you're going to go down in flames, you might as well do it in style. Great dress. You buy that here?"

I wanted to throw something at him, but the only thing available was a pretty new shoe, and I didn't have the heart. I settled for a superior *hmph* and settled down on the pillows again, a forearm over my eyes.

"Want an aspirin?"

"No."

"Good for you, tough guy. Now, you want to tell me what all that display downstairs was about?"

I massaged the bridge of my nose, where the headache seemed to be hiding. "I wanted to get to Kevin. To warn him."

"About . . . ?"

"You're going to kill him."

"Well, yeah." He sounded surprised. "Obviously."

"You don't have to do that. And there's a girl with him. She's got nothing to do with this."

"Siobhan?" Quinn made a raspberry noise. "You're talking out your ass. She's a pro. She's still there, she's there to take him for everything he's worth. I'm not going to worry about a whore getting in the line of fire."

"You know her?"

"Busted her a few times." He shrugged. "She's a tough girl, and no civilian. She gets caught in the middle, I'm not wasting any tears."

He finally found what he was looking for in the bag and brought it out. A long black case about the length of his arm. He set it on the bed, flipped it open, and started assembling pieces.

He meant the line-of-fire thing literally.

He was putting together a rifle, a fine shiny one with a red-tinted scope. I stared at him in silence for a few seconds before I realized what he was showing me.

"You're going to shoot him," I said, and sat up. I didn't let the rodeo-bucking world stop me. When things got uncertain, I wrapped a hand in the collar of Quinn's shirt and used him for a brace. "You're going to just *shoot him?*"

"You say that like it's easy." Quinn removed my hand and dumped me back on the bed. He continued snapping things together with metallic clicks. "Not like he'll be standing still for it, I'd imagine; probably have to correct for wind, maybe worse. Don't worry, though. He won't feel a thing. As soon as he drops, Jonathan goes back in the bottle, we pick it up, and decide what to do with him after the fact. Zim, zam, zoom. Problem solved."

I had to admit, he was right. It *was* a solution. So long as you didn't have any qualms about putting a high-velocity round through a kid's brain, it was the perfect answer. "You can't do this, Quinn. He's just a boy!"

"He's a killer," Quinn said. All of the false joviality was gone now, and what was left was hard as bone and ruthless as razors. "This is what I do, sweetheart. I take care of problems. So you just be a good girl, stay in bed, and don't become a problem, and we'll get along just fine. Right?"

"Yeah? Does the AARP executive committee downstairs know what you're about to do?"

Quinn snapped back the bolt on the rifle, sighted down the barrel at the window, and smiled. "Don't play a player. Of course they know."

"They know you're a cold-blooded killer."

"Sticks, stones. You know why you've got a headache? You think too much." Quinn leaned the rifle back against the door. "By the way, somebody's been asking after you."

"Nobody I want to meet, I'll bet."

He ignored me. He picked up the telephone and dialed four numbers. "Yeah," he said. "She's awake. Better get over here. She's kind of feisty."

I subsided, waiting. Realized that I was still wearing the über-expensive raw silk dress. Unfortunately, Quinn was totally immune to my charms, so far as I could see; no point in even trying to be seductive, and frankly, with the headache and bruises, I'd be more likely to barf on him than kiss him. Speaking of kisses . . . had David really been here? It must have been a dream. If he'd really been here, he'd have taken the time to get rid of these little bumps and bruises, wouldn't he? Unless he'd been afraid they'd know.

Maybe David was even deeper undercover than I was.

Knock on the door. Quinn checked the peephole, then opened it for my visitor.

Oddly, I wasn't surprised to see that it was Lewis. Well, I *was* surprised, but seeing him again seemed inevitable, really. I'd been expecting the other Lewis-shoe to drop, and now, looking at him, it did. He'd made it to Vegas—actually, for him it had probably been easy; the wards would have passed him right through without any Warden powers, and besides, I'd been waiting for him to make an appearance. He'd arranged for me to get abducted. He'd stood by and allowed me to be *killed*. He had a plan, and it just had to be a jim-dandy one, so long as you weren't on the receiving end of it.

He looked terrible. Grayer in his flesh, and his eyes were bloodshot. Hands trembling as they gripped his cane—unlike Ashworth, his wasn't for flash; it was for support. He moved like an old man. Quinn grabbed an elbow and guided him to a chair; Lewis eased himself down with an almost inaudible sigh of relief.

I would *not* feel sorry for him. No way. I refused.

"You okay?" he asked me. His voice sounded exactly the same, a warm tenor, slightly rough, like velvet stroked against the grain.

"Oh, hell, yeah. Never better," I said, and tried to look as if I were leaning against the headboard for effect rather than support. "I should've known. This had your smell all over it. I was such an idiot, you know; here I thought all these years you'd spent avoiding the Wardens you'd been out doing good, spreading rainbows and happy horseshit. You were working for the opposition."

"No," Lewis said wearily. "I *started* the opposition. Not that it was totally my idea; there were a lot of us who saw what was happening with the Wardens. I was just the force that pulled it together. The Ma'at started operation about seven years ago, officially. Since then, we've been doing our best to mitigate the worst of the Wardens' excesses."

"Yeah, you're the hero here. Modest as usual," I snapped back. "So what's your excuse? The Wardens wouldn't let you be king of the world, so you found a bunch of stodgy old farts who would?"

Quinn eyed me grimly. Evidently, he didn't like me bad-mouthing his bosses. "Want me to get Lazlo?"

"No." Lewis continued meeting my eyes solidly. "Jo, after I ran from the Wardens, I spent a lot of time trying to find out just why they were so afraid of me. I found out a lot more than I bargained for. I know you want to believe the Wardens are good . . . I did, too. We trusted them with everything we are— we let them mold us and train us and shape us. But they shaped us *wrong*. And what they've done to the Djinn . . . I know you saw what David endured. That's not the exception, Jo. That's the *rule*."

One thing I could tell—he believed what he was saying. Lewis was speaking from the heart, speaking with unmistakable passion. He wanted me to understand. To become a true believer.

"They're corrupted," he said. "I'm not talking about individuals . . . there are still a lot of good Wardens, who believe in what they're doing. But it can't last. Power corrupts. You know that better than most anyone; you faced down Bad Bob and Star. You *know* it's rotten at its heart."

"You're so full of shit." I wobbled up to bare feet and took up a belligerent stance that was only a little compromised by having to lean myself against the wall. My collarbone shrieked a protest at the move, but I ignored it. A shivering coat of sweat broke out on my forehead. "Listen to yourself, Lewis. You think you're the *good guys?* You stood by while my heart stopped! Quinn kidnapped me at gunpoint! Your precious Ma'at *tortured* me!"

"Yeah, but we gave you five grand after," Quinn put in. "And holy shit, can you shop or what?" When I glared, he dropped the cute act. "They interrogated you because you're a Warden. Don't you get it? Half the Wardens Association is Demon Marked, and the other half might as well be. You're the first one I've seen that isn't a fuckin' killer with a rune. They're totally corrupt."

"You're one to talk."

Ooooh, wrong thing to say. Quinn gave me his dead-eyed cop stare. It was effective. "You're gonna want to shut up now before you piss me off."

No, but I was ready to adjust my sails to the prevailing wind. I turned back to Lewis. "What makes the Ma'at any better? They wear more expensive suits? They're all bitter old men too moral to sin?"

"No," he said quietly. "They don't have enough power to be tempted. They're all below the line that the Wardens consider as a material gift."

He walked slowly over to me and put a hand under my elbow. I didn't know why until I realized my knees had started to buckle. He guided me gently back down to the bed, lifted my legs, and got me prone again. My head throbbed so hard I saw flashes of red behind my eyes, and bit back a groan.

"She needs a doctor," Lewis said somewhere beyond the strobe effect of my headache. Quinn grunted. "Got someone we can trust?"

"We've got bigger problems. Look, just patch her up and let's get moving. We don't have time for this."

"I said that she needs a doctor." When Lewis got that particular tone, it wasn't worth wasting the breath to argue. "See to it."

I cracked open my eyelids to look through the lashes. Quinn was staring at me. Stone-faced was his natural expression, but I could see that he was deeply worried. Not *for* me. *About* me.

"You don't need to be getting sidetracked here," he said. Lewis didn't answer. "We can't get lost in the details. We're in the game now, and you know the stakes. If she gets in the way—"

"Quinn." Lewis's voice was soft, but inflexible. "Get a doctor. Now."

Quinn turned and left. The door clicked shut behind him. Lewis put his hand back on my forehead, and some of the sick throbbing eased.

"A month ago, I could've fixed this in two seconds," he said.

"A month ago, I wouldn't have needed it," I whispered. "Lewis?"

"Yeah."

"When did being the good guys include contracting murder?"

No answer. He was staring off toward the sunset, his face lit with gold and orange.

The saddest eyes I've ever seen.

"Lewis?"

"You don't understand." He didn't look at me. "Rest."

I didn't want to, but eventually, I slept.

With no sense of transition, I was somewhere else. I was limping, although pain was a distant, muffled sensation. My skin was red and abraded, my white T-shirt tattered and filthy, sweatpants ripped and stained.

I limped along a deserted road, one painful step at a time, and overhead the sun kept staring down. No wind. No birds. No sound at all. It was like being in a dead world, and I was dead too, I just didn't know it yet.

Dust hung like talcum powder in the still, dry air, and everything tasted like burned insulation.

I stopped, turned, and looked behind me. A ragged black ribbon of asphalt stretched toward the dim horizon. It was scoured gray in places by the wind, and there was a wreck of a car thrown off to the side. Paint gone. Nothing but junk.

I knew where this was. In the thin shade of that wreck was the body of Chaz Ashworth, and I couldn't be here; this was past, this was long past . . . *Oh, God get me out of here, I don't want to be here. . . .*

Panic surged along my nerves. It felt both over-amped and slow, dream-terror moving like cold molasses but packing the same intensity as waking fear. I was thirsty, overwhelmingly thirsty, and I ached all over, and *I couldn't be here.* I had to wake up, wake up, wake . . .

I turned and kept limping. There was shelter in the distance. A tumbled confusion of rocks that promised darkness and relief from the killing sun.

One agonizing step at a time, whimpering. Crawling, by the time I reached it, my knees and forearms scraping raw on rock and burning on sand.

Time sped up, the way time does in dreams, and I was inside, huddled against the cool darkness, shuddering in relief.

In the dream, my mind didn't know what was coming, but my body did, my nerves were screaming in panic, trying to drive me out of sleep and into the light. Better to die out there, food for ants and vultures and at the end a clean return to the earth, than go into the dark. . . .

But I couldn't stop myself. The part of me that decided to move wasn't the part that knew the future.

I heard the steady, whispering drip of water, and it

pulled me on into the shadows. I was too weak to pull water from the dry air; badly injured, I needed to drink to survive.

I crawled for some period of time, don't even know how long; all that mattered was finding the water. Finding *something* that didn't hurt. I heard the tinkling sound getting closer, and crawled toward it in the darkness . . .

. . . and was blinded by a sudden hot flare of light.

Hands. Hands in the dark, dragging me down. The stranger slammed my head into the wall, and things went gray and soft, and in the white flare of his flashlight I saw my burned, bleeding fingers scrabbling at the rock.

Digging for rescue, like the woman in the sand.

What are you doing here?

My throat was too dry to do more than croak.

Who do you work for?

I couldn't see him. He was just a vague shadow behind the light, no particular height, no particular build. A baseball cap and stained blue jeans. The smell of leather and sweat and blood. I knew him. I'd seen him before.

What do you know?

He dragged me over sharp-edged gravel and dumped me facedown in a pool of water so cold it shocked me back to consciousness. I gasped, breathed water, rolled over coughing, and then turned back to suck down greedy mouthfuls of the clean, pure taste.

He was pacing behind me, kicking rocks. The flashlight beam bounced wildly off of rock, off of boxes stacked against the far wall. Off of scuttling insects fleeing a false and unwelcome day.

The mouthful or two of water I had time to swallow wasn't enough to cure me of thirst, and I was weak and exhausted and confused. I didn't even realize he had me until I felt the cold bite of the knife, panicked as I realized it was slicing away the tough elastic of my jog bra.

Cold cave air on my bare breasts.

Tell me how much you know.

His name was Orry. I knew his name, because Chaz had told me in the car. I'd delivered myself to the same fate Chaz had intended for me; of course I had, I'd been less than a minute away from the rendezvous when I'd called the wind. . . .

I fought. The second time he hit me, I fell into the darkness, screaming, weeping, mourning. Trying not to feel what was happening to me. I wanted to leave, to wake up, but it hurt too much, and pain brought me back to the cave, to the darkness, to the knife.

He never made a sound, except for grunts and the pistonlike sound of his breath. I knew he was going to kill me; I knew every second because I'd seen what he'd done to the woman in the desert. When he was done, he would kill me.

Tell me what you know!

I lost hope.

I lost myself.

And then, when he had what he wanted, he shoved my head into the ice-cold water, and held me down to die.

I woke up screaming, or thought I did, but when my head was clear enough to register sound I realized it was just a thin, desperate moan vibrating in the back of my throat. I curled up on my side, drawing my knees to my chest, and realized that I wasn't wearing my new heavy silk sheath dress anymore. I wasn't wearing anything. The sheets clung cool to my damp skin, and I grabbed for them and wrapped them closer.

Someone in the room. My heartbeat hammered fast. I licked my lips and whispered, "David?" but I already knew that it wasn't, it couldn't be. David was far, far away, and he couldn't help me. Couldn't be with me, any more than he'd been there in the darkness of that cave while hope died.

Without meaning to, I slid my palm down from my chest to my abdomen, where a flicker of light remained. *I am with you,* something whispered, and some of the panic in me eased.

A light flicked on across the room, and revealed a sleepy-looking Quinn. He was reclining in a chair, feet up on a rich damask hassock, book folded open on his chest, a pair of reading glasses on the table next to the lamp.

Gun beside the glasses.

"Hey." His voice sounded rusty. He sat up, blinked at the book as it slid down to flop shut on his lap, and readjusted on me again. "How's the head?"

One big bruise. "Fine."

"The doc said you had a mild concussion, so somebody should stay with you. Lewis needed rest. You sleep okay?"

"Fine." Not. But I wasn't going to admit it to him.

He grunted and ran a hand over his face. Quinn was the kind of man who got more attractive from a day's growth of beard stubble, not less. "Yeah. You always whimper like that in your sleep when you're fine?"

"Mostly." I kept it cool and distant. "Clothes?"

"Sorry, I didn't figure you'd want to sleep in the three-grand dress. It's hanging in the closet." He was looking at me oddly. I wondered what my body language was saying. "Lewis took it off you, in case you're wondering."

"Thanks. You can go now."

"And you think I take your orders?" He sat up, kicked away the hassock, and holstered the gun. The glasses went into a pocket of his jacket, the book onto the table. "Coffee?"

"I want you to go." The panic was coming back, speeding up my nerves like a slow electric shock. "Go now."

"Sweetheart, I'm not going—"

"Go!" I screamed. It had the raw edge of panic. He froze. Watched me. I struggled to get my breath under control. "Just get out, okay? I want to dress."

He reached into the closet and retrieved three hangers draped with fabric, tossed them on the end of the bed, along with a sealed bag tied with a white ribbon. "You've got a selection," he said. "They cleaned your old stuff. I think they even threw in some new underwear and shit."

His eyes were dark and far too knowledgeable. "Get the fuck out, Quinn."

"I'll be in the bathroom. Oh, by the way, there's somebody outside the door, so don't bother. You won't get far."

He went in and shut the door. I crawled out from under the sheets and ripped the ribbon off the bag, shook out clean underwear, and stepped into them with a deep sense of relief. The skirt had been laundered and pressed; even the knit top looked like shiny and new. I slid my feet into the designer knock-offs, carefully bagged the midnight-blue Manolos, and draped the bag over the hanger with the silk dress.

"Okay?" Quinn's voice came through the door. I sat down on the edge of the bed, aware of a thousand pinpoint aches, of exhaustion, of an unsettling trembling in my hands. Of a headache that would kill me on other, less eventful days.

"Yeah," I said. "Fine."

He opened the door and stood there for a few seconds, watching me. I didn't look up as I focused on combing tangles out of my hair with my fingers. It was futile; the curls were back with a vengeance. Quinn wordlessly ducked back into the bathroom.

A sleek faux-ivory brush appeared under my nose. I looked up to see that he was holding it out. I took it and began dragging it through my curly hair, wishing I could make it straight again, wishing I could make everything straight again.

Straight and clean and simple.

"Better?" he asked, when I put the brush aside. I nodded. "Toothpaste and lotion and all kinds of crap in there. Probably ought to check it out."

I didn't move. "What are you going to do with me?"

"Ask Lewis."

I would, while I was hitting him repeatedly with my fist. Hitting something sounded really, really good right now. Not Quinn, though. Quinn would hit back.

I got up, fought off the various grinding aches and

pains, and went into the bathroom to inspect the damage. On the bright side, it wasn't as bad as if I'd gone ten rounds with a heavyweight; on the dim side, it definitely gave me a piratical, dangerous look. No makeup available; I did my best with lotion and toothpaste and mouthwash, ran the brush through my hair until the curls became glossy black waves. I needed sunglasses. That would complete the picture of the battered wife.

When I came out, Lewis had arrived, and he'd brought reinforcements. As in, Myron Lazlo, Charles Ashworth II, and Gnarly Guy, whose name I learned was Rupert McLeish. They also brought breakfast in the form of black hot coffee and some truly excellent pastries, which I cheerfully accepted; no sense in going on a hunger strike, especially since I planned to kick the ever-loving crap out of them the first chance I got.

Out the expansive windows, Las Vegas was still lit up like Christmas, but the clock reported it was nearly four A.M.

"So," I asked around a mouthful of muffin, "have you blown the kid's head off yet, or are you saving that for the big finale?"

The Ma'at had taken up seats in the various comfortable armchairs, except for Lewis, who—stubborn as usual—remained standing, braced by his cane. Quinn manned a strategic vantage point in the corner. I'd settled on the edge of the bed that was closest to the breakfast tray.

"We don't find any of this amusing, Miss Baldwin," Ashworth said severely.

"Really?" I said, and raised my eyebrows. "Neither do I, but I figured it was right up the rich-white-guy humor alley. And just a comment, but don't you guys ever take off the suits? 'Cause it's kind of strange. Really."

Lazlo, Ashworth, and McLeish were all still in conservative business attire—blues and grays, with perfectly knotted silk ties. Still perfectly turned out. Lewis was, as always, informal. He'd given up the denim shirt in favor of a ratty old NYU T-shirt with a hole at the neck. No flannel. I kind of missed the flannel look for him.

Lazlo looked over at Quinn. "Has she been cooperative?"

"Sure." That was nice of him, but then, being a cop, he probably had sliding scales of cooperation. I hadn't actually tried to hit him with a blunt object, at least.

Lazlo turned his attention back to me. "That was quite a display you put on in our lobby, Miss Baldwin. What exactly was the point of that?"

I was starting to wonder myself; Rahel still hadn't appeared to save my ass, and I was starting to suspect that I'd been robbed. "I wanted out."

"You might have asked nicely."

"You might have said no."

Lazlo's lips curled faintly, and he and Lewis exchanged a look. "We regret the extreme measures taken to subdue you. I trust you are feeling better?"

"Much." I noticed Ashworth wasn't providing the apology. "Nobody else got hurt, right?"

"You were surprisingly adept at rendering our operatives ineffective without harming them. My congratulations."

"It was luck." I stared hard into his eyes. "Next time I may not be so lucky."

"Next time, Mr. Quinn might just have to resort to something more than unpleasant words."

I crossed my legs and made sure they saw the bruises. "Gee. Imagine my debilitating terror. If we're done with the bluster, why don't you explain why you're keeping me here? If your great plan is just to have Quinn put a bullet in Kevin's head, why do you need me? You know I'm not going to sign up for your little club, and I'm damn sure not going to betray the Wardens for you. So why bother?"

Stalemate. Lewis stepped forward, crouched down next to me, and rested his elbows on his thighs. An entirely natural pose for him, but the pallor and strain in his face were disturbing. God, he looked bad. *Really* bad. Worse than he had earlier.

"I need you to see something," he said. "Are you up to it?"

"Well, I just ate, so use your discretion if it's going to be gross."

He didn't smile. "Laz. If you please."

And then we were *moving*.

I yelped as the world dropped away. I forgot all about my discomfort, because there was far too much to see up here. My body, for instance. All bright glass, with an aura of blue and gold, and a hard white core of light centered around my abdomen. Lewis, darker than the darkness, like a hole in space shot through with poisonous red lines.

The Three Amigos, up on the aetheric, had the look of—believe it or not—wizards. Their shapes were all flowing robes and tall hats, spangles of dark blue and star white. They had the muted, shadowy flow of regular humans, but the aetheric imaging of Wardens. Eerie.

And then there was the *city*.

Human emotions sculpt the aetheric. Human actions echo so strongly that the results can be awesome or terrible, beautiful or tragic. Sometimes all of that at once. New York had been layers upon layers of reality—you could read the history of the place through its emotional remains. There had remained an essential core of hope to the place, of fierce and abiding pride. Darkness, yes . . . but a great, almost sentient presence, too.

Vegas was nothing like that. It was *empty*. The aetheric was almost flat. There was history here, but it was layers of darkness, not light. Where the city in the real world was a blaze of light, on the aetheric it was shadow and midnight, velvet and silence. Hunger and the death of hope. This place *consumed*.

The Luxor was a lone blaze of light, burning and shimmering with power. There was a golden mist streaming away from it like a flow of dry ice, heading across an empty stretch of darkness toward . . . something else.

The absence of fire. A flickering blackness full of shadows, gravity, *hunger*.

It was consuming light, not producing it. Like a black hole, devouring everything around it in ever-increasing spirals.

We dropped back out of the aetheric. I fell hard

back into my body with an all-over jolt that pulled sore muscles. Winced.

"That's Kevin?" I asked. Lewis slowly nodded. He looked mortally tired, even by so brief a journey. "Hey. Sit before you fall."

He lowered himself to a cross-legged position on the floor. "So. You understand?"

"Not really."

"I told you, she's useless," Ashworth said, and gripped the silver head of his cane more tightly, as if he wanted to bean me with it again. "Try putting it in words of one syllable for her."

Lewis put his hands on his knees, palms up, in a lotus pose. "Kevin's not producing enough power anymore," he said. "His natural talent was fire; he exhausted that weeks ago. He's burning through what he took from me too fast, and now in order to sustain himself and Jonathan he's learning how to take power from the world around him."

I felt a sudden chill. "Like a Djinn."

"No. Djinn do it on a much more balanced scale; he's drawing power like a demon. He has to be stopped, Jo. Regardless of his age, he's becoming a threat deadlier than anything that's walked the earth in ages. He has to be stopped, *now*." Lewis sucked in a deep breath, then let it out.

Lazlo took up the thread. "We need you to draw him out of hiding."

"Excuse me?"

"He doesn't come out of that room. We were able to act once, to get you out of there, because he was about to kill you, but we can't do it again. He's ready for us now. I need you to draw him out in the open so Quinn can take him. He'll be defending against magical attacks. He won't expect this kind."

I stared at him, stunned. "You want me to be bait?"

"No. We want you to gain his trust and then betray him. And it's very possible he might kill you before we can take him down."

"Wow, I'm just *jumping* at the chance to help you out now."

Lewis reached out and took my hand. I tensed, waiting for the burn of power that had always passed between us, but felt nothing. Of course . . . all his powers were gone, drained away, leaving a huge bleeding hole that was killing him. I'd never feel that burn between us again. Even if we succeeded in . . .

"No!" I yanked my hand back. "Lewis, dammit, if you kill the kid, we can't get your powers back. You *know* that!"

I wasn't saying anything they hadn't already thought of themselves. None of them had so much as a flicker of shock. Not even Lewis. "I know." He shrugged. "That's how it has to be. He can't be allowed to get any stronger. It's tearing things apart. And that's just him sitting still. If he starts really *using* those powers, God help us all."

"No!" I practically yelled it. Lazlo glanced at Lewis. So did Quinn. "You've got power, I know it, I can *feel* it! Combine forces, get over to the Bellagio, and kick his teenage ass! All we have to do is get Jonathan away from him. Hell, you even had the *chance* when you sent Quinn to get me!"

"Jonathan doesn't want to go," Lewis interrupted me. "Believe me, we've tried. Best we can figure, Jonathan *wants* to be Kevin's Djinn."

That made no sense at all. Why would Jonathan—
who I *knew* was no one's bitch—stay a slave? Unless
there was something in it he wanted . . .

I had a blinding memory, real as the aching lump
at the back of my head. Jonathan, standing in front
of a plate-glass window that didn't really exist,
watching the world go by, his eyes dark and bitter
and angry. *There are days when every single one of
them deserves to be wiped off the face of the earth.*

He'd been looking out at the mortal world.

And Rahel had said, *He is the one true god of your
new existence, little butterfly.*

I said slowly, "Kevin's not doing this. At least, he
doesn't know he is, and he probably doesn't want to
do it. It's Jonathan. He's found a way to give the
world back to the Djinn. As far as Jonathan's concerned, Kevin's the perfect answer—nearly unlimited
power, not too bright, not too principled, too young
to know that he's being stupid. Too innocent to understand that Jonathan's using him, not the other way
around. Jonathan just says 'yes, master' a lot and goes
about his own affairs. He's killing Kevin by drawing
off every scrap of power inside of him, and he's reaching through Kevin to suck it out of the world
around him."

Silence. Lewis's expression was unreadable.

"But you already knew that," I finished softly.
"Didn't you?"

Lewis nodded.

"And you know what he's trying to do."

Another nod. Lewis wasn't looking so good. I could
almost see the blood draining out of his face, leaving
him an unhealthy yellowish gray.

"Actually, killing the human world is a bonus," he said. "Jonathan's looking for lost Djinn."

"Lost . . ." I frowned. "You mean free, right?"

"No. Lost." He sighed. "The Wardens have been losing Djinn, and we haven't been finding them. They're still sealed in bottles, best guess. And it's too much of a coincidence that so many have gone missing. Somebody's got them."

"Somebody around here?"

"Think about it. Jonathan manipulated the kid into coming here, remember? He put the idea in Kevin's head. He *wanted* to be brought here. That means the answer must be here, too."

"And you're sure it's not your friendly neighborhood Ma'at."

Lazlo looked offended. "We don't imprison Djinn. We free them."

I glanced at them each in turn. Ashworth looked like he was sucking lemons.

"Up to you, Jo," Lewis said. "You get the boy out in the open, where we can stop this. If we have to take this fight up on the magical level, it'll kill everything. That's what Jonathan wants. That's what he *needs*. You have to . . ."

His eyes rolled back in his head. I reached for him, but Quinn was there ahead of me, taking his weight and easing him down on the carpet full-length.

The seizure lasted a full two minutes this time, complete with bone-cracking, spine-bending galvanic spasms. I tried to hold him down but it felt like he was made of metal cables and stainless steel, not flesh and blood. Except there *was* blood, trickling bright red from the corner of his mouth. I wiped it away with a warm, damp washcloth Quinn brought from the bathroom. Once the convulsions stopped, he lay still as death except for the rise and fall of his chest. I ran my fingers through his sweat-damp hair and looked across at Quinn. Quinn looked as blank as marble, and just as hard.

"He'll sleep awhile," he said. "Let's get him on the bed."

I helped lift him. Now that the spasms were past, he felt like he was a disjointed marionette, all papier-mâché and thread. Lighter than he should have been. When Quinn stripped off his T-shirt I realized I could count his ribs. I put my hand flat against the bony ridges and found his skin was burning hot, hot as a Djinn's.

"Pants," Quinn said, and pointed to Lewis's jeans. "Less confusing for everybody if you do it."

I swallowed an inappropriate laugh and unbuttoned and unzipped. Déjà vu. Wasn't the first time I'd been in Lewis's pants . . .

Quinn whipped them off with medical efficiency. The boxers underneath were white with pale blue stripes, very 1950s. I pulled the covers up over him.

The three old men were looking at me expectantly. I closed my eyes for a few seconds, said a quiet prayer, and thought about what Lewis had shown me.

I'd been so arrogant to him. So self-righteous. *Since when did being the good guy mean contracting murder?*

Since standing by meant destroying the world. Or letting it be destroyed.

"I'm your only hope to get close to Kevin, which is exactly what the Wardens want out of me, too," I said. "Here's the deal. Nonnegotiable. I'll play it my way first. If I can retrieve Jonathan's bottle without a fight, that's how it'll be done. If that fails, I'll get him out in the open, and Quinn can take him out."

"I hardly think that your way—" Ashworth started in.

"I hardly think you're in any position to tell me how this is going to go," I said. "I'm the only one of you that Jonathan will let get in spitting distance of the kid."

They all paused, looking at me. I put my hand over the warm spark that lived inside me, over the promise of life that I could use to deliver death.

"I'm the only one Jonathan won't kill on sight," I said. "If I can manage it, I'll get Jonathan's bottle and stop this the easy way. If not . . ."

I looked at Quinn. Quinn nodded.

". . . there's always the easier way."

I told them to leave, afterward. Quinn and the rest of the League of Totally Ordinary Gentlemen trooped out. I spent the rest of the night curled up against Lewis's dreaming heat, listening to the steady, deep, even rhythm of his breathing. Sometime in there I faded into chaotic dreams of fire and flood, earthquake and storm, and me standing naked as the world eroded around me.

I woke up with Lewis spooned close behind me, still asleep but clearly awake in one part of his anatomy. I eased out from under the covers, went into the bathroom, and did the morning business. I struggled with the brush for ten minutes and was rewarded with shining body waves of dark hair that cascaded down past my shoulders.

Couldn't possibly be a bad day, if my hair cooperated like that.

I contemplated the blue beaded dress, but it was a little formally call-girlish for this early in the A.M. Back into the knit top and short skirt. My legs needed shaving. I attended to that, thanking the Luxor for the gift of personal safety razors, and finished up with a coating of lotion.

As I was smoothing on the last handful across the top of my thigh, I noticed I had company. Lewis was standing there watching me, eyes half-closed but not in the least sleepy. He'd put on his blue jeans, but nothing else . . . very sexy. I couldn't help but take in the view.

"Hey," I said, and took my bare foot down from the counter. I hastily wiped the extra lotion across hands and arms and tugged my skirt down to a more modest level. "You're alive."

"Barely," he agreed, and indicated the toilet. I vacated, closing the door on my way out, and fished my shoes out from under the bed. When he flushed and opened the door again, I was sitting on the bed, waiting. He sat down heavily in a chair and rested his head in his hands. "I'm tired, Jo. Really tired."

"Yo, boy, join the club."

"I'm going to get you killed, you know."

"Yeah, well, you look like you're going to drop dead at any minute, so I'll try not to hold it against you."

He wasn't smiling. "You were right. This was my idea. Mine and David's. We knew you'd never get to Kevin alive. . . . I came up with the idea of stopping your heart temporarily, transporting you past the wards, and reviving you. He didn't like it much. He liked the idea of sending you in to Jonathan even less."

I remembered thinking how easy it would be for Jonathan to swat me like a fly. That would put an end to David's divided loyalties. "He found a way to protect me." The hot spark tingled under the press of my fingers on my abdomen. "We *will* be having a conversation about that later."

Lewis looked at me through latticed fingers. "What?"

"Nothing." I sucked in a breath and let it out. "So. Good move, getting me inside, but why didn't you use your business-suit buddies?"

"We've tried. Kevin's stopped us cold, and he's been sucking power at a faster and faster rate. We can't balance what's happening anymore. It's out of control. That's why we have to do this, Jo. It isn't that I want—" He broke off, shook his head roughly. "This isn't what I ever wanted. And using you to do it . . ."

"Sucks," I said crisply. "Well. There you go. Anything else I should know?"

He leaned back in his chair and regarded me through bloodshot, half-lidded eyes. "Yeah. Djinn are supposed to be returned to the vaults when Wardens die. There's always been attrition—some bottles breaking, some lost. But two hundred years ago, there were fifteen hundred Djinn known to the Wardens. Do you know how many there are today?"

I frowned at him. "No. Why does this matter?"

"Because there are fewer than six hundred in the vaults and assigned in the field."

"How many showed up free?"

"Maybe three hundred of them. Now, there will be losses. Bottles get buried, sunk in the ocean, there's predation by the Ifrit. Even then, there have to be a lot missing, and most of them have disappeared in the last six years. I think that's why Jonathan's resorted to this. He either believes we're behind it, or that we don't care."

"So somebody's stealing from the *Wardens*? And they don't know?"

"They suspect." Lewis rubbed his face as if he were trying to rub away exhaustion. "Marion's been investigating. I helped her for a while. It all comes back here. To Las Vegas, or nearby. We can't find the bottles, since they don't show up on the aetheric, but there's this sense of . . ." He hunted for the word. "*Evil.* Jonathan manipulated the kid into bringing him here. He's looking for the same thing we are. He's just more ruthless about finding it."

"So our enemy isn't Kevin."

He shook his head. "Make no mistake, it is. Kevin's out of control, and Jonathan doesn't care what kind of damage the kid does, so long as he's left free to do what he likes. In fact, Jonathan's using the kid as a conduit. It all comes down to the kid. We have to stop him."

"And the missing Djinn?"

"One thing at a time."

I nodded. "Okay. How do I get over to the Bellagio?"

He gave me a genuinely sweet smile. "Nice day for a walk, or so I hear."

"You're coming with?"

"I'm not letting you out of my sight." When I raised my eyebrows silently, he did echoed the gesture. "David will kill me if I let something happen to you."

I cleared my threat. "Yeah . . . speaking of . . . is he . . ."

"Around?" Lewis's smile turned positively cruel. "You'd know more about that than I would. We work together, sometimes—doesn't mean we're the best of friends. Especially not where you're concerned. If he knew I'd just spent the night here—"

"Hey! Nothing happened!"

"Only because I'm at the point of death." He clutched his chest and mimed an elaborate choking. Except it wasn't really funny. He *was* at the point of death. "Sorry. It's sort of weirdly amusing from this end. It's the first time in my life you considered me safe to sleep with."

I lowered my gaze to contemplate the practical. As in, shoes. I had the left one on and was toeing the right when I heard a rumble of thunder, and felt the flashover of power. Hot and fast.

I looked up. Lewis was already heading for the windows. "Were we expecting rain?" I asked.

"Not in the forecast."

"That doesn't exactly feel natural. . . ."

I stopped, because he hauled back the curtains, and we both saw it at the same time. There was a storm forming outside. A *big* goddamn storm, purple-black, swelling like a tumor. The anvil cloud stretched dizzyingly high, a gray-white tower thrusting up practically to the troposphere. The amount of power in that monster was growing exponentially.

Worse, it had rotation. *Big* rotation. I watched the edges that were rapidly expanding to the horizon, counting seconds and cloud motion.

"Shit," I breathed. "I don't think we'd better plan on walking to the Bellagio."

Lightning laddered down from the massive clouds in three or four places, shattering like neon glass against the ground and buildings. I saw the hot blue flares of transformers bursting somewhere near the edge of the city.

Lewis cursed softly under his breath, then said, "I can't *see* anything. What is it?" Without his powers, he was barred from the aetheric. I rose up and took a look.

Not good. Not good at all.

"Tell me it's somebody we can stop," he said.

It wasn't. In fact, it wasn't *somebody* at all.

It was *nobody.*

Weather is mathematical, in a certain very basic sense . . . warming and cooling the air simply means controlling the speed at which atomic structures vibrate. In any normal situation, no matter how dire, atomic structures vibrate in harmony, in groups, like a grand and glorious choir. In storm situations, there is dissonance.

This was complete and utter noise. There weren't bands of heat and cold; there weren't *winds,* exactly. Or if there were, they couldn't sustain themselves; they began and died and shifted in the blink of an eye. Hot and cold vibrations were jamming up against each other at the subatomic level, not just as a leading edge of an event, but interwoven.

"What the *hell* . . ." I whispered, appalled. This

wasn't nature gone crazy. This was nature without any mind at all.

Over at McCarren Airport, a wide-bodied jet angled in for a landing; I saw it seem to stutter as a wind shear hit it. The tail came up; the nose came down.

"No! Jo, do something!" Lewis yelled, and slammed his hand flat against the window.

I threw myself up fast to the aetheric, saw the chaos and destruction raging. I focused on the plane. It was full of terrified screaming people, burning like straw in Oversight; I had to ignore that and try to make sense of what was attacking the area around it.

Chaos. No sense to it at all . . .

I felt a harsh ripping flash, and saw particle chains snapping together.

Lightning hit the plane dead-on, frying the electronics with a hard white *pop* of energy, a fountain on the aetheric that just further contributed to the mania.

I reached out and crammed together a layer of air beneath the plane, forced it to behave like normal air under normal circumstances. It took a huge amount of effort, and I felt the strain vibrating through me like stretched steel wire. I propped the plane with an updraft, smoothed the air around it, and fought back another wind shear that attacked from the side. The plane was heavy, and the wind kept fighting back, trying to slip away, swirl like a matador's cape. It *wanted* to rip the wings off of that 737. I forced a straight runway of calm air ahead of the screaming engines.

I was shaking all over. Human bodies couldn't channel this kind of effort, not for long, not without the help of a Djinn, and David wasn't here. Wasn't connected to me.

A little farther, just a little . . .

The plane was a hundred feet off the ground. I felt the air trying to spin apart under the wings and grabbed hold, wove the chains together and forced it to stay connected.

Fifty feet.

Twenty.

"Hold on," Lewis whispered next to me. "You're almost there."

Ten.

Just before the wheels touched tarmac, I felt something give way inside me with a bloody rip, and everything fell apart. The plane bounced, landed, skidded, was slammed right and left by wind shears like fists.

I couldn't stop it, but I kept trying, grabbing for control. I fell to my knees, breathing hard, tasting blood in my mouth and seeing bright red spots in front of my eyes.

"Jo!" Lewis had hold of me. I struggled to stay out of the dark. "Let it go! They're down!"

The plane had come to a stop, through a panicked superhuman effort on the part of her pilots.

When I let go, the wind forged itself into a hard edge and came straight for *me.*

"Lewis!" I yelled, and pulled him down on the carpet, covered him with my body.

The wind shear slammed into the pyramid full force, at least a hundred miles an hour, and the window blew like a bomb. I felt a hot burn across my back, then an ice-cold burst of rain. I rolled off of Lewis and grabbed his arm, pulled him to his feet, and shoved him toward the door.

Before we made it there, another wind shear blasted

in, hit me in the back like a freight train, and slammed me down to the carpet. Lewis turned and grabbed for me, but my hand was slick with blood, and the wind shear became a backdraft, sucking me out into the storm.

I felt gravity let go as I spun out of the broken window, hundreds of feet above the Las Vegas streets. The fountains at the Bellagio were still booming, but the water was ripped to mist as soon as it exploded out of the water cannons. I tried to grab control of the winds holding me, but being suspended in midair like Fay Wray in King Kong's hand didn't do a lot for my concentration.

The wind sensed my attempt to manipulate it and dropped me.

Straight down.

I screamed as I hit glass and started to slide down the side of the pyramid. I tried to reach to cushion the fall, but it fought back, flowing away, creating a downdraft that sucked me faster toward the concrete. I flailed at slick glass windows, cold metal, left bloody streaks behind.

This is it. I felt a sick, nauseating terror taking hold, shredding what was left of my magical control. One second closer to the ground. Two. I was going to hit. . . .

I stopped falling with a jerk, like I'd come to the end of a bungee cord, was yanked back upward in a spiraling whirl. The pyramid's glass blurred by, reflecting white streaks of lightning. Rain hit me so hard it felt like strikes of hail, and I couldn't breathe, hadn't taken a breath since I'd begun screaming. . . .

I passed the broken-out window, caught a glimpse

of Lewis standing stark-pale, shielding his face against the fierce wind, blood-streaked from flying glass cuts.

He reached out to try to catch me, but it was too late. I felt the hot graze of his fingers against my bare ankle and then I was going up into the storm.

Taken hostage.

EIGHT

I had time to take about six breaths before I was too high up for it to matter, and then the gasping started. The elevator kept rising. *I can't breathe.* . . . No, I was breathing, but it wasn't doing any good. Oxygen content too low. I was filling my lungs to no effect. *Create oxygen. You can do it.* Sure, I could; it was just a matter of forming new molecules out of the available surroundings, but God, I couldn't think, I couldn't . . .

I just couldn't. For the first time, I found myself unable to do what I knew I had to do.

Which left dying. Normally, that would have been one hell of a motivator, but my brain was fraying into threadbare strands, and I couldn't feel my body anymore. Dying was more like fading. It hardly hurt at all.

Something white exploded through me like a surge from a cattle prod.

No, please, I just want to rest. . . . *Tired* . . .

Another white flare, crawling up my spine to catch fire in my brain. Panic. Panic from some part of me buried so deep it couldn't even express itself in words, just flashes.

I opened my eyes.

It had hold of me. It had been a Djinn, once . . . I could still see the furious liquid-aqua eyes in that distorted, screaming face. Not a Djinn anymore. Not even an Ifrit, which was at least a coherent entity, a being. This was a tumor of magic, cancerously overgrown, swollen with . . .

. . . with a black, glowing Mark that burned and rippled on its distended chest.

This wasn't a Djinn anymore; it was a cocoon for a demon. I sensed the Djinn trapped within, but it was failing, dying, being consumed slowly and horribly by the *other*. It was desperate.

They were both desperate.

Black spots danced madly in my vision. Lack of oxygen. I blinked and tried to remember again how to fix that, but there were too many missing pieces, and it was much too difficult. . . .

The Djinn opened its mouth, and I saw something black move inside it.

Crawling toward me.

I had a helpless, suffocating flashback of coming to on Bad Bob Biringanine's couch, his cold blue eyes on me, a bottle full of demon in his hand. *Hold her down*, he'd snapped at his Djinn, and pried my mouth open. . . .

Maybe I didn't mind dying so much, but I minded *that*. Without even a second's thought, I grabbed at the energy around me, channeled it, and slammed it down in a hundred million volts, blue-white plasma, right on top of the thing that had hold of me.

At the last instant, I remembered that if I hit the Djinn, the Djinn was still holding *me*, and that meant I was going to fry with him. As the particle chains whipped together, as the charge began to flow like liquid through the ripped sky, I jammed together air molecules between us and sent them hurtling toward the Djinn, shoving him away. He wasn't corporeal enough for it to move him far, or misted enough for it to make him disappear, but it gave me a precious foot of space as the sky turned white around me.

The lightning hit the Djinn with the force of a nuclear bomb, shredding it into shadows. I saw it even through closed eyes and covering hands, and then the shock wave hit, knocked me flying, and gravity started to claim me.

The sky was screaming.

I emerged from the clouds, falling like a star. Friction heated my skin, lashed my clothes into shreds around me. I was spinning helplessly, spiraling toward the brilliant spilled jewel box of Las Vegas.

One good thing: plenty of fresh air. I breathed, fast and hard, pumping up the oxygen in my bloodstream, and began working on slowing my fall. My head was clearer. It almost felt like a nightmare, except that nightmares generally didn't come with partial blindness and singed hair. I still saw the afterimages of the flash, the frozen, distorted scream of the demon-infected Djinn.

I hadn't killed it. You don't kill a thing like that, or at least humans don't; David had succeeded in destroying a demon once, but he was a Djinn, and second only to Jonathan in power at the time.

I wasn't slowing much, and the ground looked

closer. My skin had gone numb from the cold rushing air. I'd stopped spinning, but I could feel the greedy suck of gravity pulling me down, and no matter how fast I grabbed for air to create a cushion it was too slow.

At this rate, I'd manage to break my fall just enough to die breathing through a tube in ICU.

I went up to the aetheric. Instinct and panic, rather than a conscious plan, like rats climbing the spars of a sinking ship . . . up there, the demon-infected Djinn was still raging, black and furious, and the whole plane was roiling with power.

Below me there were some brilliant lights—not the neon glare of the strip; the blaze of Wardens, channeling power.

One was an orange torch big enough to light up the entire aetheric . . . that had to be Kevin. The other was a rich golden color, like summer sun.

Kevin had Lewis's stolen powers, and he could act if he wanted to, but I knew better than to assume he'd save me, even if he understood how. And the other Warden, glittering like summer, wasn't a Weather Warden.

I was so screwed.

I sucked in a deep breath and concentrated, *hard,* managed to slow my descent enough that it didn't feel like terminal velocity, but when I opened my eyes again I saw that the ground was rushing up, close, God, closer than I'd thought, and there was no way I could stop myself in time.

I wasn't going to hit the street. I was heading for a stretch of desert somewhere near the airport. Dirt and thornbushes and a death that was going to hurt—a lot.

A flash of lightning lit up the patch of pale sand that was going to be my final resting place.

I screamed, threw up my arms in a useless, instinctive move to cover my face, and hit the ground.

It was like hitting a bed full of the softest down feathers. It exploded up in a fluffy cloud, and I sank, slowly.

Drifted. I felt weightless, floating.

I felt oddly giddy, and realized I was holding my breath; my eyes were squeezed tightly shut. When I opened them, I didn't see anything. The air I gasped in tasted dusty.

It was dark.

I reached out and felt loose, drifting particles, fine as talcum, and then there was solid ground under my feet, lifting me up.

I emerged on my feet, borne out of the ground in a shower of powder-fine quicksand.

Oh. The other Warden had been an Earth Warden. Not to mention favorably inclined. I'd have to thank somebody, big-time. . . .

I took one step forward, and keeled over to my hands and knees, coughing and gagging. Somebody patted me helpfully on the back, raising dust clouds.

I looked up to see the face of my savior.

"Marion?" I paused to cough up some more of the desert. "Jesus—"

"Breathe," she advised me.

Marion Bearheart looked pretty much exactly as she had back at the Denny's, before I'd been driven off to die and go to Vegas . . . even down to the black-fringed jacket. Her hair was still neatly braided, tied off with turquoise-beaded accents. She looked untroubled by the storm, the demon-Djinn howling overhead, or the fact that I'd just plunged a couple of miles straight down, feet first into the ground like the stupidest Acapulco cliff diver ever.

"Thanks," I finally managed to gasp out, and spat grit. *Uck.* I *so* needed a toothbrush. She gave me a faint smile. "What . . . how . . ."

She ignored me, looking up into the clouds. "Can you stop that thing?"

"Not really." I wiped my hand across my mouth and struggled up to my feet. Bare feet. *Damn.* My clothes were in tatters. I looked like a reject from *Les Misérables.* "The Djinn up there has a Demon Mark."

She nodded, as if she already knew that. It was always hard to tell just what Marion knew, because nothing really seemed to surprise her all that much. She took out a bottle from her pocket. It was simple, square, and looked sturdy enough to survive most ordinary disasters. Nice, thick glass. She held it balanced on her palm and looked up into the storm.

"Keep it busy," she said. "Keep it off of me if you can. I'll have to get it caged."

The clouds boiled, as if they sensed what she was about to do. I heard the wind start to howl, and knew it was coming for us. I braced myself, but even so, the sheer fury of the blast that hit me almost knocked me over; Marion's fringed coat flapped and belled, and her braid frayed into waving strands of gray hair. Sand whipped away from me in pale streams, and in the tangled glare of light on the other side of the fence, where Las Vegas really began, I saw streetlights pop and transformers spark.

Keep it off of her? Was she *kidding*?

I felt the storm turning its attention on us, and shook the residual haze away to focus on the aetheric. I couldn't do much about the Djinn, but I could fight its effects . . . flip polarities, break up the wind shears. The lightning continued to flare, but I was able to keep it in sheets, high up in the ionosphere.

"Be thou bound to my service!" Marion shouted into the wind.

I felt it coming. "Hang on!" I screamed, and threw up a wall of still air around the two of us, a lame-ass attempt at a shield that shattered under the fury of the Djinn's attack. Marion clutched the bottle and held on to my arm; I wished there were something nice and solid for *me* to hold on to, like a mountain, because the gust that hit us even through my buffering knocked us back at least ten feet, lifted us off the ground, and flung us flat on our backs. I immediately scrambled up and grabbed for Marion. She still had the bottle.

"Be thou bound to"—the wind hit us again, lashing, and I felt the hot ozone burn of a lightning strike trying to form. I focused hard on it. Marion swallowed a mouthful of wind and choked out—"my service!"

Hurry the hell up, I thought, but I didn't have enough time to say it, because a face roared down from the circling clouds and headed straight for me, accompanied by a curtain of sideways-blown rain that felt like tiny silver nails on my cold skin.

It opened its mouth, and I saw the demon in it, staring out, hungry for warm, fresh screams. I had another flashback to the black, slick taste of a demon squirming down my throat, burning itself into my flesh. *Never again.*

The Djinn whirled in the wind, picking up a lethal dose of rocks, sand, thorn-spiked branches, tin cans.

It was going to strip the skin right off of us.

I hit it with the strength of panic, compressing air molecules and freezing the rain, blowing it backward and into a shredding minitornado that trapped the Djinn inside.

"Finish!" I screamed. I didn't know if Marion could even hear me; I couldn't see her, in the confused darkness with my hair whipping wildly over my eyes.

Whether she could hear me or not, I definitely heard her.

"Be thou bound to my service!"

It rang out, loud and clear, and there was a sudden sense of indrawn breath and a pressure drop so sharp it made my ears pop, and in a last, blue-white flash of lightning, I saw blackness streaming into the mouth of the bottle in Marion's hand.

She slammed the cork down and collapsed to her knees, breathing in convulsive gasps. There was blood trickling from the corner of her mouth, and as she slipped the bottle into her coat pocket, she hugged her right arm close to her ribs.

The wind blew on for another few seconds, then faltered and began to calm down. Overhead, the bruise-colored clouds, stained by sodium and neon, began to shift and break against each other.

"You okay?" I asked her. My legs were shaking, and I realized how cold I was. My heart galloped on, ignoring the message my brain was sending about the danger being over. Hearts are funny that way. *Prove it*, it was saying.

"Yes," she said. She sounded faint and exhausted.

She had reason, I supposed—she hadn't been blown a couple of miles up and tossed straight down, but she definitely had carried her weight. Not to mention saved my ass from pancaking on the desert floor. "Broken rib, I think. It'll mend. The boy did this, you know. Broke the bottle, freed the Demon Marked Djinn. He has to be stopped."

I extended a hand. She needed a lot of help getting up. With her hair blown into a wild tangle, she looked much less like the intimidating Marion I knew and feared.

"How did you get here?" I asked. The faint smile she gave me had a tinge of pain to it.

"Never mind that now." She probed her side, and winced. "You need to get moving. They'll be looking for you, and I'd rather not take on anyone else just now, if you don't mind. If you're going to stay here, we could use your help. The boy needs to be neutralized. Soon."

She didn't look up to it; that was certain. I held her dark eyes for a few seconds.

"I'm going there now. Listen, if I leave you here, will you be okay?"

The smile etched deeper and spawned little lines of amusement at the corners of her eyes. "Joanne, I've survived far worse than you. And I'm not so old as all that."

To prove it, she pulled free of my grip and straightened up. It almost looked credible. Overhead, the clouds scudded fast, moving south, as the wind pushed and searched for its path.

Moonlight wandered through a slit in the clouds, and bathed us in a circle of silver.

"Get moving. I'll see you later," Marion said, and turned and walked away into the desert.

I limped barefooted through sand, wincing at the rocks and stabbing thorns, and came up against an eight-foot razor-wire-topped cyclone fence.

"Great." I sighed.

I was *really* starting to miss being a Djinn.

There didn't seem to be any reason to go limping back to the Luxor, particularly since it was at least a half a mile hike farther than the Bellagio, and I'd just have to turn right around and go do the bidding of the Ma'at, not to mention the Wardens. Since no cabbie in his right mind would be stopping to pick up a shoeless, windblown, ragged waif in the predawn darkness, I hit the sidewalk. It was marginally easier than scaling the fence had been, which had involved layers of scrounged rags, a piece of old tire, and a fine collection of lacerations. I kept to the shadows, avoiding any unnecessary attention from the pervs and the cops. The fountains were quiet in front of the hotel; I suppose it had something to do with the wind, which was still kicking up hot and fast.

Even as early—late—as it was, there were plenty of people entering and leaving. I paused, considering the brightly lit front entrance, and looked down at myself.

Nope. Not happening. The Bellagio did have standards.

The parking lot was a sea of cars, all nicely docked at anchor. I limped through a couple of rows, spotted a few—there were always a few, even in these suspicious times—with doors left unlocked. The first two yielded nothing but nice velour upholstery and change in the drink holders; the third had a gym bag lying on the back floorboard. Black leggings, T-shirt, socks, and cross-trainers, all smelling of recent use. I went with the leggings and T-shirt, couldn't stomach the socks, and jammed the too-large shoes on over my abraded feet. My in-shape benefactor had included a hairbrush. I put it to use, wincing through the tangles, and tied the lot back with a scrap of fabric from my trashed skirt.

I'd pass. Sort of.

I jogged through the parking lot, trying to look as if I were enjoying the exercise instead of wincing with every step, went the long way around to work up a good coating of sweat, and then jogged into the lighted portico. Uniformed doormen held open double glass portals, and I threw them a jaunty wave and walked in without so much as a raised eyebrow. Bent over to pull in some deep, gasping breaths, which weren't at all feigned.

"Glad you made it back, miss," one of them said pleasantly in a lovely British accent. "Quite a storm out there."

"Was there?" I put my hands behind my back and stretched. "Didn't notice."

I tossed him a grateful smile and escaped into the lobby. Most of the desk clerks were off duty; only a couple maintained the graveyard shift. The casino continued its constant money gulping, to the accompaniment of pleasant electronic beeps and the glittering metallic tinkle of change. I turned and walked down the endless stretch of carpet, to the hallway that held the elevators.

There was still a uniformed security man on duty. I

made a production of wiping sweat from my face as I walked toward him, gave him my most vapid smile, and waved. He ignored me. Evidently no self-respecting hooker would go out looking quite so bad.

I punched the button from memory and leaned against the wall, trying not to catalog the ways I hurt, starting with the still-throbbing headache that was re-asserting its claim, and the various aches, bruises, and near-death experiences. I needed a week at the spa, with deep-tissue massage and hot stone therapy. Not to mention some intensive chocolate care.

The floor was deserted when I arrived, a long chan-nel of expensive carpet and closed doors. No sound. I walked down the hall to the door where Kevin and Jonathan had made their little home-away-from-hell.

When I reached out to knock, it swung open. Very *Addams Family.*

"Hey," Jonathan said. He was sitting on the couch, exactly as I'd first seen him—lean, athletic, military without the uniform. A black round-necked knit shirt that was somehow more formal than a simple tee, some kind of khaki cargo pants with lots of pockets. Sturdy lace-up boots. "Jo," he greeted me, and nod-ded at the armchair across from him. "Come in. Take a load off."

I did, without comment.

His salt-and-pepper eyebrows quirked as he gave me the merciless once-over. "Bad day?"

"Not the worst I've ever had. Which doesn't say a lot for my life, does it?"

"You look like you could use a beer."

There were two bottles on the end table next to

him. I twisted off the cap of one and took a swig. A little harsh and hoppy, but acceptably cold and refreshing.

"Nice cuts and bruises," Jonathan said pleasantly. "How's it going?"

"Good. You?"

"Can't complain." His eyes were dark, dark like the space no stars could ever shine. "And that takes care of the small talk. You *do* understand that I'm going to kill you if you so much as think about getting in my way, right?"

"I don't want much. I want a halfway decent massage, an herbal scrub, and to put a stop to this before we all get killed." I leaned back and kicked a leg over the arm of the chair, casual as could be. After the night I'd had, Jonathan didn't really bother me all that much. "You knew about the Djinn with the Demon Mark. You let Kevin set him free."

He didn't confirm or deny. He just tilted his beer bottle slightly in my direction, and I saw the Djinn's past go by in a blur. Enslaved to a bottle. Working for a hated master. Being called one day and commanded to stretch out its hand . . .

. . . and take a black scorched Mark on its master's chest as its own.

Locked away in a bottle, sealed for all eternity with an enemy it couldn't defeat and couldn't ever surrender to. Dying, but never dead. Infected.

The bottle being grabbed and stuffed in Kevin's pocket, at the Wardens Association vault in New York. A distorted, wavering view of Kevin, Jonathan, David, Lewis . . .

. . . me.

"Not that you care," he said remotely, "but that's a friend of mine trapped and dying."

"I can't save him."

"No," he agreed. "You can't. Neither can I. Sucks, right?"

He tipped his beer back upright and took a sip. Dark eyes never leaving me.

I sighed. "Come on, Jonathan, let's quit playing games. What do you want from me?"

"You trying out the Rule of Three? I wouldn't." His smile warned me of all kinds of unpleasantness. "How's it feel when the chickens come home to crap all over you?"

I leaned forward, rolling the beer bottle between my palms, and looked him directly in the eye. "David's here. In Las Vegas."

"Bullshit. You don't have his bottle."

"Somebody does. Maybe it's the same guy who's been bogarting Djinn for the past decade. You know, the one you're looking for?"

"You're lying."

"I could be." I deliberately upended my beer and drained it dry. Burped. "Explain something to me. You didn't give a shit about freeing him the whole time he was Bad Bob's property." The second the words left my mouth I wished I could rewind the tape, but he didn't react. Much. "You didn't rescue him when Bad Bob was whoring him out to Yvette Prentiss for her little games. It occurs to me to wonder why you're so hot to protect him from *me*. Who doesn't mean him any harm, as well you know."

He shrugged and took a pull off of his own beer.

His eyes never left me. "He hated Bad Bob," Jonathan said. "He hated Yvette. You . . ." He kept the heat off the words, but the air felt electric and harsh. "I can deal with the others. They only enslaved his body. You've gutted him."

"And you want things back the way they were?" I set the bottle down on the shiny antique side table. "That's not mine to give, Big J. Take it up with him. Oh, wait, you did, right? And when you told him to choose, he picked me. Wow. Bummer."

I felt a sharp pain go through my chest. Arrhythmia. Jonathan took another casual sip of beer.

"How's it feel, being back in the old body again? Working out for ya?"

"Famously." I wasn't going to beg. Another stab of agony, this one longer. "I need your help."

"Kinda figured you might."

"If you care about this kid at all, you need to help me get your bottle away from him."

Jonathan raised his eyebrows. "So *you* can be my new owner? Sorry, I dance with the one that brung me."

"You mean that you're not through with him yet."

"You've got to admit, the kid has talent. And one hell of a lot of power."

"Which he stole."

"Some of it." Jonathan shrugged. "Hey, his idea, not mine. Don't shoot the messenger."

"Not that it'd do any good to shoot you."

"There's that. . . . The Ma'at are ready to move, is that what you're telling me?" Jonathan adjusted his position slightly, rolled his head to the side, but kept me pinned in his stare. "Time's up?"

"They'll kill him," I said softly. "You know they won't hesitate if they think there's no alternative."

No answer. He tipped his beer up, and his throat worked.

And he smiled.

"Hey, kid," he said, and put the bottle aside. "You're awake."

I looked around to see Kevin standing in the bedroom doorway. He looked pale and nervous and small, hair stuck up at odd angles as if it had never seen the toothy side of a comb. Next to him stood the thin tattooed girl, her short red hair gleaming, her hands clasped around Kevin's arm. Siobhan. The hooker.

Kevin stared at me with dead eyes. "I thought I told you to kill her," he said.

"Didn't tell me when," Jonathan pointed out, and when Kevin opened his mouth to rectify the mistake, Jonathan held up a single finger and waggled it.

Kevin shut up.

"Hey!" Siobhan glared, and took a step forward. She had cheap plastic high-heeled hooker shoes, but great balance, and the orange toenail polish was all that. She was too sharp in the chin, too narrow in the eyes, but the whole package was effective as hell in a knit top and low-rise jeans. "He *owns* you, man! You have to do what he says!"

"Siobhan," Kevin said quietly. "Don't."

"Yeah. Don't." Jonathan's tolerance for Kevin clearly didn't extend to girlfriends. "Butt out, Red, and I won't feel the need to show you the curb the hard way."

That gave me a nice, cold shiver. When Siobhan

started to fire back a retort, I shook my head. "No,"
I said. "He's not kidding. Just relax, okay?"

"Like you care." She had a glare identical to Kevin's. Interesting. Maybe he actually had found a soul
mate, all the way out here. A soul mate with her picture plastered on call-girl cards all over the street, but
hey, it wasn't like Kevin was fresh out of the Innocent
Academy. Kevin *would* find someone more screwed
up than himself to fall for. It was inevitable. Since
he'd been powerless for so long, someone in worse
shape than him would have a powerful appeal.

"I care," I said gently. "I'm trying to keep him alive.
Just do what this guy tells you, okay? And let me
handle the witty banter."

Jonathan was looking bored. When I turned my attention back to him, he did an exaggerated lift of his
eyebrows to indicate just how extreme his ennui was.

"What do you want?" I asked.

His eyes flickered, and for a second I thought he
really *was* going to swat me like a fly. And then he
smiled. "Okay. Here's the truth: I want you to be
careful."

"And you care because . . . ?"

His eyes focused briefly and pointedly where the
warm spark of life fluttered inside me. "Got reasons."

"I'm not naming him after you, if that's what
you're thinking."

Jonathan's lips curled into a deeper smile. A real
one, nothing sinister or sarcastic about it. When he
looked at me like that—no, at what was *in* me—I
felt faint. He had the same supernatural power David
possessed to make women's clothes fall off; he just

rarely bothered to show it. I was grateful. If he'd looked at me like that before, I might've handed over David's bottle without a fight.

Well, not really. But I would've thought about it.

"Because of Imara," Jonathan said. Purred, actually. It was that kind of a word.

"Excuse me?" Before I could react, he stood up, reached over, and put his hand over my stomach. His touch was hot enough to scorch, almost painful, and I opened my mouth to yelp . . .

. . . and it ceased to hurt at all. There was a fast whirl of images that burned through me: a young woman with luxuriant black hair that fell in cascades to her waist. Laughing, talking, moving with the supernatural fury and grace of a Djinn. Her lips were David's. Her eyes . . . God, her eyes. Stern and burning, and the color of pure gold. She smelled of warm things, vanilla and cinnamon and woodsmoke; she was smiling and then she was gone, a whisper, a memory.

I caught my breath and felt tears run cold down my cheeks. Where Jonathan's hand had rested felt branded.

"Imara," I whispered. *My child.*

He was still next to me, close as a second skin, and his lips were warm at my ear. "Djinn can be born only out of death."

"So why are you keeping me alive, then?" I wiped at the tears, angry. He took a step back.

"Not human death. Not powerful enough."

I felt a cold flash, and said, "The death of a Djinn?"

No answer. Just that look from him, unexpectedly unguarded.

"And not just any Djinn."

"No," he said. "Not just any."

I felt light-headed and sick, every cut a nuclear fire, every ache another notch on the torture rack. My head throbbed hard and continuously, a strobe light of pain. I was aching and weary, and my hairline-fractured collarbone screamed every time I dared to move it, which now that adrenaline was fading I didn't even attempt.

I slowly let myself sit down again. "You mean David," I whispered. "David has to die for her to be born. God, I can't do this."

"Can't what?" he asked me. "Can't survive? Sure you can. That's what people do. They survive. It's the one thing about them I admire."

"I want to stop hurting." I was cold, wet, exhausted, wrung out. My *daughter*—the daughter I couldn't have without losing someone else I loved—my daughter had looked superhuman. I wasn't. "I want to be out of this, Jonathan. Let's end this."

He nodded, not unkindly. "Then get out. Walk away."

Kevin stepped up again, chin jutting out. "Hey! I said I want her *dead*, okay? She's trying to screw us! Just do it right—"

Jonathan, in a lightning-fast move, reached out and thumped him on the forehead. Just once.

Bop.

Kevin's eyes rolled back in his head, and he dropped. Siobhan yelled and went down on her knees next to him, fingertips pressed to his neck, but she needn't have bothered; Jonathan couldn't kill his own master. No matter how much he wanted to.

Kevin was sleeping like a baby.

"We'll take that up later," Jonathan said, and fixed Siobhan with a warning look. "Don't say a word."

She swallowed a mouthful of curses and ducked away.

I should do something, I thought. But honestly, what did it all matter, anyway? The kid was going to either get me killed or kill me himself. If he formulated the order right, Jonathan wouldn't have any choice but to carry it out.

I didn't have to care about any of this. Jonathan had already told me I could walk away. The Ma'at weren't my buddies. The Wardens . . . well, the Wardens hadn't exactly stepped up to shouldering the burdens. They'd sold me down the river when I most needed their support. And maybe Quinn was right . . . maybe the Wardens were corrupt and venal. I'd certainly seen enough of that to make it credible. I'd never taken money to change the weather, but I knew it went on. Rain on some farmland here for an extra sweetener . . . starve some folks over there to get them to cough up. As chaotic in nature as it all was, who'd know?

Worse . . . who'd care? Yvette Prentiss had violated every code the Wardens possessed. She'd ignored her duties, abused her stepson, used her Djinn for purposes even the Marquis de Sade might have found repulsive. Had anyone stopped her? No. Not until I made it impossible to ignore.

The Ma'at had some clear ethics—not to be confused with morals—but it was a chilly kind of arrogance, an icy view of the world. Human suffering didn't even factor into the equations. They concerned themselves with numbers, not faces. I could see why that appealed to Lewis; as caring and vulnerable as he was, numbers must have been an escape from the constant agony of feeling the weight of the world.

But I couldn't be that. I couldn't reduce people to numbers and trend lines. Ma'at's principles said that the forest had to burn, but I'd fight the fire every step, protect every tree, until the smoke choked me or I went up with the rest. That was my nature. *You know what you look like in Oversight? Goddamn Saint Joan the martyr. You burn real bright, Joanne, but you're burning yourself right up.* Chaz Ashworth had said that, before I'd started the fight that had killed him and left me in a cave, trapped and wishing I was dead.

You're burning yourself right up.

I didn't want to burn anymore. I was entitled to a little not-burning. Just for a while.

I clasped my hands over my stomach, over the tiny spark of potential life that was our child, and mourned something that wasn't even gone.

I felt a warm hand on my forehead. Not Jonathan's; his touch didn't comfort; it seared. This was something easier and gentler.

"She's burning up." For a second I thought it was Imara's voice, but then I cracked my tear-caked eyelids and saw it was red-haired Siobhan, perched next to me on the couch in her hussy jeans and cheap shirt and chipped nail polish. She had a fading bruise under one eye, concealed under makeup, and she smelled faintly like sex, as if it had soaked into her clothes. "She sick or something?"

"Or something," Jonathan said. He sounded remote. "Better get her a blanket."

Siobhan left, and a few seconds later I felt something heavy and soft settle over my sweating, aching skin. Her hand explored my forehead again. "She's been beat up pretty good," she said, with the authority of someone who knew the subject well. "Her eyes look funny."

"She has a concussion," Jonathan said. "She'll live."

"Yeah, well, you can't tell me you couldn't fix that shit." Siobhan sounded scared and mutinous. I felt a quick pulse of alarm and sat up, pulling the blanket close around me for comfort as I did.

Sure enough, Jonathan was giving her the hairy eyeball.

"I'm fine," I said, and sniffed when my nose ran. "You got any tissues?"

"Sure." She moved off again, came back toting a white box blooming with pastel sheets. I took a handful, thinking I was going to blow my nose, but then the unpleasant watery feeling let loose with a flood.

Nosebleed. I gasped and put the tissues to my nose, listened to Siobhan talking authoritatively about ice packs and putting my feet up, and watched Jonathan. He never stopped sipping his scotch. Never stopped watching me.

"You're not going to make it," he said finally, when Siobhan's fussing had me flat-out on the couch again with ice chilling my nose and my feet propped up on pristine down pillows. "You're not built for this kind of thing anymore. That body's taken enough abuse. Time to hit the showers."

I sniffed and swallowed a metallic taste of blood. "Don't snow me, Jonathan. You don't give a crap about me; you're worried about Imara. Assuming Imara isn't just some little illusion you conjured up out of your bag of tricks." I shifted the ice to a less painful angle. "How long is Kevin going to sleep?"

"As long as I want him to."

Valid answer. "Why are you here? Don't give me any bullshit about the kid. You could run rings around him. You do already. If you didn't want to be here, you'd be gone."

He went very still for the space of three or four seconds, then looked down into his drink. Which magically kept refilling. "I hear the shows are great."

"Why are you here?" I asked. His dark eyes flashed to me.

"Don't play games with me." It was an unmistakable warning, followed by a wintry smile. "Besides. Philosophy's really not my strong suit."

I chickened out on the Rule of Three. "Never mind. I already know. Don't tell me it was because Kevin ordered you to bring him here. You *arranged* for that kid to claim you. You made it easy for him, because you knew it would be simple to do exactly what you've done. Manipulate him like Gumby and get whatever you wanted." I sucked in a deep breath. Siobhan was sitting on the couch next to me, and I wasn't entirely sure how much she knew, but knowing Kevin, he'd probably told her everything he knew and lied about a whole lot he didn't. "You're killing him, you know. Just like you're killing everything around you. You need to stop this."

"Stop what, exactly?" he asked mildly.

I was tired, aching, pregnant, and fed up. "Jonathan, you look like the kind of guy who gets what he wants, and damn the consequences. Which is why you and Kevin are a match made in heaven. Look, I know why you're on a crusade. Lewis told me about the missing Djinn. You're using Kevin to suck power out of everything and everyone around us to try to find them, but more power won't do it. This isn't a situation that calls for a bigger hammer."

"I suppose *you* know what it calls for."

I moved the ice pack from my nose to my throbbing forehead. "Not a friggin' clue. Why, should I?"

For answer, Jonathan took me up on the aetheric. It wasn't like what had happened when the Ma'at had dragged me up, kicking and screaming; this was more like he made the aetheric descend to *us*. I never even moved, and yet suddenly everything was in that deep Oversight color palette, ringed in translucent shell-like auras. Siobhan turned to a shadow, sparkling with jealous-green and envy-red; she looked positively festive. Kevin was . . . nothing. A hole in the aetheric through which energy poured, draining into Jonathan. Dispersing . . . elsewhere.

That wasn't what he was trying to show me. As I watched, Jonathan dipped his fingers into shadow and tugged, revealing thin spiderwebs of lines. Lines that ran from several different directions . . . and connected to me.

"What . . . ?" I reached down to touch one, but my aetheric fingers passed right through it. I could barely see it, and I was pretty sure that was because Jonathan was allowing me to see it. It wasn't anything humans were equipped to sense . . . or, I thought, Djinn.

"Everything connects," he said. "The important thing is *who* connects, and when, and why. And the missing Djinn? They connect to you. I never knew that until I saw you here."

"How?" I asked, mystified. He shrugged.

"You tell me."

Another eyeblink, and the aetheric disappeared, melting into the expensive luxury of Kevin's stolen suite. Outside the windows, thunder rumbled.

"The lines connect to you," he said. "You know where my Djinn are."

I sat up, felt my nosebleed threaten to start up, and went flat again, ice pack in place. "I don't."

"Do."

"Don't," I said definitely. "Look, if I'd seen a whole bunch of bottles lying around someplace, don't you think I would have said something?"

I happened to be looking at the bar, with its gleaming ranks of scotch and gin and tequila, with its crystal glitter of glasses catching the light.

If I'd seen a whole bunch of bottles lying around . . .

"Holy shit," I murmured. I sat up, headache forgotten, nosebleed forgotten; the ice pack thumped to the carpet.

If I'd seen a whole bunch of bottles . . .

Goddamn. Pretty smart, kiddo.

"Wake him up," I said. Jonathan frowned, put aside his drink, and stood up as I did. "Wake him up right now!"

He didn't do anything that I could see, but Kevin groaned and flopped and came upright with a jerk. Siobhan got up and teetered over on her high-heeled hooker shoes to his side; he grabbed her hand and held it, and for a second I saw the scared kid under the surly adolescent.

"He knocked you out," Siobhan told him. "I told him it was a mistake. You should punish him."

Kevin groped her thigh awkwardly. She hauled him to his feet, and he put his arm around her and faced Jonathan squarely.

"Don't do that again," he said. His jaw muscles flickered, trying to hold back anger or fear. "I mean it. I'll put you back in your bottle and I'll toss it in the nearest sewer, I will, I swear."

I looked at Jonathan, who shrugged. "Hey, you're the one who wanted to wake him up. I guess you have a reason."

I did. I hugged the blanket closer around my shoulders and walked over to Kevin and Siobhan. He took up a defensive stance and—how weird was this?—moved the girl behind him. Kevin, the knight in slightly tarnished armor.

His eyes darted from me to Jonathan and back. I must have looked fierce . . . bruised, bloody, wild-eyed, wrapped in a blanket like some Red Cross rescue. He opened his mouth to order Jonathan to do something, then gave it up with a visible effort. Smart kid. Starting to realize just how little owning and operating a Djinn of Jonathan's quality was doing to help him in the first place.

"I need to talk to you," I said to the kid. "In the bedroom. You." I pointed at Jonathan. "You stay here."

He gave me that thin little look that clearly said, *Make me.* All righty then.

"Make him," I said crisply to Kevin, who flinched, but nodded.

"Yeah," he agreed. "Back in the bottle."

Jonathan had a lot of power, but that was one command he couldn't resist. *Whoosh*. Vapor. Gone.

"And don't come out until I say so!" Kevin called after him.

"You ought to cork the bottle."

"And show you where it is? Blow me."

"You wish." I sighed. I trailed blanket all the way over to the bedroom door, opened it, and stepped into Shangri-la. "Oooooh," I said, and rubbernecked. "I could get used to this."

It was a palace. Space, expansive views (of clearing skies), carpet so thick and glorious it begged to be petted. A huge fantasy of a bed, heavily rumpled, with thick down pillows dented and disarranged. The entertainment center had a plasma TV. It was on mute, but it was tuned to a sex channel. . . . I cleared my throat and walked over to hit the power on the remote.

"Hey!" Kevin protested.

"Trust me, you're not missing any plot points." I nodded across the room to a small grouping of elegant gilt-and-brocade chairs. Two were covered with piles of newspapers and room-service trays with half-eaten burgers. "Mind making a hole? I'm a little under the weather."

As jokes went, it was weak, and besides, neither of them got it, but Kevin shoved newspapers out of the way and Siobhan piled trays off on another piece of furniture—some kind of priceless antique that would have had dealers weeping at the abuse. I made sure the blanket cushioned the chair, and let myself relax.

A little.

"You know I'm not going to hurt you," I said to

Kevin. "Number one, well, I can't. You're too power-ful, and besides, I'm too damn tired."

"You can leave," he said. Being—for Kevin—magnanimous. "I'll let you walk out. Just go."

"That's nice, but if I go, so does your last hope for getting out of this thing alive. Those people out there, they're not going away. You're not going anywhere, because they've got this place locked down, and even though you've got Jonathan, you have to know that he's got his own thing going." I watched his eyes, and saw the flash of resentment and fear in them. "You're a means to an end, Kev. Have you tried to leave Las Vegas?"

He didn't answer. Siobhan did. "Once," she said. He frowned at her, but she ignored him. "He told that guy to get us out of here, but then there was this whole debate. It was stupid. I told him so."

Jonathan didn't want to leave, and if he didn't want to, Kevin had very little understanding of how to make him. Hell, Kevin hadn't even been able to control *me*, and it wasn't as if I were the most difficult of Djinn, back when I'd been all floaty. He was completely out of his depth.

"These people are going to kill you." I didn't pull any punches. There wasn't really any time. "It won't be like the movies, Kevin—it won't be some big blaze of glory, some badass villain ending. They'll just kill you, and then walk through your blood to get what they want. I can't stop them unless you help me."

"Jonathan will—"

"Jonathan," I cut him off, "will do just as Jonathan sees fit, and if you're not useful to him anymore, kiss your ass good-bye. Get me?"

He didn't want to, but he got me. Kevin played with a frayed hole in his jeans, glared at me from under a fringe of ragged, unwashed hair, and didn't seem to notice that his hooker girlfriend was rubbing his back for comfort. I took a second to scan her over more closely, then took a good hard look up on the aetheric.

She wasn't more than she seemed. Just a girl, nothing special, no Warden powers, no Ma'at glyphs. The longer I stared at her, the more I saw . . . a fragile blush of gold in her aura, like soft morning. Black slashes beneath of greed and pain. She had a bad history, but so did Kevin . . . that was what drew the two of them together. The dark gravity of desperation.

"You're running from something," I said to her, and saw her flinch in both the real world and the aetheric. "Someone."

"Maybe." Bravado wasn't her strong suit. "None of your business."

"Someone here in town? Who is it?" I had an instinct, and followed it. "Quinn. Quinn has something on you."

No answer. Siobhan stared at me with pretty, empty eyes, and I switched back to Kevin. He'd reached out for her hand, like a boyfriend, not a trick. And I saw the corresponding flicker and glow of her aura.

True love. How romantic.

Kevin took in a deep breath, glanced at his girl, then back at me. "You're right," he said. It was the most adult tone I'd ever heard him use. "I got stupid. I shouldn't have taken that guy Lewis's powers. . . . Hell, I don't even know how to, you know, do stuff with them. Well . . . I did some things. . . ."

"Like what?"

"You know. Things. Like . . . made girls' T-shirts see-through. And there was this flower garden—I made it grow and gave Siobhan a rose."

"That was nice," she said.

He shrugged, indifferent. Only someone his age could be bored by ultimate power. He brightened up and continued, "I got GWAR to do a free concert downstairs, you know, in the lobby. With the blood and everything. It was cool, especially when they were cleaning it up later—they all kept yelling at each other about who let it happen. Pretty funny."

That was the human race, all right; a thrash-metal band shows up, plays at ear-bleeding volume, and everybody blames the next guy. Management was probably still shaking in their Bruno Maglis. I wondered why security hadn't put a stop to it, and realized that Jonathan had probably found it just as funny as Kevin.

Guys. What can you do?

"And there was that fire; that was cool." Siobhan said, eyes gleaming. Kevin shot her a look, and she got off the subject fast. "I said he should rub the lamp or whatever and say he never wants to work again, but he said that was stupid, that he'd end up paralyzed or dead or something."

Which was what I'd threatened him with, back in the bad old days of Kevin being my lord and master. I couldn't restrain a smile. Kevin's answering one was thin and fragile, and shattered when a far-off rumble of thunder sounded. He turned his face to the windows and looked out.

Even tired and drained as I was, I felt the pulse of power that went out of him—unfocused, overdone, like a cruise missile swatting a gnat. The clouds literally exploded into vapor, veiling the sun, and then vanished completely.

In three seconds, it was hot and clear as far as the eye could see.

Kevin turned back to me and saw me staring, lips parted.

"I don't like rain," he said flatly.

He'd always had Fire Warden powers, but it was surprising he was doing this kind of weather manipulation with Lewis's stolen bag of tricks. And that he was learning to use it without Jonathan's tutelage. No, on reflection, not surprising: alarming. "You shouldn't—"

He interrupted. "You don't tell me what to do. *Nobody* gets to tell me what to do, ever again."

I shut my mouth. No percentage in arguing with him, not now. His mood had changed again, just like the weather—gone dark and morose, in contrast to the bright shininess beyond the glass—and I'd seen Kevin in dark moods before. Not good. When he was scared he lashed out, and right now I didn't have the strength or the ability to go toe-to-toe with the little jerk.

We stared at each other in silence for a few long seconds, and then Kevin blinked and, still surly, said, "You want I should fix that stuff?"

"What stuff?"

For answer, he reached out and took hold of my wrist. I tried to pull back, but he was stronger than he looked—weedy, but roped with muscle—and then I felt the hot tingle and knew what he was doing.

I stared down at my exposed skin as the cuts turned pink, puckered closed, and sealed up. I felt things shifting inside, healing. The heat made me break out

in a fast sweat, and the tingle turned to a more local-
ized heat. Deep down. *Really* deep.

"Stop," I panted. Kevin kept holding on. "Stop it!"
I yanked free, breaking contact, and knew my face
was flushed. He'd been healing me, but he'd also been
playing with me. Siobhan had taught him some tricks,
consciously or not. He gave me a smug grin and settled back with a proprietary arm around his girl.

I wiped blood and sweat from my arms with the
blanket and saw that he'd done it perfectly—no cuts,
not even faint scars to mark where they'd been. I even
felt energized. He'd pumped up my blood supply, too,
made my bone marrow go into overdrive. Dangerous,
but effective.

I looked down at the rest of me, sighing at the over-
size T-shirt and too-large black leggings, and
Siobhan—who had a professional understanding of the
importance of wardrobe—jumped up and ran to the
closet. She dug around and pulled out a pair of low-
rise blue jeans and a crop top that would, with imagination, just barely manage to be decent.

I accepted the jeans, and found a red mesh T-shirt
with a Chinese design to cover up the crop top. Since
I'd gone without a bra this morning, and rejected the
sweaty jog bra from the car, some layering was going
to be crucial.

The Bellagio had thoughtfully provided a lovely
stained-glass screen in the corner, probably just for
decoration, but I went behind it and changed. The
jeans fit, barely; I had to bite my lips and suck in a
breath to get them zipped up. The crop top felt like
hookerwear, but the mesh top redeemed it. When I
stepped back out, Kevin had turned on the plasma

TV again and was watching a writhing knot of bodies on screen.

"Get your head out of *Penthouse Letters*; it's never gonna happen," I said, and reclaimed the remote to flick the power button again. I sat again, leaned elbows on blue-jeaned knees, and looked from one of them to the other. "Here's the deal, kids. You've got exactly three options. You can give up—"

"Never gonna happen," Kevin said.

"Or you can die, because those guys out there, they *will* kill you. And believe me, they want to do it sooner rather than later."

Kevin's throat bobbed as he swallowed. He must have read the sincerity in my eyes. "You said there were three options."

"Yeah." I leaned back. "You can help me."

"Help you do what?"

I smiled slowly. "Save the world."

He hesitated just exactly the right amount of time to indicate how cool he was, and then said, "Yeah, whatever."

NINE

First things first. I picked up the hotel phone, dialed a number from memory, and when Marion answered, I said "Hello, pizza delivery? I'd like to order a large special."

I listened to the buzz of cell phone static for a few seconds, and then she said, "Are you in trouble?"

"Ain't I always? Just look for the biggest pile of crap; I'm usually neck-deep in it. You know that." I rolled my eyes, for Kevin and Siobhan's benefit. "You never answered me earlier. How'd you get into Las Vegas?"

"The same way you did," she said crisply. "I died. And, I might add, I'm not doing it again. It disagrees with me."

I smiled; there was something about her that I just couldn't help but like. "I'm in the Bellagio, and Kevin's ready to talk. Look for us downstairs in the casino, the far end near the restaurants. It's quieter there."

"Fifteen minutes," she promised, and hung up.

I replaced the phone in the cradle and looked over

at Kevin. "Don't start anything," I warned him. "And give me the stopper."

"What?"

"The stopper for Jonathan's bottle." He looked wary, but there was nothing to be gained from holding it back. He fumbled in his pants pocket and found a little plastic thing. It hardly seemed big enough to hold in something like Jonathan.

"You're not gonna screw me, right?" he asked. I shook my head. He dropped the stopper into my hand. "Better not, or I'll go nuclear on your ass."

I walked out into the living area again, which was drenched in early-morning butterscotch sunlight. The place smelled faintly stale; they hadn't let the maids in for days, maybe weeks. I walked straight for the wet bar, picked up the bottle of Jim Beam, and poured myself a splash in a crystal tumbler. Kevin appeared in the doorway, and I saw him go pallid—more than usual—and then try to cover up.

"Pour me one, too," he said, and swaggered over.

I gave him a lovely, warm smile. "No." I screwed the cap back on the whiskey and put it aside, turned to the bar, and let my eyes sweep over the glittering array of crystal. "Your idea? It's not a bad one, kid, really. Purloined-letter stuff. Classic."

"Jonathan!" he yelled, and I hardened the air in a thick shell around him, creating a thick, opaque bubble that kept sound from penetrating. He'd break it, but it would take him a few seconds to figure out how; that was the advantage I still had over him. Training. I started pulling out decanters, one after another, and shaking them. No, no, no, no . . .

Yes.

The muffled rattle of glass on crystal. I put the decanter down, took a firm grip, and held my fingers over the mouth as a rough sieve as I poured the (no doubt expensive) booze down the stainless-steel sink.

A glass bottle hit my fingers with a wet, heavy impact.

Kevin snapped the bubble around him with a wild flare of power, wild enough shatter the mirror behind the bar and send heavy furniture tumbling. I ducked, almost fumbled the heavy, slick crystal, and heard him yelling Jonathan's name again.

Not that Jonathan could respond. Kevin had clearly told him, *Don't come out until I say so,* and he hadn't said so, not in so many words. It would require a direct command to counteract his previous instructions, and that gave me precious seconds.

So long as I didn't drop anything . . .

. . . which, of course, I did, as Siobhan tackled me from the side. We both tumbled. I fetched up against the hard edge of a cabinet, the crystal decanter thumped to the carpet, spraying the last amber drops, and a glass bottle about as big as a purse-sized perfume slid halfway out the round mouth.

Siobhan lunged for it. My turn to tackle. She pulled my hair, which hurt, and I rolled her over and reached for the crystal. It slid greasily under my fingers, scooting another four inches away. Kevin was still desperately yelling for Jonathan, not quite comprehending what was going on except that there was a girlfight on the floor and he was kind of liking it.

I kicked loose of Siobhan's grabbing hands, rolled, and took the decanter with me.

"Jonathan, come here!" Kevin yelled frantically,

and jumped over Siobhan to come at me with a swing-ing fist. I upended the decanter.

My fingers closed around the slick, wet glass of Jon-athan's bottle, and the world . . . changed.

He was now *my* Djinn.

Everything stopped, crystal-clear—Kevin, suspended in midswing; Siobhan, clawing her way across the car-pet toward me; the discarded liquor decanter, heading for the floor.

Everything . . . just . . . stopped.

I sucked in a deep breath and held it, felt my mus-cles and tendons and blood and bone and tissue as if they were all new, brand-new, made in this second. Then the world formed around me. Air, in its complex and beautiful lattice of molecules, moving in waves and eddies, a life-form of its own. The stunning crystal perfection of the bottle in my hand. The world, God, *the world*, so huge, so astonishing, so wondrous in its clockwork precision.

The enormous, dreaming strength of the world liv-ing in every pulse beat, every breath.

And there was Jonathan, standing before me. Not in his normal human form, with its easy-to-underestimate casual grace; no, this was something else, something bright and unknowable and wild in its magic.

The seduction of it . . .

The next breath, Jonathan was back in human dis-guise, staring at Siobhan and Kevin, who were still frozen in time. Light gleamed in his brown-and-silver hair, and the darkness of his eyes was the darkness of the end of things.

"I don't like you," he said, without even glancing my way. "You know that."

"I know." My mouth felt strange, my voice even stranger. "Sorry."

He shrugged. "Well, that's the way the world crumbles. Sometimes you get surprised."

And he turned and pulled me close to him. His touch was fire—not the soothing heat of David's skin, but the scalding burn of an open flame. I tried to pull away, but that wasn't possible here, now. He put one hand at the small of my back and moved the other to splay an open palm across my stomach.

Too close. Too intimate. *Very* personal.

Stars in those eyes, like an endless sky. Unknown and unknowable, to anything human. And there was passion in there, too, the passion of gods that insects would never know or understand.

"This saves you," he whispered, and put his lips very gently against mine. A closed-mouth kiss, but it set my blood on fire, made my knees weak and rubbery. "*She* saves you. Count your blessings, Jo. This could have had a different ending."

. . . and time snapped back together. Jonathan stepped back, smiling.

And Kevin's fist hit my chin, snapped my head back, and instead of visions of mountains and gods I saw stars, but I hung on grimly to what was in my hand, even as his fingers scrabbled at it to take it away.

I slid sideways to the carpet, worked my jaw experimentally, and said, "Jonathan, restrain them, please."

When I opened my eyes and blinked away the blurring, he was holding Kevin by the scruff of the neck and Siobhan by the arm. They were both struggling—

Kevin was screaming curses, mostly directed at me—
but they weren't going anywhere.

Jonathan raised his eyebrows in my direction. "Nice
bruise you're going to have."

I glared. "Let's get this over with," I said. "Take
the powers Kevin stole from Lewis, and put them back
where they belong." He just stared at me. We did
several long seconds' worth of that. "I said, take the
powers Kevin stole from Lewis, and—"

"Heard you," Jonathan interrupted me. "You don't
want me to do that right now."

"You want to play Rule of Three with me?"

"Trust me, you *really* don't want me to do what you
just said."

"I—" I shut up and looked at him, deeply, and
changed my mind. "Okay, I'll play. Why not?"

He gave me a Djinn smile, all slyness and misinfor-
mation. "I thought you wanted to save the world."

"Meaning what?"

He shrugged. Siobhan was trying to bite his hand.
He gave her one sidelong look, and she went limp and
fell to the carpet.

"Hey!" I protested, and scrambled over next to her.
She was still breathing. In fact, she had a sweet little
smile, when she lost the 'tude. She was a natural red-
head, with the soft pink skin to match, and the light
was kinder to her than the world. "Watch it, buster.
I'm the one with the—"

"You got nothing," Jonathan said. "We both know
you can't make me do a damn thing I don't want to
do. Yeah?"

"Yeah," I agreed glumly. "So why don't you want

to return Lewis's powers? What's the point in that? He'll *die!*"

The smile continued on Jonathan's sharp, handsome face, but there wasn't any amusement in his eyes.

"Trust me," he replied. "It's better this way. Just for a while."

We could have played the game for hours, I knew that; I had Jonathan's bottle, but I didn't have Jonathan himself, not by any stretch of the imagination. He'd been newly under thrall when Yvette had him, and he hadn't figured out the boundaries properly in the heat of the moment; otherwise, he never would have carried out half the commands she'd given him.

Lucky me, I got him farther along the learning curve.

"Fine," I said. "Wake Siobhan up. We're all going downstairs."

He didn't so much as glance at her, but the girl came straight up, gasping, and immediately launched herself at me again. Jonathan rolled his eyes and, without my asking, stopped her in midlunge.

Freeze-frame.

He shook Kevin by the scruff of the neck and said, "Explain to your girlfriend how stupid that is."

Kevin licked his lips, darted glances from Jonathan to me and back again. "Can she hear me?"

"Sure."

"Siobhan . . . uh . . . cool it, okay? It's not like this is a bad thing. Maybe they'll all quit chasing us now."

Jonathan released her from the pause button. Siobhan, off balance, windmilled her arms and legs but stayed upright.

And a pout. "You don't want it back?"

"His bottle?" Kevin gave Jonathan another cautious look. "Uh, no."

"Loser," she muttered. She threw up her hands and scooted her butt up on a bar stool. "Coulda been rich, you know. Living in some big white mansion with servants and shit. Swimming pool."

I didn't dare leave her behind; she knew too much. "Okay, kids, let's go. Play nice and maybe I'll give you some good toys."

Siobhan, no fool, lowered her mascara-thick eyelashes. "Like a big white mansion?"

I reached out and shoved her off the bar stool. "Don't push your luck." I nodded at Jonathan. "Let him go."

"You're a bitch," Kevin said.

"And you say that like it's a bad thing." I grabbed Kevin by the shoulder and steered him and Siobhan in the direction of the door. "Move it."

I took Jonathan aside in the elevator, turned our backs to Kevin and Siobhan, and whispered, "The Ma'at have a sniper on call. He's under orders to take Kevin out. I need you to make sure that doesn't happen." No change in Jonathan's expression. No acknowledgment, either. I sighed. "Can we agree to a decent working rapport, here? Because I really don't have time for this, and I can always stuff you back in the bottle and shove a tampon in the top instead of a stopper, and all the other Djinn will point and laugh—"

"Fine," he said. "I'll make sure Kevin doesn't get shot."

I smelled a rat. "I'd rather not be shot, either."

Jonathan shrugged. I took it as a gift and saw that Kevin and his girlfriend had taken the opportunity to whisper together, too . . . probably not soft little nothings, from the glances they were tossing us. Great. Now I had to worry about treachery from Jonathan *and* the simpleminded scheming of the juvenile Bonnie and Clyde.

The elevator glided to a smooth, elegant halt and deposited us back in the marble hallways, rows and rows of doors all opening and closing, people always moving. They say New York is the city that doesn't sleep; Las Vegas doesn't even *nap.* I wondered when they got the basic cleaning done. Even Disneyland closes long enough to empty the trash and polish the brass.

We joined the flow out into the main concourse, turned left, and went past the cashier stand, into the wilderness of gently chiming slots. To our right were trendy restaurants—the kind that didn't post prices— and somewhere at the back was a walkway that led to Caesar's Palace next door. *Next door,* in Las Vegas terms, meant about a ten-minute walk through a sky bridge that seemed to go on forever.

I halted us near a bar at the back corner, chose a table, and got everyone to sit. Everyone except Jonathan, who was examining slot machines and entertaining himself by making random ones spit coins. Kevin watched him raptly. I could tell by the greedy flare in his eyes that he'd figured out what the Djinn was doing.

"Don't even," I said. The security cameras wouldn't see Jonathan at all, most likely; they'd just see machines randomly vomiting tokens . . . but if Kevin started flouncing around making the bells ring, there'd be a fast, heavily muscled presence and a windowless office, followed by some harshly worded questions we couldn't afford to avoid just now. "Play later. Just sit."

Kevin, still watching Jonathan, said, "I know they're going to kill me." His expression didn't change. "You might as well just take him and go. Siobhan and I can hide on our own."

Surprisingly, that was probably true. He and Siobhan could blend in, get out of town, find some big city like Chicago or Detroit where two more teenagers wandering homeless wouldn't attract any notice. Providing Siobhan didn't just blow him off once she realized he wasn't the bankroll she'd thought. But I couldn't lose him now. I needed him, for Lewis's sake.

I caught a flicker out of the corner of my eye, and turned my head. Marion Bearheart was coming our way. She looked, as always, cool and composed. Her hands were in her coat pockets, and she didn't hurry; she stopped to admire some items in a shop window, checked out the menu at Le Cirque. She made a slow circuit of the area, checking the aetheric, I was sure.

Then she pulled up a chair next to me and said, "Nice to know you made it."

"Yeah, likewise." I shot a look at Kevin and Siobhan. "I guess you know Kevin."

She nodded politely to him, as if she weren't planning to get him behind closed doors at her facility and strip him clean of power and potential just as soon as the opportunity presented itself. Kevin didn't move. He was giving both of us his patented bad-boy glower.

Marion dismissed him, and focused her dark eyes on me. "You have it?"

I opened my fist to show her Jonathan's bottle. "I'd like to trade for something more valuable than your word. Not that I don't trust you, but . . . well, I don't trust you."

She removed a hand from her coat pocket and mutely displayed the blue glass bottle that Yvette Prentiss had used, not so very long ago, to trap a man willing to give up his life for me.

I reached out, slowly, and took the glass. No stopper in the bottle. It felt warm. "David," I whispered, and closed my eyes for a second in relief as the connection between us hummed tight between us.

"Right here." I heard a chair scrape, and saw that he'd joined us at the table.

He looked utterly unchanged—auburn-flecked hair worn a little untidily, brown eyes flashing behind round gold-rimmed spectacles. An old-fashioned olive-drab coat over a faded blue plaid shirt. Blue jeans.

I sucked in a startled breath and felt my eyes sting with tears; the vision of him turned into a colorful blur. A blur that reached across empty space and cupped my cheek in its hand, and *yes,* that was his touch, warm and sweet and gentle. I leaned against it, breathing in the smell of old wool and cinnamon, leaves and woodsmoke. "Oh, God," I whispered, and it sounded like the prayer it was.

He was leaning close; I could feel the aura of him against me, the barely-there touch of his lips against my ear as he whispered, "I've been watching you." The shimmer of heat that ran through me turned me into honey and butter, made me think thoughts that I shouldn't be having in public, much less in front of people who might want to kill me.

"Could've helped me out a little," I said.

"You did fine." He kissed me, and all the thoughts were refined into sheer, unadulterated longing. I wanted him to keep kissing me, forever if that was possible. I couldn't imagine it ending, but of course it did, a slow withdrawal of those soft, delicious lips from mine.

I opened my eyes and looked straight into his, and saw them burning copper and gold, molten with love and longing and power.

This was what I'd been fighting for. What I'd fight for with every breath, every remaining day of my life.

"Anything I can do for you, master?" he whispered to me. "Or to you, anyway?"

I sucked in a superheated breath, trembling, and managed to be practical. "A purse to put this bottle in would be great, actually."

He reached under the table and pulled out a black leather bag, nothing designer—my bad for not specifying properly, really—and he'd thoughtfully included padding material. I slid the bottle inside and zipped it shut, then looped it bandolier-fashion over my head. I was *not* losing him. Not again. I'd break his bottle when we were out of this mess; I didn't like keeping him prisoner, but right now having David's power amplifying mine might keep us alive.

"Joanne?" Marion's distant voice. I blinked and pulled my attention away from David; it was like ripping off a limb, but I managed. Absence didn't make the heart grow fonder; it created a kind of magnetic lock that didn't seem humanly possible to break. "Jonathan's bottle, if you please."

Oh. Right.

Jonathan had given up on slot machines and had wandered back. He was standing behind my chair, and without turning around I knew that he was watching David. I could feel the crackle of power in the air. They weren't speaking, but there was conversation going on. Levels of power, emotion, give and take.

"Glad to get rid of it," I said sincerely, and held it out for Marion to accept.

Kevin had been waiting, and he took advantage of the chance. He slapped my hand, and the bottle went spinning out of control across the tabletop, skittering and bouncing, straight toward David—who, being Djinn, couldn't physically or aetherically touch it. He reached out for it, but his hand went right through it as if it didn't exist, or he didn't, or some combination of the two; the bottle slid through him and disappeared. I heard the muffled thud of it hitting carpet.

"Jump ball," Jonathan murmured, and then turned serious again. "Crap."

I felt the surge at almost exactly the same time, and so did David, who threw himself over me. Something was coming. Something *big*. I could see it blowing up in the aetheric, big as a dragon and twice as fiery—no idea what it was, but it was huge and very, very scary.

"Get down!" Jonathan's voice roared through the casino, supernaturally loud, like an enraged drill instructor on the world's largest loudspeaker, and it wasn't surprising that every single person in sight who wasn't Jonathan dropped to the carpet like they'd been chopped off at the knees. There was some muffled screaming, but surprisingly little. I started worming my way across the floor toward where Jonathan's bottle had fallen, but David was in the way, and Kevin was elbow-walking that way, too. I lunged across David at the faint sparkle of glass in shadow, but I was too late; a hand was there before me.

Siobhan. She grabbed it and stuffed the bottle into the pocket of her jeans.

Jonathan had turned, watching her with narrow, dark eyes, like a predator about to eat something. I grabbed the girl's wrist. "Siobhan. He'll kill you. *Give it to me!*"

She went very pale. She hesitated, then pulled it out of her pocket and handed it over just as Kevin got into position to try to snatch it away. We had an undignified little wrestling match, which consisted of me yanking my hands away from his and him trying to pry my fingers open, muttering things about my mother that weren't very complimentary. Siobhan crab-walked backward, away from the fray.

"Quiet!" Jonathan snapped at us. We all froze. Then there was a surprisingly weighty, profound silence. And then there was the faintest tinkle of glasses on tables, going on for a few delicate seconds.

And then an earthquake hit like a bomb.

Maybe people screamed, I don't know; the first tremor rippled through the floor like a wave through a stormy ocean, and I was tossed sideways, rolled, fetched up against a railing that I grabbed onto for dear life as the building continued to pitch and roll. It was too loud to hear screaming over the jangling of alarms and bells and dying slot machines and breaking glass and shattering steel.

I had a lot of power. It was all useless. Weather was an ephemeral power; this was something deep, strong, relentless. I caught a flash of someone moving faster, coat flying, and saw David leaping over the rolling, rippling floor to land hard beside me. He threw himself on top of me, smothering my scream— I *had* been screaming, I realized from the raw ache in my throat—and I felt impacts against his body. Things hitting him. Things that would have crushed me.

Even a minor earthquake has a deeply unsettling effect, but a major one, like this, robs you of the ability to do anything but hang on and pray. I prayed, my hand locked a vise around the wrought-iron railing, and I heard David whispering in that liquid language of the Djinn. It might have been a prayer, too, for all I knew.

And then I realized that I had the power to stop it. My left hand, the one not holding on in a death grip, was clutching Jonathan's bottle—which was, thankfully, still intact.

"Get off!" I yelled in David's ear. "Off!"

He rolled away into a fluid, inhuman crouch—the first time I'd really seen him betray his Djinn nature in body language. He was moving like Rahel now, like something built out of alien parts into the semblance of a human body. His eyes were blazing so brightly it was like they'd caught fire.

I held up Jonathan's bottle, coughed against a choking cloud of crumbling dry wall, and yelled, "Jonathan! I command you to stop this earthquake, *now!*"

He was the only one still upright. Tall, slim, untouched by the shattering concrete and flying debris as the hotel ripped itself apart. Marion was motionless at his feet. Kevin. Siobhan.

He looked utterly composed as he turned toward me and said, "I can't."

The wave of disbelief almost drowned me. I hadn't left him any room for equivocation; I was *holding his damn bottle.* . . .

He nodded toward it.

"That's not my bottle, kiddo," he said. "Sorry. Nice wording, though. Eight out of ten for style."

I stupidly shook the bottle in my hand—why, I have no idea; trying to make it work?—and before I could get my head around it, the moment was past. Jonathan was doing something. Not what I'd wanted him to do, of course, but *something*, which was more than the rest of us were capable of trying.

He grabbed Kevin by the scruff of the neck, yanked him to his feet, and yelled something in his ear. Then he grabbed Marion, got her standing, and yelled something to her, too.

Then he steadied the ground under them. I could see it, even in this reality—a golden shimmer, spreading out around him in concentric, growing circles, and inside the gold, a small island of calm. Marion and Kevin were talking, or rather yelling; I couldn't hear a thing. I couldn't even hear David now, who was wrapped around me—he shoved me back into a thick recessed doorway and braced himself there, holding me in. I peered over his shoulder at what was happening.

Marion had taken Kevin's hand. The two of them were facing each other now, and as I watched she went into a trance state, eyes slowly closing. She took the kid with her. As his face went smooth and calm, he looked ten years older and, at the same time, amazingly childlike.

Alight with power.

This was a shallow quake, I knew that much; deeper-seated disturbances usually do less damage, because the energy gets absorbed by the bedrock on the way. Shallow ones are much more dangerous to the surface, and this one was a doozy. No way to objectively measure it by Richter scale standards, but I'd been taught the Mercalli intensity scale, and this was damn sure an IX. The damage was being caused by exactly the same things that happen when you drop a stone into a pool of water—waves bouncing back from harder objects, then from other waves of greater intensity. Energy in dissonance, deflected constantly back against itself. It ripped things apart in its madness.

I felt the shaking and rolling subside to a mere sickening tilt and jerk and shudder. As it did, sounds became clearer again—screaming, crashing, slot machines tipping, walls collapsing.

And in the circle of gold, Marion and Kevin opened their eyes and smiled at each other. Pure smiles of delight and pride.

The shaking stopped. One last sifting of dust from above, and then it was over. What emergency lighting there was flickered on, bathing everything in a sickly halogen glow, but the shadows stayed deep and secret.

Marion let go of Kevin's hands and reached up to put her palms on his cheeks. She leaned him closer and kissed his forehead gently as she stroked his oily, tangled hair.

"That was lovely," she said. "Very fine work. I commend you."

Kevin looked rapt. His face was shining and, for once, the light in his eyes wasn't one of greed or fury.

It was something close to love.

"Now we need to help," Marion said. "There are a lot of injured. Come with me."

She stepped over a chunk of fallen concrete and held out her hand to him.

"Kevin!"

Siobhan's shrill voice. She was getting to her feet—Jonathan not helping—and brushing dust off her shorts. There were bloody cuts and scrapes on her, but nothing serious, I thought.

She looked royally pissed off.

Kevin hesitated, looking back. His fingers were just a couple of inches from Marion's beckoning hand. *Go*, I begged him. *Learn what the real Wardens do. See what a difference you can be in the world.*

I wished I'd duct-taped the girl to a chair. Hindsight.

"Kevin," Marion said, in a much more adult tone. Not commanding, not wheedling, just reminding him of what was important.

The light faded out of his face, and he took a step back. "Why should I help them? What'd they ever do for me?"

Marion dropped her hand back to her side, turned, and walked away to kneel by the side of the first person she saw. Marion was an Earth Warden. Healing was so much a part of her that she couldn't deny it, and I could see from the torment in Kevin's face that he was feeling that part of the heritage he'd stolen from Lewis, as well. Earth powers had a hell of a lot of strength, but also a carried a great load of compassion and responsibility.

I watched as Kevin turned back to Siobhan, and I felt myself mourn inside for the lost opportunity.

"Joanne." David's voice drew me back to the here

and now, to his body pressed against me in the narrow space. "Are you hurt?"

I shook my head and saw dust sift off my hair. Sneezed. "Just my image. Go help Marion. Save whoever you can."

He kissed my forehead without comment, and left me. I picked my way across rubble and almost slipped on a wide round plastic tray piled with glasses; I looked around for the waiter, but he was gone. At least it didn't look like there were too many casualties. Amazing.

Jonathan had righted one of the unsplintered chairs and seated himself, staring out at the mess. I stopped next to him. Siobhan and Kevin were hovering nearby, Siobhan whispering, Kevin listening.

"Not your bottle?" I produced the one I'd been clutching. He shook his head mutely. I took a closer look—not that I'd memorized the one I'd taken from the decanter, but this one *did* seem different. And I no longer had the sense of Jonathan's presence in me, either. "Then who's got it?"

Jonathan gave me a bleak smile. "You already know who—" He stopped short. Someone was approaching through the rubble, walking with the fluid ease of a tiger. Even through the dust-choked haze, her clothes blazed with color.

Neon yellow.

Rahel sidestepped the wreckage of a slot machine bleeding tokens, and walked toward us. Beautiful as ever, confident and easy.

Smiling.

Her eyes were black. Jet-black, lid to lid.

"Crap, I don't have time for this. Rahel, dammit—"

Jonathan said, and that was all there was time for, because she threw herself on him, turning into angles and glittering coal, a thing made of cutting edges and teeth.

The Ifrit had just found the meal of her life.

I screamed and tried to grab her, but I wasn't a Djinn any longer, even if I still had some kind of Djinn second sight; my hands went through her like a ghost. And through Jonathan, too. He'd become ghostly, trapped in her embrace. They fell and rolled over rubble, fighting and clawing. Jonathan lost his human state and turned to something brilliant and hotly dangerous as a star, but the darkness engulfed that heat.

"David!" I screamed, but I didn't really need to; he was already on the move, leaping over obstacles and landing on the back of the Ifrit. Taking her sharp-edged head—*was* that her head?—in his hands and twisting with vicious strength.

She didn't so much turn as just . . . reverse. What he was holding grew teeth, the back of her grew claws and spikes and arms. They pierced him and held him, and I felt the sharp vibration of agony go through me, too. It made me stumble and fall to my knees.

"Rahel, no!" I cried. "Stop! God, *stop!*"

She couldn't. She was totally out of control.

There was a sudden odd sense of pressure changing, and my ears responded with a painfully abrupt pop. I lurched forward, falling, and caught myself as I felt David scream. It rang through the aetheric like a shattering bell, and I knew there was no time, no time, he was being torn apart by her hunger. . . .

I had no idea if it would work, could work, but I had to try.

I held out the empty bottle—the decoy bottle—in one shaking fist and yelled out the first iteration of the ritual. "Rahel! *Be thou bound to my service!*"

The Ifrit turned on me with a roar. David was bleeding. That wasn't real blood, any more than his was a real body; it was a physical representation of an aethereal energy; he could heal himself from anything so long as he had enough power left to form flesh. . . .

But it looked so real. He was pallid, shattered, broken. The copper of his eyes was dying.

"*Be thou bound to my service!*" I shouted, and crawled backward as the diamond-sharp claws raked at me.

Through me. She couldn't touch me. I felt a hot spark of triumph.

"*Be thou bound to—*"

She lunged at me and the claws plunged deep, deeper . . . snagged on something.

No! No no no no no . . .

Not my baby.

She could destroy the life inside me, I knew that. I *felt* that, just as I felt David trying to get to me, determined to protect me or die in the attempt.

Rahel hesitated. Her claws were caged around Imara, holding that fragile spark. One instant's pressure would be enough.

As she hesitated, torn by whatever remnant of reason was left to her, I gasped it out. "*Be thou bound to my service!*"

She went entirely still. Ice and angles, coal and glass. A three-dimensional sculpture visible only to Djinn eyes. Living? Breathing? I didn't know, couldn't tell. There was no sensation of power from the bottle I held, and no sense of connection to her. Had anybody ever tried to bind an Ifrit before? Probably not . . . humans couldn't see them, and Djinn wouldn't be able to do it.

I was the only one who could see them, *and* bind them.

"Let go of my baby," I whispered.

The hand inside of me unclenched. Claws withdrew. It was the only part of her that moved at all.

"Rahel," I said. "Can you hear me?"

No answer. I shuddered and opened the black leather purse still slung around my body; there was enough padding in there for two bottles. I shoved Rahel's in, careful that it wouldn't knock against David's, and left her frozen there to fumble my way to where David was lying.

His torso was a mess of shredded meat. Blood, so much blood. His eyes had gone as brown as dying leaves, and his lips were a light shade of lilac.

She'd almost consumed him whole. I couldn't get my breath as I knelt next to him. He felt so cold to the touch—David, who was always burning warm. Like a fire going out.

I whispered his name, over and over, like a chant. I ordered him to heal himself. He didn't respond, although his eyes fastened on me like I was the only thing in the world.

His hand found mine and held it. There was no strength in him. His fingernails were the same pallid shade as his lips.

He whispered, "Leave me."

"Like hell!" I snapped. "God, *please*, don't do this—David, I *order you to heal*—"

Kevin was standing next to me. "He's dying," he said. "Whoa. I didn't know they did that."

"*Shut up*, you little bastard." I looked up, and for a second I thought the dancing red dot on his chest had something to do with the tears distorting my vision, but then I realized late and cold what exactly it was.

I'd forgotten all about Quinn and his sniper rifle.

The red dot was a laser sight, focused on Kevin's heart.

"No!" I screamed, and shoved Kevin with one hand flat against his chest. He tripped, fell on his ass. I stood up, waving my arms. "No, Quinn, stop, it's over, it's over—"

Kevin leaped up, the idiot. A clear target.

The red dot settled over my heart. Steady as a rock.

It was focused on *me*. Not Kevin, *me*.

What the hell . . . ?!

I had just enough time to throw myself backward, and I swear, I felt the supersonic hiss of the bullet's friction burning the air as it passed over me.

Missed, I thought, and then I saw that there had been someone standing behind me. Like her boyfriend, Siobhan had been stupid enough to bounce up like a pop target on a shooting gallery.

Her mouth was open in amazement. She stared down at the red hole—about the size of my thumb—through her chest. She didn't really make any noise. Just a quiet coughing sound, like someone trying to clear their throat, and then there was a sudden shocking flood of red out of her mouth.

She pitched forward over me. I raised my head and saw the hole in her back, the size of a clenched fist, full of blood like a deep well that spilled over in gouts and splashes. She was shaking all over. I yelled something—it might have been Marion's name. Kevin was already there, reaching for her, but I felt her going.

We both felt her die.

Her body collapsed against me, limp and empty, and for the first time I saw that her eyes weren't hazel at all; they were a beautiful spider's-web pattern of moss and brown, flecked with gold.

Her body felt heavy as sin, draped over me.

I don't know how many seconds that was—it felt like an eternity—and then Kevin was there, screaming. He rolled her limply into his arms. I felt the surge of power as he tried to force her body to live; the flesh jumped as nerves conducted electricity, but that was nothing but reflex.

"She's gone," I whispered. There was blood all over me, splattered; I wiped at the mess with shaking fingers. "Kevin, stop. She's gone."

He kept trying. Breathing into her mouth. Flooding dead flesh with jolt after jolt of raw power as he tried to change the immutable.

"Do something!" he shouted at me. His face had gone zombie-white, but his eyes were furious, his lips smeared with her blood from the mouth-to-mouth. "You've got a Djinn! Save her!"

"No," I said.

"I'll kill you, I swear I will!" I could feel the fury coming off of him, but the words were little-boy words, broken and afraid. The power he had was nothing like little-boy power, though; it was Lewis's power, and it could crush me, burn me, rip me apart.

There are three things you aren't supposed to ever ask your Djinn to do. Give you eternal life. Give you unlimited power. Raise the dead. That's the one that gets most people, if they live long enough. In that first chill of grief, too many turn to their Djinn and blurt out an order they shouldn't. The consequences were tragic and legendary.

Because when you do those particular things, the Djinn act under a totally different set of imperatives. The magic that drives them to obey you also drives them to turn on you.

I bit my tongue, *hard*, and swallowed a scream.

"No," I finally whispered. "She's gone, Kevin. I'm so sorry."

I thought for a second he really would kill me, kill me with his bare bloodstained hands, but then tears spilled over and he was sobbing hopelessly.

"Stay down," I said, and crawled to where David was still lying on the floor. He wasn't any better. In fact, he looked worse. Breathing in shallow gasps. His eyes weren't brown anymore; they were turning darker.

"Trying to kill you," he murmured. "*You*. Not them."

"Yeah," I agreed shakily. "I saw. Why would Quinn try to kill me?"

He reached up to touch my face. I felt no warmth, only a faint, insubstantial ghost of contact.

"Don't leave me," I whispered. "You can't leave me, David. I won't let you."

His pale lips parted to shape my name, silently. I felt the love in it.

"I need you," I said. "I need you with me. Stay." My breath was doing something funny in my chest, turning sour and thick. I couldn't seem to gasp in enough air. "God, David, don't do this to me. Don't you dare."

He tried to answer me, but then his back arched and he cried out. His open eyes shifted from a violent storm-black to a bright orange, running through the spectrum. I remembered that. I'd seen it before.

Flesh corrupted and melted away, revealing wet stripes of muscle. Bone. Layer by layer, he died.

What was left turned hard and cold and black.

Frozen.

Ifrit.

Soft human hands were on me, pulling me back into a sheltering embrace, and I was being rocked against someone as I whimpered. Unable to weep now. Unable to scream and let out the fury and horror.

Cold, cold, everything was cold.

David was a thing of ice and shadow, burned by darkness. Lying on the floor and motionless.

Marion had me. She was saying something to me, but I couldn't understand her; she unzipped the purse at my side and took my strengthless hand and wrapped it around David's blue glass bottle.

She was telling me to do something. It didn't matter anymore, but I numbly echoed the words. "Back in the bottle," I said. The words sounded odd in my head and tasted flat on my tongue.

The Ifrit that lay like some twisted sculpture in David's place misted into an oily whisper and disappeared. Marion fumbled the stopper in place.

Rahel. No one else could see her, but I couldn't just . . . *leave* her here. I took the second, empty bottle. I whispered the words. Rahel's frozen body disappeared, too.

There were rescuers coming. Flashlights dancing wildly in the dust-filled air. Marion zipped the purse shut and held me close as the first of them got to us. Paramedics and firefighters. One of them forced Kevin to put down Siobhan's body, and the three of us—the three survivors—were wrapped in blankets and led out through the tangle of steel and broken glass and darkness.

I remembered the sniper only then. It no longer seemed to matter, but there were no merciful red laser dots coming to dance on my chest. Quinn had missed his chance, and he'd given up the field of battle. I didn't care. If he wanted to shoot me, shoot and be damned.

We walked out a twisted side door into hot sunlight, and I blinked and shaded my eyes.

Oh, God. I don't know what I expected to see, but not this.

The rest of Las Vegas was untouched. Literally untouched. Windows intact, buildings still standing. The Eiffel Tower still climbed toward the sky, and the half-scale Statue of Liberty raised her torch.

The Bellagio was barely damaged, overall. Just the casino area, and just *our* casino area.

The Ma'at had targeted us. They'd done all this just to get *us*. Or worse . . . maybe, considering who Quinn was shooting at, to get *me*.

I felt the comforting ice of shock start to break up around me, dumping me in the cold water of reality.

Sink or swim, now. Give up and die, or make it mean something.

"Marion?" I licked my lips and tasted blood, swallowed grit and bitterness. "How many people—"

She looked exhausted under the paling layer of dust. Her hair was coming loose from its meticulous braid, and her leather jacket was ripped and shredded in places. When she wiped her forehead, she left streaks of still-wet blood.

"No fatalities. We were able to minimize it," she said. "Me and the kid." She cut her eyes toward Kevin, who was wrapped in silence and his own blanket, sitting on the curb while a paramedic tried to get information out of him. Miraculous. There'd be news coverage twenty-four/seven for the next few months, going over and over the freak earthquake, the survivors. Pundits would come on the airwaves to talk about all kinds of crackpot theories, everything from international terrorists to James Bond superweapons. None of them would get it right.

Please *God,* nobody would get it right.

"He could be great, you know. If anyone cared enough to show him how."

Marion was still watching Kevin. I nodded. "If nobody kills him first."

"See that they don't."

The paramedics were working their way around to us. "We need to get out of here," I said. "Before they get our names."

Marion nodded. She understood the need for secrecy now, as I did.

"Better use your Djinn," I finished. She looked down at the ground. "Marion?"

"He's gone," she said. "He was taken from me five years ago."

No wonder I'd never seen him. "Why? What happened?"

She heaved in a silent breath. "He was stolen from me."

"And you never told . . ." No, of course she hadn't. Losing a Djinn was practically a hanging offense in the upper ranks of the Wardens. It was something you kept quiet while you got your bottle back, and your life with it. You were supposed to *die* before losing your Djinn. Oh, it happened—bottles broke, bottles were lost in catastrophes—but there were penalties, and very few replacements.

"I was told," Marion said softly, "that if I reported it, they'd torture him. I believed it."

I wanted to ask a million questions, but this wasn't the time or the place. Too exposed. My skin kept crawling, trying to feel the nonexistent pressure of a laser sight.

I felt a hand on my arm, and turned.

Jonathan. *God*! I'd forgotten all about him. . . .

He had on his most rigid, focused expression. "Not much time," he said. "He found the bottle. Listen, I'll delay him as much as I can. You know where to find him—"

"What the hell are you talking about? I don't understand!" I grabbed for Jonathan's shoulder, made a fist out of the black fabric of his shirt, and tried to pull him closer. It was like trying to pull a pile of lead. He had the specific gravity of a mountain. "Tell me what's happening, dammit, and no goddamn Djinn evasion!"

His dark eyes glittered and went to narrow slits. "I've been claimed. You *know* this guy! We're going to fant—"

Blip. He was gone, instantly gone in midsyllable. I caught a flicker of something in his eyes—impotent rage, maybe a tiny flash of fear—and I sucked in a startled breath. I spun around, hard, and plunged back toward the casino, where emergency workers were swarming like hornets. Marion wrapped her arms around me and dragged me to a stop.

"No!" she said sharply. "You can't go back."

"I left him! Jonathan's bottle . . . have to get it back!"

"It's too late." She was too strong, and her voice was too compassionate. "Someone just commanded him. You can't get it back."

"Son of a *bitch*!" I sucked in a wet, trembling breath. "Let go. *Let go!*"

I wrenched free, but she'd convinced me; when she released me, I stopped trying to bull my way back inside. I'd left Jonathan's bottle, somehow, some way . . . how the hell . . .

I remembered in a blinding flash.

Siobhan, slipping the fallen bottle into her pocket. Me demanding it back.

She'd switched bottles. And now someone— probably Quinn—had taken it off her corpse. Siobhan had been working for him. Son of a *bitch*, I couldn't believe that I'd let it slip past me.

Marion raised her head to look, and her face went blank and grim. Eyes like flint, ready to spark.

"Don't look now," she said, "but the cavalry's arrived."

I turned my head.

A group of maybe twenty, pushing through the crowd of looky-loos; the one in front was a distinguished-looking older man in a spotless blue suit, with a silk tie in tasteful gray.

Myron Lazlo. Next to him, Charles Ashworth II flourished his ebony cane. No sign of Quinn at all in that pack of grim-faced men (and a few women).

The Ma'at had come to restore the balance.

TEN

The Ma'at manhandled Kevin somewhat—impersonally, at least—but Marion and I went willingly. We slipped through the chaos behind the hastily erected disaster barriers, heading for the Luxor. The heat quickly made the blankets unbearable, so we shed them at the first available park bench for the homeless.

I kept a hand clenched on the leather of the purse slung around my body, the other splayed over the still-warm spark of life in my womb. I was carrying too many lives. Too much responsibility.

None of the Ma'at said a word as we headed for the Luxor. We were going against the flow of traffic, everything and everyone moving toward the smoky smudge that marked the Bellagio event. The lobby of the Luxor was deserted, except for a marked security presence who eyed us nervously but waved us past when Lazlo displayed some kind of credentials. Back to the private rooms again, but to a larger one this time. Ballroom-sized, but with the feel of an old-school gentlemen's club, the kind without strippers. Lots of dark woods and deep carpets, port and sherry and uniformed butlers in tails.

Their symbol, set in stained glass above the door, was an ankh.

"Sir." The head butler, who looked as severe and professional as any of the Ma'at, headed straight for Lazlo. "What do you require?" British accent, of course. Nothing else would do for a place like this.

"I think some brandy might be in order. Thank you, Blevins."

Blevins inclined his head. I wondered what school you attended to learn how to be arrogant and servile at the same time, and still maintain that enormous amount of personal dignity. His eyes—blue as summer skies, startlingly—swept over me, then Marion, then Kevin. He turned on his heel and walked away.

We were led to chairs. Kevin was forcibly planted in one, and held there by a Djinn I remembered. Mr. Clean, he of the heroically bare chest, little brocade vest, and puffy trousers, not to mention shaved head and earring. The one that Rahel had taken a bite out of earlier.

He smiled at me with shark teeth. There was no welcome hiding there. "I remember you," he rumbled. "You came looking for trouble before."

"I found it," I said. He inclined his head.

A solemn voice behind me called my name. "Jo."

I turned, winced at the bite of bruises, and saw Lewis approaching. Or rather, being rolled up to us. He was in a wheelchair now, faded and thin, worse by far than he'd been when I'd been sucked out the window. He was crashing. There were hectic spots of red high in his cheeks, but his hands were trembling and he looked feverish and not altogether sane.

He wasn't looking at me, even though he'd spoken my name; his eyes were fixed on Kevin, and I didn't like what I saw there.

"We come to a turning point," said Lazlo solemnly. "Boy. It's time to give back what you stole."

I could have told him what Kevin would say, so I wasn't surprised when the kid snapped back, "Bite me, Grandpa. I'm not giving up anything."

"He no longer has Jonathan," I said. All eyes went to me. I straightened my shoulders under the pressure. "The bottle's gone."

"Gone?" Lazlo repeated softly. There was danger in there, hiding in the silky half-whisper.

"Quinn has it," I replied. "As you probably know, right? He's your dog."

Lazlo shut his eyes wearily.

"You killed Siobhan!" Kevin yelled, and tried to get out of the chair to lunge at Lazlo, or anyone else in reach. I wasn't sure whom he was directing the accusation toward, but I figured it was probably all of us.

"I'm afraid we did, but not deliberately." Lazlo rubbed his forehead and forced himself back to dignified attention. "And I'm afraid we put you in danger as well, Miss Baldwin. It was not our intention."

"It's been Quinn all along," I said. "Right? Quinn wanted Jonathan. I'll bet it was his idea to 'rescue' me, too, when I first arrived."

Nobody made a sound. I turned toward Kevin. "Quinn put Siobhan in there to try to steal the bottle. Kevin, I think she did like you, but I'm pretty sure

Quinn had some kind of hold over her. He was a cop, after all." Siobhan had picked up Jonathan's bottle when I'd dropped it. She'd put it in her pocket. She'd given me back the decoy.

Like I'd noticed from the start: She was a professional.

"He's the one who shot Siobhan?" Kevin asked. His hands were still shaking, but he looked feral now, especially spattered with her blood. Ready to gnaw his own arm off if it would get him a step closer to Quinn. "Why? Why would he do that?"

"Because I ducked," I said flatly. I turned toward Lewis, knelt down next to his chair with my arms braced on his knees. "He was shooting at me, and it wasn't about Jonathan. Not that time."

He looked at me through bleary eyes. "Then what?"

"Question for a question. What's his first name?"

Someone made a sound halfway between a *huh?* and an *uh-oh, she's lost her mind*; I didn't bother to check who. Lewis looked at me with feverish, red-rimmed eyes and said, "His name is Detective Thomas Quinn."

Which wasn't what I'd expected. It threw me for a second, but then Lazlo cleared his throat. His lips twisted like a man having surgery done with a sharp spoon and no anesthetic, and he said sourly, "Thomas *Orenthal* Quinn." Laz was already ahead of the curve. He'd heard my story. He knew.

"Orry," I said. "No wonder he wanted me dead. He couldn't know how much I remembered. He didn't know whether or not I'd recognize him—I didn't; it was too long ago, I never really saw his face, but he couldn't take the chance that I was running some big-time double-crossing game. I think he would have killed me earlier, but he was afraid to do it in the Luxor. Afraid you'd know. He felt better after he heard me tell the story to Ashworth, but he still didn't trust me. When I ended up over there again, he figured I might have figured it out. Couldn't have that."

Jonathan had said it: The lines connected through me. I was the nexus of so many things here, including—especially—this.

Thomas Orenthal Quinn: Orry. Chaz Ashworth III had died taking me to his boss, Orry . . . and at the time, I'd assumed that Orry's business had been all about drugs. It probably was, in the beginning. Easy money for both of them.

I'd been right in the same room with the man who'd inhabited my nightmares for years, and I never even knew it. Hell, I'd even *liked* him.

Suddenly the enormity of it crashed down on me . . . David, turning to ash and shadows; Siobhan, dying in my place; Lewis, dying right now, dying as I watched. I could see it happening. I'd let Jonathan be taken away when I'd had the answer in my hands, because I hadn't been fast enough or good enough or smart enough to see.

"Joanne?" Marion's voice, Marion's warm hand on my shoulder. I looked up at her and realized how tired she was. Her Djinn had been taken from her, held ransom for her good behavior. Quinn had been working the angles for a long, long time.

A cold shiver went down my spine. "When did your Djinn disappear?"

"Five years ago." From her expression, I'd bet that

Marion could have told me down to the day, hour, minute, and second.

I felt my hands curl into fists. *Five years ago.* "How long have the Djinn been disappearing?"

"In numbers?" Lewis asked. "About six years. Maybe less."

Since Chaz. Since Orry in the desert.

Since I'd gone into that dark, dark cave and he'd asked me questions.

I felt Lewis take my hand, and despite the weakness I knew was ravaging his body, he managed to squeeze it tight enough to make me wince.

"David?" he asked. He read the answer in my eyes. "What happened?"

"Rahel. She . . ." My throat threatened to close up when I thought about it. "She was after Jonathan. David wouldn't let her . . ." I couldn't get the rest of it out. It had been a battle nobody else had seen, *could* see, except for me—the Ifrit would have been invisible to most human eyes.

"Where are they?"

My hand went involuntarily to the leather purse hanging slung around my body. "I put David back in his bottle. Rahel . . . I claimed her. Put her in the bottle Siobhan used to switch for Jonathan."

Lewis let go of me and held out his hand. "Give her to me." I started to unzip the purse, then hesitated. "Not a whole lot of time left, Jo. Do it."

I took out the bottle and gave it to him. No sensation one way or another; I hadn't felt any click of connection with Rahel, and I didn't feel any loss of it now. But Lewis did, clearly; I saw him suck in a breath

and sit up straighter, and for just a second his dulled
eyes took on a ferocious gleam.

"She fed off of Jonathan?" he asked.

"Not really sure how much of it was Jonathan and
how much was David, but she took a lot." I felt my
stomach do that slow drop and roll again. "David—
he's bad. I don't know if he's—"

"He's not dead," Lewis said. The way he said it,
almost dismissively, made me give him a sharp look
and want to follow it up with a sharp right hook, except it wouldn't have exactly been a fair fight. In a
tussle between Lewis and a plastic grocery sack, I'd
give two to one on the bag.

He opened his fist, and I realized that Siobhan's
blood had transferred from my hand to his; it was
smeared in dull red clouds over the bottle. I squinted,
because it looked as if those dull red clouds were *moving*. Swirling over the surface of the glass.

Being absorbed.

I felt a fast, hot surge of nausea. *What's the matter,
Rahel, eating Djinn wasn't enough for you? Now
you're snacking on human blood, too?*

"What the hell are you doing?" I snapped at him,
and pulled myself back upright to step away, glaring.
He considered the bottle balanced on the palm of his
hand for a few seconds, then looked up at me with
an unreadable expression.

"I don't think I have to do anything. Mazel tov,"
he said, and dropped the bottle to the carpet. Then
he levered himself out of the wheelchair, lifted his
foot, and stomped on the glass hard enough to shatter it.

Something pulsed through the room in a silent explosion. It was a ruffle of wind in the real world, a white wave of pure energy in the aetheric; I felt it tug hard inside me as it passed, and the Djinn-child inside of me vibrated like a tuning fork. I instinctively took another step back and covered my stomach with both hands, but the kick I felt wasn't pain; it was something like delight.

A flash of hot gold from the corner of my eye, and then a shadow, moving . . . shadow taking form, function, grace. Walking with a loose-limbed stride as she formed herself out of the air, out of legend and memory and power.

Rahel's hair was short now, the cornrows reduced to an elegant half-inch crop around the perfect noble sculpture of her head. It set off the line of her cheekbones, the full, lush curve of her lips.

Her eyes blazed hot, hot, hot amber.

She was wearing black, which I'd never seen her do. Black silk shirt flowing over her lean, muscular body, showing off just enough curves to make her feminine. Kind of a retro look for her, very seventies. Hip-hugging black pants, wide belt, no-nonsense kick-ass boots.

"Snow White," she said, and the smile looked real. Not exactly comforting, but certainly real. She gave me a slight, significant bow, then turned her attention to Lewis as he sank back down in his wheelchair. It was sort of a controlled fall. "You seem unwell, my friend."

"Yeah," Lewis croaked. "Had better days."

Rahel reached down and put her hands on either side of his face. Quite a contrast; her skin was a deep blue-black, unsettlingly reminiscent of the hard, glistening shade she'd worn as an Ifrit, and instead of an Ifrit's diamond-sharp claws she had fingernails again, painted a rich, hot gold.

"So I see," she murmured, staring into his eyes. I couldn't have held that stare, not for any price. Lewis blinked, but managed not to flinch too much. "I have suffered, Lewis. Like you. I understand what it is to lose yourself, to know hunger and pain and rage. I understand what it is to face an eternity of it, without relief."

"I'm still human," he said. "Eternity's a little shorter for me."

"So you think?" She shook her head a little. "Eternity is the same for all things."

"Why are you back here?" I whispered. "How did you—"

Rahel's attention turned my way, but her eyes didn't. She made her reply directly to Lewis. "Because there was death."

"*Human* death," I said, and then I shut up fast, because I remembered just how Jonathan had become a Djinn in the first place, along with David . . . on a battlefield, surrounded by human death. Then the death spreading, spiraling, fueling a transformation . . . "Death gives life. That's what Jonathan told me." It meant that there might be another way for Imara . . . no. I couldn't think about it now. Not now.

"The power is very strong," she said. "Though if I had not drawn so much from such powerful sources, I could not have managed it. Human death tipped the scales; it did not balance them."

She leaned very close to Lewis, so close she was

inches from kissing him with those lush, glistening lips. "I can give you what you need."

His smile jerked into something oddly humorous. "You're an exhibitionist now?" His voice had fallen into a silky lower range, resonating in his chest. I knew that tone. It had dropped my knickers on the floor in a lab back in college.

"Tell me you want it." Rahel's voice had gone into the dark, too, ripe and sexy and barely more than a whisper. "Tell me what you will give me for it, my love."

"Undying gratitude?"

"You'll have to do better than that." Her lips just grazed his, and I saw his skin flush redder.

The whole room—the twenty-odd members of Ma'at who had trooped in with us, the silent waitstaff, Marion, Kevin, the muscle-bound security men—we all stood, spellbound, watching this. I don't know about anybody else, but I was starting to expect clothes to come off, which would have had the virtue of being completely, wildly inappropriate, and would scandalize the socks off of the Ma'at.

And then Rahel smiled wider. "Tell me what you'll give me."

"Freedom," Lewis said, and kissed her. Big-time. A hungry, openmouthed kiss. I heard the shocked gasp go through the room. Butler dude—Blevins?—looked so disapproving that I felt like I'd wandered onto the set of a Merchant Ivory film.

Rahel pulled away, standing straight. Lewis's pulse was beating fast; I could see it pounding in his neck. Rahel looked perfectly composed.

"You already gave me that," she said. "I require your love."

I finally saw Lewis look completely idiotic. Yep. That was an utterly blank look, blank as a codfish. "What?"

"Love," she said distinctly. "Devotion. Shall you give it? Or shall I go now and leave you to deal with this as you please?"

He licked his lips. Probably still tasting her there. Myron Lazlo's shock finally wore off enough for him to step forward and say sternly, "This is neither the time nor the place to—"

"Silence!" she hissed, and snapped an open hand his direction, gold talons suddenly looking a lot less like a fashionable manicure and more like something you'd use to gut fish. "I do not speak to *you*, man. It was not a general invitation."

Lazlo wisely decided to back off. In fact, everyone backed off a couple of respectful, precautionary steps. It was just Lewis, his wheelchair, and the Djinn.

She looked good in black. Strong, lethal, sexy as hell. I wondered if it was something she'd picked up from Jonathan or David, in that free-for-all fight for survival.

"Tell me you want to live," she said to him.

"I want to live," Lewis said, and his eyes flicked from her to Kevin, behind me. I heard the kid's feet shuffle on the carpet. He was scared. The sight of Rahel had clearly given him a bad turn, and now he was starting to really feel claustrophobic. "He doesn't die, Rahel. That's my condition."

"Lewis, I don't know what kind of game she's play-

ing with you, but she can't fix this," I said. "I asked
David. He said no Djinn had the power to reverse
what Jonathan had done without killing them both . . .
except Jonathan." It had been a constant topic of conversation for close to a week as we drove around Las
Vegas, trying to figure a way to solve the problem.
David had been definite about it.

"True," Rahel purred. She turned to face me. Rahel
had always had a certain feline quality, something as
natural to her as breathing to me, and I felt the force
of that again. A cat playing with her food, watching
it run and squeak and hide. Djinn were scary people,
when they had no reason to regard us with affection.
"*I* can't. But, you see, little flower, I'm not really *me*
anymore. I am more than I was. Less than I will be.
And I never said I would do it alone."

It happened so subtly that I almost missed it—*did*
miss it, at first. It was only when an empty space behind her filled that I realized she meant it literally.

She really wasn't alone. Not in the least. The gray-
haired, gray-eyed man behind her, with the pale, perfect skin . . . I remembered him, not fondly. *Ashan*.
Jonathan's second-in-command, with David stuck in a
bottle. Chilly bastard, full of power that boiled off of
him in the aetheric like heat waves.

More of them, silently appearing in the room, mixed
in and around us. A girl with raven-wing hair and
elaborate eye shadow, dressed in crimson. Eyes like
neon signs in a peculiar shade of magenta. A little girl
named Alice in a blue-and-white pinafore. A skele-
tally thin, tall creature so androgynous that I couldn't
decide what he/she was, except a fashion fatality.

Djinn. Lots of Djinn. *Free Djinn.*

I focused on little Alice, who favored me with a shy smile. "Hey, kid," I said. "Aren't you supposed to be somewhere?"

"Cathy isn't one of the Wardens anymore," she said. "She had enough. I'm free now." Alice's blond head inclined toward Lazlo. "She's with them now. Me too."

The room wasn't big enough to hold all this power, all this humming, vibrating *potential.* I heard glass rattling in a steady, musical jitter. Too many of them, too close together; I could feel the place heating up.

Lazlo could feel it, too. He said, "Enough. Your point is made, Rahel; there are a lot of you, and I know that you can help or hurt us, as you like. We trust you to make the right decisions, as you trust us. That's the principle of Ma'at. Balance."

"Balance," she agreed. "The Free Djinn have no quarrel with you. But we will not allow one of *yours* to go unpunished. Or *ours* to go unrescued."

Whatever second wind Lewis had gasped in was fading fast; his skin had taken on that ivory cast again, white around his mouth and eyes, and I could tell he was in pain. Maybe it was the presence of the Djinn. Maybe it was more than that, his body degrading and folding in on itself as it raided its own tissues in a search for power. He was burning himself from the inside out.

Rahel slowly crouched in front of his wheelchair and laid her golden-tipped fingers on his knees.

"Ashan," she said. "Grant me your strength."

He moved to place a hand on her shoulder. Mr. Clean silently came to take Ashan's hand. The black-haired girl in red parted the humans in her way and laid fingertips on the back of Rahel's close-cropped head.

They came, one by one, moving like ghosts. Those that brushed past me made me feel sparks and chills from the contact. Each touching Rahel, or each other. Forming a network of power, in a very specific configuration.

Lazlo realized it first. He grabbed my elbow, hustled me over to Kevin, and said, "Take his hand."

"What? No!" Kevin yanked free. His eyes were huge and panicked. "You're not fucking with me, man! You'll kill me!"

"Kevin, shut up and do it." When I reached for his hand, he gave it to me in the form of a punch. It landed solidly in my solar plexus. I felt breath evacuate as if I'd been vacuum-sealed, and croaked for air as I doubled over.

But I grabbed his fist and held it in both hands, tightly. Death grip. Lazlo, bless him, held on to the kid's other arm. Once gravity and leverage were on our side, I transferred my grip to Kevin's shoulder to keep him down.

"Let me go, you fucking bitch!" He was screaming it now, writhing, trying to get away. I felt the air curdling. He was lashing out with powers, too panicked to do something targeted, but he could cause a lot of damage even unfocused if we let him. I sharpened my hold on my own energies, began to weight the air around him to damp down the chaos he was causing . . .

. . . and Myron Lazlo said, "No, Joanne. That isn't how we do things. Let him try."

"He isn't just going to *try*," I gasped breathlessly.

Tough to talk when my diaphragm didn't want to pull in air. "He's going to make what happened at the Bellagio happen here, don't you get it? Only worse!"

"I know." Lazlo closed his eyes. His face went serene. Not empty, just . . . peaceful. Behind him, Ashworth laid a hand on Lazlo's blue-suited shoulder, and then there were more of them, forming a human chain that matched the Djinn's across the room. Two circles of power.

Balancing.

What the Ma'at were putting out wasn't energy; it was *absence.* Where the Wardens concentrated on the subatomic world, manipulating molecules, adjusting the vibration speed and makeup to rebuild the world in our image, the Ma'at went deeper. I couldn't see how, until I let myself go still and quiet with them.

Kevin's energy raged like a forest fire on the aetheric, power enough to destroy the city, level forests, break the land into rubble. And power *moves*.

But the Ma'at surrounded it. Contained it.

Negated it.

"For every action, reaction," Lazlo murmured. "For every vibration, a cancellation. We don't seek to win the struggle. We seek to stop the game."

I remembered the card game. The cards floating over the table. Even as it formed in my head, I heard Lazlo sigh. "You see power where no power exists. We didn't float the cards. We simply negated the forces that acted on them to make them fall."

Kevin, furious, screaming, red-faced, tried to rip the walls of the room apart by digging deep into the bedrock below the hotel. He didn't care anymore who he hurt. Maybe he never had.

My instinct was to act, to *do something*, but I waited, watching.

Marion's hand slipped over my shoulder in a warm, gentle touch, and when I looked at her I saw tears in her eyes.

"I see," she said. "I see what to do. All this time we destroyed them, and we could have saved them. . . ." She was talking about the Wardens she'd been ordered to neuter—or kill. This was a revelation for her, and it couldn't possibly be a happy one.

The Ma'at, in their quiet, invisible way, focused their powers to still the vibrations. It was a basic principle of wave motion; hit the right frequency, and the wave disappears. At a molecular level, everything resonates at specific speeds, to specific notes.

Even the earth.

Even Kevin.

The Ma'at didn't fight what he did; they fought what he *was*, at the source . . . stilling him, quieting him.

Stopping him, as a mother's hand stills a child's lips.

Kevin wasn't screaming anymore, I realized, and I looked down. His tear-streaked face was open and vulnerable. Defenses gone. I felt him trying to get beyond his own skin; he had Lewis's earth powers, and that meant that if he wasn't particular about how he used it, he could easily blow my heart open or crush my brain into jelly inside my skull. The temptation to do something, anything to protect myself was almost overwhelming, but I had to trust Lazlo. The best I could understand it, if I introduced a chaotic vibration into what the Ma'at were laying down around him, it would destroy any chance of success.

Boy, Kevin wanted me dead. Really, really dead. I

could feel it coming off of him in red waves, see it like a poisonous cloud curling around him on the aetheric.

The cool whisper of the Ma'at was keeping that in check. It was a little like a piece of Saran Wrap holding back a heavyweight boxer's punch. I tried not to let the analogy make me nervous.

"Now," Lazlo breathed. "Take her hand."

Her, who?

I looked down.

Alice. Her innocent smile clashed with the vastness of the power I sensed in her. She was old, this little one. Far up on the Djinn scale of People You Don't Want to Mess With.

I extended my hand. She wrapped her small fingers around it.

We completed the two halves of the pattern.

Yin and yang.

Human and Djinn.

Positive and negative.

On the aetheric, the pattern swirled, lit up in glorious glowing color, and it was breathtaking. Complex and graceful as a sand painting, each piece in exactly the right place. I watched the colors race around . . . green for earth, blue for air and water, red for fire, sparking off of each human they touched, then shading subtly lighter as they moved through the chain of Djinn, gathering strength . . .

. . . to cascade through Rachel's touch into Lewis. A rainbow of light, turning brilliant white as it coiled inside of him. His body—a failing ruin of shadow and darkness—took on form and color. Not healed—that would take time—but no longer destroying itself.

No longer dying.

Let him keep what he is. I heard that through the clasp of hands, felt it move through us like a breath. Human and Djinn, formed into one living, thinking thing. Lewis was part of that. So was Kevin. There was a bright red bonfire burning inside of him—his natural powers, the ones that the Wardens expected Marion to rip away from him. It could be done now, without risk. Even without risk to Kevin, for that matter. He'd survive it. We'd all see to that.

But that was Lewis's voice, whispering, *Let him keep what he is.* Because he understood, maybe better than anyone, that Kevin couldn't live without that touch of fire in his soul. He wasn't demanding, or ordering. The Ma'at was a strange kind of democracy—the exact opposite of the Wardens, which was (for good or bad) an association of independents. In this formation, this . . . symbolic machine . . . we debated in silence, on the strength of emotion and feeling rather than words or logic. We argued from our souls.

And, in the end, we knew what we had to do.

Marion took her hand off of my shoulder, and the pattern dissolved into silence. Into forty-odd human and Djinn, each with their own agendas, their own hates, loves, needs. Each separate and apart, as the Wardens were separate and apart.

That was why the Wardens had never truly succeeded. They *couldn't.* They didn't understand.

This was power.

Kevin burst into tears.

I left my hand on him, not to hold him down, but to give him comfort.

"You hurt me," he was whispering. "She's dead,

and you hurt me. Siobhan's dead. I couldn't protect her."

He kept crying, rocking back and forth. His whole body was shaking. I looked across at Marion, whose face was luminous and calm again.

"Yes, he's still dangerous, I know that," she said. "And he has a lot of potential. Now that I know it can be nurtured and controlled, I'd be a fool to destroy that for him."

"Guess he's going to need a mentor," I said. And, when she opened her mouth, "Don't look at me. I don't even like the kid."

Oh, that smile. That self-satisfied, knowing smile on Marion's lips.

"I *don't*," I insisted.

Kevin continued to cry.

"Oh, give me a break." I turned toward Rahel, who was still kneeling next to Lewis. "Rahel."

She rose to her feet in one of those smooth, inhuman motions that comes standard-issue with Djinn DNA—assuming they have such a thing—and turned to face me, chin down, eyes fierce, smile fiercer.

"Snow White," she said.

"My turn," I said. I saw people stepping away from what they saw in my face. "You fixed Lewis, you fixed Kevin. You know what I want."

She studied me without fear. "I can't. You already know that. What David is can't be fixed so easily."

"You were worse off, but you're just fine now, aren't you?" I gestured to indicate the whole Rahel package. "Don't give me any crap, Rahel. I'm not in the mood."

"It doesn't work that way."

I took one step closer and refused to look away, no matter how hard it was. My fury gave me strength. "You heal David, or I swear, I'll tear you apart. I'll make it my *mission*."

Silence. She didn't answer me. Alice did, little-girl Alice with her neon-blue eyes and ancient smile.

"She can't," Alice said. "She was healed because she took power from the stronger, and because of the death. There's no one here stronger than Rahel now. And no death."

"I could arrange that." I glowered at Lazlo, who raised his eyebrows fastidiously.

"It wouldn't matter," Alice said. "You need Jonathan, and he would have to give of himself."

Rahel nodded. "I will go with you to retrieve him. He can't remain in the hands of a . . ." She made a face and said a word in Djinn. A few of the other Djinn looked shocked. Alice actually blushed.

Whatever. "Good. Anybody else want in on this?"

The Djinn looked at each other. One by one, they voted silently with their disappearances, until all that were left were Ashan, that cold bastard, and Alice.

Ashan gave me an utterly subzero stare and said, "I will hold you responsible if you fail," and then he was gone.

Alice gave me a wide-eyed regretful look, shrugged, and skipped off into the shadows.

So much for Djinn loyalty, apparently.

"Fine. Me and Rahel." I leveled a finger at Lazlo, who was conferring quietly with two more of the Ma'at. "Yo! Laz!" He didn't respond immediately. When he did, he turned toward me with a genteel frown, as if I'd made some sort of rude biological noise. "I'm going after Quinn. Who have you got?"

"I'm going," Marion said immediately. "You'll need me."

"You're in. Thanks." I waited for Lazlo to step up to the plate. "C'mon, man. He's your guy; don't you think you ought to at least come along? Maybe present a nice distraction while I find a way to take him down?"

Lazlo retained his dignity, even in the face of my sarcasm. I didn't consider that a positive.

"Detective Quinn has been of assistance to the Ma'at from time to time, but only as an associate," he said. "We encountered him several years ago when he helped save one of our members. Since then, he's been very useful to us in keeping tabs on the movements of Wardens through this area, and also in locating and freeing Djinn from imprisonment. But he's got little or no power of his own, and we don't see him as a functioning member of our organization."

"Really." My voice had gone flat. "Don't hurt yourself, covering your ass like that. The Ma'at are in this up to their necks. Sure, Quinn was in with Chaz, smuggling drugs, back in the day, but then Quinn discovered something more interesting. How much would a Djinn in the bottle be worth on the black market, Laz? Millions, to the right rich bastard. Even a regular human can use them—not as effectively as a Warden, but they'd be pretty damn cool toys." I glanced over at Kevin, thinking involuntarily of his stepmother. "You guys made him your enforcer, right? When you heard about Djinn that you might be able to retrieve and set free, you sent him out to 'rescue' them. How often did he fail?"

Lazlo looked unsettled. "Failure was expected. No one can retrieve every—"

"How many times did he come back empty-handed?"

Silence. And then Ashworth said, "At least twenty in the last few years."

Marion indicated Lewis. "What about the ones Lewis took when he left the Wardens? Where did they go?"

Left was euphemistic, at best. *Escaped with his life* might have been a little more accurate, but I held my tongue. Wasn't Marion's fault that she had the job of getting rid of the Wardens' most dangerous problems. In fact, I was happier that she had it than anyone else I'd ever met; at least she was fair, gentle, and strong. Nobody liked an incompetent executioner.

"Freed," I said on his behalf. "Lewis set them free himself because he doesn't believe in keeping Djinn as slaves."

And then I realized what I'd just told her. What she'd witnessed, here in this room.

She *knew* that Djinn could exist outside of the bottles, now . . . that they could live on their own terms, with power and significance. That they could interact with us freely.

Just what I *didn't* want the Wardens to know.

Only Marion hadn't exactly looked shocked.

"You already knew about the Free Djinn?" I asked. She inclined her head. "How?"

"I'd be a fool if I didn't."

"Does anyone else—"

I got her warm smile. "There are many fools wearing the symbol of the Wardens. You ought to know that, Joanne. Truthfully, they're so caught up in their own lives, I doubt they notice much else. The world is full of secrets, anyway. Most people see what they want to see, and nothing more. I sometimes think it's the secret to sanity."

The Ma'at were buzzing around me. Lazlo was saying something, fairly loudly, about the Ma'at not being soldiers, which was true enough; I didn't hold it against them. Besides, I wasn't absolutely sure I trusted any of them to have my back, not against Quinn. He'd been part of their organization for too long for them to disavow him now.

Rahel was watching me, arms folded. Smiling.

"Well?" I asked. "Just the three of us?"

"Four," said a new voice. Lewis levered himself out of the chair, took a second to get his balance, and walked toward us. Around him, the Ma'at's frantic discussion fell silent. "I'm going."

"You can't—" Charles Ashworth began querulously, then shut his mouth with a snap when Lewis cut a look his way. "Fine. Kill yourself, then. For my part, I'm finished with this nonsense."

He turned and walked away, flourishing that damn cane to shove people out of his way. Rahel evidently thought by her grin that this was the best entertainment she'd had in years. She got in his path and blocked the door. They played a silent game of keep-away until Ashworth decided his dignity was worth more than a dramatic exit, and tried to look like it was his own idea to stay.

"That is, if you want me to go," Lewis said dryly,

and I realized that I hadn't acknowledged the effort it had taken for him to rise and walk. Maybe his pride was hurt. I hadn't exactly come over to weep on his collar about how glad I was he'd survived.

I *was*, in fact, glad, but damn if I was going to show it now. There was work to be done.

"Depends. You going to fall over?" I demanded. He had his own cane in hand. It was starting to look like as much of an affectation as Ashworth's.

"Why? You going to catch me?"

"I never could resist a fainting hero," I said. As a gift horse, he was pretty creaky, but the color in his face was better, and I could feel that soothing vibration coming from him again, the one that made me feel all was right with the world in his presence. I experimentally reached out and touched his hand.

Zap. Blue sparks jumped. We both made faces and put more space between us. Things were definitely back to normal—electricity and that deceptive, seductive burning in my skin from his touch that had nothing to do with current taking the path of least resistance. I wouldn't be sharing any beds with Lewis again soon, no matter how innocent the intention. Couldn't totally guarantee my own willpower.

"So that's it? The four of us?" The Ma'at were taking themselves off as quickly as the Djinn had done . . . if in a less ethereal manner. A few younger ones were hanging around, mostly fascinated by the spectacle of enemy Wardens in their midst (I still couldn't bring myself to think of Lewis as Ma'at, even though I knew he was), not to mention the magnificence of Rahel in her sleek black silk.

"Five," Kevin said. His voice cracked on the word.

We all looked at the kid, then at each other. "Not like I'm joining up or anything. It's just . . . he killed Siobhan. And you can't leave me here. With them."

Whether it had been true love or not, there was suffering in Kevin's eyes. An awareness of something beyond himself, even if it had just been for one other person in the world. *Even psychopaths can love.* I couldn't remember who'd said it, but it seemed applicable.

We reached a sort of silent consensus, à la Ma'at, and Lewis said, "Stick close to me, kid."

Kevin's never-flat hackles rose. "So you can what, suck the rest of me dry?" We all stared at him. He flushed. "You know what I meant."

"Well, *I* meant stick with me because Quinn's going to see you as the biggest threat, since he'll think you've still got my powers," Lewis said. "I plan to use you as a human shield."

Kevin eyed him. "Yeah?"

"Would I lie to you? Besides, you kicked the crap out of me, kid. I'm still weak. I need the support." Oh, clever Lewis. The one thing Kevin craved and never got . . . respect. Responsibility.

Kevin tried not to look impressed. "Yeah, okay. Whatever."

Marion sent me a clear you-trust-him? look. My feelings for Kevin were too complicated to put into squints and eyebrow moves, so I just deadpanned. Truth was, I suspected Jonathan felt something for the kid, too, and that would help us. Quinn had a lot of liabilities he didn't yet understand.

"Stupid question," Marion said apologetically, "but exactly where will we find him? We can't track the

Djinn, not even Jonathan. Unless you . . . ?" She addressed it to Rahel. Rahel shook her head. "Okay, then how do we find him?"

"Jonathan told us," I said.

She looked mystified. "He was cut off in midword."

"Doesn't matter. I know what he was trying to tell me." I turned to Ashworth, who was glaring at me with undisguised contempt. We weren't mending any fences, I sensed. Not that I was worried about it much. "Your son's house," I said. "Fantasy Ranch. The one in White Ridge. Do you still own it?"

"No," he said, and turned to go. Rahel blocked him again. Glaring ensued.

"Who bought it?"

Ashworth's hand tightened on the cane; I watched the knuckles go white. "I'm sure you already know," he said.

"Thomas Orenthal Quinn." I didn't have the slightest doubt. "Keeping it all in the family."

"I never liked the slippery bastard." Ashworth kept walking, cane stabbing carpet. "Go and be damned. Do me the courtesy not to die in my son's house, if you please." This time Rahel stepped aside and let him exit with dignity intact.

White Ridge. Fantasy Ranch. Orry.

I was going back into my worst nightmare, but at least this time, I wasn't going alone.

ELEVEN

Rahel, not being claimed anymore, couldn't jump us magically from one place to another. A drawback, but not a huge one . . . I didn't think that Quinn could use Jonathan to do any transportation, either. *I'll delay him as long as I can,* Jonathan had said, before he'd been yanked out of the world. I grabbed Myron Lazlo, who was having some sort of old-guys meeting in the corner of the room that seemed devoted to snuffboxes and cigars and brandy. Literally. By the arm. He didn't take it well, but I'd come to realize that manhandling the Ma'at was a whole lot less dangerous than taking on a militant Warden. Ashworth had caned me pretty handily, back in the lobby of the Luxor, but Lazlo had done nothing but called one of the associated Free Djinn to take care of me.

Lazlo just retained his personal dignity and shrugged free of my grip.

"Yes?" he asked neutrally. "I've already made it clear, the Ma'at will not—"

"Provide transportation? Think again. We need to get to White Ridge. What've you got?"

He frowned at me for a full thirty seconds, then said, "Are you asking me for the loan of a vehicle?"

"No, Laz, I'm telling you that I'm taking a couple of cars. You pick which ones, but the faster the better." Warmth registered near my back. Lewis, Marion, Kevin, and Rahel had tagged along with me, to lend support. Lazlo's eyes skipped over them, unreadably, and focused back on me. "Time's wasting. He's your mess, in case you forgot, which means you're just as bad a judge of character as I am."

"I liked him," I said. It burned me to admit it, made parts of me flutter uneasily as memory reasserted itself. Darkness, pain, violation. I'd looked him in the eyes and I hadn't recognized him, not even the capacity for violence. I'd trusted him, like a complete brainless moron. "Cars, Laz." I snapped my fingers.

Behind me, Rahel murmured, "I believe you'll find them outside at the valet stand."

"Oh?"

Lazlo's face shut down hard. "Take what you'd like. We'll speak of this when you return. *If* any of you return. I don't give you very good odds. He'll know you're coming, of course. By now, he will know that his attempt to silence you failed."

I waited for him to wish me luck. He didn't.

I turned and led the way out to the lobby. It was still mostly deserted, thanks to the excitement over Bellagio way, and we walked straight out the doors, past Ma'at security, to the covered portico where uniformed valets waited. They were clustered together, nervously gossiping, but sprang into action when we approached.

"Rahel?"

She pointed to two matching Dodge Vipers. One was a deep, glistening midnight blue, flirting in the sunlight; the other was silver.

I knew the blue one. She was unmistakable.

"Mona?" I felt stupid asking it, but Marion nodded. "You had David bring it with you when you came here?"

"I thought we might need it," she said. "And he knew it would please you. I confess, I thought it would be to make a quick escape, not to go riding off to . . . whatever we're riding off to. . . ."

"And the silver one?"

Rahel buffed her talons on her shirt. "It wasn't being used." She opened her palm and dropped keys into my hand. I tried to hand them back, but she stepped away with an expression of distaste. "I do not *drive*."

It was, apparently, a Djinn thing; David had claimed not to, either, but he'd come around when I'd needed him to. I tossed both sets of keys in the air, thinking, and then underhanded one set to Marion. The silver car.

"Take Rahel and Kevin," I said. "Rahel, watch out for trouble." I didn't look at Kevin, but I didn't think I needed to. Her hot amber eyes glowed just a little brighter. "Marion—"

"I'll watch out for it, too." Neither one of us trusted Rahel completely either; I could see the acknowledgment of it in her serene face. I wouldn't have trusted anyone but Marion to shepherd those two. "How fast are we driving?"

I stepped out from the thick shade into the molasses-thick glare of the Las Vegas sun and walked to the driver's side of the blue Viper. It was too hot to put my hand on the blue finish, but I held it a couple of inches above the blazing metal. Petting her was almost irresistible.

"What?" I asked absently. Marion, unlocking the silver Viper, repeated the question. I looked across the car at Lewis, who had opened the passenger side.

I laughed, and said, "Just try to keep up." It sounded hollow, felt worse. I should have felt free, opening the driver's-side door and easing into Mona's comfortable seat, feeling the potential of her ignite at the turn of the key. Cars had always made me feel safe. Powerful.

But I was driving this one into the past, and that was one place I didn't want to go.

What surprised me was that I hadn't recognized his voice. Not recognizing his body or face, sure, that was understandable; the only clear look I'd ever had at Orry was that morning in the desert, and it had been fifteen seconds long, at a distance, with a baseball cap shadowing his face and panic jittering my focus.

But the voice. I should have recognized the voice.

When the shadow in the dark grabbed me in the caves and held me underwater, I'd honestly thought that I was dead. Coming awake again in the darkness, I still thought I was dead; combine the trauma with the heat exhaustion and dehydration, not to mention the head injury, and dead was what I probably should have been.

Instead, I opened my eyes in the dark and for a few seconds there was nothing, nothing but the drip of water and the sound of my own heart slowly, steadily working its way toward death, one beat at a time.

I licked dry lips—even though there was water beaded on them, they felt dry and painfully cracked—and whimpered as pain stabbed through my head. I tried to pull in a deep breath, but it gurgled in my lungs, and I coughed.

Coughing with a head injury, not recommended. My head exploded in pulsations of white agony, and I couldn't stop hacking. By the time I stopped I was huddled in a sitting position, my back against what felt like wood. It creaked when I moved against it. My chest was on fire, but that was nothing compared to the complete devastation of my headache. I carefully leaned my skull back against the wooden boxes, in the hope that not moving it anymore would help the nauseating throbbing to settle down. I had both hands clutching my temples, but that didn't seem to be helping—it felt like it was holding the pain inside—so I let them fall back into my lap. The air tasted damp and cool. Not a breath of wind.

I heard the scrape of footsteps. My first thought was to call for help, but my second was a memory of being held underwater, and I kept still. I stared into the dark—which was complete—and saw nothing. Not a flicker of light. *Maybe I'm blind.* That was a freak-inducing thought that I tried to put well behind me.

The sound of someone coming got louder. Pebbles rattled. He must have misstepped once; I heard someone curse softly—male voice—and there was some scuffling that sounded like things being rearranged. Metal, maybe, dragged over rock. Tough to say.

I was still trying to figure out which direction the footsteps were coming from when he flicked on a flashlight, and I was hit squarely but a rush of light so bright it felt like he'd set my eyeballs on fire. I screamed and covered my eyes, turned my face away, but even then I could see the halogen flare, burning bright red on my eyelids.

He'd meant to do that, just in case. He wanted me blind and disoriented.

I felt something grab my foot and drag me suddenly forward; I was able to save my head from smacking into the rock, which might very well have killed me, and then there was a weight astride me, a belt buckle digging painfully into my stomach as he leaned forward. The light was still in my face. I couldn't see him at all.

"Open your eyes," he said. I couldn't have, even if I'd wanted to; I was already crying from the blaze of light. I tried to bat the flashlight away, and he grabbed both my hands in one of his and slammed them back to the stone. The light loomed closer, bloodred on the other side of my eyelids, like a giant blazing eye. "Open your eyes!"

I tried. I think I must have managed to get them open just a little, because I heard him say, "Blue. Huh. I'd have bet they were brown."

He didn't sound crazy. In fact, he sounded very normal, as if we were standing at a cocktail party with our little drinks, making small talk. As if he hadn't just tried to drown me and killed another woman and was kneeling on my chest with a light in my eyes.

"What's your name, sweetheart?" he asked. I could almost see him smiling, saluting me with a martini.

No reason to lie. "Joanne." My voice sounded weak

and fractured. Nothing like what I wanted it to be. "You already know that."

"Smart girl. Indeed I do know. Chaz told me." He leaned over closer. That made it harder to breathe. I coughed again, and couldn't help a sobbing moan when the headache dug claws deeper. "You're in sad shape, Joanne. Wish I could say that I was here to help you out, but you already know that's not true, eh?" I felt a sharp sting as he slapped me to keep me focused. "Eh?"

I nodded.

"What did Chaz tell you? Oh, by the way, I saw what you did out there. Very impressive. Chaz tells me most of you can do that by yourselves, right?" He bent very close, close enough that I smelled aftershave and a hint of herbal shampoo. "Without a *Djinn*. That how you say it? *Djinn*?"

"I don't know what you're talking about." It didn't matter. He wasn't a Warden. When I went up on the aetheric—I could barely catch a glimpse of it in Oversight now—I saw no power in him. No potential. He was as absolutely normal as the guy next door. "I don't know what that is."

"You don't have one." He sounded definite about it. "Chaz didn't have one, either. Guess it's just the really high ups that get them, huh? Or . . . the ones who need them? Out in the middle of nowhere, storm central? Places that get out of control quick?"

He was too close to the truth. There were more Wardens with Djinn in trouble spots; half of the ones in Oklahoma and Kansas were equipped, and an even greater portion of the ones in California. He understood an awful lot more than he should have.

Starting with the fact that there were Wardens. "Chaz told you," I whispered.

The flashlight switched off. It was like being doused with cold water in the desert—sweet, shocking relief. Felt like the darkness was a place of safety, a place to hide, even though I knew better. I heard the soft sound of plastic and metal on stone as he set it aside.

"Chaz told *you* things," he said. "About me. Blabbed his stupid head off. Right?"

I didn't answer. Saving my breath for the screaming part.

"This is going to go better if you just tell me now. The end's the same, but like the Chinese say, it's the journey that counts."

"He told me you were running drugs," I said. "That other Wardens went along with it. Look, I was going to take the money. I'll still take it. You don't have to kill me."

"Honey, I wish I knew that for sure, because I kinda like you. You don't fold under pressure, and that's a gift." He straightened up and let go of my hands. I didn't try to hit him; there was no percentage in it yet. He still had me pinned. "No, I figure you . . . you'd take the money and run right back to your little friends, and next thing you know, I'm out of business. Can't have that."

I was too weak to really use my powers, but I had one advantage: He didn't know it. I concentrated hard, readying myself. I wasn't going to get a lot of opportunities, and I'd better act fast and with perfect timing when one came.

"Tell me about the Djinn," he said. "Chaz didn't

know much, or at least he said he didn't. It's interesting."

"It's a myth," I said. "It's a TV show. He was putting you on."

"Oh, I don't think so, because I asked him with lots of nice folding money. You, unfortunately, money won't do it. I'll have to be more persuasive." I heard something metallic tap the rock. "You know what that is?"

It could have been anything. A nail file. A ring. A bottle opener. "Knife," I whispered. "It's a knife."

"Good memory." Suddenly the sharp edge of it was under my chin, pressing, and I felt myself start squirming. I couldn't help it. My body wanted to get away so badly that it refused to listen to reason and stay still. "Here's how this works, Joanne. You tell me what I want to know, and you never even feel this knife move. You *don't* tell me, and this knife knows how to do things the hard way, the slow way. Get me?"

"Yes." I was sweating. I couldn't afford to sweat. My brain felt slow and stupid, desperate for moisture. There was so much around me, in the air . . . and I couldn't reach it.

"Now answer my question."

"You haven't asked one," I heard myself say.

"What?" The knife moved at my throat, pressed harder. I squeaked. "You playing with me, honey? Because you won't like the way I like to play."

"They're Djinn," I whispered breathlessly. "They live in bottles."

"What kind of bottles?"

"Any kind." No, that wasn't true. "Glass bottles. Crystal. Has to be breakable."

He made a gratified sound. The knife moved away. Where it had touched me, I felt a core of cold that stung hot after a few seconds.

"How do you use one?"

I licked my lips with a dry, rough tongue. "First you have to have the scroll—"

The knife plunged into my skin. I screamed. It was buried about a half an inch deep in my arm, and he kept moving it. Cutting. When he finally stopped, I didn't; the screaming dissolved to helpless sobs, but I couldn't shut up until I felt him prick me in another place with the sharp, merciless tip of it.

"There's no scroll," he said. "Right?"

"Right." I swallowed tears. "You're right, you son of a bitch."

He seemed to like that; I heard him chuckle. A warm, friendly sound. He patted my cheek.

"Tell me the truth," he said. "We got all the time in the world to cut through the lies."

"Quinn's been stealing them for six years," I said aloud. The road was blurring in front of my eyes.

"What?" Lewis had drifted off into a twilight state, nearly asleep; he jerked back awake at the sound of my voice. We were about two hours outside of Vegas, heading north. Mona was running at close to top speed. We were lucky in a lot of ways, but mostly because Rahel was keeping us off the radar, both literally and figuratively.

I swallowed and felt my throat click. "The Djinn. They've been disappearing for six years, and that's

exactly when . . . when I told Quinn about the Djinn.
That's how he found them. He gave up drug running
to take up black-market Djinn, and I'm the one who
taught him how to do it."

Lewis listened to me as it poured out—the fear, the
pain, the dark, Quinn's questions. When I stopped,
the air tasted poisonous. He didn't look at me.

"You don't know how much Chaz told him," he
said. "Don't assume this is your fault, Jo."

"It's very much my fault, Lewis, and you know it.
Chaz was a low-level functionary; he knew the basics
of the Djinn but nothing else. I'd gotten the advanced-
level training because they were grooming me for bigger things. I had the practical info he needed."

"Theoretical," Lewis pointed out. "You didn't own
one. You'd never worked with one. You were telling
him what everybody knew."

"The thing is," I said, "it doesn't matter. If he'd
gotten the information from Chaz, he might have
blown it off as the bullshit of an amateur. Chaz
couldn't back it up, after all. But I confirmed it, and
that means he started to take it seriously based on
what I said. That means I'm to blame. This happened
because I cracked."

He looked somber. "Everybody cracks. You stayed
alive. That matters."

I didn't think so, at the moment.

Lewis checked the side mirror to make sure that
the silver Viper was still behind us, then glanced at
the speedometer. It registered two hundred, but I was
pretty sure we were doing better than that. I'd helped
us with a strong tailwind, and screw the balance. The
headwind was a bitch, and it kept trying to shove the

car sideways. My arm was getting tired, and my whole body was vibrating with tension.

I kept waiting for something, anything to stop us, but it was clear sailing all the way to White Ridge.

The gates to the Fantasy Ranch were wide open when we arrived, tarnished silver girls arching their backs to the sky; I pulled the Viper in cautiously, alert for trouble from any direction, but apart from the creak of iron and the skitter of tumbleweeds, the place was utterly still.

"He's got a rifle," Lewis warned me. "Let Rahel do this."

Rahel, in fact, was already out of the silver Viper and moving fast as a blur toward the house. She didn't pause for the door. It blasted open ahead of her, and we sat tensely, in silence, waiting.

She appeared in the doorway a few minutes later and shook her head. I let out an aching breath.

"He's gone."

"Looks like." Lewis popped the passenger door. I found myself looking at the separated garage off to the side; the doors were rolled up, and Quinn had left behind a dirty green Cherokee and a black Explorer. The Explorer had boxes in the back window, neatly stacked, labeled GLASS, FRAGILE.

They were full of sealed bottles. I turned them over in my hands, wondering, but Rahel wandered over and checked them out simply by reaching over to pick one up.

"Decoys," she said. "There are many like these inside. He hid the priceless among the cheap. He's been gone for a while."

I dumped the box over, furious. "How are we going to find him? Can you track him?"

Her eyes were dark and serious. "I can try. It's difficult. Jonathan is masking their movements."

"Try." I kicked the scattered bottles. "Let's move it."

Back on the road. Rahel and Marion led the way this time, and I concentrated on staying right on the gleaming silver bumper, drafting. We were back on the freeway, and then made an abrupt turn to a farm-to-market road that wasn't built for speed. We were forced to slow down.

"Jo," Lewis said. "You need to accept that he may get away, for now."

"Bullshit. He's not getting away. No way in hell."

I kept a paranoid watch, but there was no sign of Quinn trying to pick us off with a sniper rifle. Although I doubted even Quinn could have made a hero shot at this speed. There was nothing to do but think, or talk, and neither one of us seemed to want to do much talking. The sun crawled over the sky, and we were losing time.

Rahel directed us down another road, this one heading into the desert. It was a little better. We edged the speed higher, heading for what looked like even more deserted country.

Lewis said, "Let me have David's bottle. Maybe there's something I can do to help him."

The purse was still slung across my body, under the seat belt. I resisted the urge to clutch it close and settled for a quick, definite headshake. "He's sick, Lewis. You can't take him out of the bottle right now.

If he isn't an Ifrit, he's close. Just . . . leave him alone."

"Do you trust me?"

"Don't start."

"Do you?" He reached over and unzipped the compartment.

"Swear to God, Lewis, if you touch that bottle I'll rip your fingers off."

"I'm trying to help," he said, and reached inside.

I grabbed his wrist. It was like grabbing a ground wire—enough power to make me jerk and swear and have to quickly put both hands back on the wheel so that we didn't veer sideways around the tractor-trailer rig to our left, spin out, and flip like some Hollywood stunt gone horribly right. As it was, Mona fought me. She was stubborn, like my lovely Delilah, scrapped back in Oklahoma and still bitterly mourned. At this speed, steering was razor-sharp and as temperamental as a bipolar opera singer. Her tires were shrieking against the urge to turn. I held her straight, blindly concentrating, and didn't let my breath out until I felt her unclench first.

And then I remembered what had set things off.

David's bottle was in Lewis's hands. Held casually, catching the light through the tinted window in a pretty home-decorating sparkle. It looked empty, but then, it always did. What David was had no weight in the aetheric state, and when encased in glass, failed to even register at all on any plane of existence we could reach.

"It took a human death and Jonathan's and David's power to bring Rahel back," he said. "It'll take Jona-

than's power and more death to bring David back.
Are you prepared to pay that price?"

"Sure," I said grimly. "Quinn might as well serve
some useful purpose. And hey, Mr. Morality, you were
willing to sanction Quinn's putting a bullet through
Kevin's head, as I recall. Don't break anything climbing off that soapbox; it's awfully high."

Lewis kept turning the bottle in his hands. "Does
he make you happy?"

I didn't answer. I didn't have to. Lewis knew well
enough. "Put it back, Lewis. Don't make me hurt
you."

"I have an idea—"

"I have an idea that you're going to put that back
right n—"

I never finished that, because all of a sudden I was
just simply . . . not there. I'd been yanked out of the
car with tremendous, magical force, far up into the
sky. Below me, a dot of a blue car veered wildly,
corrected, and shuddered to a screeching halt. The
silver one braked after a two-second delay.

Then I was spinning out of control, heading . . .
. . . down.

Thump.

I landed in a dusty sprawl, out of breath, sweating,
gasping, and blind. I clawed hair back from my eyes
and saw that I was in shadow, lying on a soft bed of
sand. To either side of me, canyon walls crawled up
hand over hand toward the sky. They were
astonishing . . . harvest gold shading to brick red shading to dull brown, a muted but glorious rainbow of

layers. Overhead, the sky was the perfect, supernaturally bright blue of a Djinn's eyes. Where the sunlight hit, it hit hard and woke glassy sparkles from the sand.

The place wasn't completely devoid of life; there was a raw scuttling in a thin, straggly cactus that probably meant either a lizard or a rabbit, or both. It wasn't even devoid of hints of human visitation. There was a cool silver moon slice of a beer can partially visible near the canyon wall.

But nobody in sight.

I licked dry lips and called, "Jonathan?" I couldn't think who else would have had the ability to yank me out of the driver's seat and deliver me here without also delivering me in pieces. I got up and slapped dust from my jeans—what use it was, I have no idea, since the rest of me was thoroughly caked. I ached. I stank. I was grimy and horribly itchy and pissed off as hell.

I was also scared to death.

"Quinn?" I tried. "Hello?"

His voice came down to me like God from the mountain, amplified into a divine echo. "Shouldn't have come after me, Joanne. I didn't come after you."

Like hell. "You tried to *shoot* me!"

"You wouldn't leave well enough alone," he said. His voice sounded hollow but self-satisfied; I couldn't see a thing, couldn't tell if he was up at the top leaning over or standing on some concealed ledge. "Sooner or later, you'd have figured it out. You're like a bulldog. I respect that. I was just removing a risk. And now you just won't leave me the fuck alone, will you? I'm just trying to leave, you know. Get on with my life."

"News flash, now the Ma'at know. And the Wardens will know. And whether you've got Jonathan or not, there's no place you can hide. They'll hunt you down and—"

"And kill me, yeah, I know. Very dramatic."

An explosion echoed through the canyon, louder than a scream; I felt stone chips dig hot into my shoulder, and dived for the dirt again. As if that would help. He was shooting down at me, and I had no place to hide. But then, if he'd been all about the shooting of me, he could have easily put one or two through my head.

"What do you want?" I yelled, and spat sand. "Hey, grab a knife, come down here, and stage a rematch, you bastard! I'll give you a really good time!"

"You know, I used to just want to get away with this, but you're pissing me off. Now I'm thinking, maybe I need a little recreation before I hit the road."

Another shot pinned me to the sand. He could drill me anytime he wanted; I knew it. And there wasn't a lot I could do to stop him.

"You remember what I asked you at the end? In the cave?" His voice sounded worse than hollow now. It sounded like a shell, and something lived in it that wasn't human. I stayed very still. "Joanne?"

"I remember," I said. I didn't know if he could hear me.

"Is it still what you're most afraid of?"

I felt the vibration coming up through the rocks. Next to my eyeline, sand jittered madly, and I felt a sudden cool, damp breeze.

I clawed my way up to my feet and looked at the canyon walls. Far, far up at the top, I saw a black dot of a head looking down.

I knew how he was going to kill me.

Fuck him. I wasn't going to die like this. Not like this.

I kicked off my shoes, ran for the wall, and grabbed for my first handhold.

I'm going to ask you one last question, he'd said, there in the dark, when all my screaming had died down to whispers, when he'd stopped cutting me and left me to bleed for a while. The scrape of his fingertips over my sweaty, bloody face had made me want to crawl away, but I'd been too weak. Too afraid.

What are you most afraid of? What's the one way you don't want to die?

And because I'd been too numbed to lie, I'd whispered, *Drowning.* As soon as I'd let myself say it, I'd tried to take it back, tried to pretend I'd lied, but he knew.

Orry knew fear when he heard it.

He'd dragged me to the edge of the pool, and he'd held me underwater until I'd stopped moving.

I'd had just enough power left, just enough skill, to keep the oxygen in my lungs refreshed as his hand shoved my face down to the bottom of that shallow pool and held me there with his fist knotted in my hair.

He was careful. Let me stay under for a full two minutes before he let go, and he left me there, floating facedown.

When I was sure he'd gone, I'd rolled out of the water and huddled in the dark, trembling. Weeping without sound and without tears. Then crawling, inch by torturous inch, back out of the caves into the hot sunlight.

Four hours later, I'd made my way outside to the highway, where a passing motorist had found me.

Just another victim.

What are you most afraid of?

I'd told him, and now he was going to use it against me again.

Son of a bitch, screw you, I'm not dying like this.

I hauled myself up with my right hand, found a grip for my left, and jammed fingers in. Nails broke, but I barely felt it. My bare toes scrabbled at the rock wall and clung to a tiny outcropping.

Three feet up. I found the next handhold, and hauled against the shattering strain in my arms and shoulders. *Need to lose some weight.* That was the crazy, insane, stupidly optimistic part of my brain that just never quite failed to see the funny side of dying horribly.

I could feel the vibration in the canyon walls. The breeze was picking up speed. *Climb!* The air in the canyon was unstable, already swirling. Trying to control it was a sucker bet.

I climbed another three feet, painfully achieved.

"Give it up," Quinn said from somewhere way up there, hundreds of feet above. "You know how this goes. A flash flood rips through these canyons, it pulverizes boulders, rips up trees like kindling. You won't even be a little bitty scrap of skin by the time it dumps you out in the river. Maybe you won't even have time to drown. Would that make you feel any better?"

Two more feet. My sweating toes slipped, then my

left hand; I bit back a scream of rage and reached again. Pulled. Felt the burning tear in my triceps grow stronger.

A whip of wind lashed my hair back, and I heard the low grumble.

"Holy shit," Quinn said. "Looks like a real gully washer, there. Sorry. Want me to shoot you, put you out of your misery?"

"Fuck you," I gasped, and lurched another two feet higher. I glanced down. I was maybe ten feet up now, enough to make me dizzy but no way enough to save me. The low grumbling sound was getting louder, and the wind stiffer. It smelled like wet sand and death. Nothing clean about the water hurtling down the canyon toward me. It had started out as a flood at least half a mile back, maybe more, picking up speed and debris by sweeping the canyons. Foaming and raging like a sea, taking with it birds, rabbits, snakes, people, cars, anything in its path.

It was coming fast.

"*Sure* you don't want me to shoot you? 'Cause if you're waiting on your friends, they're a little busy. Jonathan's helping out with that."

I lunged upward. My fingers were bloody, the nails ripped off at the quick, and my shoulders and arms were trembling. I flailed for a right handhold, found one and shifted my weight . . .

. . . and the shale under my fingers shattered like glass.

I screamed, clung to my left handhold, and felt my shoulder pop hot as a gunshot. The wind turned cold, flapped my hair like a flag, and when I reached up again for a grip my bloody left hand slipped. I scrabbled like a doomed cartoon character, managed to find something to cling to, and hung there, trembling.

No way could I get high enough. It was going to lick me off the wall.

I turned my face toward the first damp breath as the roar burst open. The flood was rounding the corner up ahead. It was a wall of black of mist and foam and death, thirty feet high. I saw the bloody, torn hindquarters of a cow being tossed on the leading edge.

I felt my fingers slip again, and there was no point in trying to stop it this time.

As the wall of water slammed into me like a speeding truck, I let myself fall.

What are you most afraid of?
Drowning.
That wasn't actually true, after all. It hurt, but what hurt worse was the knowledge that Quinn was going to get away. He was going to take Jonathan's bottle and he was going to get in his SUV and go bouncing across the desert, and if there was revenge to be had, it wouldn't be had by me, and *dammit*, I couldn't let myself go down like this. I couldn't. I'd survived him before, in the dark, when there was no hope.

I felt something warm move inside of me.

I might let you kill me, you bastard, but you will not kill my daughter.

The current had knocked me fuzzy and gray, but the real problem was the debris churning in the water with me, and the impacts with canyon walls that were going to rip me limb from limb. I had seconds left, maybe less. The water was moving so fast that the walls were a blur sweeping past, and all I could do was try to stay on top of the roiling cold surge. Swimming was stupid. I focused on the water itself, but it was driven by so much force and so much chaos that I couldn't grip anything, couldn't hold it. . . .

Ma'at.

It wasn't about gripping and holding.

It was about removing the need for the water to move at all.

I took a deep, scared breath and ducked under the surface. It was almost black, laden with silt and debris, and the silk of the water swallowed me whole.

I left myself go. Drifting. Listening to the water's heart.

Letting it flow through me like a river. Surfing with it, undulating. Finding the frequency of the water and creating the countervibration, exactly opposite.

Waves began to still instead of amplify. Surges became still patches.

Slowing.

I opened my eyes and bobbed up to grab another breath, and saw that the flood was still fast but no longer the roaring monster it had been. I could try to swim, at least. Stay ahead of the heavier debris, ride the crest of the—

There was a boulder straight ahead, jammed in a narrow part of the canyon, and I was heading straight for it.

Five seconds left.

Two.

Oh, God . . .

I felt myself lifting on the surge of the wave, and waited for the fall, the impact, the end.

I kept rising.

Rising out of the water.

Someone was holding me from behind, arms clasped around me under my breasts, and I felt a wild and burning heat that turned water between us to steam.

"Rahel?" I asked, and turned to look.

Not Rahel.

It was David.

He smiled at me with so much love and relief that it broke my heart, and said, "You think I'd let you go, after all this?"

I cried out and turned in the circle of his arms, and held him as we floated over the foaming, churning flood.

At the top of the canyon we had a welcoming committee. It consisted of Rahel, Lewis, and Marion. Rahel, of course, was spotless; Marion and Lewis were sweaty and dirty and breathless.

We touched down, and I winced at the burn of hundred-degree sand on my bare feet, but then David was collapsing in my arms and I forgot all about the discomfort. My shoulders couldn't take the strain. I had to let him fall.

"David?" I hovered anxiously over him. His eyes were flickering copper, turning brown. "David—"

"He's too weak," Lewis said, and fumbled the blue glass bottle out from his pocket. "David, back in the bottle."

He faded into mist. I rounded on Lewis in a fury, but he held up a hand to stop me. "If we leave him out, he'll fade again. The bottle is all that's keeping him alive right now. Djinn life support."

"And you called him out?" I didn't know what made me more angry. "Do me a favor—don't help, okay?"

"I was supposed to let you get smashed to pieces?"

"You were supposed to take down Quinn!" I yelled. "Did you?"

They looked anywhere but me. Rahel said, "We will."

"We will," I mocked. "Yeah, fine, whatever. Just let me find him and do this thing." I staggered when I tried to get up. Marion took my arm and hauled me upright, frowning.

"You're in no shape to take on anything more dangerous than a week in bed," she said. "You've torn muscles, damaged your shoulder—"

"I don't care." I bit the words off furiously and wiped wet hair back from my face, wishing that I were still a Djinn so I could clean myself up and smite somebody with a truly righteous amount of smiting. "He's got Jonathan, and he's got God knows how many bottles, and he's not getting out of this without a fight, and where exactly is Kevin?"

I ran it all together, alarm sharpening my voice, and saw Marion and Lewis look around in shock.

"He was right here," Marion began, but I wasn't watching her. I was caught by Rahel's expression. Alone among us, she wasn't surprised by his absence.

"Let him do this," she said. "It's his right."

"Do *what*?"

She shrugged. I shook free of Marion's hold and turned around, looking down the edge of the canyon. It couldn't be that far, a few sand dunes in the way, maybe a thousand yards of desert in the way. . . .

Something blew up out there.

Something very, very big.

The shock wave rippled over me, and the noise whited out my eardrums; a fireball the size of a blimp rose up into the air, curling in on itself in reds and crimsons and ropes of hot yellow, in waves of smoke like tattered silk.

A shattered metal frame rose up off the ground, powered by another explosion. The massive steel monster, turning end over end, sailing out over the canyon and dropping down to smash into the foaming water with a hiss of superheated steam.

"That was a Hummer," I said numbly.

"And I think that was Kevin," Lewis said.

The kid had finally found a decent use for his powers over fire.

Then we were running.

The explosion had left a crater the size of a meteor strike, black in the center. Sand had turned to glass.

Quinn was down near the edge of it, bleeding from ears and nose, coughing up mouthfuls of red. The second I saw him, memory clicked into place: baseball cap, windbreaker, the same lean, whipcord body. Sunglasses hiding his face.

Quinn. Orry. One and the same, not that I'd had any doubt.

Jonathan was standing over him, staring down. When we pelted over the sand toward him, avoiding the burning scraps of what used to be a hugely expensive SUV, I saw Kevin kneeling nearby. He looked . . . blank. Exhausted. That explosion had taken everything out of him.

No time for him now. I fixed my attention on Jonathan, and held out one hand in a calming motion. "Easy. Let's not get crazy here. We come in peace."

"No, you don't," Jonathan said absently.

"Okay, I lied, we don't. But it looks like Quinn's not going to make it, so let's not increase the body count, okay?"

"I don't have a choice." *Ouch.* The bleak fury of that was painful. "I thought since he wasn't a Warden, I'd have more chances. But he's good. He knew exactly what to say, what to do. . . ."

The first command you give is to restrict them from using any power without your express order. The second is to order them to protect your life unless you expressly countermand it. The third . . .

I'd told Quinn how to do it. I'd screamed it out in the dark, under his knife.

I'd taught him everything he needed to know.

I'd told all that to the Wardens, of course, during the debriefing, and they'd said, *It doesn't matter. He's not a Warden. He'll never be able to use the knowledge.*

Except he had, hadn't he? Quinn was nothing if not ruthless and resourceful.

But I hadn't told him the most critical things, even so.

"Can he talk?" I asked Jonathan. It came out cold and even. Quinn's eyes rolled toward me, wild and rimmed with white.

"No."

"Then his last commands to you remain in force."

"I'm supposed to protect his life," Jonathan said. He was watching Quinn, not us, but I knew that he'd have no choice but to act if we moved. "The kid was clever. He went for the car, not Quinn. Took the bottles out at the same time. I didn't have to stop him."

I felt a flashover of hope, hot as the sun beating down on us. "Where's *your* bottle?"

Jonathan gestured down at the kneeling man. "On him. In his jacket pocket."

I looked at Lewis. He made a little after-you gesture.

I snapped my head around, lifted a hand and gathered the wind like a hard coil, and sent it arrowing for Quinn.

It slammed into him hard. A microburst, containing a wind shear not strong enough to do him any harm—physically—but plenty strong enough for just what it had to do.

Break a bottle in his front jacket pocket.

I felt it pop, like a sudden change in air pressure.

Quinn flopped down on his back, twisting silently in agony. For a few seconds Jonathan didn't move, and then he slowly bent down and reached in Quinn's pocket.

He took out a handful of broken glass and sifted it onto the sand.

"You don't own me anymore," he said, and crouched down next to the dying man. "Do you have *any* idea how much this is going to hurt?"

Quinn managed to choke out a few words, after all. ". . . ordered . . . defend . . . life . . ."

"I didn't let her kill you," Jonathan said, and smiled. It was the most princely, evil smile I could imagine ever seeing. "It'll probably take you days to die. I'll watch over you the whole time, maybe remind you of all the good things you've done in your life. It's the least I can do."

Quinn's eyes widened. Whether it was mercy or luck, something inside his body snapped. Blood gouted out of his mouth and nose, and he arched his back once, for an aching ten long seconds. . . .

Then collapsed.

"Is he dead?" I asked quietly.

Jonathan leaned over and studied him closely. Then he reached down, hauled him up by the arm, and before anyone could stop him, pitched Quinn limply over the cliff into the swollen, rushing floodwater.

"Yep," he said, and walked away. He called back over his shoulder, "I'm going home. Take care of the kid. Keep him out of trouble."

"Wait!" I yelled it, desperately. "What about David?"

He stopped walking, but he didn't turn back. His shoulders tightened, and then slowly relaxed.

"You broke him," he said. "You fix him."

He vanished before I could get out more than half a curse.

The Wardens agreed to a meeting back at our old stomping grounds, the Holiday Inn outside of White Ridge. I'd spent an entire day showering, bathing, showering, and sleeping with David's sealed bottle resting in my arms; when I came downstairs the next day I looked rested, relaxed, and heavily abused. Bruises up and down my body. Wrecked fingernails. Sunburn on my face, not to mention the muscle tears and sprains that made holding on to a smile an effort.

Thank God for aspirin and Vivarin.

Paul was waiting, along with Marion, Lewis, and a few others. Wardens all, at least in name.

"Jo." Paul tried to put his arms around me. I backed

him off with a look and took a seat on the couch. After a pause, he followed suit. He glanced from me to Lewis, me to Marion. "I guess we can call this a qualified success."

"Qualified," I repeated. "What did we qualify for? Bonuses? Free parking?"

"Look, it's just . . ." Paul fidgeted, then fixed me with a steady stare. "The kid's missing—Kevin. Jonathan's gone, and I don't have to tell you what kind of a loss that is for us. We're just lucky that things are moving back toward normal."

"Normal?" I sounded like a parrot.

"The earthquake thing, it's better. There's going to be a couple of big ones, but in remote areas and not too much damage. The warming trend's slowing down. We're still heading for an ice age, but I don't see that we can do shit about it without—"

"Without Jonathan." I rested my aching, torn hands in my lap. I was wearing jeans again—hip-huggers, in memory of Siobhan—and I'd gone for open-toed flip-flops, considering the state of my cut and bruised toes. "Jeez, sorry about that. Guess we'll just have to hope for the best."

Paul clearly wasn't liking my polite, nonconfrontational attitude. "What's up with you? I'm telling you that you *failed*. If you'd stayed out of things like we agreed—"

"Then we'd all be dead," I said sweetly. "But hey, next time? I'm booking a spa, getting a massage. Wait for the end in style, you know?"

He didn't respond. I dropped the sweetness from my tone. "Fine. Let's get to the important parts. What's the damage?"

"You've been lying to us, sweetheart."

No kidding. Where to start? "About what?"

"Jonathan, for starters." Paul's eyes were full of bitterness. "He's not in the goddamn register. He doesn't fucking exist, Jo. Where'd he come from? You know, don't you?"

"No."

"Are there more like him out there? More Djinn?"

I kept quiet, watching Marion's impassive face. She knew. And she wasn't talking.

"Jo, I'm giving you a chance to speak up, here. Take it."

"Gee, thanks. But no."

I moved from looking at Marion to looking at Lewis. He was a closed book, too. Quiet. Self-contained. He'd taken Kevin in hand, as I'd known he would; the kid was safely tucked away with the Ma'at, back in Vegas. Lewis would watch out for him.

Whether he would be able to watch out for me was an open question. I was the one thing that could break the secrecy of the Ma'at *and* the Djinn.

We'd all said the same thing: David's bottle had been destroyed. He was lost. The blue glass was hidden in the bottom of my purse, wrapped safely in a cocoon of bubble wrap.

I still had him, if he lived. If he could recover.

Paul was getting impatient. "I want you to understand that you're part of the chain of command, kiddo. You have a boss—that's me, in case you didn't know—and you do what your boss says from now on, or I'm going to have to consider removing you from the association. You get me? That means you give up your powers—Marion and her guys see that it's done humanely, but it's done. That's how it would have to happen."

Over his shoulder, Marion gave me a tiny, definite shake of her head. Behind her, a shadow flickered into existence, then into three-dimensional life. He was beautiful . . . tall, broad-shouldered, with impenetrable midnight eyes—not brown, a true, lightless black—and long dark hair frosted lightly with gray. Lines at the corners of his eyes that softened him into something more human. He was dressed, like Marion, in blue jeans and cowboy boots, but his shirt was a matte blue silk, something that begged to be petted.

Marion's Djinn. Marion's lover. He was back. That was the silent message from her. I didn't know if it meant she'd openly disobey orders, but she wasn't following them with a whole heart.

I said, with a weird sort of calm, "Oh, yeah, Paul, I totally get you." I stood up. "Thanks for the opportunity to get reamed out for doing the right thing, and by the way, doing it better than any of you seem to have managed. But I hope you don't mind if I decline the verbal abuse."

He opened his mouth, and shut it again fast when I turned and headed for the door, for the bright, merciless sunshine. I had brand-new credit cards, provided courtesy of Rahel. Wads of cash, from the same source. A fast car, waiting outside.

I could go back to Vegas, catch a tan, heal up. Eventually, I'd need to figure out what to do, but hell, I figured I deserved a vacation.

And the Ma'at damn well deserved to fund it.

"Jo," Paul called after me. I turned, slid on sunglasses, and gave him my best, brightest smile.

"Bite me," I said. "I'm not playing Warden anymore. Go save the world without me. I quit."

My favorite songs contributed to the craziness of Jo-anne's Las Vegas adventure. Support the artists, buy the CDs!

"Harder to Breathe"	Maroon 5
"Gotta Serve Somebody"	Bob Dylan
"Burning Hell"	Joe Bonamassa
"Disease"	Matchbox 20
"Woke Up This Morning"	A3
"Professional Widow"	Tori Amos
"You're So Real"	Matchbox 20
"She Cries Your Name"	Beth Orton
"Blues Deluxe"	Joe Bonamassa
"Blood Makes Noise"	Suzanne Vega
"Mr. Zebra"	Tori Amos
"Crucify"	Tori Amos

Each of these songs contained something that evoked the mood of the book or the characters for me . . . and hey, damn cool driving music, too.

Enjoy,
Rachel Caine
www.rachelcaine.com

Finally, someone is doing something about the weather...

ILL WIND

BOOK ONE OF THE WEATHER WARDEN SERIES

by Rachel Caine

Joanne Baldwin is a Weather Warden. Usually she can control the strongest hurricane with a wave of her hand. But now she's trying to outrun a different kind of storm: accusations of corruption and murder.

Her only hope is a powerful warden named Lewis. The only problem is that he's in hiding. Now Joanne is racing to find him—and the bad weather is closing in fast.

"A FUN READ. YOU'LL NEVER WATCH THE WEATHER CHANNEL THE SAME WAY AGAIN."
—JIM BUTCHER, BESTSELLING AUTHOR OF THE DRESDEN FILES

0-451-45952-0

Available wherever books are sold or at
www.penguin.com

What's the good of being dead if you're still on the run?

HEAT STROKE
BOOK TWO OF THE WEATHER WARDEN SERIES

by Rachel Caine

Mistaken for a murderer, Weather Warden Joanne
Baldwin is hunted down and killed by her colleagues.
Reborn as a Djinn, she senses something sinister
entering Earth's atmosphere—something that's making
tomorrow's forecast look deadly.

"AS SWIFT, SASSY, AND SEXY AS
LAURELL K. HAMILTON!"
—MARY JO PUTNEY

"A FAST-PACED THRILL RIDE THAT
BRINGS NEW MEANING TO STORMY WEATHER."
—*LOCUS*

0-451-45984-9

Available wherever books are sold or at
www.penguin.com

R737

THE
DRESDEN FILES
By
Jim Butcher

"Fans of Laurell K. Hamilton and Tanya Huff will love
this new fantasy series."
—*Midwest Book Review*

STORM FRONT: Book One of the Dresden Files
                                    0-451-45781-1

FOOL MOON: Book Two of the Dresden Files
                                    0-451-45812-5

GRAVE PERIL: Book Three of the Dresden Files
                                    0-451-45844-3

SUMMER KNIGHT: Book Four of the Dresden Files
                                    0-451-45892-3

DEATH MASKS: Book Five of the Dresden Files
                                    0-451-45940-7

BLOOD RITES: Book Six of the Dresden Files
                                    0-451-45987-3

Available wherever books are sold or at
www.penguin.com